**Also available from Tricia Lynne
and Carina Press**

Book 2 in the Unlovabulls series, coming soon!

Also available from Tricia Lynne

Moonlight & Whiskey

Protective Instinct deals with topics surrounding animals some readers may find difficult, including animal abuse. This book was written with careful consideration for those triggers and does *not* contain any on-page depictions of animal abuse, neglect or death.

PROTECTIVE INSTINCT

—

TRICIA LYNNE

carina
press

Recycling programs
for this product may
not exist in your area.

ISBN-13: 978-1-335-47470-4

Protective Instinct

First published in 2020. This edition published in 2021.

Copyright © 2020 by Tricia Lynne

For questions and comments about the quality of this book, please contact us at CustomerService@Harlequin.com.

Carina Press
22 Adelaide St. West, 40th Floor
Toronto, Ontario M5H 4E3, Canada
www.CarinaPress.com

Printed in U.S.A.

To Dad, who taught me to never be afraid to lead instead of follow.

Love,
Buzz

For Brennan, Orion, Sugar and Jock

Hello Lovely Reader,

For many, animal abuse and neglect are difficult topics to discuss—myself included. *Protective Instinct* was written with careful consideration for triggers and does *not* contain any graphic on-page depictions of animal abuse, neglect or death.

The subject matter, however, requires I provide basic information about the nature of puppy mills and their treatment of breeding dogs. Please know I went to great lengths to keep any on-page dialogue/discussion about these issues as nontriggering as possible.

If you'd like more information on puppy mills and how to spot a puppy mill breeder, please visit the following.

www.humanesociety.org/all-our-fights/stopping-puppy-mills

www.aspca.org/barred-from-love

www.rover.com/blog/spot-puppy-mill-puppy-mill-ad

As Lily says, it's not an easy rabbit hole to go down, but it's an important one. If you suspect animal abuse or neglect in your area, I hope you'll be their voice and report it to your local animal welfare agency.

All my best,

Tricia

PROTECTIVE INSTINCT

Chapter One

Murphy's Law: Shit can ALWAYS get worse.

Lily

"Oh, goddamn. I ain't got time for this now." I clenched my teeth as traffic slowed to a crawl. Heading south on the Dallas North Tollway—yes, I knew how ridiculous that sounded but it was accurate—I was late to a meeting with a new client. At four p.m. on a Friday, you could always expect traffic going north on the tollway, but going south? Frisco was far enough from the city that it shouldn't have been a problem. Instead, there I was, doing five goddamned miles an hour.

"Well, shit." I pulled the rubber band from my hair and regathered it at my nape.

I hated Dallas traffic on a good day. Today it was the cherry on top of my shit sundae.

It had started first thing this morning. I'd been in Starbucks when an asshole in a dually parked so close to my driver's side door that I didn't have a prayer of squeezing my butt through the opening. Already running late to teach my morning puppy kindergarten class, I crawled across the passenger seat. As I was shimmying over the console, I kicked over my coffee. Then, the dually driver emerged, glanced through my window, shrugged, and left.

Next, I got peed on.

After puppy class ended, I was speaking with Pickles the Pupper's mom when Cassie (or Casshole, as her mother referred to her, because of her need to destroy all puppies in her general vicinity) came through the door. Cassie was nearly thirteen. She had agility and nose work titles, and she'd earned the right to be a bitch if she damn well pleased.

She was also the reason the Unruly Dog Training Center had a no-greeting-between-dogs policy.

The next part happened in a matter of seconds. Pickles the Pupper's tail started wiggling at helicopter speed as she pulled her leash tight toward a barking Cassie. Knowing the dachshund's barking wasn't a friendly hello, but an *Ima tek yo face off, puppeh!* I quickly scooped up Pickles as Casshole snapped out, nicking the puppy's lip.

That was when Pickles peed on me. Down the front of my last clean work shirt, over my khaki pants, and right on the inside of my sneaker.

Now, I'd hit traffic when I was late to a client meeting. *Can this day get any worse?*

The cosmos threw her head back with a witch cackle. *Oh child, ask and you shall receive. Muahahahaha!*

Contemplating the merits of anger-management

classes, I didn't bother to check the caller ID when my phone rang. I hit the Bluetooth button on the steering wheel and immediately wanted to punch myself in the face.

"Yeah?"

"'Yeah'? We don't say 'yeah' when we answer the phone, Liliana." My mother's voice was like nails on a chalkboard sending hair on my nape up.

"What do you need, Mom? I'm late for a training appointment."

She huffed. "That's why I called. Your father—"

"Stepfather. Dick is not my father." My father was Billy Costello—one of the foremost linebackers in Dallas Bulldog history. Unfortunately, he'd died when I was younger. Not long after he passed, my mom turned to Dick as her meal ticket.

A weary sigh filled my car speaker. "Please stop calling him Dick. Richard detests when you do that. Speaking of training appointments, don't you think it's time to let the dog thing go?"

"Umm, no? Is that why you called? To harass me into working for *Richard*? Because you might as well stop there. I won't work for the team."

"Liliana, the Dallas Bulldogs have been good to us. Your stepfather needs someone he can trust in the head trainer's position, and...well, playing with dogs all day instead of using your expertise...it's an affront to the family."

"Hmphf. To Richard, right? Don't you mean it's an insult to Dick?"

Her voice got higher. I could hear the annoyance. "We've discussed this. You are the daughter—"

"Stepdaughter."

"*Step. Daughter.*" I was sure that ugly vein in her overly Botoxed forehead was starting to bulge. "As the stepdaughter of the general manager of the Dallas Bulldogs football team, you knew Richard expected you to use the degree *he* paid for by working for the team."

Dick needs someone he can trust in the head trainer's position. Uh-huh. Sure, he did. Dick could give a good goddamn that working with dogs was what made me happy. He saw me as a tool he could use to better the team—*that* was the reason he'd paid my tuition. Now, he was pissed he wasn't getting any return on his investment.

"I'm not having this argument again." I seriously thought about beating my head on the steering wheel. Instead, I looked over my shoulder and turned on my signal, trying to nose my way into the exit lane. No one was budging.

Yes, I had a master's in kinesiology, but my undergrad had been in political science. I'd planned to go to law school, but a guy happened, and law school didn't. Long story. Anyhow, when I was little, my real dad took me to the *Bodies* exhibit when it came through Dallas—you know, donated human bodies dissected, preserved, posed, and displayed? I'd been fascinated with human mechanics ever since. Instead of applying to law schools, I applied to the Master of Science in Kinesiology program at UNT.

Dick had almost been as gleeful to have me slotted

in the head trainer position for the Bulldogs as he was to have a lawyer he thought he could bring on staff. I never had any intention of working for my stepfather. As it turned out, I didn't have the highest peopling threshold. Hence, me not using said degree. Besides, Dick had shady written on his forehead. He had to have an ulterior motive for wanting me working for the Bulldogs—Dick didn't do anything that didn't benefit him—I just didn't know what the reason was. Best guess was because of who my father was, but I didn't think that was entirely it, either.

Why were most humans such asshats?

Like the person driving the F-150 sitting in my blind spot. *Ignoring. My. Turn. Signal!* Dogs, however, were as close to the divine as people would ever get. If they only lived longer…

"I'm not going to work for the team, Mom. I don't want anything to do with the Bulldogs. Ever. I don't give two shits *who's* disappointed in my job choice." Dammit, if this jerk would only speed up or slow down…

"Language. I raised you better." *Screeeeech*, went the nails on the chalkboard. "Besides, isn't it about time you let all that ugliness go?"

Raised me? Ha. I raised myself. And ugliness? She made it sound like a pimple on prom night. Not only did Dick have the word *shady* written on his forehead, the Dallas Bulldogs employed my cheating, creepy ex-fiancé. I'd rather dig out my eyeballs with a spork than work for the team that employed *that* prick. The little voice in the back of my brain told me this conversation would go a lot faster if I kept my mouth shut.

"Liliana, Richard is serious. He made it clear that if you refuse to work for the team, we'll be forced to cut you off financially."

Oh, whatever. "Okay, thanks for the info gottagoby-eeeee." I pushed the hang-up button, shooting meta-phorical lasers with my eyes at the pickup truck driver through its tinted windows. Cut me off, financially? I didn't know why they thought that would work.

Why the hell was he so desperate to have me work for him, anyway? I wasn't buying the whole you *owe me for paying for college* thing. As far as money went, besides tuition, I'd only asked my mother to help finan-cially when my dog, Joker, had needed surgery, and when a couple of my foster dogs needed medical help I couldn't afford. Even with the expensive surgery, I still lost my boy, Joker. But both of the rescues went on to forever homes. The couple of times my mother *had* helped me out, Dick admonished her for "setting a bad precedent and using his money to do it."

My mom was a lot of things. Vain. An unfit mother. A social climber. A former Dallas Bulldogs cheerleader who moonlighted as a jersey chaser.

Audrey Costello-Head may have been a flake who needed a man to take care of her so she could go shop-ping at Neiman's and get on the committee for the Cat-tleman's Ball. Still…

She wasn't a Dick Head.

Finally! Someone left me enough room to squeeze in behind the jerk in the pickup. "Yassss, biiitchesss!"

DFW drivers believed our daily commute was a contact sport. As such, we took that shit as seriously as we took our Friday night football or the Red River Rivalry. Pushing my way into the exit lane felt like my very own touchdown dance. Slowing down, I moved over to the right, rounding the truck on its left side. The pickup driver turned on their signal to move into the lane in front of me. Refusing to let the truck over, I pulled even with the passenger side, rolled down my window, extended my left arm, flipping the driver off with enough force that surely the sonic boom reverberated through his cab.

Asshole.

Yet, somehow, he managed to slip in behind a Tesla two cars back. I didn't think anything of it until I took the right toward the apartments where my appointment was, and the truck turned behind me.

Oh, shit.

There was a scene in *Miss Congeniality* where Sandra Bullock tackled a guy in the crowd during the talent competition. She told the pageant director that the dude had a gun. The pageant director replied that in Texas everyone has a gun.

Yeah. *That.*

I tried to hold it together, except when I turned in to the garage for the building, the truck followed. Convincing myself I was being paranoid, I found a guest spot and put the car in park. It was a nice building. The first floor had a gym, spa, coffee shop, restaurant, dry cleaner. Good. That meant people were close by. A thought that gave me little comfort when much to my horror, the truck whipped into a numbered spot catty-corner from me.

Fuck. I double-checked to make sure my doors were locked then put the car in reverse. The truck bounced as the sound of the driver's door shutting echoed off the concrete walls, and a large man in basketball shorts walked to the bed and grabbed an athletic bag.

I knew that neck-length messy black hair. That scruff. Those wide shoulders. The breath rushed from my chest. I rested my forehead against the wheel hoping he wouldn't notice me. Only, when I chanced a peek, his maple-syrup-colored eyes met mine, his pink lips turned up at the corners. Shit. I would have rather faced a gun.

Shutting the car off, I grabbed my bag while he leaned against the bed of his truck. I made my way over knowing I wasn't getting out of this without saying hello.

"Well, well. Liliana Costello. Fancy meeting you here." Brody Shaw's voice was all dark, sweet hot fudge, and I was the ice cream melting under the sound.

His lips curled in something like flirty amusement. "Especially after you flipped me off."

My heart sped up. "Hi, Brody. It's been a while." The term "sex on a stick" was invented for this man. At six foot three and 252 pounds, Brody used to run the forty in five seconds flat. The man was built like a brick shithouse. Though he'd had shoulder issues the past couple of seasons, Brody Shaw was the archetypal middle linebacker for the Dallas Bulldogs. Big and fast, he had a Mastiff-sized set of shoulders and his ass resembled two bowling balls trapped in a pair of football pants. The man's arms were surely a gift from some long extinct Roman god, and those legs…oh my God, they were my crack. I had a thing for strong legs—the kind of thick, ripped thighs a guy only got from squatting four hundred pounds or digging into the turf to push other men around.

I know. Very cavewoman of me.

We'd chatted a few times before, when my mother forced me to attend team functions. I knew the dude was witty, quick with his devastating smile, and flirty as all get-out.

The first time we talked, he'd approached me during a rooftop gala. I knew him, of course, but he didn't realize who I was at the time. He'd spent a solid thirty minutes making me feel like the center of the universe. We'd discussed politics, books, a shared love of the TV show *Supernatural*, and the foundation we were there to support—an organization working to minimize the instances of concussions in high school sports. He'd even asked me for my number before one of his teammates interrupted and mentioned I was the GM's stepdaughter.

An hour after that convo, he left with a tall blonde he hadn't arrived with. Not that I would have given him my number, anyway. I didn't date my stepdad's players—if being Billy Costello's daughter had taught me anything, it was that football players were fickle, hedonistic, and volatile.

It didn't stop Brody and me from gravitating to each other at any and all subsequent events before he inevitably left with a different woman. Between that, and the very recent fantasy suite scandal, it was clear Brody Shaw was bad news with a capital Bad Boy.

Fun to look at, even to flirt with on occasion, but that's where it ended.

I swept a stray hair behind my ear as I tried not to stare. It wasn't easy. "Yeah, I'm sorry about that. I'm running late for an appointment. In fact, I should get going. It was good to see you." I started to sidestep him to head for the elevator. Brody slung his bag over his shoulder and matched my strides. The lines in his forehead deepened as he squinted an eye shut, catching his bottom lip between his front teeth.

Jesus. Ten years into his career and he looked even better than he had in college. The laugh lines, the bronzed skin, and hard muscles underneath. I'd watched Brody play football at UNT when I was a student. *That* Brody was a boy. A boy who did things to my lady parts, granted, but still a boy. This version of Brody was a man. The sharp jaw, the crooked nose with the scar across the bridge, the dimples hidden by his dark scruff and eyes that warmed every part of me.

My breath came out in a pant. Annnd *that* wasn't embarrassing at all.

"Lily, aren't you a dog trainer?"

I peeked sideways as I pushed the elevator call button. "Yes. And a certified canine behavior specialist."

A grin crept over Brody's face.

No! My mouth fell open. Not long ago, Brody had made the news when his dog bit a pet sitter. "Are you… Erica?"

"Yep." His smile was enormous. "Well, she's one of my neighbors, but yeah. My publicist made the appointment for me. I had no idea it would be you. She always gives my neighbor's name and address to make sure I don't get psycho fans knocking on the door."

No. This cannot be happening. The elevator opened, and we stepped in. *Not no, but hell no.* I needed to get through his dog's evaluation and recommend another trainer for Brody to work with. Given my body's reaction, Brody's reputation with women, and his affiliation with the Dallas Bulldogs, this was a really bad idea.

Really. Bad. Idea.

Chapter Two

Everything happens for a reason.
Sometimes the reason is that you're stupid
and make bad decisions.

Brody

After pushing the button for three, I leaned against the adjacent wall and watched as Lily pinched the bridge of her nose and repeatedly mumbled the word *no* under her breath. Goddamn, she was cute as hell. She smelled a little bit like pee—I'm guessing dog. Her glossy black hair was in complete disarray, and she had dried drool on a green polo shirt that said The Unruly Dog Training Center, along with some kind of stain on her pants.

That road rage of hers, too…when she flipped me off, it cracked me right the fuck up. I didn't know it was her in the little SUV. She'd been weaving in and out of traffic, running up on people's bumpers or slamming on her brakes. There wasn't a chance in hell I was letting her over in front of me. When she realized it was me, the expression on her face had been fuck-ing priceless.

Lily Costello was a tough nut to crack. Gorgeous—I'd always thought that—and her ass was something to behold, all round hips and cheeks with a softness that I really, really wanted to squeeze. Not that I would with-out her permission. Texas gentleman, born and bred. Besides, with Lil, it would for sure get me nutted. I al-ways seemed to seek her out at team functions—even after I'd learned she was the GM's stepkid. I knew I shouldn't. Not smart to have the hots for the GM's step-daughter. But she was something to behold.

The first time I'd met her, she hadn't smelled like pee. Instead, she'd smelled like some exotic flower that drove me insane. It wasn't until I smelled it on another woman that I asked and found out it was jasmine. On Lily, the scent was darker, headier, sexy as hell. As far as I was concerned, the scent was Lily's alone. I couldn't smell it without thinking of her. She'd had on a deep purple dress that night. With silver studs. It left her soft, strong arms bare. Thighs of the same compo-sition peeked out of her hemline. Again, with that ass in the form-fitting dress, and I could see the outline of a small belly under the fabric.

She had a wicked sense of humor, not an ounce of pretension, and she rarely bit her tongue with me. I'd gone home with some completely forgettable jersey chaser that first night. I had to. To try to rid myself of the scent, the sound, the sight that was Lily.

Something she'd called me on the second time I ran into her. The thought made me smile. We were at a team fundraiser, expected to mingle with the guests in order to give them their money's worth. Instead, I'd spent half the night trying to find her face in the crowd. When I finally did, she'd playfully busted my balls about asking for her phone number and then going home with someone else before we'd talked a bit about her dad's playing days and the structural superiority of waffles to pancakes.

Things flowed so easy for us. It didn't matter what we talked about; we fell into a rhythm. She was never nervous or forced, she didn't stroke my ego or tell me what she thought I wanted to hear, and she sure as hell wasn't starstruck. More like the other way around.

She was real, unrehearsed, and I was in awe.

Yeah, I was for damn sure attracted to Lily Costello, but my brain was on board, too.

She was my magnet. "Am I really so bad, Lil?"

Her dark blue gaze snapped to mine as she tucked loose hair behind her ear. "No. Sorry. I've had a bad day is all. Is this the dog that made the news?"

"Yeah. I've only had her a couple weeks. She was wandering outside the practice facility, limping, skinny as hell, and skittish. Got her to a vet and they had to muzzle her to clean her up." The wound on her foot had been badly infected, and she'd had two clusters of ticks attached to the skin above her tail. But the wound on her neck had nearly sent me into a rage. She'd been knifed. Like somebody tried to slit her throat. The vet had bathed her, removed the ticks, and put her under to clean and stitch the wounds. She was so damn scared in the vet's kennel it broke my heart, yet the warning in her eyes was all *you don't wanna fuck with me, buddy.*

I understood that look on a gut level.

Hiring the pet sitter was a stupid idea. I absolutely blame myself for that. When I couldn't get the dog to go outside to pee or poop, I should have hired a pro trainer right then. Instead, a friend told me to try a dog sitter when I wasn't home for the day to clean up after my girl. I paid the guy's hospital costs—which were as extensive as antiseptic, Band-Aids, and a precaution-ary round of antibiotics—as well as offering him five large because I felt bad. Hell, he returned to work the same day. Then he realized who I was, and the scratch on his forearm became a traumatic event.

Now he wanted a seven-figure settlement.

The elevator door slid open on my floor, and I mo-tioned for Lily to go first, wondering what kind of pant-ies she had on under those pants. What would that ass look like bent over my couch?

My dick twitched. *Fuck, don't go there.* I was al-ready on thin ice with the Bulldogs, and my no-trade clause was contingent upon my conduct. I was sure after all the shit I'd stepped in lately that banging the GM's stepdaughter would be crossing the line.

The fantasy suite scandal had been an epic cluster-fuck that was still in the news. I'd been in the down-town Dallas hotel that night, but when my teammates started getting naked with those chicks, I took off.

My reputation with women wasn't great, I freely ad-mitted it, but I didn't screw around anymore. I hadn't in a while. Boring Brody didn't sell magazines, and the girl from the fantasy suite who'd tried to blackmail us had doctored the pictures, inserting me into the thick of things. I owned that I'd been there, but I left before shit went sideways. The fact that the news broke only a couple months after I slept with someone who turned out to be the team owner's granddaughter didn't exactly help matters with the organization.

She never told me who she was, and it was a one night thing when I'd needed to blow off some steam.

Now, the owner wanted me gone, pronto. I was hanging on by a thread, especially at my age. I was planning on retiring once my contract was up, anyway—the rookie linebacker from Florida was breathing down my neck. I wanted to finish my career in Dallas. I'd played all my ball here, from peewee on up. Hell, my mom still lived in Plano and came to my home games.

The GM was clear—if I didn't keep my dick in my pants and my face off the news, I wouldn't get to play out my two-year contract and retire from my hometown team.

So, yeah. As much as I liked Lily Costello, she was strictly off limits.

"Is she a mixed breed? How big is she?"

I forced myself to pull even with her as we walked the length of the hall. "Yeah, she's a big girl. One-ten, maybe? Some kind of Pit Bull, but bigger? Looks intimidating as hell but she sticks to her kennel like she's scared.

"I think if it'd been a yorkiepoodleretriever that nipped that sitter, he wouldn't have made a fuss. My girl barely broke the skin. Honestly, I'd watched the nanny cam footage I set up to keep an eye on the dog during the day. I would have bit the sitter, too. I told him to check on her, let her out to potty in the bedroom on the pads because she wouldn't tolerate a leash. If I try to take her outside, she locks up on me before I can get her out of the room.

"The sitter tried to drag her out of the crate by looping a leash over her head and pulling. Now this guy is playing it for all it's worth to get into my pocket." I felt the lines in my forehead deepen.

"A lot of those folks don't have a ton of experience when they take a job as a dog sitter and don't have the proper training in canine behavior. Working with dogs sounds like a fun and easy way to earn some money. Until it isn't.

"Most of the time, when a dog bites a person, it's either because they've been trained to, or the human isn't reading their behavior correctly. She likely panicked on the leash. Since you found her outside, I doubt that will send her into a panic, but getting her out there might be an issue. How did you get her to go with you?"

Meeting Lil's eyes this close with the light from the end of the hall filtering in, I discovered that they weren't blue like I'd thought. They were the most amazing shade of violet. "Uh, protein bars. I unwrapped one and threw it in the back seat of the cab. I held another and sat on the parking block. Took about twenty minutes before she came up to me and took the pieces from the ground. Another ten, and she was eating from my hand. She'd let me touch her side, but if I reached for her head she ducked away. The emergency vet found a gash in her neck. It's healed, and the stitches are out, but it was bad. Vet said it was a knife wound and barely missed her jugular. I'm guessing whoever tried to slice her throat is sporting some serious wounds of their own because they obviously didn't finish the job."

Lily's nostrils flared and I could almost hear her molars grinding together.

"When I stood up off the parking block, the dog skittered back. I thought she was going to run away, so I opened the door of my truck and threw the last of the bar in the back." I shrugged. "I got lucky, I guess, because she jumped in."

I slipped my key into the lock. I knew I was staring, but I couldn't stop trying to get another peek at those purple eyes. "I figured, out there in the north forty at the training facility, there's coyotes and bobcats. Even heard tell of a couple mountain lions. I didn't want her to be something else's dinner. Hey, are your eyes purple? They're mesmerizing, Lil."

She nodded, chewed on the inside of her lip. "It's a mutation. They're not actually purple. It's a shade of blue that appears violet in certain lights. But that really wasn't smart, Brody. A dog that big could have attacked you from behind while you drove and taken your head off. You should have called the nearest rescue or animal control. And dude, the way you're staring is full-on creeper."

Like I said, Liliana Costello did not sugarcoat shit. I huffed a quick laugh. "Sorry, don't mean to be creepy. I've never noticed it before, and I've never seen anything like it." Lily cleared her throat, forcing me back on topic. "The dog stayed curled in a ball on the floor-board. But, yeah. I realized that after the fact."

Pushing the door open, I motioned for Lily to go first, resting my hand on her back without thinking. The small touch sent a shock of heat through me and a shiver through her.

"Wow. This is… I expected it to be bigger."

I snickered as she surveyed my apartment. "That's what she said."

She let out the most inelegant snort. Yet, that beautiful purple hue sparked with her smile. I liked making the woman smile.

My apartment was open and airy with comfortable furniture and two bedrooms. "I really don't need much. The flashy stuff isn't my thing."

Lil nodded. "Smart. I don't need a lot either. Where do you keep her kenneled during the day?"

"In the guest room." I led her down the short hall, tennis shoes squeaking on the floor.

"What's her name?"

"I haven't given her one yet. I was hoping her personality would show itself."

"Well, that's your first assignment. If you're keeping this dog, give her a name."

I nodded, opened the door. Huddled in her open-doored kennel, she was folded into a small ball. All black brindle, with cropped ears laid back tight against her massive head, she missed nothing as we entered. "She doesn't like to come out of there. Especially when someone is in here with her. I come home and check on her, and she'll wait till I leave the room before she emerges. She'll leave it to eat and do her business on the pads, then she turns around and goes right back in. And I already learned if I shut the door to it, she'll do her business in the kennel if she has to. I didn't want to have to give her a bath as scared as she's been. As long as the door stays open, she won't do her business in there. So, I took out everything of value and now it's her room."

"Mmm." Lily scanned over the monster of a dog and took everything in. "I'll need to get her out of the kennel, but I'm already seeing two things. First, she's not a Pit mix. She's a Cane Corso."

Huh. "Never heard of that breed."

"It's an Italian Mastiff breed derived from an extinct breed called Molosser. Actually, all bully breeds come from Molosser. Even the little guys like Frenchies and Boston Terriers." Her voice was soft and even, soothing, as she spoke. "Corsi are a working breed with highly developed guardian instincts. Very loyal, but they need firm, positive reinforcement combined with continuous socialization to be good family pets. A lot of people want Corsi because they have the 'tough' look. However, when people don't have the skill set or knowledge to handle a powerful breed with guarding instincts, bad things happen."

Her voice was getting louder. Not sharp, but firm. Confident. The dog's ears twitched at the sound; her head turned in Lil's direction. "The breed gets a bad rap because so many owners pick them for the wrong reasons. They don't think about how the breed will actually fit into their lives. An unsocialized Cane Corso is a bite waiting to happen. But, properly socialized, they are some of the most loyal and loving companions you can have."

"Cane Corso. Huh. I think I'll call her CC. You know, your stepdad wanted me to have her put down. I couldn't do it. She's not a bad dog. She's misunderstood. She needs somebody to believe in her is all." I let my head drop forward a bit. I wanted so much to give her a good life, yet I didn't know where to start.

Lily smiled, put a hand on my arm. The touch kicked up my heart rate as heat rode down my spine. "I get it. And I love that Brody Shaw, big mean linebacker, goes all soft for his rescue pup."

I didn't think it was possible for me to get embarrassed, but I felt the tips of my ears turn red.

"She'll come around with time and patience. If you don't think you have those, plus the energy to put into her day-to-day care and training, tell me now. I'll make other arrangements for her, because she's going to be some work. Right now, that kennel is where she feels safe. I'd guess she's spent most of her life in one. Wherever she came from, she's not had an easy life, and it's going to require a lot of work on your part to earn her trust."

I didn't have to think about it at all. "No, she's my dog. I'll do whatever needs to be done to make her life with me stellar."

Lily gave a solid nod, her lips turning up at the corners. "Okay. I'm going to get her to come out. Why don't you have a seat to give us some room?"

I sat in the corner chair and watched the raven-haired trainer work her magic. She moderated her voice the entire time we'd been in the room, but now her tone changed to one that held more authority. CC's ears perked, her massive head coming up from her paws to watch the trainer.

Lil knelt in front of the kennel. She didn't baby talk or coo; she simply spoke in the same confident tone that perked the dog's ears. She told CC how brave she was. That she was safe. That she wouldn't let anything hurt her. It didn't matter what she said because the point was the delivery.

Within a couple of minutes, the dog moved to the open door to investigate the trainer, who offered a palm to sniff. After a gentle nosing, Lil scratched her behind an ear and my girl's eyelids drooped in pure bliss. She stopped before the Cane Corso had had her fill, and a question filled CC's puppy-dog eyes when Lily pushed back a few feet. While she spoke, Lil produced a treat from her pocket.

It proved too tempting, and my girl emerged from the kennel to investigate. It was something to see. Lily was in control of the situation, the dog picked up on it, and as a result, started to relax. She peered around as if seeing her surroundings for the first time. The dog ducked when Lily stood to her full height, and nearly dropped to the floor. As soon as her new friend reached into her magic treat pocket, CC's heartbreaking reaction was replaced with curiosity.

"She's inquisitive, eager. That's good, but you're going to need to repeat this process until she comes out on her own to find you. You'll want to keep treats with you whenever you're with her to reward her for good responses."

Lily's patient yet firm voice was doing it for me, too. The woman was totally in control and it was hot. "What about bad behavior? Housebreaking and all that?"

When CC sat next to Lily's leg and nosed her pocket, Lil offered her another treat. She patted CC's head, examining the dog's scarred neck and the smaller scars on her ribs. I had no idea how she'd gotten those. Barbed wire maybe, or a cage that was too small. Like they came from some repetitive action and the scar tissue was so thick hair no longer grew.

When Lil started moving around the room, the dog followed. The trainer rewarded her with another treat. "For now, ignore any unwanted behavior until she's more confident. What puts her at ease is feeling like you'll keep her safe. You want her to feel that all the time before we worry about bad habits. Once she's sure of herself in the apartment and seeking you out on her own, we'll worry about the rest."

I propped my elbows on my knees. My voice came out grated. "Make her feel safe. I can do that."

Whatever my girl had endured before she hopped in my truck, she'd never have to worry, or scrounge, or shiver, or fight again. Lil must have noticed the emotion swimming through my eyes because her own softened.

"I'd like to get her out to your living room so I can look her over better." She reached into her pocket, producing a handful of treats. "Hold on to these. I'm going to lead her into the hall behind you, and then you'll take her out to the living room the same way I get her to go with me. Sit on the living room rug and let her come to you. Reward her when she does. If she asks for more treats, reward her again. If she asks for affection, give it to her with a gentle touch, but don't lean over the top of her or make prolonged eye contact because those are threatening gestures in dog language, okay?"

I nodded.

"You go in front of me and hold the treats in your left hand. Once we're in the hall, I'm going to move away, and she'll slide up next to you. As soon as she does, give her a treat and say her name in a gentle voice."

CC circled around Lily's legs, sniffing. Patting her hip, Lily took a couple steps forward and the dog stayed with her.

I fell in ahead of them and moved into the hall. In a seamless transition, a massive brindle head appeared next to me, nosing my hand for a treat as Lily stepped away. "Good girl, CC." My voice was even, calm. "You're such a pretty girl. Wanna come sit down with me?" She stopped nosing my hand, instead contemplating me with interest, and when her mouth fell open, her enormous tongue lolled to the side.

As soon as my butt hit the rug, she dropped down to her haunches and began nudging my hand for treats. I talked to her, rattled nonsense, told her about my workout and the pretty girl who flipped me off. She listened to it all. Ears pulled forward, her head cocked from side to side like she was trying to comprehend what

I said. My smile must have been a mile wide because Lily chuckled as she sat down with us.

"What do I do when I run out of treats?" I only had a couple left.

"She'll be fine. We're going to watch what she does and I'm going to look her over." Lil's smile was soft. "Corsi are intelligent, loyal animals, but they need a strong owner, or they'll walk all over you. Your job is to remain gentle and confident, and trustworthy in her eyes." While Lily spoke, she watched my girl with intense precision. "She's going to need a job at some point, too, or she'll take it upon herself to make sure guarding is her job. She'll need socialization. Lots of exercise. She's obviously been bred a lot in her short life. I'm guessing she's around three, maybe four years old? A vet would be more accurate. The way her nipples protrude indicates she's nursed several litters. What the..." Lil squinted, scooting closer and leaning down to study something on the dog's belly.

"Something wrong?" CC lay down, resting her chin on my leg.

"She's got... Fuck." Lily blanched. "She's been branded. And I've seen this brand before. Six times. Only once on a dog that was alive, and it was a close thing. My dog, Mack, has that brand."

"What? Are you sure?" I leaned over and spied the number sixty-three and the letters DA burned into the dog's abdomen. I felt like a shit for not seeing it sooner. With her curled up in the kennel all the time, I didn't have much of a chance. The rage monster I saved solely for the football field was dangerously close to the surface. "Who the fuck would do that?" CC jumped up, skittering away from me to hide behind her new friend.

Lily patted the dog's shoulders, scratched her ears to settle her. "A puppy mill. Dogs are livestock to them. With less freedom. I'm guessing the number is so they can keep straight which dogs have been bred to which and who produced." Anger crested her cheeks, but Lil stayed calm to keep from upsetting my girl. "Shit, Brody...her behavior fits the mold of a mill mama, too. Not wanting to leave her kennel because she's only lived in a cage, likely in deplorable conditions, expected to churn out litter after litter. Even the scars on her flank."

"Are you fucking kidding me? I mean, I've heard the term before—I know what a puppy mill is—but exactly how bad is it?" I was desperately trying not to lose it and blow all the progress we'd made today. I knew the basics—a puppy mill was a large-scale "breeding" operation that sold puppies for profit. They were nothing like legitimate breeders. In mills, puppies were a means to an end, not a part of the family.

"She must have escaped. I'm guessing when they did this"—she tapped the angry skin on CC's neck—"it went wrong and CC got away. Damn it. I'd give anything to get rid of these puppy-for-profit operations. This particular mill hasn't been easy to find. Five of the other dogs with this brand were killed and dumped in the woods a few miles from the rescue that picked up Mack. Every time I've tried to find this mill, I've hit dead ends."

"I could help you? I wanna help you find this place

and close it up for good, Lil. I'm all in." I was out of treats, but when my own emotions settled from anger to determination, a large black snout inched forward and nosed my hand. As I ran my palm over her massive head, she pushed back against me.

In my career, I'd had some real highs. I once had three sacks in a single game on the most prolific quarterback in the league. I'd been to the Pro Bowl four times, and I currently held the single season record for tackles.

Yet, *nothing* compared to the elation, warmth, and love I felt the first time my dog pushed her head against my palm and asked me for a pet.

Absolutely nothing.

Chapter Three

If it sounds too good to be true...

Lily

I've seen that expression on a dog's face a hundred times before. The moment they choose the person who chose them. It was one of the most heartwarming things a trainer could witness, the first time a dog—especially a rescue—decides to give its love freely and without presumption.

I choose you, human. You will be my whole world until I take my last breath. I will give you my unconditional love because you will not fail me.

Of course, it didn't always work that way. We failed them plenty. In the worst possible ways for reasons a dog could never comprehend. Yet, as often as we failed them, they had an unparalleled capacity to forgive. To move forward and continue to love with open hearts and minds.

I envied them that.

There are people who simply don't notice that moment when it happens. The light bulb doesn't go on for them, and they don't realize the commitment the dog is making, or the one they're making in return. For those folks, a dog is only a dog. They are things, possessions, like the new Mercedes sitting in the driveway that they might trade in on a new model in a few years' time.

With Brody, the light went on.

He and I had been acquainted enough over the years that I knew the man wore a few different faces—and no, I did not want to think about how much I'd studied his face. On the field, Brody was all business. Be it practice or game time, he was the physical manifestation of determination and testosterone. He used the charming face during interviews and parties. It made him seem approachable even though he was guarded—a nifty little trick of his. Then, there was Brody's flirty face. When he leaned in a little too close and made you feel like the only woman in the room. The cocky smirk that said he knew he was good in bed. The promise of dirty sex sparking in his eyes. It was hypnotic and he knew it.

But this Brody…his face was open, his gaze wide. Knowing. His forehead absent of lines and his lush lips the slightest bit slack.

He got it. He understood the gift his dog was giving him and received it with awe and reverence.

He cleared his throat and his eyes turned glassy. So did mine. "I'm…do you see this? She's never done this before. Never asked me to pet her."

I grinned. "It's a wonderful thing to feel, isn't it?"

"I…yeah. I think I just fell in love." His lips quirked to one side as he stroked CC's cropped ear.

Avoiding touching the dog so as not to shift her focus to me, I rose and sat on the leather sectional to get some much-needed distance. "I'm pretty sure you were already in love. Now you realize it." Brody's nod was small, his smile, adorable. "You need to spend as much time with her as possible to build on this bond. Encourage her to follow you around the apartment. I'd like to give you two a couple days' bonding time before our next session, but I want you to move her out of the guest room into your bedroom. Dog packs sleep together. You want her to think of you as her pack. We're going to put an ex-pen and a soft-sided crate in there for you. I have one of each in the car. You can borrow mine until you get your own."

"What's an ex-pen?"

"An exercise pen. It's a gated area to give a dog room to get out of their kennel but limits where they can go." I whipped out my phone, started searching the web. "Give me your number, I'm going to text you the link for a crate. It's a bad idea to put her back in the wire crate in the guest room because she associates it with fear. We don't want you forcing her into a fearful state right now. The ex-pen will serve two purposes. It should give her the security she feels with confinement, while keeping her from tearing your stuff up. I'd move anything valuable out of your room."

Brody rattled off the numbers and I texted him the link. "Should be able to get it in few days' time. I'm also going to text you links for some helpful products, like floor cleaner and big dog poop pads."

"Am I always going to have this pen in my bedroom?"

"No. In time, you'll be able to keep her in the crate without the pen. It will become her safe place. Dogs are den animals. She doesn't want to relieve herself in her kennel and we want to keep it that way. Yet, we can't crate train her like we would with a puppy because she may have never known life outside of one until she escaped."

Something was perplexing me about CC. Her ears were cropped and her tail, docked. It wasn't likely a mill would go to the trouble with their breeding stock because the buyer would never see the dog. Which meant CC was either born in the mill and they docked and cropped her because they had planned to sell her as a puppy. Or, she came from a decent or backyard breeder and somehow ended up in a puppy mill.

"When the new kennel arrives, we'll be able to start working on housebreaking. As long as you're home, let her wander with you and explore. If you need to use the treats again to get her to follow you, that's okay, too."

"Treats are my friend, yeah?"

"For now. After a while you won't have to use them anymore except for new things. Before I leave, we're going to put on her collar and leash. She'll scratch at the collar but don't take it off. We'll try taking her outside, too, to see how she does on leash. I'm also going to give you a few basic commands to start working on."

I put a hand on his shoulder and the hard muscle

beneath flexed tight. "There will likely be setbacks, Brody. This process is two steps forward and one step back for most dogs. Some dogs make leaps and bounds. Some take baby steps. Some never recover, but I'm quite sure CC is going to be okay. She's smart, motivated, and starved for contact she didn't even know she wanted."

He pushed his huge body up on the sofa with his triceps, let his elbows rest on his knees. Shaking his head, his voice was nearly a whisper. "I just…what the hell is wrong with people? I'll never understand how they can be so cruel. For the sake of money." I understood the sentiment more than he knew. CC curled into a ball between his spread ankles. This man…there was so much worry and concern on his face. Maybe not all the time, or for everyone, but when it came to his dog, Brody was a softie.

No, I didn't want to know this side of Brody. This face. It made me want to let my guard down. To see the man underneath.

"This is why I work with dogs," I reminded myself and told him at the same time. "Dogs are loyal. Guileless."

"Truth." Brody's chuckle set CC's ears to twitching as her nub tail gave a wiggle. She liked the sound of his laugh.

I did, too. Which meant it was waaaay past time to wrap this up.

After I brought up the ex-pen and spare crate, I offered to help him set them up before I left. *Miiiiista-aake*, I thought, as he pushed the door open. The scent of fabric softener, men's soap, and unicorn tears hit my nose. His bedroom was large. Of course, it would have to be to accommodate the bed…which I couldn't stop staring at. All garnet and charcoal sheets with a gray leather headboard. In the corner, next to a floor-to-ceiling window, sat a buttery leather recliner of the same color. Next to it, a table stacked with books.

I could see him there, shirtless—no, naked—on top of the sheets with it all hanging out as he air-dried from the shower and watched *Sports World* on the ridiculously expensive TV across from the bed.

Jesus, I needed to get out of there before I threw myself at the man and rode him like a horse at the Kentucky Derby.

As I squatted to adjust the pen's gate, I heard a thick inhale and shot upright realizing I'd just made my ass his focus. Brody stood at the end of his bed, feet spread, biceps bulging, arms crossed over his chest. The expression on his face was not flirty Brody. But damn if the promise of filthy sex wasn't written in every shadow and contour. From the lined forehead to the clenched jaw. A quick glance at the sheets, however, and all I could imagine was blond hair fanned over his crimson pillow.

Brody's smirk turned downright dirty. *Yeah, no. Time to go, Lily.* I not-subtly-at-all rolled my eyes. "Stop."

"Stop what?" His grin grew.

"I am not that girl, Brody. I'm not the leggy blonde I was just picturing there." I pointed at the pillow. "And you are in a shit-ton of trouble as it is for sticking your dick into a few too many women. Frankly, I'm not sure where that thing has been."

His mouth fell open and he barked out a laugh, but I kept on. "Rather than dancing around it, I'm going to come out and say it. Yes, we have chemistry. Yes, you're shit hot and you know it. But, if you're going to help me find this mill, there isn't a chance in hell we're getting into that bed."

"Oh, darlin'. First, nobody but me has ever been in that bed. Second, my dick is immaculately clean. I get it, though. You see things on TV, or hear it through the grapevine. I'm not going to say it wasn't true at one time." He shrugged a massive shoulder. "People grow up, Lil." Brody turned and walked to the doorway, giving me a shot of that spectacular ass. "However, I happen to agree with you. If I'm gonna help you find this mill, us sleeping together is off the table."

He refused to give me an inch to get through as I slid through the doorway. I had to choose—I could contort like an idiot to avoid touching him and give him the satisfaction of watching me try. I could ask him to move, essentially letting him know I didn't think I could control myself if I touched him—which, to be honest, was a real concern. Or, I take his dare, and either rub my boobs against him or brush my ass against his junk.

Boobs, it was.

"But…" He glanced down at my nipples pearled against his rib cage as I attempted to shimmy by. "Don't think for a second that I'm not gonna enjoy every dirty thought I have about you."

Chapter Four

*Whoever said diamonds are a girl's best friend
never had a dog.*

Lily

After arranging another session with CC in a couple of
days, I headed home for a shower to finally get the dog
pee off. Thankfully, CC gave me a lot to think about on
the drive, other than Brody, and I was grateful.

I'd gotten the collar and leash on her with minimal
fuss and a handful of treats, which led me to believe
that her biggest issue was all about trust. She hadn't
trusted Brody until today. The sitter had only made
things worse. Sigh. Stupid humans. Another handful
of treats got her through the door and out to a walking path surrounded by grass that belonged to Brody's
building. That had aroused another suspicion.

I showed Brody a couple simple commands he could
practice with her, but she already knew Sit and Down.
She also peed twice and pooped. As an aside, Jesus H, I
was glad Brody's hands were bigger than mine, because

he was going to need them in order to get that dog's poop into a baggie in one shot. I would have needed both. But besides the massive piles that come with having a massive dog, I thought maybe CC wasn't born in the mill. Someone had worked with her on the basics. I'd have to ask Brody if the emergency vet scanned her for a microchip.

My hooligans greeted me at the door to the garage. "Hey, puppers. Were you good dogs?" Mack, my Staffy, bounced around with a toy in his mouth grunting while circling my feet. Jet, my Australian Shepherd, pushed her head against my hand before circling to the back door.

I pulled it open and watched as they galloped into the backyard. They couldn't be more different. Jet was all elegance and refined femininity until it was *time to go to work*—her command for it's time to focus on her task. Be it obedience, rally, nose work, fly ball or agility, Jet was ready to kick ass and take names. And she loved to compete.

Mack, dork that he was, hit the step off the patio crooked and tumbled ass-over-head into the grass, where he proceeded to roll around snorting. Poor guy hadn't always been so carefree. I wondered about his inauspicious start in life quite a lot.

The brand on his tummy read 12DA.

Mack had come to me through a rescue. He was a good-looking Staffordshire Bull Terrier—not a Pit Bull or Pocket Pit like people assumed. He sported cropped ears and a docked tail, too. That alone suggested he hadn't been born in a mill either.

I preferred the floppy ears on bully breeds because I thought it made them appear softer, sillier, less intimidating. Some people liked that tough-dog look, and some breed standards required it as part of the dog's history and/or original purpose.

Unlike CC, Mack had zero training. Which made me think the mill swindled him out of a decent, or maybe backyard, breeder.

He worked hard to become a good companion animal. His fear response was more than the rescue could handle. It paralyzed him. I'd taken him home to work with him and the goofball stole my heart so completely he never left.

He was my one and only foster fail. And I didn't consider him a fail at all. I loved him too much to do that.

Mack Truck wasn't the brightest crayon in the box, but he more than made up for it in smiles, kisses and disposition. He did agility, too, but Mack didn't have the body or uptake to be as good as Jet. His command in the ring was *ready to play*? Because he wasn't going to do what you asked him in the correct sequence, but he had a grand time trying. He was so much fun to watch. Both my dogs loved agility, but Jet was born to compete; Mack wasn't. There was nothing wrong with that as long as they both had fun.

I gave my doofus the belly rub he was asking for then went back in. After fixing their dinner, I stripped off my clothes and turned on the hot water in the tub for a nice long shower.

What a day.

I wasn't worried about Dick's threats. I didn't care if he cut me out of the will, or off, or whateverthe-fuck. I lived modestly, within my means. Originally, before my douchebag ex, Trey, cheated, we'd planned to buy a McMansion when he finished his residency. Then I caught him with his sidepiece and threw his shit out of our apartment. Using money I'd saved, I bought this place after I finished my master's. Trey had harassed me for several years after the split, and he worked for the Bulldogs. Yet another reason to stay away from the Bulldogs altogether, as if Dick and my dad weren't enough.

Billy Costello had indeed embraced the pro football lifestyle. I loved my daddy, dearly, but I remembered with absolute clarity the fights with my mom after he'd been on a road trip and she'd found the proverbial lip-stick on the collar. How I'd lock myself in my room and listen as dad trashed the house, and then he wouldn't come home for a few days. Or when he couldn't get out of bed to come watch my soccer games.

Slicking my hair with shampoo, I lathered up. I won-dered how long it would be before Brody flaked on the mill. I wanted to believe he'd come through like he'd promised, but the reality center of my brain told me he'd ghost.

Fickle.

The man was fickle. He had a short attention span. I think he'd had one relationship in his pro career. It was the only time period he'd been photographed with the same woman more than once.

My body's reaction to Brody was also highly inconvenient. The few times where he and I chatted at some event or another were always…flirty. Eyes lingered too long on each other. Mouths would get dry while other parts of me ran slick from even the politest conversation. We focused too much on each other. Flowed too easy together. I'd even catch him eyeing me as I spoke with other guests. Yet, at the end of the evening, he always found someone else to leave with. Chemistry was a bitch when the man you wanted most was also the last one you'd sleep with.

Of course, in the past, we'd always been in public, and our flirts had stayed polite. On the up-and-up.

Until today.

Being alone with him in his apartment had set off all kinds of slippery slope warning bells in the back of my brain. Yet, when heat flooded his rich chocolate irises, I could have used a change of panties.

Turning, I let the hot cascade of water beat on my shoulders to loosen the knots in my neck. The fantasy suite scandal was still making headlines on the regular, too. I mean, the dude had been caught participating in a team orgy. I wasn't judging. If that was his thing, more power to him, but it was something straight out of an episode of *Ballers*. I only knew what I'd seen in the news, but at least seven Bulldogs players had been identified in the pictures one of the women sneaked, and Brody was in the thick of things. On top of that, they'd trashed a $20,000-per-night presidential suite.

No matter how much I wanted to rub my naked self all over his naked self, Brody Shaw was look but don't touch.

He was beyond pretty to look at, though.

I lathered my washcloth, letting the conditioner sit in my hair. God, that guy's shoulders, and arms. His thighs and butt. The hair and jaw and scruff, the lips and… Gahhh!

Then there was the gaze when he fell in love with his dog——so soulful, with an unexpected softness and complexity from a guy who could snap a quarterback like a twig. His eyes were totally at odds with the easy-going facade. Brody Shaw had a lot more depth than he wanted people to see.

Then, there was the intensity on his face when I slipped through the doorway. I'd always wondered what he'd be like in bed. The whole football thing made me think he was likely all rough and raw. But those eyes…they spoke of slow and easy. Rocking back and forth while I straddled his hips, and Sunday mornings under the covers.

Of course, that was ridiculous. Sundays were for football.

That thought killed the fantasy fast. It was a good thing, too. Thinking about sleeping with Shaw would only make it harder for me to concentrate around him—coveting what I would never let myself have.

I considered my handheld showerhead snuggled into its spot below the regular one…sigh.

Flicking the water to cool, I rinsed my conditioner, and got out before I thought better of it. Mack had pushed the bathroom door open. He was curled up on my bath rug, little nub tail going in circles.

Mommy's little monster, that was him.

I slipped on an old Donnas T-shirt and a clean pair of undies, Monster following me around tight on my heels. Jet was more independent than Mack. She was confident in her place in the world, and that place was on a stack of mattresses. With a pea hidden somewhere in the middle. Mack needed to be closer, to be reassured more often that he was safe and loved. Understandable, given his start. "Hey pally, who's a good boy, huh?"

His tongue lolled to the side. That big old smile melted my heart every time. I put on my much deeper Mack voice and answered for him. *"Me mama, Iza good boy. Iza the bestest."*

"Yes, you are." I smooched the top of his head. "You're the bestest boy ever." After kissing his snout, I pulled a comb through my hair. "Guess what, pally. I met a pretty girl today who has a scar on her tummy like yours. Her dad said he's going to help find the fuckers who did it to you." I hoped.

Following me to the spare bedroom-turned-office, he watched as I pulled out the folder I'd stashed in my desk over a year ago. It was time to study it with fresh eyes. Seven dogs with that scar, two that had barely escaped with their lives. Five weren't so lucky. One with a failed attempt at a slit throat, and my boy with scars from buckshot that had been stuck in his nose, neck, and shoulder.

Collapsing on the couch, I pulled my legs under me. It was never fun to go down this rabbit hole, but Mack had no voice. I would be the voice he didn't have. With his head on my hip, and Jet's fluffy butt brushing my other thigh, I cracked open the file. Nothing killed lady-wood quicker than puppy mill research.

Sometime later, I woke up on the couch to a text alert. My open laptop was sitting on top of Mack's snoring body.

I picked up my phone. Eight thirty p.m. Jesus, I was tired.

Then, I saw who the text was from. Wide fucking awake.

Brody: Shit. I left a Hershey bar on the counter for five seconds, and when I turned around it was gone, wrapper and all. CC has foil hanging from her lip. Do I need to take her to the emergency vet?

Brody sent a picture of the offending counter surfer with Hershey wrapper stuck to her lip. I barked out a laugh.

Me: First, I didn't think you guys were allowed to eat stuff like that. Second, don't panic. Was it dark chocolate?

Brody: First, off-season. Second, it was milk chocolate.

Me: She probably doesn't need to go to the vet but keep your eye on her. Dark chocolate is worse for dogs. Also, CC's a big girl—it would take a lot of chocolate to poison a dog her size. If she starts acting agitated, has muscle contractions, excess vomiting—then you need to call the vet. Chances are she'll be fine.

There was a long pause.

Brody: What about the wrapper? She swallowed it, too. Do I just wait for her to…you know?

Talking about dog poop was a way of life for me. I forgot now and then that it made other people uncomfortable.

Me: It'll pass. Keep an eye on her poop to make sure she's going normally. If she gets diarrhea or seems constipated, call your vet. CC is a big dog who produces big piles. Much less chance of her having an issue than a Yorkie.

When he didn't answer right away, I plugged in my laptop and put the dogs out for the last time that night. After whistling them back in, I crawled into bed, huddling down in the covers. It was my favorite season in Dallas—that two days between winter and summer when it was cold at night, but the sun was warm during the day. Spring, that was it. I wished it lasted longer than two days.

After I patted the bed, both dogs jumped in. Mack bracketed my left side while Jet curled into my ribcage on the right. I was starting to doze when the phone pinged with another text. Sigh. I'd given Brody my number because I knew he'd worry constantly for the next few weeks. I was beginning to think it was a mistake—I couldn't stop thinking about his handsome ass if he wouldn't stop texting.

Brody: I took her out, seems fine. not the least bit bothered, but I feel horrible.

Me: If it makes you feel better, Mack once ate a sock. I didn't know until he threw it up on the couch. It wasn't blue anymore.

Brody: LMAO! I gotta meet this dude.

Brody: Our first manners class is in two weeks. Is there anything special I'll need?

Me: We have private lessons at the center, if you'd rather? They'll email you a list of stuff you'll need for class.

Brody: Are you offering to give me…private lessons? Why, Ms. Costello, I'm scandalized. ;)

Me: Did you really just send me a winky emoji?

Brody: Hey, it wasn't a dick pic.

Me: Classy, dude. Real classy.

Brody: Is anyone else sending you flirty winky emojis or dick pics?

   I felt my eyebrows pull together, but a part of me really, really wanted to go down the flirty text road. Sigh. Time to nip it in the bud.

Me: First, none of your business, but no. Second, your attention span with women is like a spider monkey on meth. I don't date my stepdad's employees, Shaw. And I don't hook up with guys I'm working with.

Yikes. That was blunt even for me. It was a solid minute before the dots popped up.

Brody: You know all the orgy stuff is a bunch of bullshit, right?

Honestly, I didn't know if I believed him or not. The evidence was pretty damning.

Me: I know we have chemistry, okay? But the dogs come first. Always.

Brody: Yeah. TBH, getting involved with you would be a shit storm. If the media got ahold of it, they'd say I'm sleeping with you to get in good with Dick…and that's not why I want you under me.

Brody: At. All.

Me: Brody!

Brody: Not gonna lie. I've been thinking about having you under me since we first met. You in that purple dress. The way it showed off your ass-sets… I wanted that particular ass-set filling my palms.

Me: BRODY! You have to stop.

Brody: One condition.

Me: Thank God, anything.

Brody: Tell me you've never thought about me? How we'd...fit, Liliana? How we'd move?

The truth was I'd thought about what it would be like having Brody between my thighs a lot.

He was the kind of man that took up all the air in the room. Not only handsome and built, but engaging *and* smart. When I talked to Brody Shaw, I felt like he was invested in listening to what I had to say. Every word of every sentence. Even discussing football, he never tried to mansplain it to me like other players had.

His reaction when he'd found out my father was a Hall of Fame linebacker, was comical. We'd been talking about his lucky streak of playing his entire football career in Dallas, and I told him that even my dad had played for another team before I was born.

Brody leaned against a pillar, his legs crossed casually at the ankles as he sipped bourbon from a tumbler. "Oh? I didn't know your dad played. Where at? What position?"

Damn, the man could wear a suit. Navy, with a crisp white shirt and a red pocket square. One corner of my lips lifted. "Yeah, my dad was a linebacker, too. Billy Costello."

I watched as the wheels turned in his head and he put two and two together. The way his eyes widened to ridiculous proportions and all traces of cool Brody vanished.

Then he proceeded to fanboy all up in my face. "Holy shit. Your dad was Billy Costello?"

I nodded, sipped my champagne. "The one and only."

I hadn't been surprised he didn't realize. It had been going on two decades since my mom married Dick. The media made plenty out of it, at the time, but as the talk and speculation about Costello's widow marrying his former team's GM slipped out of the media, people tended to forget those little nuggets.

"Seriously? Billy Costello revolutionized the position! Linebacking changed forever because of the way your dad played. I learned so much just watching his films and studying his form, his nose for the ball. I can't believe I didn't know he was your dad, Lily, I'm... This..."

Brody gestured wildly with both hands splashing the rest of his bourbon over the rim, on the floor. "Oh, shit. Did I get you?" His cheeks turned pink as he sputtered before trying to pull it together.

It was completely endearing. Honest. Guileless.

Dangerous.

There were plenty of men in the world I'd fantasized about—Jason Momoa, Dean Winchester, the UPS dude that always made fuck-me eyes when he delivered packages at the Unruly Dog—yet, Brody Shaw... He ticked all my boxes in a way no one else ever had.

Even Trey hadn't done that.

Which meant the man was too damn good to be true.

Me: G'nite, Brody.

Brody: Night, Lily

I got up the following morning to another text.

Brody: Woke up at 2am with this new growth against my side. Don't think the ex-pen is going to hold her. P.S. She snores. Loud. :P

Below, was a picture of CC curled into a ball against his torso. His very muscled, mostly naked torso. To his credit, it appeared he'd *tried* to cover up with the sheet, but CC had stolen a good portion of his covers. She'd also pushed him to the edge of the bed.

Sweet Jesus. Was there anything better to look at than a hot, half-naked man cuddling his dog?

I hadn't expected the ex-pen to hold CC if she wanted to get out—it was only four feet high—but seeing her snuggled into Brody like that? They were going to be just fine.

Brody Shaw had finally found a woman he could commit to.

Chapter Five

Boners in public are sooo fourteen-year-old me.

Brody

Spring was my favorite time of year in the Metroplex. The sun was shining, not a cloud in the sky. In
April, it was still cool enough to run outside. Soon
enough, life would revolve around workouts, my diet,
OTAs—Organized Team Activities, or unofficial training camps—and two-a-days.

Sitting in damp grass, I stretched my hamstrings
while I waited on my running partner.

Sun warming my face, my eyes slid closed. It was
like Lily's ass had been tattooed on the inside of my
eyelids. Dear God, those khaki pants of hers had been
screaming *pull me off, Brody. Pull me off!*

I would have moved out of the doorway if she'd
asked me to, but, goddamn, did she rise to the challenge.

I had, too. When her hand brushed over my semi, I
went full hard-on and had to trap my dick in the waist-
band of my shorts.

There was so much more to Lily than her appearance. She was confident and smart, commanding even. She'd never been intimidated to talk to me or tell me her opinion because she was afraid I might disagree.

Instead, she met me head-on and shot straight. Something I truly appreciated.

"Brody. My man."

I rolled my lids open with effort. "Hmm."

"Are we running, or are you going to continue to sit here and think about whoever is giving you that semi?" Once upon a time, Hayes Walker was one of the best tight ends in football. Unfortunately, this was a young man's sport.

I'd rounded thirty this year myself. I felt it in every bone of my body, too. Even before I'd dislocated my shoulder last year, I was in so much pain, I was having cortisone injections in that shoulder right and left.

But Hayes had a few years on me...

He was a great sounding board, and an even better player. But midway through last season, the organization moved him back on the roster to make way for a younger version. The stats didn't lie. He wouldn't be getting his starting spot back.

Hands on his hips, he proceeded to give me shit. "Now, don't get me wrong, bro. I'd much rather plop my ass in the grass next to you and see who can get the biggest hard-on, but we really oughtta go for that run, don't you think? Plus, we both know I'd win." He stuck out a hand and helped pull me off the ground.

"Dude, you killed my wood the minute you said

you eyeballed my dick." We took off, feet padding the ground at a pace comfortable for talking.

Hayes squinted into the sun. "The trail is a little over three miles. Howsabout we take it easy. My hamstring has been bugging me."

I nodded my agreement.

"So, you going to tell me who you were thinking about? Not sure I've ever seen you that way before." Hayes's side-eye was accompanied by an asshole grin.

"What way?"

"You were thinking about a woman you obviously haven't fucked, but you want to."

"How do you know I haven't nailed her already?"

"If you have, and you're sitting on the ground with a hard-on like a park perv, then I'd be even more worried. Once you hit that, you don't backtrack. Not that I blame you. Andra was a piece of work. I'd go strictly hit-it-and-quit-it too after someone like that."

Sweat crept down my back as our feet struck the crushed granite path and the day warmed.

Andra.

Most people—including Hayes—seemed to think that Andra had broken my heart and I'd never recovered. That wasn't it at all. I don't think I ever really loved her. I think deep down part of me knew Andra wanted a lifestyle, not a partnership. She wanted me to let her run wild with my black card and live in a penthouse downtown. She'd slipped right under my radar. That's why I didn't do relationships anymore. Because she was someone I thought I could love who'd played me like a damn fiddle. I brushed away the thoughts.

"It's my new dog trainer. She's someone I really, *really* shouldn't touch." It probably wasn't a good idea to tell anyone I had a thing for her, either. I wouldn't have if it had been anyone other than Hayes, especially after the owner's granddaughter. But Hayes was a vault. Leak proof like Rubbermaid.

That girl... I had no idea who she was, and she came on to me. Not the other way around. At the time, I assumed she was any random jersey chaser—she'd hidden the crazy-obsessed thing entirely too well. Plus, I made it clear from the outset it was one and done.

She thought she was the exception, because when I didn't call her, she told granddad we were in love.

Now, I was at the top of the owner's shit list and climbing up the GM's, too. Throw in my shoulder, and if I didn't walk the line, they'd trade me in a heartbeat.

"Shaawww," Hayes dragged out my last name. "You're not supposed to be touching *anybody*."

I huffed out a breath. "Damn, how stupid do you think I am? I'm capable of keeping my dick in my pants."

My running partner pushed out an inelegant snort before he grabbed my elbow and pulled me to a stop. Overhead, the live oaks provided shade with the small leaves of spring. Bending at the waist, Walker reached for his toes and hissed. The hamstring obviously didn't hurt enough for him to stop giving me shit. "I know you, brother. I know you didn't wade into that orgy. I mean, I love my teammates, but you and I both know some of those guys will stick their dicks anywhere. Following one of them, even suited up, you'd be asking for a case of the crabs and a round of antibiotics. But you're not exactly known for self-control in that area, Brody. You've been known to nail a different woman every night. I'm just saying… I know you don't screw around anymore, but…now is not the time to end up with some girl posting pictures of your naked ass to TikTok. It's not worth risking the rest of your career, my man." He righted himself.

I felt my molars grind together. That had actually happened. I'd slept with some random girl, and the next day my bare ass was on the social media app in a video the girl set to Saweetie's "My Type." It was pretty much the last straw. The women, the lifestyle—constantly worrying about who I could trust, be it a one-night stand, or someone I could see myself with long term. It wasn't worth it anymore.

I'd stopped manwhoring a few years ago, but apparently the gossip rags hadn't gotten the memo. They wrote whatever the hell sold magazines and dredged up my past as proof.

Funny, the media never really bothered me before. Until I discovered it was possible Lily believed the bullshit. Yeah, that…irked me for some reason.

Because you like *her. Is she someone you can have more with?*

That was a stupid fucking thought. She was the one person who could get me traded or fired, and frankly, I didn't know Lily well enough to be sure she could keep even a one-nighter a secret. "Thanks, Dad. You don't have to worry. I'm not going to risk losing my job."

"Hey, I'm only reminding you what's at stake. You're

the one with the something to lose here." Hayes poked me in the chest. "Don't scratch this itch, my man."

We set back to pounding the path. "I knew I never should have gone to that hotel room. Jesus, I love my teammates, but some of them…" I shook my head. "I don't want my dick anywhere near where Peterson's dick has been. That thing…last year after a practice, he came up to me, opened his towel, and says"—I put on my best Alabama accent—"Shaw, do you know what this is? It itches like a motherfucker and it hurts to take a piss.'"

Hayes half tripped as he burst out laughing. "What did you say?"

"I told him he better cover up his gnarly knob. That it was a goddamned petri dish of VD and hooker glitter that was going to fall right the fuck off."

Hayes snickered. "I'm glad I stayed home. I'm too old for that shit, anyhow."

"I should have, too. Just kept my ass at home and watched Moose and Squirrel take on the monster of the week."

"You know that's a chick show, right? Like, ninety percent of their viewers are women."

"Shut your cakehole. You don't throw shade at Dean Winchester. Bitch."

"Jerk."

"Ha! I knew it."

Hayes's arms pumped in a relaxed rhythm as he executed the combination eye roll/head shake of disappointment. "How's things coming with the dog? You get bit yet?"

"Nah. She's a good girl. She's not a Pit Bull like I thought. She's a Cane Corso. I did some research. They were bred as guard dogs in Italy, but have a bad rap because people get them without understanding the breed and don't do right by them." I lifted my shirt hem to wipe the sweat off my face.

A woman who probably did cross-fit nine days a week and could kick my ass wolf-whistled as she passed us going the other way. I turned, gave her a little salute, but she wasn't my type. Lily was my type. Soft in all the right places and strong where it counted. "This trainer knows her shit. CC lies on my lap now. She's jumping into bed with me at night and follows me around the apartment. Hell, she sits outside the shower while I'm in it. Apparently, the breed tends to form a very tight bond with one owner."

Hayes eyebrows rose. "CC?"

"That's her name."

"She sounds loyal."

"Very. It's nice for a change. Having a loyal woman in my life. Besides my mom, that is."

A flash of something crossed Hayes's face. I didn't know much about his family, but I knew it was a sore spot.

"She's a smart dog, too. She learned her name in no time and she's getting the hang of housebreaking. I worry, though. The one time I told her no a little too loud when she tried to snatch food off the counter, she cowered and hid in her kennel for an hour. I think someone's probably hit her."

When it happened, I'd texted Lily. I felt like a

douche. Lil told me not to worry, that she'd come back out when she was ready, but not to reward her for the reaction by plying her with treats inside the kennel. *That* was hard. All I wanted to do was comfort her. But she would think it was praise for the behavior and continue to do it.

When she finally came out to see me, I heaped on the love. Dogs were much more resilient than people gave them credit for. Didn't help me feel like any less of an asshole.

"What are you going to do with her when the season starts?"

"Not sure yet. Maybe my neighbors will keep her for camp and away games. I think Lily would choke me if I tried to board her somewhere this soon. She's not ready for that. I could ask my mom. She can't say no to me." My grin spread wide.

"Do you know how lucky you are to have played all your ball for your hometown?"

"Jealous much?"

Sticking out a hand, he gave me a shove before he took off at a sprint.

"Sonofabitch." Huffing out a breath, I set out to chase him down. Finally caught him stopped at a water fountain.

When he lifted his head from the spout, water ran down his chin as he wiped the sweat from his face. "Lily, huh? This wouldn't be Dick's stepdaughter, Lily the dog trainer, that I've seen you mooning after before, who also happens to be Billy Costello's kid, would it?"

Fuck. I hadn't realized I'd said her name.

He shook his head. "Wow, Shaw. You *do* know how to pick 'em."

Truer words.

Chapter Six

*The sexiest thing a woman can do
is have her shit together.*

Brody

I sat on a park bench outside my apartment building staring over the man-made pond, with CC's leash wrapped around my wrist. CC amazed me with how smart she was. The commands Lily had given us to learn, she had down in two or three repetitions. She also hadn't had an accident since she started letting me take her out on a leash.

The dog could be deceptively calm. While we waited on Lily, CC lay on my foot in the grass. Her watchful eyes missed nothing, ears twitching with every new sound. Today, we were going to see how she reacted with other dogs.

I was worried. Everything I read about Corsi said they weren't good dogs for first-time owners, which is exactly what I was. She was big, and strong, and had a powerful set to her jaws, neck and shoulders. If she decided to get aggressive with another dog, she could inflict serious damage, and the last thing I wanted was for another dog to get hurt, and/or CC put down because of it. As a guardian breed, Corsi didn't always do well with other dogs or strangers if not properly socialized. In inexperienced, or the wrong hands, they could be ticking time bombs. Which was how the breed got a bad reputation. They were on a lot of banned breed lists. Early and continuous socialization and proper training methods were essential. They also needed a human that didn't lose their cool—apparently, the fastest way to make a Cane Corso obstinate was to act irrationally. Scream and yell, and they assumed you were a head case and not fit to lead. Also, you should never hit.

I was fairly certain someone had taken *that* approach with my girl.

Any quick movements toward her, or over the top of her, and she'd cower. It hurt my heart and made me want to commit murder at the same time.

I'd spent plenty of time after that first appointment researching puppy mills, too.

Jesus Christ, they were abhorrent. Dogs crammed into kennels in the worst conditions imaginable, infested with disease. Puppy farmers didn't give a damn about the dogs, only the money they brought.

"Hey, there. Lost in thought?" Lily had stopped about ten feet away. Damn, every time I saw her it hit me in the chest and knocked the air out of my lungs. She was pretty. But I didn't have nearly enough time to admire her.

CC got to her feet, checking out Lily's dogs with

wariness. One of them was a little gray fireplug of a thing. His ears were cut like CC's and his stub tail was going so fast his whole ass-end wiggled. A wide scar over one eye and several small scars on one side of his neck and shoulder made him look like a dog you didn't want to piss off. His build reminded me of a running back who'd pound the ball up the middle with brute strength play after play. And the jaws…this dude could tear your arm off if he wanted, yet his lips were split into a mammoth doggy smile as he wiggled and snorted.

He was kind of adorable.

The other dog was gorgeous. Dignified and refined. I'd never seen a dog appear feminine before, but this one had to be female with her delicate features. She was about forty pounds, her fluffy white coat stippled with red, brown, and gray patches. Ears set high on her head were folded over forward. She stood tall and relaxed on her front feet, a curious expression on her face as she checked out CC. Regal was the word.

Lily watched CC's reactions.

"That a Border Collie?"

"Australian Shepherd. This is Jet. She's a confident dog. You'd be amazed how much one confident dog can teach another about how to behave. Right now, Jet is super curious about CC and how she's going to reac— ah, see? There it was. CC looked away."

I watched my girl, who I was keeping on a very short leash. She'd turned her head to avoid Jet's eyes.

Lily went on. "In dog language, prolonged eye contact is a challenge. When CC glanced away, she deferred to Jet. I think we're good to introduce them one at a time. Mack first." Lil turned to Jet. "Sit, girl. Stay." The dog did as she asked and Lily dropped Jet's leash and started toward us. Damn if I didn't admire those yoga pant thingies she had on. The woman had powerful thighs. The kind I wanted to feel wrapped around my waist.

Shit. Knock it off, Shaw. I was doing a piss-poor job of not thinking about Lily and all manner of dirty things I'd like to do to her.

Standing, I put a hand up to keep Lily from coming closer. "What about that dude?" I eyeballed the running back.

She glanced at the Pit Bull then back to me. "Trust me, big guy, you and CC have nothing to fear from Mack Truck. He doesn't have a fight response."

As Lily neared with Mack, CC's ears dropped back against her head. When he went to sniff her rear, my girl jumped, letting out a little growl. My heart hurtled into my throat, but Mack dropped down to his belly and rolled to his back right under CC's chin.

CC sniffed his junk, sans jewels. Her own tongue lolled in greeting. I couldn't help my smile when both of their nubs began to wiggle. It made my chest warm in a way I hadn't experienced in a long time. After Mack got to his feet, the two dogs danced around each other, sniffing.

I patted CC's head, then Mack's. "Hey, buddy. Aren't you just a little meatball?"

A soft grin spread over Lily's face. "I'm going to call Jet over, okay?"

My shoulders tensed and Lily paused.

"Brody, CC takes her cues from you. If you relax, she will, too."

I rolled my neck, tried to let go of the tension, but I couldn't help but think of the damage my enormous dog could do to the little Aussie.

Lily turned to her dog. "Jet, come." The animal rose from her sit with grace, her neck elongated and her weight over her toes as she trotted forward to Lily. "Sit." The dog did as she asked. It piqued CC's curiosity. My girl pushed forward to the end of her leash and sniffed at Jet's mouth. However, when Jet stood to sniff CC's rear, my girl spun around and let out a low growl and my heart jumped. "CC…"

"Brody, let them be," Lily whispered.

Jet quickly flipped around to face my much bigger dog as she met CC's stare. As soon as the bigger dog looked away, Jet continued over to me to sniff as if CC didn't exist.

Lily smiled, patted her dog's fluffy butt. "They're going to be just fine."

Letting go of some of my tension, I turned to say hello to the Aussie. She allowed me to touch her for only a few seconds before walking to the end of her leash in the opposite direction as if to say, *Well, are we going or not, humans?*

"Did…did she just give me the brush-off?"

Lily chortled. "First female to give you the brush-off, Shaw? Don't take it personally. It's Jet's world. We're only living in it."

I held up two fingers. "Second. Second woman to give me the brush-off." My gaze made a slow trip from

Lily's heart-shaped face to her curvy legs and back up. "Of course, her owner's given me the brush-off several times."

Her cheeks turned pink.

Dammit, why couldn't I stop flirting with this woman? I was in enough trouble. Besides, one night was my limit, and Lily Costello definitely wasn't one-night-stand material.

I liked her, found her brain fascinating. I wanted to get to know her better. Find out why she was so guarded, and that was relationship talk. I'd learned the hard way that as long as I played football, I couldn't have my cake and eat it, too. Relationships were a no go when you didn't know who you could trust.

It didn't matter how much I liked Lily; she had a direct line to the man who could ruin my career. Pursuing her would be monumentally stupid. This whole arrangement was too tangled up with my career for me to be sure Lily could like me for me instead of the number 58 on my back.

I shook off all the thoughts, pushed them to the back of my brain and pasted an affable smile on my face. "Let's not keep Jet waiting, shall we?"

As we set off down the path around the pond and into the wooded area, CC stayed tight to my leg on Jet's side.

When a squirrel took off across our path, CC lunged after it, and Jet emitted a little growl. My big girl shrank back to my side.

My surprise must have shown because Lily chuffed out a laugh. "It's okay. Jet's telling her to behave herself."

"Jet is the alpha."

Lily grinned. "No. Technically, I am. I prefer the term leader to alpha since dog pack behavior is a lot more watered down than their wolf ancestors. Jet *is* a dominant dog. Most dogs defer to her, but she takes her cues from me. It's fairly simple, really. If Jet trusts me, she'll follow me. The other dogs follow her. I only need to be in charge of one dog, Brody. But it has to be the right one."

"I mean, how do I do that? Become CC's leader?"

"First off, you're lucky. She already watches you for cues. She's wary of her surroundings, but you're okay with them, so she's trying to be okay with them, too. You have to keep that up by making her feel safe anywhere you two are. It's like running the defense. If you're confident in your abilities, and in control of your emotions and reactions, the other players will be confident in your ability to lead them. If you're indecisive or worried, panicked all the time, so are your teammates. They won't trust you to lead them anymore. You and CC are a team, too."

Lilly was putting it into language I understood. "I did a lot of research on Corsi."

"Oh?"

"I don't want to screw up with her, you know?"

"I'm glad you're taking being a responsible dog owner seriously. What did you learn?"

I observed Lily's profile. Her creamy skin had a pink glow. Soft, full lips I wanted to nibble on. Lily's nose turned up just the slightest. My granny would have said God made it that way to keep the rain off her lip. She even had cute ears—tiny little things that might've belonged to a fairy.

I mentally slapped myself in the nuts. "I know they have a bad rap. That people think they're dangerous and there are certain cities that have outlawed the breed. But it seemed to me that most incidents happen because of the people involved. Like, let's get the dog, then slap it on a chain in the backyard where the trash man throws rocks at it, and hell yeah, I'd bite somebody, too."

"Mmm. Truth is, every breed has bad owners, but as bully breed owners, we *have* to be diligent and put more time into training and socialization because of breed bias." She blew out a long sigh. "Because, honestly, Brody, you should know, if CC were to bite, whether it's a dog or person—even if she were defending herself against an attack—it will always be her fault. Whether she is or not, people will *say* she was the aggressor."

"That's bullshit." I felt the lines in my forehead deepen. "I mean, I get it why we need to be cognizant, but it's—"

"Unfair?" Lily pulled to a stop. I could see both the frustration and resolve on her face.

"Yeah."

She nodded, continued walking. "It is."

Stopping at a fenced area, she swiped a card. An electronic gate buzzed open and Lily led Jet and Mack inside, unclipping their leashes. I followed, hesitant to do the same with CC. Particularly after the conversation we'd had.

"It's okay. Let her off leash. Leaving her on will make her feel vulnerable because she can't run if something happens." Bending at the waist, she unhooked CC's leash and gave her a scratch on the head before she told Jet and Mack to go play.

"I know about dog parks. I just worry she'll hurt another dog, and that will be the end of CC."

Lily began to saunter through the grass. "First, this isn't really a dog park. It's a training area. The Unruly Dog owns it. Second, we're the only ones here. I signed the area out just for CC. Next time we'll introduce her to more dogs, but today it's just us."

"Ahhh. Controlled environment."

"Exactly. Now, we're going to let CC be a dog and explore her surroundings." Lily meandered through the short grass as Jet led Mack and CC around the perimeter of the park at a trot.

CC sniffed at everything. Sticks. Holes in the ground. Bushes. A bird carcass. Eventually, she even broke away from Jet and explored on her own with Mack following her like a mooning teenager.

I knew the feeling. "How did you get into dog training?"

"I used to work with my own dog all the time. As I was finishing up my master's degree in kinesiology, I went through an ugly breakup with a cheating asshole who got borderline obsessed. I needed to hit the reset button on life. Do what made me happy. I love the mechanics of the human body, but dealing with people all day… I have a low threshold for bullshit and my bedside manner is similar to my level of road rage during rush hour. Teaching my dog became my sanctuary. My escape from the people I had to deal with daily. That time with my dogs was wholly satisfying and made me happy in a way working with human subjects never had. So, I got certified.

"Besides, I never wanted to work for the Bulldogs anyway, and I knew that's where things were headed."

"Why not? With who your dad is, it seems like a natural progression."

She shrugged. "I don't get along with Dick, and football is...complicated for me."

I could understand that. Lots of people in the league speculated on Billy Costello's death, and some guys played too long because football was all they knew. Billy's accident came only a couple of years after he retired, and long before the league recognized concepts like Concussion Protocols and CTE.

I nodded, watched CC sniffing a tree. "I get that. If I could just play, I might feel differently about football now, if I didn't have to deal with all the extra shit. The media and the politics. It's lost a lot of the appeal for me." I shook my head. "The celebrity thing makes me a target. Like with the pet sitter. And I have no desire to be famous. My goal is to retire when my contract is up. To go out on top in my hometown *before* my body gives out and get away from that aspect of it."

Lil nibbled on her lip. "That's a smart plan. So, tell me what else you learned in your googling? Did you do any research on mills?"

"Besides pictures that made me so mad I had to go for a run before I put a hole in the drywall?" Remembering had my stomach turning.

"Yeah, they can get pretty graphic. It's an uncomfortable rabbit hole to go down, but an important one, too, to understand what a mill is and the difference between mills and reputable preservation breeders."

"I can't believe these things are legal in Texas."

"They're legal in most every state. In Texas, as long as they stay in compliance with the Texas Department of Licensing and Regulation, it's perfectly on the up-and-up. Texas passed a bill in 2012 to regulate and exact penalties if they fall out of compliance. The problem is, they're supposed to inspect the facilities and dogs every eighteen months. One, that's too long between inspections—more than enough time for a breeding operation to spiral. Two, there are too few state inspectors to actually do the job. The mills often go longer than the eighteen months without actually being inspected. Plus, there are plenty of inspectors who will look the other way in exchange for a big fat wad of cash."

I could see the frustration on Lily's face. As my own frustration started to build, CC wandered over to me, pushing her massive head into my leg. I scratched her ears to calm us both. "If mills have to register, shouldn't it be easy to find this one?"

"You'd think. There's a public list of breeders who register and don't meet the appropriate standard of care. There are also countless mills that choose to operate illegally. They never register with the state to save themselves the hassle. Why do that if they can do everything below board? I'm certain we're dealing with one of those."

I glanced down at my girl. "Why don't people just adopt?"

"That's the right answer for many folks, but there are also reasons people started breeding dogs for specific traits, too. Huskies are bred to pull, Labs to retrieve, Corsi for guarding the castle, Aussies for herding sheep. You can't always guarantee what traits or possible physical issues you'll get with a mixed breed. Even purebred rescue dogs like Mack and CC can come with a ton of baggage. Not every owner is capable of retraining, or perhaps they have reasons for wanting the dog to come without baggage. For me, I'll always have a rescue dog in my house. I work with a few rescues to rehabilitate dogs to increase their chances of being adopted, too. But I also understand the inclination to purchase a specific breed from a reputable breeder."

Lily raised her eyes and that violet hue hit me in the chest. "When I got Jet, I'd just lost my dog Joker. I'd finished my training certification and I needed a highly intelligent dog confident enough that she could do anything I asked of her. She needed to be an example to my students of what they can accomplish with their own dogs. I also love dog sports and wanted a dog I knew would be physically sound and fast as hell so we could compete."

"But how do you tell if a breeder is legit?"

"First things first, study the breed you think you want and make sure it's the right breed for your lifestyle. You're active, Brody, so you're fine with a Cane Corso, but you can't exactly take a Basset Hound running with you, can you?"

"Actually, I kind of run like a Basset Hound."

Lil's laugh was a quick burst. "I know for a fact you don't run like a basset."

I waved her off. "I get what you're saying. One of the reasons dogs end up in shelters is because people don't research. There are people who want dogs like Mack and CC, so people think they are badasses, but when they don't understand the breed's traits, the dogs end up with the bad rep, and overcrowd shelters."

Her face brightened. "Exactly. Same goes for health issues, exercise needs, grooming, how much time you can dedicate to the dog. I tell people to check out the breed's national dog club to find reputable breeders. Talk to potential breeders; ask to see the litter's parents. Ask for references. Do your due diligence. Dogs should *never* be an impulse purchase, either. Jet's breeder had *me* provide references. She called my regular vet and two of my instructors to make sure my dogs were healthy, happy, and that I trained with positive reinforcement."

Lily's voice was vehement. "Most people aren't worried about where a dog came from when they see the adorable French bulldog puppy at the pet shop." Mouth forming a small frown, she flashed a shadow of pain on her face.

"The puppy mill thing… I imagine in your line of work you see a lot of pups that come from mills. Is that how you got involved with rescue?"

She nodded, tucking her hair behind her ear. "Puppies gotten from mills cause so much heartache for people who don't know any better.

"Pups people buy in pet stores or from internet ads, odds are high they're coming from dogs that shouldn't be bred for health reasons at best. At worst, they're mass produced, born in filth, inbred, and predisposed to a host of serious health problems. Both genetically *and* because of exposure. They're never healthy, and they die young." She fiddled with her napkin as regret passed over her features.

"What happened, Lil?"

Exhaling, she leaned back in her seat. "Before I decided to go into dog training, my ex gave me a French bulldog puppy for my birthday one year. It was an adorable little baby with a round tummy and ears too big for its head. His name was Joker. The ex bought him from a pet store. When I took him to the vet the first time, I learned he came from a mill." Her face softened. "Joker was—it was heartbreaking. He had a ton of health problems. The older he got, the worse it was. Serious joint issues, constant respiratory problems. Really bad allergies. Then we discovered the hole in his heart."

Glassy eyes caught the sunlight. "He was six when I lost him. A dog that size should be capable of living into its teens. Plus, the vet bills and procedures trying to help him be a healthy dog. So many dogs end up in shelters because owners aren't informed. There are lots of legitimate reasons for surrendering a dog to a shelter or rescue, but owner inconvenience and a lack of due diligence shouldn't be among them. It's not the reputable breeders' fault shelters are overcrowded. It's the mills and unprepared owners." Glancing down, she wiped at her cheeks. "I know the heartbreak unsuspecting owners go through when they pay a small fortune for a mill puppy and unwittingly line some puppy farmer's pockets."

It hit home for me. This was personal for Lily. She wasn't judging. She was trying to educate people to stop others from experiencing the pain she'd been through with her own dog and the fallout that became the unwanted dogs in shelters. My heart hurt for her. I could tell this dog meant the world to her, and she'd lost him too young.

"I'm sorry you went through all that, Lil. I haven't had CC long at all, but I already know my life is richer, fuller with her in it. I'd be crushed if I lost her now. The love she gives me, it's pure. Uncomplicated. Unfailing."

Of its own volition, my hand drifted to her arm and slid until her tiny palm was in mine. "Unconditional."

"Yes. Inherently good. People don't…"

I stepped in closer and her eyes drifted up my chest, landing on my face. "Most people either don't or can't offer that kind of love."

Taking a step back, Lil pulled her hand away, crossing her arms over her chest, and the moment was gone. "Look." She tipped her head in the direction of the dogs.

Jet and CC were running together, playfully nudging each other with their shoulders while Mack tried to insert himself in the middle.

"Poor dude. They're totally ignoring him."

Lily grinned. "Oh, don't you worry about Mack. They'll come around."

Chapter Seven

Who the hell talks in hashtags?

Lily

Brody had been watching CC since we left the park. "She doesn't seem overstimulated now, and her ears are standing up. She's always so watchful. Every little thing seems to put her on alert." CC walked on leash beside Brody, buddied up to Jet like she'd been doing it her entire life. "But now, she seems relaxed. I can't believe it's that simple."

I snorted. "It's not. Some things come more easily than others. Depends on the dog. Right now, she's physically and mentally too exhausted to give a damn, but some of her caution will return. I think her curiosity will always win out. She'll always be watchful—that's ingrained in her DNA. You need to get her out for exercise every day and start exposing her to new surroundings. A tired dog is a good dog." A thought occurred to me. "Have you had her spayed?"

He nodded. "The emergency vet took care of it when

they put her under to stitch the gash closed. They gave her shots, ran heartworm tests and all that. Told me I was lucky she was heartworm negative. She was dehydrated and underweight, but I don't think she'd been wandering for too long. I need to find a regular vet. I have to follow up with the rest of her immunizations."

"I'll give you the name of my vet."

As the coffee shop in Brody's building came into view, he seemed antsy. "Got time for coffee? Unless, I mean, you have a class or client or something."

"Sure, I've got some time. And that surrounding will be good for CC. It's best to expose her to new situations after she's well exercised. Plus, I wanna talk to you about some of my observations." It took everything I had not to grin. He sounded like a nervous teenager and I was fairly sure the tips of his ears turned red. Truthfully, I'd been enjoying his company. Probably a little too much. The scene back in the park was…not something I did with my clients. Or anybody, for that matter. I had friends in the dog world who knew Joker's story, but it wasn't like me to be quite so transparent. The way Brody and I had connected back there… I'd never been so thankful for Jet's timing.

Pulling a folded ball cap out of his back pocket, he slapped it on his head. Slipped on the sunglasses he'd hung on the neck of his shirt. After grabbing a table in the shade, I took CC's leash and Brody went inside to order. By the time he reemerged with our coffee, the dogs were drowsing on the sidewalk.

"I worried about you handling all three dogs. Obviously, I didn't need to."

Flicking my gaze up, I took my coffee, and Brody's lips parted. "Jesus, Lily. Those eyes…"

"It's not polite to stare, Shaw."

Brody cleared his throat, stared at my mouth. "Uh, sorry."

A slow smirk crept across my lips. "I'm messing with you. I've gotten that my entire life. They're unusual. People stare." I shrugged, sipped my flat white.

"They're just…arresting. I can't believe I hadn't noticed them before."

"We've always chatted at night. Not a lot of changes in light." I felt my cheeks shift to pink. Time to change the subject. "Something occurred to me with CC and Mack's mill."

He leaned both elbows on the table. "What's that?"

"I think there's a distinct possibility that this mill owner has answered free-to-a-good-home classified ads to find some of their breeding stock."

One eye squinted as he sunk his teeth into his lip. It was all kinds of yummy. "Why is that?"

"The rescue I got Mack from found a handful of dogs that didn't get as lucky as Mack. They'd been dumped in the woods back off a road."

Nostrils flaring, Brody's lips thinned as his molars got a workout.

"They took pictures for the authorities, and one of them had its ears and tail cropped."

"Yeah, but a lot of these bully breeds have that, right?"

"Yes, but it's an extra expense. It's an aesthetic for a breeding dog. A puppy farmer wouldn't care about it because they're never going to let you see their breeding dogs. They could have weaseled them out of legitimate breeders, but that's expensive. Plus, if they went through the hassle of getting dogs from legit breeders, they wouldn't cart them out to the middle of nowhere and dump them because they weren't producing. They'd sell them off at auction or clean them up and advertise them. As scrutinizing as show breeders are about who they give their pups to, mill owners are just as tenacious and deceptive."

I bit the inside edge of my lip. "I think Mack may have come from an unwitting breeder. He hadn't had any training when he came to me, but confirmation-wise, he's a good example of his breed. CC... I'm ninety percent sure someone has worked with her on basic commands."

"You think she was someone's pet?"

"At one time. Did the emergency vet scan her for a microchip?"

Brody nodded. "Yeah, she didn't have one. They gave her one, but I need to send in her registration."

"Don't forget to do that. Otherwise the chip isn't much good."

Two lines appeared between Brody's brows.

I rested an elbow on the table, covered his hand with my own. "I don't think anyone is out there looking for her. If she didn't have a chip, chances are they weren't real concerned with losing her anyway. But all the little clues did get me thinking.

"Nearly all pups in pet shops come from mills, but mills are also known to sell pups online. I think this puppy farmer may have ran across CC's owner trying to give her away and picked her up to breed her. If this mill owner cruises classifieds to find cheap or free breeding stock, we may have another avenue to finding them. It's essentially the same way fighting rings find bait dogs. It's also why I tell people not to use classifieds or social media to get rid of a pet."

Brody rubbed his plump bottom lip with his index finger as he mulled over the logistics.

"We can search classifieds for phone numbers—message them if we need to, like we're interested in a dog—and narrow down the area. I can work on that since I probably shouldn't go to pet shops with you anyway."

"Spill it, Costello."

I was never going to live this down. "I, uh…might have gotten arrested at a pet shop."

Brody choked. Almost full-on spluttered coffee on me. "You did what, now?"

"It's no big deal. I got belligerent with an owner, who called the cops. They cuffed me, but they didn't process me or anything. After one glance at my driver's license, they cut me loose." One of the perks of being Billy Costello's kid.

"It's no big deal?" The way his eyes widened reminded me of a cartoon character.

"Anyhow, I didn't get much info. Mill circles are incredibly tight lipped. And I'm fairly sure my picture is behind the register at most pet shops now." I tried not to grin but failed. Truth was, this was why I needed Brody's help. I needed someone on the ground who wasn't affiliated with dogs or dog rescue like I was. Brody was that person, and the fact that he was a football player in a football town would go a lot further than some crazed dog trainer screaming obscenities.

While he held up a finger, amusement danced over his features. "I...want to revisit this. Particularly the part about you in handcuffs. But I don't see how that rolls into finding the mill? I get we can narrow it by area code. I don't mean to piss on your boots, but are we supposed to just drive around and hope we get lucky?"

"Mmm, I've thought about that. I mapped where each of the dogs was found after I left your place. They've all been within about twenty miles of each other. If I can narrow it down further, we can place our own free-to-a-good-home ad."

"That's smart. Find out where they're selling most of their puppies and then bring them to us. What can I do to help?" The excitement on his face was pure and bright, contagious.

Yet, my gaze shifted to the woman who'd stopped behind him and put a hand on his shoulder.

"Hey, Brody. I thought you could use a refill." As the barista set another to-go cup in front of him, I didn't miss how she brushed his back with, um...all of her, really. "Oh em gee, is this your dog? Why haven't you brought him before now? Hashtag whosagooddoggie."

Seriously? Have you been under a rock? Although, she didn't particularly seem the type who diligently watched the five o'clock news. She had spray-tanned giraffe-length legs she used to great effect when she bent to greet CC, and as far as she was concerned, I didn't exist. Hand to God, I strained my macular nerves with my eye roll.

An amused expression crossed Brody's face.

"What's his name? Can I pet him?"

CC sat up, scooting back under the table.

"It's a she, and she's not crazy about strangers. Best give her some time. She's still learning to trust people."

The barista jerked her hand back. "Oh, okay. Well, just let me know if you need anything else."

I was pleased to see him reading his dog's body language. He hadn't hesitated to tell the woman no. Actually, he'd surprised me a lot today. Particularly his empathy when I talked about Joker and the way he'd hinted at having his own issues with the game he played. He was kind and thoughtful, unfailingly sweet and so concerned he would screw up with CC. Surprisingly easy to blush when he got nervous or felt like he was out of his element. How fricking adorable was that?

Then, there was his research. He truly wanted to help any way he could. Most people got a glimpse into puppy mills and decided it was easier to write checks to soothe their conscience than to go down the rabbit hole. Experience told me that would be when he would bail—when things got hard and hands started to get dirty.

"Actually, you forgot to bring my friend another flat white." Brody's voice cut through. "Could you get her another, too?"

The woman's eyes bulged.

That...did not make things any easier for me at the moment. Letting Miss Handsy know that she was being rude? My pink parts gave an involuntary shiver and I could have climbed him right then.

I sent the barista a completely petty grin. "In a to-go cup, please." Because this morning had been way too revealing. I already had a hard enough time distracting myself from all the tingle feels I had about this man.

Leaning forward, a grin crept over his face as he fished his wallet out of his back pocket, producing a twenty. He slid the wallet back in and I'd never wanted to be a beat-up piece of leather so much in my life.

Mercy.

Clearing my throat, I forced myself to stop thirsting. "I have to get going, but let me talk to my dog peeps to see if they can help me send messages and make calls. You can do some of that if you want. Oh, and CC's not reactive with other dogs, which is a very good thing given her breed. I do think she should spend some time with a group of dogs, to see how she does. My Sunday playgroup meets at that park around nine in the morning. If you're free, I could meet you around eight thirty and arrange for the other folks to trickle in."

"Wait. You're leaving already? I have questions about commands and stuff. And handcuffs." The puppy dog eyes he gave me were totally by design. Bastard.

"Sorry, big man. You think you're all I've got to do today? I have a life." Though, not much of one.

He arched a sexy eyebrow. Question: When the hell did eyebrows get sexy? Answer: Brody Shaw. "I'd love nothing more than for me to be the only thing you *do* today."

I couldn't help but laugh. Until his knee brushed mine under the table and I jumped like a schoolgirl with a crush. Seeing my reaction, he decided to let it linger. Lord help me. "Clever, Shaw. You give good…" Leaning forward, I let myself flirt even though I knew I shouldn't, shifting my knee to brush the inside of his thigh. Now it was his turn to jump. "…innuendo, I'll give you that much."

The barista dropped off our coffees without looking at me. I said thank you anyway as she glanced at Brody over her shoulder. The fact that he ignored her when she did it…yeah, it was time to go.

"But, I'm not worried about you, Shaw. Something tells me you've got enough women lining up to crawl into your bed to last your lifetime. You don't need me to be one of them."

"You think I sleep around."

I gave him the *duh* look. "Brody, the night you asked for *my* number, I watched you leave with some woman you hadn't come in with hanging all over you."

I thought I saw a quick flash of disappointment. "People grow up, Lil."

I watched him, weighed his words. Was I selling the man short? Maybe, but I'd rather sell him short than give him enough rope to hang me with. Standing a bit slower than I should have, I enjoyed watching him track my movement while Jet and Mack got to their feet. "You can call me with your questions. I'll text you some info about taking private lessons...with Rob. He's our doggie basics instructor."

Brody's playful grin returned along with hooded eyes. "What, you mean my private lessons won't be with you?"

"Or, if you'd rather, he has a group class starting soon. I hear tell groups might be your thing, Shaw." I threw a wink in with the comment.

He barked out a laugh, tipped his head in a nod of defeat. "Round two to Ms. Costello. Two women brushing me off in one day. I know exactly where Jet learned it."

I wondered about the whole fantasy suite thing and how much was true. The evidence was pretty damning, yet the man I'd spent this morning with made me want to hear Brody's side of the story. It made me wish he didn't play football and all that came with it.

Still, curious kitties...besides, I really didn't need to like this guy any more than I already did.

Patting her head, I bent to whisper to CC loud enough for Brody to hear. "You tell him, girl. If he can't run with the big dogs and all that."

On that note, Jet and I sauntered off.

It might have had the desired effect, too.

If Mack hadn't stopped to whiz on a patch of grass as we walked away.

Later that day, I was in the checkout line at the grocery store flipping through the latest edition of *Dallas Life & Style* when I came across their "Spotted" column. It was a *people-around-Dallas* thing, meant to highlight where to see and be seen.

The photo captions always read similarly. *Spotted: Neiman's flagship store—oil heiress Bitsy Anderson seen leaving the Zodiac Room with party girl and former college roommate Blake Wyatt.*

Letting my gaze wander, I picked up on a familiar face. *Spotted: Midnight Rambler—Baylor Fairchild, recently divorced heir to the Fairchild cattle fortune— seen making out with It Girl Mercedes Hanes before leaving with unidentified redhead.*

I huffed a laugh. I'd known Baylor when we were kids. Once a dog, always a dog. Actually, that was insulting to dogs.

Spotted: Bourbon & Banter—tarnished golden boy Brody Shaw seen leaving with unidentified blondes under each arm. Things appeared cozy as the threesome shared an Uber to Brody's home north of the city last Saturday.

It was Brody, all right. Leaving a bar with a pair of stunning women. The photo was split. In the second picture he and both women were getting out of a car in front of his apartment building.

I felt the lines in my forehead wrinkle.

Damn it. He's exactly the guy I think he is. The quintessential baller and all that came with it.

After putting my groceries away, I took the dogs out to the backyard and curled up in my hammock with my Kindle, but I couldn't concentrate on what I was reading. Honestly, I didn't know why the magazine bugged me. It wasn't anything I didn't already know about football players. It was a hot-tempered sport played by overindulged men, and it allowed them access to a way of life I wanted no part of.

I loved my daddy, but life with him hadn't been easy. He was on the road half the year, cheating on my mother with God knew how many women and pissing his money away at some poker game or another. When he was home, he could be the doting father and husband, or the angry drunk who put his fist through a plateglass window because he'd run out of the two Vs—Vicodin and vodka. All retirement did was take away the women and the money, leaving Billy to sink deeper in on himself until I didn't recognize him anymore.

Sadly, the football hero facet of my father was also the very reason Brody would likely understand me. He could be someone I could talk to, but never someone I'd allow myself to depend on.

Catch-22 at its finest.

I needed to be smart about Brody Shaw *because* we had that connection. Not just the attraction and chemistry, or our shared love of all things Dean Winchester. We had the capability to understand each other on a level that had shaped us as people. As much as I might like to find out how deep that connection went, I wasn't about to put up with cheating or volatility the way my mother and I had again. I could be friends with Brody, partners in this mill search, even have a harmless flirt, but any secret thoughts I'd entertained about letting it go further died in the checkout line at the grocery store when I thought about my mom screaming at my dad and my dad trashing the house.

Jet pushed her head under my hand, and I gave her an ear scratch followed by a scratch on Mack's wiggly rump.

No, guys like Brody Shaw were like rescue dogs: you could only count on them being there for so long. Whatever you do, don't let yourself get attached. Because they always move on soon enough.

Chapter Eight

"Resistance is futile." —Borg

Brody

Eight o'clock Sunday morning, CC and I pushed open the chain-link door at the park. Lily was already inside, and I could see Mack hauling ass to the gate as quickly as his short little legs would carry him to see his best girl. "Hey, buddy. Did you miss CC? You've got it bad, don't you?" I squatted down to unclip CC's leash and rub Mack's head.

Lily came out from behind a pile of dirt and several straw bales with Jet in tow and smiled.

"It's okay, pally," I whispered to Mack. "I know exactly how you feel."

After I stood, CC trotted by Lil to get a head pat before she commenced her perimeter check and ignored Mack as best she could.

"Morning," I called. "What's with all the construction?"

"There's an Earthdog trial next weekend."

"What's Earthdog?"

"It's generally for smaller dogs. Terriers, dachshunds. Dogs bred to hunt rodents. They dig tunnels underground and place rats in ventilated tubes for the dogs to hunt. It plays on their natural instinct to both hunt and dig."

"Huh. Never heard of such a thing."

Lily smiled. "Next month we're having a Lure-Coursing trial. It's part of the reason the center has this land, to do some of the dog sports better suited to outdoors. The owner is talking about putting in an above ground pool for DockDogs events, too." Walking into the sun, she shielded her eyes. "How did CC's class evaluation go?"

I literally felt my chest puff up. "She's a star pupil."

"Rob said she tested out of the beginning training class and is going into manners building class instead. That's awesome, Brody."

The pride I felt... I was turning into a dog dad and I didn't even care. I understood on a whole new level why dog people got as excited to show off pictures of their pooches as most parents did of their kids. "She's so smart, Lil. He ran her through some of the baby agility equipment, and after we finish up this class, we're going to start agility for beginners."

Lil's grin was a mile wide and sly as hell.

"What? What's that look about?"

She tried to school her face. "Nothing."

"No, tell me."

"I'm just really glad that you and CC are finding your normal, is all. That you've turned into a hard-core dog lover. It's the best part for me—when someone *gets* it and becomes a dog person for life. You are such a dog dad. Like, soccer level dog dad. When are you getting your minivan and Who Rescued Who sticker?"

I felt my cheeks turn pink. "Pfft. Like I'd do that. I'm a truck guy." Shooting her a slightly embarrassed smile, I mumbled, "Besides, I've already put the sticker on my truck."

Lil busted out laughing and the sound was a shot of adrenaline straight down my spine and into my boxer briefs.

"I'd suggest before you start her in agility that you get her Canine Good Citizens certification," Lily added. "Because she's a Cane Corso, when you tell people she has her CGC title, it can go a long way to change how people see her and treat her."

"Hmm. Rob mentioned that, too. I'll check into it. Hey, you gotta see this picture I took of her sleeping on the couch." I pulled my phone from my back pocket and started scrolling through pictures as my girl finished her perimeter check and wandered back up to sit on top of my foot.

"She was just sleeping like this. With her head on a pillow on the floor, and her ass on the couch."

Lily chuckled as she scratched CC's head. "Silly girl, how'd you even get into that position?" She leaned in closer as I scrolled through pictures, and the smell of her shampoo drifted to my nose. She was so close. All soft curves, confidence, and strength. Turning my head, I took her in. She was so totally at ease, content. In her element and so beautiful like that. Whether she realized it or not, Lily dropped her guard a little when she was with dogs. I understood why she called working with them her sanctuary. It was so fucking alluring, that little crack in the shell. It made me want to continue to chip away at it, to let her behind my own curtain. Lily would understand more about the ups and downs of life as a football player better than any other woman could—how this life weighed on me and played with my head.

Then, I thought about my last girlfriend and how completely blind I'd been. I'd trusted that she wanted me for me instead of what I could give her. It was the first and last time I made that mistake. Once bitten, twice shy and all that. Besides, I had an endgame and it wasn't getting myself traded to another team.

When the gate slammed closed behind us, CC startled, and I went on high alert. It was time to stop mooning over what I couldn't have and meet some more dogs.

"One of us. One of us," a short blonde in a Nike jacket chanted as Lily continued to flip through pictures of CC. A light gray Miniature Schnauzer sniffed around Lily's ankles.

"I guess so," I said through a crooked grin.

"How's she doing?" the blonde asked Lil.

CC watched the new dog, but didn't move away from me.

"Cautious," Lily answered. "She's taking her time, but you can see the wheels turning. She wants to check Jasmine out."

Finally, my girl got up and went to sniff the Schnauzer's rear.

"Brody, this is Kate." Lily gestured to the blonde. "Jasmine's indifferent to other dogs so we're starting with her." For the most part, the small silver dog ignored CC, but I couldn't help it. I was tense all over. CC could've easily made a snack out of the little dog if she wanted to.

"She's quite curious." Kate said. "Confidence will come, don't you think?"

Lily nodded, but never stopped watching CC. "Brody, you need to relax. If you relax, CC will, too."

Making a physical effort, I twisted my neck to each side to stretch out the tension just as the gate slammed again.

A short lady with sandy blond hair and kind eyes wearing a T-shirt with dogs doing yoga walked up next to me. "Darlin' it's going to be fine. Let Lily work her magic."

"Ahh, sorry. I don't have a lot of experience with dogs and it's all making me nervous."

"Naturally." Her smile was soothing. "I imagine it would be much the same if any of us were to step on the football field with you. My goodness, you're handsome up close. The TV doesn't do you justice at all. And so big. Lily, did you see how large this boy is? What size shoe do you wear? I'm Carrie, by the way." She batted her lashes, putting a hand on my biceps. "Oh my, Lily. Have you felt these? They're so firm. Arm porn, isn't that what you girls call it? Brody's got the arm porn."

Amusement marched across my face, and I felt the

Tricia Lynne   99

tips of my ears turn red as an older gentleman walked
up next to her. Carrie was at least in her fifties. Lil
wasn't even trying to hide her giggle, and my cheeks
flamed to match my ears.

"Damn it, Carrie. Stop flirting with the boy. He's
half your age. I apologize for her, son."

I grinned, sent him a conspiratorial wink. This man
was clearly her husband, and this wasn't the first time
they'd been through this routine.

I noticed absently that two more dogs were running
in and out of our group. "To tell you the truth, I never
mind flirting with a pretty lady, ma'am."

"Oh, flattery will get you everywhere. You could
take some lessons, Everett." She pointed at her husband
while squeezing my biceps.

"Which dog is yours?" I asked, and slowly turned
to extricate my arm from her grip.

"Oh, the red merle Aussie."

A laugh burst from a woman coming through the
gate with another red merle Aussie. She had a warm
brown ponytail sticking out of a baseball cap and
a smile to match. Behind her came in a tall, curvy
woman with mermaid-colored hair. "Sorry, it's a running joke in this group," Baseball Cap said. "Carrie's
dog is Sasha." She pointed to the dog circling Jasmine
trying to get her to play. "I'm Regan. Ping is my red
merle." She pointed after the dog chasing Jet. He was
bigger than her, his build heavier.

"The Aussie chasing Mack right now is Kiwi,"
Regan continued. "That's Melissa's dog."

The woman with mermaid hair waved.

"The yellow Lab swimming in the pond over there? That's Gus. He belongs to Dave, who's currently preoccupied with throwing the ball into the water for him." Dave was a big guy, but probably in his sixties if he was a day. Yet, I'd bet he'd delivered a sack or two once upon a time.

"And I'm Everett, in case you hadn't figured it out." The gentleman in beat-up Wranglers and a John Deere hat stuck his hand out. "Glad to meet you, son. Mine is the German Wasteofur over there chasing Gus into the pond. Orion is his name." He pointed to a big Shepherd mix.

The group chuckled, but it took me a minute to get the joke. "German Waste O' Fur." I laughed.

"How's the shoulder treating you?" Everett nodded toward it. "Gonna be ready for camp come July?"

"Yes, sir. I believe so."

"Glad to hear it. You got a nose for the ball, that's for sure. Gonna be a helluva addition to the Hall of Fame someday."

"Thank you, sir."

"Oh, Lord, here we go." Melissa shook her head. "I know down here you all think this man is the second coming of Dick Butkus, but will you get real? Seriously."

Not able to stop it, I barked out a laugh. She was passionate, I'd give her that. Most people who followed football were. I didn't blame her for defending her team. Besides, I happened to agree.

"True enough. Nobody will ever be number fifty-one but number fifty-one."

Everett waved her off, leaned over with a stage whisper. "Melissa's from Illinois."

But Melissa didn't slow down. "Every year with you Bulldogs fans. Win two games in a row and you start talking championship."

A funny thing happened around then. As I was listening to them argue about my Hall of Fame prospects, it dawned on me they were distracting me on purpose. I'd relaxed like Lily had asked me to and CC wasn't by my leg anymore.

Lily was engaged in a conversation with Regan and Dave, but she brushed me with her shoulder to get my attention and nodded at my dog. My girl was circling back and forth under Kate's hand as the woman cooed to her in a soft voice.

My mouth fell open. She'd never willingly let anyone touch her except me and Lil. Not even Rob.

"Her issues aren't with dogs. They're only with people. She approached Kate on her own. Which means she's learning to trust." Lily's near whisper had my abs tightening as I wondered what those lips would feel like against my ear. I turned to her. When she saw the heat in my eyes her own widened.

Fuck if I didn't want to kiss her.

Something told me that mouth with its perfect little bow and slightly larger lower lip would taste like fine wine against my tongue. She must have read my mind because she took a step back and exhaled a heavy breath.

Shit. This woman was dangerous to my self-control.

Then, the most remarkable thing happened. Mack

cut a swath straight to CC, all wiggles and smiles and drool.

Standing in front of my girl, he slapped his paws against a patch of bare earth and the smell of clean, cool dirt rose to meet my nose. Ass-end in the air, elbows on the ground, Mack twisted his head this way and that while making grunting noises that had everyone smiling.

My girl's nub tail went a million miles an hour, but she hesitated.

Lily mumbled under her breath, "C'mon, CC. Play with him."

Jet circled behind CC, pulled up shoulder-to-shoulder with my girl. Jet broke into a bouncy run and CC launched a split second later. When Mack joined them, most of the other dogs fell into the chase.

My girl was playing! The first time we'd come, she'd followed Jet, tolerated Mack, but was more concerned with her surroundings. Now, it was as if she'd woken up and said, "Look, there are other dogs for me to play with!" Swear to God, I knew what the Grinch from the children's book felt like when his heart grew.

Out of the blue, the little red Aussie turned on the afterburners, and I figured out why Lily had named her Jet. But then CC did the same.

Holy shit. CC. Was. Fast. Especially for a big dog.

Not as fast as Jet, but her long legs made up some of the difference. When Jet hit the brakes and cut back, so did CC. Mack—who'd taken a line-of-sight to catch up—plowed into CC's shoulders, bowling her over. My heart jumped into my throat, but my girl shook it off and slapped the ground with her massive paws. The two of them bounced around, pushed and shoved each other as the other dogs came to check out the wrestling, as Mack mouthed the skin on CC's face and CC swung her butt around, knocking him over.

"Mack's found himself a wrestlin' buddy," Carrie said. I hadn't realized that the conversations had stopped to watch the play. "That's a fine dog you got there, sugar. With that kind of speed and athleticism, we'll see her in novice agility class in no time."

Regan spoke up. "You can tell she hasn't been given a chance to be a dog, and people are scarier for her, but her confidence will come in no time."

And that's when CC nipped Mack. Hard.

The little fireplug howled, and I tensed, started for the dogs, but Everett grabbed my elbow. "Wait, son. She's about to find out if she gets too rough, he won't play with her."

"Not gonna let a fight break out."

"Watch, young Skywalker. There are things other dogs can teach her quicker than you can. They won't fight. The energy between dogs about to fight is different. If you're paying attention, you can sense the shift when a fight is coming."

Lily was watching the interaction closely. She gave me a short nod of reassurance. "Everett's right. Besides, Mack won't fight with her. He'd run. Jet would fight *for* him."

Princess Jet trotted between the two with her nose in the air and CC turned to sniff at the wet Lab, who'd come to check things out.

Crisis averted.

"How did y'all know that?"

"Time and experience, Shaw." Lily grinned. "When you have a defensive player about to lose their temper, what do you do?"

"I get in front of him, tell him to take a walk. Cool off." Jet had done what would have been my job on the football field.

Lily sent me a cocky smirk. "I'm going to give you a couple of books on canine body language." Taking a step forward, she let out an ear-splitting whistle. Jet's head turned, and all the dogs followed as the Aussie returned to the group of people.

This woman.

She couldn't be more than five foot two. But I had no doubt that Lily led this pack. If Jet ran the defense, Lily was her coach.

And damn if that didn't turn me right the fuck on.

Chapter Nine

Brody

After CC's class, we wandered into the retail portion of the training center to kill time. Lily's class would end soon, and then we could talk about the mill progress. After I bought a bag of CC's favorite treats, I let her make the rounds in the large building.

She used to avoid strangers. One by one, the people at the Unruly Dog had won her over with treats and affection. She was more confident now, her ears perked up instead of laid back against her head. She'd also started seeking out strangers to say hello.

We wandered to the indoor dog fountain next to the shop and she slurped up a decent amount. After I wiped her jowls with a golf towel—something that went everywhere with us now—we walked around the training center. A puppy class was going on in one area, everyone trying to get their dogs to sit on a mat, and the sound of clickers punctuated their success. Another had a tricks class where a dog was balanced on her owner's upstretched feet. In a third area, a white-faced dachshund wormed her way through straw bales. "Rat!" the woman yelled, raising her hand. The instructor pulled a transparent, ventilated tube out of the straw where the dog had been sniffing. In another area, two teams of dogs from Chihuahua sized up to husky sized competed against each other, jumping a series of hurdles to retrieve a ball from a machine. As soon as they hit the platform and the ball launched into their mouths, they dashed back so the next dog could go.

Outside the agility ring, I watched Lily teach as CC found a cool spot on the concrete at my feet and started snoring. The space was big, probably fifty yards by thirty yards, with obstacles all around. Lily was sitting on the floor at one end of a tunnel with her legs crossed. "Snorts, you're up!"

Snorts's owner stepped up to the opposite end of the tunnel with the bulldog. "Snorts, tunnel!" she yelled, but the dog hesitated.

Lily peeked through the far end and called him. "Let's go, buddy! C'mon!" The dog reared up like a bull, throwing his butt to one side before dashing through the tunnel only to crash into Lily's lap. "Yay! Good boy!" She scratched his ears as the dog snorted and licked at her chin. Once his mom clipped his leash on, they headed for the back of the line of students.

"Murphy."

His owner unhooked his leash, but this pup didn't hesitate—he dashed through, got his treat, turned around and ran back into the tunnel, only to fly out of the entrance.

"Murphy is a tunnel sucker."

Lily's laugh hit me low in the gut.

Dusting off her pants, she adjusted the height on two jumps—one before and one after the tunnel. "Okay, let's put it together.

"Your dog is going to go jump, tunnel, jump. Then, you're going to bring the dog around the side of the jump, back into the tunnel, ending with the first jump. Got it?" Class nodded, though I could see their nerves. "Khloe, first. Then, Snorts, Phineas, Nelson, Murphy, and Bandit."

Each dog took their turn, some better than others, but all of them were having fun while Lily called out adjustments to the owners. "Call Murphy's name as he's taking the jump, so his attention is on *you* when he lands. Keep your feet moving when you reach the tunnel, too. Or you're communicating to him it's okay to stop."

When it was Snorts's turn, Lily kneeled at the end of the tunnel to make sure he got a treat for going through. "Okay, gang, that's all today. Next week, we're going to start learning the dog walk." She pointed to a long, narrow bridge painted yellow on each end.

That was when Snorts's mom made her way over to Lily while glancing up at me.

As they came my way, I couldn't help but admire the sway in Lily's hips. "Good class?"

"Hey, Brody, come meet your namesake! His mama was hoping you'd sign his jersey." Lily's grin was something to see. So was the bulldog's smile.

"He has a jersey?"

"Yes, in my car! If you wouldn't mind, I mean." Snorts's mom had a shy smile.

"Don't mind at all. Snorts is the kind of dude I could use on the line."

His mom chuckled, handing Lily the leash before taking off for her car.

I bent to scratch the dog and couldn't help grabbing his snout in a playful shake. "Hey bud, you wanna job on the defense? You look like a tackle if I've ever seen one." The bulldog danced around, making happy snorts while he chased my hand. "My namesake?" I turned to Lily.

"Snorts is a conformation dog. He has a registered name and a call name. Prepare yourself for some selfie-love. I think Snorts's mom has the hots for you." She grinned, pushed her hair back, gathering it into a ponytail that exposed the creamy skin of her neck. Damn, I wanted to put my lips there.

"Too bad all I can think about is you." It slipped out, but it was for damn sure the truth. Lily was on my mind more than I'd like to admit.

At least for a second, she looked caught off guard. Then she stepped it up. "Pfft. Yeah, right. I saw the photos in *Dallas Life & Style*."

"What photos?"

"You, leaving a bar with a blonde under each arm. They had a picture of the three of you getting out of a car in front of your apartment, Shaw. Like I said before, you've got a line of women waiting to hop in your bed that get off on that whole football thing. You don't need me to be one of them."

I didn't know anything about photos, but Lil sounded bitter. "When was this?"

She picked at her nails. "This month's issue."

That would have been Staci and Erica.

I scrubbed a hand along my scruff. Much to my dismay, I *did* care what Lily thought of me. That hadn't happened since Andra.

Andra had tried to make me into something I wasn't, and Lily believed what she saw rather than seeing the truth. I wasn't that guy anymore—and the lengths people would go to, the lies they would fabricate for money, were infinite. How could I trust Lily if she took everything the media said about me as gospel? Hell, how could I trust myself when I was a bad enough judge of character that Andra had slipped under my radar?

I wished what Lily thought of me didn't bother me so damn much.

Not only was she interesting and funny, brave and strong, she stood for what she believed in and loved deeply, I could see it with her dogs. Lily Costello was a boss. If there was a woman made for me—to understand how this game molded me, now and long after I've hung up my pads—it was her alone.

"Lil, please don't believe all that shit. It's meant to stir up gossip because it sells magazines." CC whined, and I reached down to pet her head. "You're entitled to think what you want about me—most people believe what they see, what the media says—but I didn't sleep with anyone that night."

When she angled her head to weigh my words, the lights caught her eyes. I was so fucked.

"Found it!" Snorts's mom waved the jersey and a marker in the air as she came back down the hall.

I laid the tiny jersey out across the bleachers and chuckled. It was my number—number 58—with Shaw printed above. "Huh, I'll be damned. I didn't even know they made these. I need to get one for CC so my girl can wear my number." I put on an affable smile as I uncapped the marker, but all I really wanted to do was make Lily understand. "Tell me about this name-sake thing."

She giggled. "Snorts's registered name is Champion Bello, Brody Shaw's GOAT."

"I don't know about Greatest of All Time, but thank you. I'm honored, little dude." Bending over, I scratched his noggin, to which he wiggled with great amusement. I signed the jersey *To my man Snorts: Greatest Bulldog of All Time*, and handed it back to his mom. "There you go." She seemed thrilled. After Lily took a few pictures for her, Snorts left with his mom.

It had gotten late. The center had fallen quiet except for the two of us. Lily opened Jet's crate, letting the dog out to join us.

"This class was entry level? Doesn't seem too hard to get your dog to go through a tunnel and over a jump." I was sure there was more to it. I wanted to see Lily run with Jet. Something told me it would be spectacular.

"It doesn't, huh?" She jutted her chin. "These dogs are athletes. The handlers, coaches. We do strength and conditioning workouts. They get injured. So do we.

There's a lot more to this sport than you saw with this class, Shaw. You don't have to be good at it to enjoy it. Most of my students are here for fun. To build their bond with their dogs. However, a select few agility teams travel the world with their dogs, even represent the US at the World Championships."

Why the hell did I love it when she called me by my last name?

She glanced down at the Aussie. "The dogs in this class were beginners. Many may never compete; I always have a handful of students who give it a try, though. A few of those will go on to earn titles with their dogs."

I crossed my arms over my chest. "How?" This sounded like something CC and I could do.

"There's a class system. Each dog has to earn enough points from clean runs to receive a title and advance to the next level." With pride in the set of her shoulders, Lily patted Jet's head. "Jet has her MACH—Master's Agility Champion—title. We're working on her premium title so we can make the world team."

Now I really wanted to see them run. "Are you going to show me what she can do?" I nodded at the dog.

The curl of Lily's lip was sly.

She turned on her heel, opening the door to enter the ring with Jet at her side. Annnd, once again I found myself staring at her ass. For fuck's sake. Maybe if we just slept together… *BAD IDEA*.

Was it? Or would we get it out of our system?

Hmm. Was I really entertaining this? Would she? If it was possible to get her out of my system, why did it rankle that she believed the hype? I understood what it looked like, but if she'd only try to see past it...

I watched Lily set Jet in front of a jump on one of the outer edges of the course.

"Jet, time to go to work."

The Aussie's entire demeanor changed. Her body was stiff, coiled, her eyes laser-focused on her human. Putting the dog in a sit, Lily walked twenty yards ahead. Jet's front legs literally shook, vibrating with energy waiting to be released.

Finally, Lily yelled, "Jet, break."

The dog took off in a streak of red and white fur, taking two jumps on her own before catching up with her handler, who was also off and running.

Lily's instructions came swift and clear as she pointed where she wanted Jet to go while yelling out instructions. "Tunnel!" Jet hit a curved tunnel under the dog walk at breakneck speed. The thing rattled like tectonic plates had shifted underneath it. When the streak that was Jet reemerged, her coach had moved on.

"Back!" She made a pushing motion with her hand, and Jet crossed behind the jump and took it from the backside, jumping toward Lily. Before the Aussie's feet hit the floor, her handler was yelling the next direction.

"Walk it!" Jet flew up one end of a long narrow bridge and galloped along the plank. "Hit, Jet, hit!" Jet's paws slapped the yellow-painted end of the bridge before she launched off.

It was poetic, the way they worked together. Lily had to mind where she was in relation to the dog to make difficult turns, avoid running over her dog, take each

obstacle in the correct order—at the correct angle—
and as quickly as possible without going off course.

It was a ballet of plays called and audibles made.
Even Lily's body language communicated with the
dog like a receiver's did with me before he made a
grab at the ball.

"Frame!" she yelled, and Jet scampered up a large
A-frame, flying over the top without her feet touching
down. Lily's directions never stopped. "Jump! Right!
Jump! Tunnel! Go bang!" The dog scampered over a
teeter-totter that fell to the ground as Jet moved over it.

How in the hell did you even teach a dog to do that?
To ride the movement all the way to the ground. Jet
didn't budge until the end she stood on hit the floor
with a bang. Next, she snaked through a difficult set
of jumps that required Lily use quick hand signals Jet
interpreted with ease.

"Weave!" This was the most spectacular thing to
watch. Entering on her left shoulder, Jet weaved in
and out at light speed, snaking her lithe body through a long,
straight line of flexible poles. It reminded me of an
old-school tire drill. Jet didn't miss a single one; she
managed to appear as if she were dancing instead of
weaving between poles.

After the poles, the Aussie took one more jump
and her trainer threw her hands in the air. "Yes, girl.
Yesss!" The dog jumped into Lily's arms, tongue lolling wildly as both dog and trainer pushed out hard
breaths.

I whistled and applauded. I'd never seen Jet look
more doglike. She always had a feline quality about

her, but right then—in Lily's arms—she was all happy, goofy puppy and they were a kick-ass team.

And Lily... I was in awe. All those curves and strength. Legs churning, arms pumping. My thirst was real. I was damn impressed with Lil's own agility, speed, and ability to think as she moved.

Remind you of someone?

Sideways. I was fucked sideways. Because I would have given up my MVP trophies, pro-bowl selections, my left nut, and my job to be with her at that moment.

Setting Jet on the floor, she walked toward me with an exaggerated sway of her hips, the upturned lips. The flint in her violet eyes as she made her way to me.

Damn, I wanted her. All of her. The confident trainer. The sexy siren. The smart and brave crusader.

You stupid asshole.

Yep. That about summed it up.

Chapter Ten

"Eh, screw it." —Lily Costello

Lily

I watched the slow slide of Brody's Adam's apple and an exhale escaped my chest. I knew what I must have looked like. Hair wild, sweat on my face, and for real swagger in my walk.

I loved running my girl. The team she and I made. All the hard work we'd put in to get to where we were. Jet was a beast on an agility course, and it was my job to set her up to succeed. We'd run that course flawlessly. And I'd found I didn't mind showing off a little bit for Brody.

He was thirsting, too. His eyes, hooded and dark, carried over me like electrical current against my skin. "So. Whatdidyathink? Is Jet an athlete?"

"I think that was damn impressive, and yeah, you and Jet are both athletes. How long have you guys been training in agility?"

"Since Jet was old enough to safely take the jumps."

"I could see your dad come out in you just now."

"How do you mean?"

Brody's grin was sinful as he put both palms on the half wall and leaned in. "Speed, strength. Precision and determination. The way you think on your feet and adjust to your teammate. Hell, even your footwork. I would wager if your dad could see you do that, he'd be damn proud."

Grinning, I turned and started resetting bar heights for the following morning's class, knowing he'd be checking out my butt as I bent over. Realistically, I knew Brody was a bad bet. Yet, I couldn't control the way my body reacted when he was around. I liked him watching me. I wanted his hands everywhere his gaze touched.

Chemistry was a bitch, and this little interaction was turning into an eighth-grade science experiment with Brody as my lab partner. Two milliliters of perspiration. A couple of ounces of dog hair, and a beaker full of easy banter. A healthy dose of mutual respect and understanding. Then, the teacher turns her back and you both know you really, really shouldn't, but you pick up the vial labeled connection, and he picks up the other labeled attraction, and you pour them both into the mix at the same time.

Suddenly the smoke alarms are going off and you have no way to stop the impending explosion that will ensure your mutual destruction.

When I turned back to face the half wall, Brody was leaned over at the waist, forearms rested against the edge, head hanging forward as he mumbled under his breath. The only words I could make out were Jesus Christ and sonofabitch.

I crossed my arms under my chest and watched him have whatever argument he was having with himself as he cussed a blue streak.

He lifted his head and saw me watching him. The expression on his face was somewhere between barely banked heat and amused resignation. Why was it I couldn't have this man, again? Something about his job and my family and cheating men?

I'd be damned if I could remember, because all I could think about was the rise and fall of his shoulders, the pink of his upturned mouth, and mutually assured destruction.

Standing to his full height, Brody put both palms on the top of the half wall. In a swift move, he jumped while swinging his legs out to his left and sailed over with absolute grace.

I felt my mouth drop open and my cheeks pink. Mercy. Had anything in the history of sexy men ever been sexier than that little leap?

The answer was a resounding no.

"Lily." Moving slowly, relaxed, he came toward me.

I let him get in my space. That particular distance where one magnet could feel the pull of the other. He smelled like cut grass and rain. Somewhere in my brain, a voice shouted at me not to do this, but I shut it down.

I was allowed my share of bad ideas in my lifetime.

Brody stood there, nostrils flared, shoulders rising and falling a little too rapidly. But he didn't touch me.

It reminded me of that scene in *Hitch* where Albert is supposed to go ninety percent and wait for the Will Smith version of Allegra to come the other ten.

That.

And I was the "overeager sonofabitch." On the tips of my toes, I steadied myself with a hand on his waist and stretched up to sip from his lips.

Those full, consuming lips that I'd thought of kissing so often. Wondered what they tasted like.

Mint.

How they felt.

Soft, warm, and damp.

His lower lip was bigger than the upper, the seam where they met the perfect space to cradle my own. The scar at the top of his cupid's bow. I'd never noticed that before.

His name was a whisper as I pressed my soft body against his hard one. "Brody."

His absurdly long lashes fluttered, his lips parted. "Huh."

"Do you want to kiss me back?"

When his eyelids rolled open, the brown had turned so very dark. If I didn't know better, I could've mistaken them for black. Calloused hands found my waist and I was in the air. He spun us both, taking a couple of steps. Then I was on my feet again, a full wall at my back and my front pressed into his.

"Hell yeah I do." Brody's voice was raw and so deep.

"Then you should go with that feeling."

He skated his palms around to my nape. Strong fingers slid into my hair. Brody tilted my head where he wanted it, but his mouth didn't meet mine right away. His breath fanned over my parted lips instead.

Heat and need pooled in my abdomen, air crackling around us. He held us there, suspended on that precipice as the tension built inside me and his bedroom eyes searched my face. A minute passed, or maybe it was an eternity, but when Brody brushed his mouth against mine, I couldn't help the moan. He sank into me all warm and wet and perfect. Each glide of his tongue along mine, the way he pulled my lower lip in and nibbled. Brody's kiss was a flawless dance of push and pull, give and take, chase and retreat.

I savored every velvet glide, every nip, every penetration, each brush, stroke, and caress.

I ached low in my belly, warmth flooding my body. The tenderness of it all.

He wasn't what I'd thought he would be at all. I'd figured kissing Brody would be demanding and controlling. Instead, it was *come that last ten percent. Tell me you want me as badly as I want you.* It pulled at me, pulled at my gut, and at something I'd long ago tucked away in my chest and believed would never again see the light of day.

"Jesus, Lil." Voice little more than a breath, he slid his hands to my waist, and I arched against the hard line of him. Abs taut, he slid a palm between the small of my back and the wall, his thick arm a cushion against the painted concrete blocks. He tightened that arm and lifted me a couple of inches off the floor.

"Look at me, Liliana."

My eyelids were heavy, hard to raise. I was lost in

sensations. The cool wall against my butt, the warm heavy length of him trapped between us, that rain-and-grass scent of his, the lingering feeling of his mouth on mine. Brody was consuming. Immense around me. I was not a tiny woman—short, yes, but not tiny. Yet, Brody's size made me feel downright petite. Like I was swallowed up, cocooned inside his scent and body. Safely surrounded by all his strength and grace.

With effort, I focused on his unfathomable face, taking stock of all the little scars I hadn't noticed before. His lip, chin, a cheekbone. Dark eyes full of a need that bordered on desperate. That's when I heard the rusty groan of the latch on the metal chest where I kept my heart hidden away.

Brody made a slow roll of his hips against mine, and we swallowed each other's gasps, disappeared into each other's mouths. We forgot all the consequences as his hand fisted the fabric of my shirt, and my own found purchase on his shoulders, his biceps, the thick black hair at his nape.

"Mmm," I moaned.

"Shit," he whispered, breaking the kiss to press his head to mine.

That was the moment Jet chose to let loose a bark. Both of us startled. I could see the *what the hell are we doing* on his face as sure as I felt it galloping through my brain.

Slowly, he lowered me until I was on my feet and righted to his full height. We stood like that for a moment, both of us trying to decide if we should keep going or turn back.

In the end, he made the decision for us. Huffing out a heavy exhale, he placed a chaste kiss on my forehead before stepping back.

Okay then.

I tugged at the fabric of my shirt before smoothing my hair down. Brody ran a hand over his face, the other resting on his hip while he expelled a heavy breath. I knew this was the wise decision, but a part of me ached for what might have been.

If he didn't play football and all that came with it. If we weren't working together. If I didn't come with so much baggage.

He said the rumors aren't true.

"Look, Lily—" His voice was dark and raw.

I cleared my throat. "No, it's fine. It's your job on the line, and…" *My feelings.* "…the mill search, too."

"Darlin', if it weren't for all this bullshit…"

I nodded. "This is the smart play." I wished my body felt the same. "I've got the research in my backpack. You can let CC in to stay with Jet if you want."

He whistled for CC and she jumped the wall with ease only to lie next to her bestie and go back to sleep. In the break room, I pulled the research, but I could feel him behind me. His presence was larger than life; Brody sucked all the oxygen out of the room.

Trying to steady my nerves, I cleared my throat. "Dividing up the listings made quick work of it. Having Carrie and Everett, Kate, and Melissa and you really helped, too." I turned to him and wished I hadn't. He obviously wasn't dealing with this tension and heat between us any better than I was.

Popping open my laptop, I clicked on the map I made. "I think we should rent a place here. In one of the little towns. They're in the right area code and within a few miles of the Bulldogs practice facility.

"It helps us that the dogs couldn't have gotten too far from the mill. The red pins are where dogs have been found. The blue ones are where we located phone numbers we were able to trace back to that general vicinity."

"Do I even wanna know how you got those?" He leaned over my shoulder and his scent tickled my nose.

"Let's just say I know a guy." Who I wasn't ratting out. "But see how they're grouped near these two towns?" I tapped the screen. "There's a ton of unincorporated land there. Developments have sprouted up, so the towns have started to grow to cater to the team, but it's spotty. My mom and Dick are even building here." I pointed to a cluster of acreage.

"Backroads and cattle. Looks promising." His voice made the skin on my shoulders prickle. "For an ad on Craigslist to work, we'll need to rent a place in the area. Otherwise, it won't be believable."

"That was my thought, too. We need to get a look at, and be able to follow, these people. That area is expensive, though. I can talk to my crew to see if they can help field calls and be there when someone is coming to see a dog, but I can't afford—"

He shook me off. "I'll take care of the rental. Make it seem legit and handle the expenses. I'll call my realtor tomorrow. Will we need a dog?"

"I'll handle that part." I met his gaze over my shoulder, and it hit me in the gut. "Are you sure about this?"

Thankfully, he took a half step back. "Yep. I take care of my money. There was never a better reason to spend it than this... Anything for the dogs, darlin'. Anything you need."

What *I* needed was a stiff margarita.

Because with Brody throwing statements like that around, it would take a damn miracle for me not to get attached.

Chapter Eleven

The douchiest douche bag to ever douche.

Brody

I hit the gym early to blow off some steam before I had to see the team doctor.

Damn. That woman. The way she tasted, the way our tongues tangled in that un-fucking-believable rhythm. I couldn't get Lily out of my head. And the more I tried, the harder it was.

So, the gym. Because my dick was starting to chafe.

Adjusting my earbuds, I sat, tightened the wraps on my wrists, and settled my hands on the bar, hoisting the weight over my head.

One. Two. Three…

I was a fairly easy-going guy off the field. I didn't give a damn how the media painted me as long as it didn't affect how I did my job or lived my life. Yeah, it was annoying, but relatively harmless speculation up until the fantasy suite scandal broke. Speculation I knew I'd rightfully earned at one point in my career.

But Lily… I didn't want her to see me like that now. Like I was the same guy as her dad because we played the same sport.

Everyone knew the stories about Billy Costello. Best lineman of his time back before concussion protocols and CTE even had a name or were synonymous with football. Players didn't openly talk about symptoms. Frankly, if they had, they'd have been ridiculed. No, teams gave you pills and injections, and you kept your damn mouth shut. Billy was a notorious skirt chaser, he gambled his money away and got hooked on painkillers. Then, one night, he drove his car off a bridge. I understood Lily's hesitance, but I wanted her to see past the bullshit to see the real me. That I was nothing like her father.

Because, dumbass that I was, I'd started to catch the feels for a woman I had no business being with. Not if I wanted to keep my damn job and retire with some semblance of my dignity left. Lily Costello was a fine line drawn in quicksand that I was dangling my toes over. I needed to be concentrating on holding on to my job, not holding on to her curves.

Racking the weight, I stood from the seated shoulder press and stripped off my sweatshirt. Balling it up, I used it to mop my face before I added another plate to each side of the bar. The weight room was fairly empty except for the die-hards and other guys rehabbing an injury.

After reseating, I lined up my little fingers again and heaved the weight over my head as Shinedown launched into "Devil" through my earbuds.

One. Two. Three...

Usually, lifting cleared my head. I sure as hell needed to do something to help me focus. The rookie linebacker from Florida was breathing down my neck. He'd taken full advantage of the crack in the door I'd left him last season when I'd gone out with a dislocated shoulder.

And the kid could play.

Yet, I'd be damned if I retired from the fucking bench.

"How's it doing today?" Devon—the team's trainer I went to most often—stopped in front of my bench, took note of the angry red scars peeking out from under my cut-up T-shirt. "That's more weight than you're supposed to be doing, bro."

I nodded, guided the bar back to the rack, brought the bottom of my shirt up to wipe away the sweat. "I'm listening to my body. I stop when it tells me to stop."

Crossing his arms over a team polo, he gave a small nod. "Honestly, your recovery has been remarkable. I don't want you to fuck it up is all. Keep those muscles strong and keep up the range of motion but take it easy. Go slow."

I nodded, swigged deeply from my water bottle.

Devon rocked heel to toe. "I heard from Doc's secretary. Jiménez rescheduled. Dr. Chase moved you up the list. Why don't we get you stretched out and then you can see him?"

Adam Chase III—our team's head orthopedic surgeon—was a fuckstick. Fuck. Stick. He treated the

Bulldogs players like cattle. Patch 'em up and get 'em to market.

I knew at least two guys who shouldn't have finished the season last year with the concussion protocols.

But they did anyway because the team wasn't deep in those positions.

A short walk to the PT wing later, I hopped up on a table. Devon started to stretch me out. I was a big guy. It took a big guy to do the job. That's why I usually saw Devon. He'd suffered a similar injury in college when he'd played ball. He knew firsthand what I was working with.

Dev put my forearm on his shoulder and started rubbing me down. "How's the dog training coming?"

I harrumphed.

"You okay, man?" Devon walked around the table behind me, stretching my pectoral while he massaged my deltoid. "You're kinda quiet today."

"Yeah. Sorry, I'm...edgy."

He barked out a laugh. "You still laying off the women? Hell, I'm surprised. Nobody should be able to tell a man he can't get his dick wet."

"Not women. Woman," I grated.

"Ohhhh." A smile crawled across Devon's mouth. "Well, c'mon, Karen. What's the tea?"

"My dog's trainer." Divulging wasn't something I'd calculated. But Devon was a good dude. He'd keep it quiet.

The door to the PT room swung open, and in walked Dr. Douche. "Mr. Shaw, let's have a look, shall we?"

Devon stepped away, washed his hands in the sink as the doctor started his exam. "Any discomfort? Grunt once for no, twice for yes."

I stared straight ahead, ignoring the dig. Devon shook his head as the doctor ran me through a range of motion tests.

After hearing my jaw crack, I forced myself to relax.

"Talkative as usual, I see. I hear you've hired a dog trainer. A dog bites a person, you put it down."

"Opinions are like assholes," I barked, then hissed as he pushed my shoulder a little too far. On purpose. *This prick...*

I could've dropped him with one punch, and it was no less than he deserved, but Dick had a hard-on for me for whatever reason. Lots of guys had complained about Dr. Douche to no avail.

Devon must have read my thoughts because he rolled his eyes as he leaned back against the wall, crossing his arms.

"Well, I wouldn't want to be *you* if that dog bites Lily Costello. Push against my hand." He put his palm out, face down, and I raised my own to meet his and pushed with all my strength, knocking him off balance. Then I grinned at the sonofabitch.

Chase righted himself. "Neanderthals. Continue with your current weight regimen. Devon, cut PT back to twice a week." Cleaning his glasses on his custom button-down, the fucker finally found the guts to look me in the eye. "Reevaluate in two weeks." With that, he left.

The question was hanging on Devon's gaping mouth. "Lily Costello is your dog trainer?"

Yep. Lily Motherfucking Costello.

Half an hour and a shower later, Devon roared by in his pickup truck, as I came out of the building headed for my own truck. That engine definitely didn't sound like stock. Dude must have made decent money as an athletic trainer.

My phone rang and I stopped to fish it out of my shorts. Hayes.

"What's up, man?"

"Uh, hey. You here at the facility?" A dog barked and growled in the background.

"Just leaving. What's up?"

"Umm, do you have Lily's number handy? There's a big-ass dog outside my truck right now that might be hurt. I think it's a Boxer, but it won't let me get out to check on it. I try to open the door and it goes nuts. It already attacked my bumper and front tire. I don't want it to run off. It's bleeding and I don't know where from or how bad."

Shit. "Yeah, sit tight. I'll call her. Where you parked?" I turned to hustle back in and drop my stuff.

Twenty minutes later, I flagged down an SUV with Lily in the passenger seat. I jumped in the back seat, saying a quick hi to Carrie before I told her where to go. "Honestly, I wasn't sure if maybe I should call animal control or something."

"No!" Carrie glanced at me in her rearview. "Sorry, I mean, I'm glad you didn't in this case. Chances are a dog like this would go straight to the shelter and have a high chance of being euthanized. Any other time, I would say that's the thing to do, but with you knowing Lily, this was the better choice. This time."

An unsettling thought crossed my mind. These two tiny women were going to take on a rabid dog to save a hulking football player. I couldn't help the chuckle. Sometimes it wasn't the size of the dog in the fight and all that.

Looking over her shoulder, Lily must have misread my amusement as concern. "Don't worry, Shaw. We got this. Carrie is…well, you'll see. She has a way with dogs who are fear aggressive."

Twenty-five minutes later I was helping Hayes load an airline-style kennel full of previously pissed-off Boxer into the back of Carrie's SUV as she fed the dog french fries through the grating.

"My hero. How can I ever repay you?" Hayes batted his lashes at Lily before letting a lascivious grin crawl across his face.

She snorted. "All of you tough guys are the same. Needing rescue from some female you pissed off."

I grunted my dissent.

Hayes scooped my girl up in a bear hug meant to get a reaction out of me. "Hayes, put me down, damnit. You always were a little handsy for my taste. Besides, you should be thanking Carrie. She's the one who has the touch with Boxers."

He sat Lily on her feet, but not before giving me a shit-eating grin. "Thanks, Carrie." He gently picked the older woman up in the same manner he had Lily.

"Lord have mercy, put me down!" Hayes acquiesced, but after he let her go, she threw him a wink that he returned.

"You have my phone number if you need anything at all," Hayes said. "Don't forget to send me the vet bills, and call me about dinner, Lily. I'm happy to visit pet shops with this one." He tapped a fist to the top of my shoulder. "Maybe someone will get stars in their eyes."

I tipped my chin at him. "*I'll* call you about dinner."

His laugh carried halfway across the parking lot.

Chapter Twelve

Nobody likes to get Dick-slapped.

Lily

This was never an easy day for me or Mom. It was my dad's birthday, though we didn't talk about it. We'd have lunch where the little insults we flung at each other faded into the background in favor of talking about the good times with my dad. The times before he started to drown, when he was larger than life and our family was happy.

But I already knew something was up. She chose Hattie's of all places. I loved Hattie's—she knew that—but it wasn't known for being the healthiest place to eat. My mother counted calories like bankers count money. She also rode me about my own weight nonstop.

We were from two different planets; the only thing we had in common was my dad. I'm sure she would have much rather had a daughter more like her, but I'd have much rather had a mother who wasn't a flake. Such was the wheel of genetic roulette.

"Hey, Mom."

She sat at a four-top, platinum blond hair perfectly coiffed in the vein of Texas beauty queens. When she stood to give me the briefest of hugs, her white pantsuit highlighted long legs that ended in five-inch Louboutins. Chanel bag placed on the corner of the table, she already had a glass of white in front of her. "Hello, darling."

I sat back, crossing my legs. "Hattie's? Really? Isn't it in your prenup that you have to maintain a certain weight?"

Brow furrowed, she smoothed her napkin. Perhaps I shouldn't have expected a war and fired the first shot.

"Not everyone is like you, Liliana. We're not all so self-assured, so confident in who we are like you are, and your father was. I'm glad you got that from him."

I took her hand. "You're right. I'm sorry."

There was a hint of shine in her eyes. For all her beauty and grace, Audrey would always see herself as the trailer park girl with a higher kick than IQ who'd never quite fit with the old money Dallas elite. Something they would never let her forget.

Dick would never let her forget it either.

"Have you ordered already?"

She nodded, giving me a small smile as she shook off the vapors. "I did. I got you the fried chicken. I know it's your favorite. Of course, it's not the best choice with your metabolism." She considered me. "Although, have you lost weight, honey?"

Ahh, there was *my* mother.

She patted my hand. "It's for the best. Didn't Trey ask you to take some weight off at one time?"

"Yes, he did, and no, I didn't. I haven't lost weight, Audrey, and like I've told you before, I have no plans to change my body to suit anybody. Ever." Trey was from the kind of family where things like harassment got swept under the rug. Dick had practically drooled when I'd told him and my mother that Trey asked me to marry him. When I'd caught the douche banging a prospective bridesmaid and called it off, Dick—and subsequently, my mother—had tried his damnedest to get me to overlook it. When the stalking got to its peak, my stepfather told me I was being overly dramatic and that I'd broken *the poor boy's* heart.

Sigh.

Her small frown revealed the beginnings of crow's feet. No matter, as soon as she saw them in the mirror, she'd get a peel or something.

"How are things at work?" she asked as our food arrived. Seriously, the plate of fried chicken the waiter sat in front of me was worth any amount of shit my mother threw my way. I inhaled deeply, my mouth watering before I noticed the waiter place a third plate on the table.

Shit. "Dick is coming, isn't he?" I started to stand but my chair hit something soft and wouldn't scoot back.

"Yes, Liliana. I asked your mother to invite you to lunch." Dick's grumbly bass gave me a case of the willies. I hadn't smelled him this time. Usually, I could smell his nauseating combination of Drakkar Noir and unwashed taint long before I saw him.

"Hmm, new cologne, Richard?"

I shot my mother a glare, but deep down I was disappointed. I expected disappointment out of her regularly, but not today of all days. Today was supposed to be about my dad. I don't know why I was surprised, really. Audrey had a long history of choosing Dick over me. God forbid she disappoint her cash cow. He might not pay for her Chanel habit.

Ignoring my question, he rounded my chair to sit in his own. "I have something I'd like to discuss with you, darling. It's come to my attention you've taken on a new training client."

Ugh. He was no more than a sleazy used car salesman in a four-thousand-dollar suit. Tall and slight, he wore his salt and pepper hair slicked straight back à la Gordon Gekko. Manicured eyebrows, and always the red power tie. Oh, and I couldn't forget the stubble. It was comical. The ever-present beard scruff was not only a little too long to give him the appearance he was going for—you know, hip—it was scraggly and slid straight into what I thought of as the Midlife Crisis shave.

I had no reason to hide my association with Brody Shaw. He was a client helping me locate a puppy mill. That was the reality. Even if my fantasy was a tad more risqué. "Yep. Helping him train his dog. What of it?" *Nothing to see here, douche bag.*

His grin made me ill. My fried chicken no longer smelled like yummy goodness. For that, alone, I hated this asshole.

"I'm sure you're aware of the scandal surrounding

Mr. Shaw and a few of his teammates. What you don't know is that Mr. Barnett would like him gone. See, Brody slept with his twenty-one-year-old granddaughter not long before the fantasy suite came to light. It wasn't made public for obvious reasons."

The news made something in my gut knot.

I knew Brody got around, but really? The owner's barely legal granddaughter? Geez. "What does that have to do with me training his dog, *Dick*?" I over-pronounced the word and caught my mother squirming in my periphery.

Dick leaned forward, rested his elbows on the table. "Ah, Liliana, I've always admired your spine. Which is more than I can say for your mother. If only you were a man, I might have made you general manager of the Bulldogs one day." He leaned back. "Sadly, you literally weren't born with the balls for this business. But there is something you can do for me that none of my male executives can."

"Kiss my ass, Dick."

"Such talk," my mother hissed.

Dick shook his head. Producing a piece of paper from his suit jacket, he placed it next to my hand and smiled. "This is my new will—there are two versions. I've come to an arrangement with Mr. Barnett. In three years' time, I'll own a majority share of the Dallas Bulldogs. Whether or not I file the version you're included in depends on you."

Dick wasn't buying me. Ever. More curious than anything, I wanted to see where he was going with this.

"I've noticed Mr. Shaw gravitated to you at team

events before you stopped attending. You two seem to have a rapport, and now you're working with his dog. I'd like you to develop that friendship with him and inform me about any more possible missteps so the team can get in front of them."

Ahh, there it was. The hair on my neck prickled. He wasn't telling me the whole truth. "I'm not a rat, Dick. And I'm not a babysitter." I leaned forward, mirroring his pose. "I don't care what you offer me."

He drew his fingers away from his chin. "What if I sweeten the deal? The Bulldogs are always looking for charitable causes to donate to. I know rescue dogs are close to your heart, Liliana. I'm sure there are any number of organizations the Bulldogs could partner with. Pick one."

Oh, this greasy bastard. On today of all days. I glanced at my mother, who was watching everyone and everything but me. At first, I thought what I felt was hate for her in that moment. It wasn't hate. It was shame with a side of pity.

"Of course, you'd have to come home to the Bull-dogs. Use the degree that I paid for? The head trainer position would be all yours along with a handsome salary. After we're done with Mr. Shaw, that is."

Why the hell did he want me to work for him so badly? In truth, the reason was irrelevant. Whatever it was, I could guarantee the arrangement wouldn't be as simple as going to work for the team. I'd undoubt-edly run into Trey a lot as well given he was the team's head ortho guy and created most of the players' treatment plans. That wouldn't set off dude's creeper penchant. At. All.

That was assuming Dick even held up his end to support a rescue.

So, Brody had nailed the owner's granddaughter. It was no less than I expected from Brody, even if it hurt more than I cared to admit. It didn't matter if he slept his way through a Hooters restaurant—no matter how much the idea made me cringe. The man's dedication to his dog, to our cause, was reason enough not to give him up. He was a decent guy—manwhore, yes, but at this point, Brody was more than a client or a partner. He'd become my friend.

I didn't rat on my friends.

I sat back in my seat. "Dick, that's an interesting offer."

My mom perked up.

I wished I hadn't seen the small glimmer of hope on her face. "But it doesn't matter how much money you offer me, I have something that isn't for sale."

I fished a twenty out of my wallet and dropped it on the table.

"Oh, really? What's that?"

"Integrity." I grinned.

My stepfather's face scrunched up, making him appear his age. But, hell if I didn't catch the slightest grin on my mom's face before I turned to leave.

Damn it. I'd been looking forward to Hattie's fried chicken.

Chapter Thirteen

Bromas and granny panties?
The fuck has my life come to?

Lily

"He did what, now?" Olive's voice curled up to a note that could have broken my wineglasses had we not been on the phone.

Olive was Casshole's mom, and a friend. We both preferred dogs to people—me because of my family, and her because of her job in public relations. Her indignation made me smile. I held the phone with one hand and combed through the fridge trying to find the block of parmesan cheese with the other. The rattle of bowls and jars on the refrigerator shelf reverberated through as I smacked my noggin. "Ouch. Shit."

After setting the phone down, I hit speaker and started grating the cheese. "Yep. He tried to buy me by writing a check to a rescue. He doesn't get it. Dogs are things to him."

"Umm, people are things to him, too," Olive

snapped. "The man would prefer it if everyone were born with their potential net worth stamped on their foreheads. Asshat."

"I'm kinda in love with you right now."

"Pfft. It's probably as close as either of us are ever going to get." We both chuckled. "Seriously, I don't get how your mom could go from your dad to Dick."

"I know exactly how. She had zero job skills besides a jump-split and strategically placed uniform mishaps. She also had a rapidly dwindling bank account. But she had her looks." Popping the lasagna back in the oven, I finished up and poured myself a glass of wine.

Olive's huff was judgmental to say the least. "Still."

"Yeah, I know." I knew, in her own screwed-up way, Audrey was trying to take care of me. I knew she loved my dad. Fiercely. But I was the result of her jersey chasing. Dad put a ring on it, and Audrey thought she was set for life. Until the call came that her husband was dead and the bank accounts empty.

I was Daddy's girl through and through. But he put my mom on a pedestal then drove his car off a bridge, and whether it was an accident or not, she and I were the ones to suffer. I was never blind. I knew, even as a little girl, that my dad wasn't okay. But this sport… The very nature of the game—which the teams reinforced—convinced the players they were invincible. Gods among men. Then, at the first sign they weren't, it showed them the door. It set them up for failure later on in life from the moment their names were announced on draft day.

Olive's microwave beeped followed by a high-pitched bark from Cassie. "Y'all doing the agility trial in Anna this weekend?" Olive asked. The trial in Anna was practice for veterans like Jet and Cassie.

"Yeah, I've got a couple of students who were interested in competing so I'm going to show them the ropes. You?"

"No. You know what Cassie's like in that horse barn. She'd rather chase mice than run obstacles." Clearing her throat, Olive deepened her voice. "So, Bulldogs are on my *I'd rather stick my head in a bag of snakes* list but at least tell me *you're* going to climb that mountain tonight, my friend."

"What? No! Brody's bringing someone with him! We're just talking about how to approach the pet stores, is all."

"Hmphf. I'm trying to live vicariously through you here, Lil."

I pinched the bridge of my nose. "I'm not going to lie, the man is gorgeous, but I'm not crossing up those wires." I felt my stomach tense, because it didn't seem to matter how many people Brody had screwed, my body wanted to get those wires all crossed the hell up. "Besides, after the whole fantasy suite thing? I don't judge—as long as it's all consensual and everyone is of age, go'on and do your thang. But orgies are not *my* thing."

"Ha. Says the woman who has Brody 'The Body' Shaw bringing a *friend* to her house for...erm, dinner." I could hear the smile in her voice. "Seriously, are you even sure it's Brody's thing? He's said publicly he didn't participate on several occasions."

"You've seen the pictures." Brody was... Even if he wasn't a participant, the man had new women on his arm all the time—case in point: the team owner's granddaughter and the Doublemint twins.

"Sweets, I've been in this business a long time—he doesn't sound coached. Far be it from me to defend a football player, but he's either a very good actor, or he's telling the truth. It wouldn't be the first time the media sensationalized something like this. You ever heard of Photoshop? Maybe you should give it a chance. If you two have that much chemistry..."

"Mmhmm." I swallowed a sip of wine. "Maybe you should throw away all of tomorrow's to-do lists, call in sick, and drop in on a pole-stripping class."

Olive cackled into the phone. "Like that would ever happen. Besides, I can't call in sick. I own the place."

"Workaholic," I said with a smile in my voice.

"Cynic," she threw back, and we both snorted as my doorbell rang.

After a quick goodbye to Olive, I went to answer the door. I'd made an unconscious, yet conscious, decision to dress down in sweats and a holey T-shirt. My feet were bare, my hair was pulled up in a knot, and I'd even worn granny panties on purpose.

When I opened the door, however, Brody looked like a snack in a thin black leather jacket, and a gray Henley with the top two buttons undone.

"Uhh, hey." His voice was the tickle of feathers over my skin.

"Hey." I took a moment to soak him in. God, he was yummy.

"I hope it's okay, I brought CC to play with Mack."

"Mmm, yep."

A beat went by.

"Sure smells good." He glanced into the house while my eyes scanned down his torso to a pair of faded jeans that fit like a glove. I was in a full-on Brody-induced coma—a Broma.

"Mmhmm. Sure does."

"Lil?" Brody's grin was slightly uncomfortable. "Are you going to invite me in?"

I wondered briefly if I had drool on my chin before I remembered to close my mouth and snapped out of my Broma.

Granny panties. Granny panties. Totally not sexy, Lil. That's when I noticed Hayes standing back off the porch with a shit-eating grin. "Shit. Yes! Sorry. Y'all wanna take CC around back to let her run off some energy? Her and Mack will do a number wrestling in my house."

"Sure." His answer was almost shy, and that blush on his cheeks? The granny panties were officially damp.

"Ohaaaiii, Liiileee." Hayes drew out my name in amusement. Then the asshole started thrusting his hips in the air like he was giving Brody the business, only Brody couldn't see him, so it was just for my benefit.

Was it that obvious that I wanted to climb this man? I went full-on face-palm. "Hi, Hayes." *Apparently, it is.*

Christ, I'd lost my damn mind.

"Uhh, I brought wine and chocolate cheesecake."

Brody handed me a bag and brushed a bright red ear with his fingers like he knew he was blushing.

I peeked inside. Ohmygod, this big, beautiful, blushing man had brought me alcohol and chocolate. If the granny panties hadn't been damp before... "Ooooh, you didn't have to do that. Thank you. I mean, it's going to go straight to my ass, but...yeah." I was babbling.

His grin was a little shy, a little sly. "Yeah, I did. First, my mama would slap me upside the head if she knew I went to a pretty girl's house for dinner and didn't take her dessert. And second, your ass is perfect."

My mouth fell open the smallest bit. "I'll just, um, meet you guys out back. Gate's over there." I don't know what he said, but Hayes earned himself a shove from Brody as they turned the corner of the house.

After putting the cake in the fridge, I poured them both a glass of wine and refilled my own. Balancing all three, I nudged the back door with my butt while reminding myself that I was not allowed to lick Brody Shaw like an ice cream cone. No-sir-ee.

Good luck with that, my brain fired at me.

"Oh, fuck off," I whispered as I let the door go.

Brody and Hayes were standing at the bottom of the steps from the retaining wall in similar poses. Legs spread apart, arms crossed over their chests. And Jesus H...those football butts.

Lord thank you for football asses. And thighs. Didn't mean to forget the thighs. Amen.

"Here you go, guys." I handed off the glasses. "How are the dogs doing?"

Hayes chuckled. "Your boy is trying to get CC to chase, but she's ignoring him to sniff the yard."

"She's been taking lessons from Jet on how to handle men," Brody intoned.

Jet trotted up next to him, nudged his hand with her nose, and his surprise was comical. "Hey girl, how are ya?" She slipped her soft head under his hand. "Well, I'll be damned. Finally decided I'm a worthy admirer, huh?" He scratched her ear as we watched Mack follow CC around making play overtures like a lovesick puppy.

"Poor guy." Hayes shook his head. "He's got it bad." I didn't miss how his eyes darted to Brody.

Brody was more concerned with the female paying attention to him than with Mack's crush on CC. Handing his wineglass to Hayes, the linebacker dropped into a squat next to Jet, letting her lean into his side while he relished finally being allowed into Jet's orbit.

After a good long sniff, CC took Mack up on his offer to chase and I watched as she broadsided my little fireplug, knocking him on his ass.

"Damn if Shaw doesn't know how that feels. I've got twenty on CC." Hayes chortled.

I pretended not to hear the first part. "I'm not taking that bet. Mack is smitten."

Finally, Jet decided to act like a dog and joined the others. When she approached, CC did a little posturing. "What do you see, Shaw?" I tipped my head to the dogs.

"They're in play mode."

"How can you tell?" I asked.

"CC's neck is arched, but her nub tail is in a relaxed wiggle. The energy is calm."

I nodded, pleased Brody had read the books I recommended.

"CC's mouth is slack, and her weight isn't on her toes. Her ears are laid back a bit," Hayes added.

"You know something about dogs, Walker?"

He shrugged, sipped from his glass. "I had 'em growing up."

With a blink, CC took off running, Jet jumping to join her and Mack cutting the yard to bring up the rear. I sipped my wine, my glass near empty already. The timer on my watch went off. "Lasagna's ready."

Brody turned toward me. "Smells good." He patted his stomach. "Not much longer and I'll have to give that kind of stuff up for the season."

Hayes chuckled. "How much weight are you gonna have to cut?"

"Hopefully only the ten pounds I've put on. I've been trying to be careful. Trying being the operative word."

That's when the dogs cut back toward us at full speed, but Brody had turned almost perpendicular to where I was standing, and I had a hard time seeing them behind his big body.

"Incoming." As quick as I said it, Hayes shushed me.

It happened fast. Jet whipped her lithe frame through Brody's parted legs and kept right on going. Brody's face lit with surprise. Then CC and Mack tried to take the same path, but CC being tall—and Mack being wide—managed to hit the big man in the backs of his knees, taking them right out from under him.

The remainder of his wine went flying over his head as he landed flat on his ass with a thud.

Hayes was cracking up laughing, and I might have been worried about Brody hurting himself, but for the enormous grin he was wearing. Instead of getting up, he lay back in the grass, his chest shaking.

Hearing the ruckus, the dogs turned back to investigate. Mack decided to apologize by splaying across Brody's chest to lick his face. "Ahh, damn, buddy. I sure am glad you're the friendly sort. It was an excellent takedown." Mack continued to lick at him while CC sniffed at her owner and determined he was okay before walking off. "Stahpp. Stahpp, buddy."

Still laughing myself, I remembered how much Mack liked openmouthed kisses. "Dude, I'd stop talking if you don't want him to slip you the—"

"Tongue! Blech." Too late. Giving Mack a playful shove he sat up. "Well, that was smooth. And I'm pretty sure Mack just licked one of my tonsils."

Walking around him, I picked up the cracked glass, thankful it hadn't shattered. "You broke my glass, Shaw."

He pushed himself up from the ground. "He did it." Pointing at my sweet boy, who had his tongue lolling to the side.

"Blaming the dog already, B? I thought that part came *after* you ate."

Brody flipped Hayes off.

"There's no such thing as smooth, Shaw," I said.

"Not with dogs around. Come in and eat. I'll open another bottle."

As I walked up the steps, I heard Brody whisper, "Seriously? Fart jokes? How old are you?"

My snort-laugh was so loud we were now all equally embarrassed.

Chapter Fourteen

"I blame cheesecake." —Lily

Lily

My house was small and older, but had a big back-yard and had been updated since I moved in. I heard the guys shuffle in behind me as I pulled the lasagna out of the oven. "Dogs follow you in?" Picking up the large pan, I set it on the stove and flipped the oven door closed.

Brody's voice got louder as they got past the mud porch and into the kitchen. "No, they're playing. Will they be okay out there?"

"They're fine." I turned, pulling another wineglass out of the cabinet. "Hey, can one of you check to make sure there's water in the bowl by the back door?"

"It's full."

I quickly threaded a corkscrew into the new bottle like any self-respecting woman who had a love affair with her wine.

"Oh man, this is really nifty, Lil." Brody's eyes made a sweep of my kitchen as I worked the cork free.

Hayes grinned. "This is pretty fucking cool. Like it belongs on I Love Lucy or something."

After pouring another glass for Brody and refilling my own, I refilled Hayes's glass as well. The light blue metal cabinets and Formica counter, the black and white tile floor, the kitchen table that was straight out of a malt shop. "Thanks, I did a lot of the work myself."

"It smells amazing in here. Can we help with anything?" Brody offered.

I waved him off. "Y'all, sit down and help yourself to the salad while I slice the bread." Which I made quick work of. After sitting the lasagna on the table, I joined them.

"This smells amazing," Hayes added. "You didn't have to cook for us, Lily. We could have gone out."

"Two problems with that. Oh, help yourselves, guys." Hayes dug into the pan with the server and scooped a piece out for himself as I continued. "One, this isn't a topic of conversation most people want to ruin their dinner, and two, y'all are a bit famous round here."

"True." Brody dug in and served me a piece of lasagna the size of my head before serving himself. "Generally, when I go out, I don't get to eat or talk to anyone but fans." He forked a bite of lasagna and moaned. "Dear God, this is good."

Hayes chuckled. "The man likes his carbs."

I swallowed my current bite. "So do I."

Brody sent a conspiratorial wink my direction that

had me thinking about his mouth closing around more than a fork.

Now, I was the one blushing.

Hayes noticed and I wished he hadn't. "So, Lily, how long have you been training dogs?"

"Mmm, six years, I think? I don't actually train dogs. I train humans on how to communicate with their dogs. What kinds of dogs did you have growing up?"

"Mostly strays. Mixed breeds," Hayes replied.

"What about you? I'd imagine Billy was the kind of guy that couldn't deny his little girl anything," Brody asked.

I let loose a derisive snort. "Ha. I wouldn't have wanted to have a dog when I was little. My house was…erm, my folks fought a lot. My dad liked to screw around at away games and he also drank like a fish and would lose his shit on occasion. Being Billy Costello's kid wasn't all that it was cracked up to be."

When I glanced at Brody, his lips had thinned. He sipped his wine and I did the same, wishing I hadn't said that. My mom and I didn't tell people about these things. Mom didn't want his legacy tarnished or whatever. As far as armchair quarterbacks knew, Billy was a model dad and husband.

But these guys would have heard the rumors, the stories that got passed on in locker rooms. That, plus wine, and loose lips were the result. I needed to squash this shit. "And Dick… Well, we all know how shit on his Luccheses would go over with him."

Hayes chuckled. "Have you ever been bitten?"

I nodded, thankful for the subject change. "As a

trainer, you've either been bit or you're going to get bit. It's just a way of life. A dog who bites generally does it because the human isn't doing a good job of reading the dog." Setting my wine down, I held out my arm, where a group of puckered scars were set together. "This one was an Akita. I was getting my certification. He was resource guarding and the owner made it worse by trying to prove to the dog who the boss was. I thought we had it sorted, but as soon as his owner came back into the room, the dog reacted to the threat. I took six stitches."

Brody leaned forward, brushing the scars with the pad of his thumb. "Damn, darlin'."

Hayes whistled through his teeth. "Geez, Lil. Akitas are big dogs. I hope you had some help."

"Eh. I'm a lot stronger than I look."

A line appeared between Brody's brows again. "No doubt, but don't you ever get gun-shy?"

I shrugged. "I guess it's like a quarterback. You either start hearing footsteps and panic because you're about to get hit, or you block out the footsteps and do the job."

"Except a quarterback has pads. And teammates," Brody added.

Hayes nodded. "An offensive line."

"And as good as I like to think I am as a linebacker, I don't have fangs."

I clenched my teeth. It was sweet these guys worried about me, but it was my job to be in harm's way on occasion. "Guys, thanks for the concern, but it's part of my job. A part that's more dangerous the bigger the dog is, but I'll take that Akita biting me over him biting the baby that just started crawling and put her hand in his food bowl any day of the week." I refilled my glass. "You guys do your jobs. You take calculated risks each play. My job also requires calculated risks that I'm more than capable of assessing."

Hayes started scooping up dirty dishes to whisk to the sink. "Yep. Sorry, Lil. Not our place to tell you how to do your job."

Brody's brown eyes were trained on mine but had a softness around the edges. "Yeah, sorry. I just thought about if he'd gotten something besides your forearm. I didn't mean to insinuate that you couldn't or shouldn't do your job."

"Accepted," I said, adding a wink so he knew there were no hard feelings. "Why don't I feed you two cheesecake and we can talk this plan through." After pushing back, I went to the cabinet to pull out dessert plates. Bumping Hayes with my hip, I thanked him for clearing.

"You cook, I clean." His smile was the stuff of Hollywood legends.

While I served cake, I heard the back door open and close. Shortly after, dogs began dancing around my legs as Brody topped off their water bowl. When I set a piece in front of Hayes, I noticed the ass bent over in my utility room getting the dogs water. Damn, those jeans hugged him entirely too well. I wanted to know how he'd react if I walked over and cupped it. Maybe slid my hands into the back pockets.

"Mmmm. Brody, man, why'd you buy this?" Hayes's

voice brought me out of my dirty daydream and I set the other two pieces on the table before I got caught ogling again. But Hayes hadn't missed it. His grin was all kinds of lascivious. "Now we're gonna have to run tomorrow. A minute on the lips, a lifetime on the hips."

"Okay, Karen." Brody sat back down, slid cheesecake in his mouth. "Mmm. Damn, that's good."

I couldn't help the chuckle. These two were obviously pretty close and entertaining as hell.

"Y'all. Game plan."

"Mmmhmm?" Brody rolled his fork in the air.

Setting my own fork down, I grabbed the list of shops out of my office and we went over them one by one. I pointed out a few places I knew sold lots of bully breeds and owners I knew owned more than one of the shops on the list, so they didn't go to another shop that person owned. I answered questions about mills for Hayes and reminded both men to turn on the charm if need be. We even strategized when to go.

"Just remember, if they have a lot of bully breeds in the store, be thorough." I licked cheesecake off my knuckle and didn't miss the way Brody tracked the movement. At least I wasn't the only one being tortured. "I think it's best if you guys go in giving as little info as possible. Make sure you ask for a manager or owner."

Hayes interjected. "A salesclerk isn't going to know who the suppliers are."

"Exactly." I poked my fork in the air. "Tell them you're interested in breeding stock if you have to, but be vague."

Brody scratched his scruff. "They're going to want to know why we want that info. Especially if mill circles are as tight-lipped as you said. What are we supposed to tell them?"

I nibbled the inside of my lip. I felt like I was taking a huge leap of faith letting these guys improvise, but it was the only way I could see the plan working. "You be tight-lipped, too. Say as little as you can get away with. You're going to have to play it by ear and find a reason why one of their pups won't do, or why you want to know about their suppliers. Maybe tell them you'd like to breed CC. If they've got a Cane in the shop, tell them you want a Neapolitan Mastiff, et cetera. You're going to have to be as cagey as they are. Hopefully, they'll get starstruck and spill."

Hayes pushed his plate away. "We should throw swag in the truck, too. Talk with some of the other customers. Autographs and stuff. That kind of stuff might go a long way."

Brody nodded. "You can't go ten feet in DFW without hitting a Bulldogs fan."

"Plus, you two have this natural friendship thing going. Play up the banter. I would suggest you decide who's going to do the talking beforehand."

Brody nodded. "We need a couple of different cover stories. Breeding stock. Breeding CC, maybe another to have on hand when they push."

"The more swag we can throw around, the less questions they're likely to ask, too," Hayes added.

"Last, but not least," I interjected. "Don't buy a puppy."

Both men nodded. "We got this, Lil."

"I mean it. It's harder than you think."

Hayes stroked his beard. "We can be some charming sonsabitches when we need to be."

I snorted, but I believed it. There wasn't much Texans loved more than their football.

"I'm gonna take off." Hayes put his napkin on the table and pushed back to stand. "I'm beat, but Lily, thank you for dinner."

I walked him to the door. "Thanks for helping with this, Walker. You're a good guy."

He kissed my forehead. "Shh. Don't tell."

After he was gone, I went back into the kitchen where Brody sat stroking Mack's head. "I'm sorry. I know y'all wanted more guidance from me on how to play this inside the shops, but you're going to have to think on your feet to make it feel organic." Plopping down in my chair again, I wished I could go with them, or better yet, take care of it myself. "I hate having to sit this out while you two do all the work."

Brody put his hand on top of mine. "It's why we're here, Lil. I want this as much as you do."

That little touch—heat licked up my spine and bled into my cheeks, but he pulled away too quickly. Did he? Want this like I did? Yes, we flirted, but did Brody want me as much as I wanted him? Because with the wine pumping through my system, and after the lunch with my mom, there was nothing I wanted more than to get lost in Brody. To feel all his hard against my soft and trace the lines of shoulders and pecs. To dip my tongue into the suprasternal notch at the base of his throat that had played peekaboo through the plackets of his Henley all night.

But Brody seemed to have other ideas. "So, the rumors about your dad…"

That banked the fire a little. "Yeah?"

"Doesn't sound like an easy guy to live with." Brody ran a hand over his scruff, seemed to choose his next words carefully. "It's not always pretty, being on this side of the curtain. I'm sorry you had to deal with any of that as a kid. It's hard enough to manage as an adult."

I shrugged. "My dad was a complicated guy. Sometimes he was an amazing husband and father, other times, not so much. But I still loved him."

Brody nodded, and as I watched him, I didn't want to know what he was thinking. The conversation was killing my ladywood and my buzz in one fail swoop. But Brody told me anyway. "You know, we're not all like your dad, Lil."

I nodded, but the truth was I didn't know that at all, and where Brody was concerned with women, all evidence was to the contrary. "What about your dad? You only ever talk about your mom in interviews."

Stretching his neck, he leaned his chair back on two legs. "Never knew him, never cared to. My mom is a badass, though. She worked two jobs all through high school to put food on the table. And a guy my size? I eat a lot."

"I realize. Between you and Hayes, I have no leftover lasagna."

He patted his little food baby with a satisfied smile. "Truthfully, I was so thankful when I got the full ride

to UNT. Mom was bound and determined I'd get a degree come hell or high water." He grinned. "I bought
her a house with my first signing bonus. Free and
clear."

That was in line with the guy *I* knew. Generous,
thoughtful. But I also knew there was a player in there
who went through women like toilet paper. I shoved
the thought out of my brain. "You know, I was at UNT
while you were. I was an undergrad in pre-law at the
time, but I had a little secret crush. I remember when
you got benched before the conference championship."

Brody laughed. "Really? I bet you were a cute little
thing in college. I wish I would have known you then.
I would have definitely asked you out."

"Uh-huh. I bet you say that to all the girls."

Something crossed his face I couldn't identify. "You
never told me you were pre-law before. Why didn't you
go to law school?"

I shifted, trying to hide my discomfort. Did I tell
him who Trey was to the team? Surely Brody had had
plenty of contact with him. "I left pre-law because
I was seeing someone who was on a medical track.
It got serious, and he convinced me if I went to law
school while he was in medical school, we'd never see
each other, so I took the GRE instead of the LSAT and
went into Kines. Less demanding. He ended up cheating and we broke up. What about you, what are your
plans after you retire?"

Rolling his bottom lip in his mouth, he nibbled on
the edge. "I haven't made up my mind yet, but I've
taken care of my money. I have time to decide."

"What, not going to become an analyst? Isn't that every former player's dream?" I teased.

Throwing his head back, he let out a throaty laugh and his Adam's apple bobbed. "Hell, no. I want as far away from the cameras and spotlight as I can get."

Damn, I wanted my mouth there. What would his skin taste like? I knew his breath was sweet mint and his lips were soft, but I'd never gotten the chance to taste his skin at the Unruly Dog.

Just this once, Lily. Maybe I'd regret it in the morning, maybe not. At that moment, I gave zero fucks. But Brody had to want me, too. In the grand scheme, he had just as much—if not more—to lose by us sleeping together as I did. Throwing back the rest of my wine, I leaned forward, met his gaze for longer than was polite.

Heat stoked in his eyes, heavy with suggestion as the air shifted and the laughter faded. When his voice came out it was grainy, raw, deeper than normal. "Lily, don't look at me like that, unless..."

Just this once.

I stood, sauntered over to where he'd pushed back from the table.

His arms dropped to the sides, his neck tracking up to meet mine.

"Do you want this, Brody?" I stared down at the man who ate up all the space in the room. The chocolatey irises and black scruff, the pink lips and slow slide of his throat as he swallowed. The way his chest rose and fell as he tried to control his breathing and failed. Before I could back down, I was lowering myself onto his parted knees without putting pressure where I wanted it most. His breath—sweet from dessert—fanned against my lips, and I knew the cheesecake wouldn't taste even half as good as the man in front of me.

Brody's hands settled on my hips, an exhale escaping his throat.

With one palm against his chest and the other framing his jaw, I leaned into him, let my soft belly brush against his hard abs. My breasts molded around the planes of his solid chest. My wide hips and thick thighs a perfect fit around the sides of his angular hips and lean waist. We were the perfect inverse, he the convex and I the concave. Flawlessly meant to fit together with all of our hollows and slopes made in universal complement.

I brushed his lips with my own, a jolt of electricity riding over my skin as I tasted wine and cheesecake and Brody, and it was goddamned intoxicating. I needed more of that flavor. That feeling. More of the current running through my system that made my senses swim and watered down my memories.

Sliding my hips forward, I swallowed his sharp inhale as I dipped my tongue between his lips. Reveling in the way his hands felt gripping me with a mix of strain and heat and raw need.

Which was why I never expected him to say, "Lil, we have to slow down."

Brody's voice cut through my haze. "Wh-what?"

"You've had a lot of wine, darlin'."

I didn't want to slow down. I wanted to lose myself in this man's body the way I'd lost myself in the wine.

Granted, I didn't normally polish a bottle off by myself on a weeknight, but goddamn the way my mother ambushed me with her shady prick of a husband.

And today of all days.

And there they were again. All the memories I wanted to let go of.

"I'm a big girl, Shaw. I know what I'm doing." Instead of relenting, I brushed my open lips along his in a not quite kiss and arched my torso into him.

"Sonofabitch," he bit out, dropping his head back to thump it against the wall. "You're gonna kill me, woman." His hands tightened on my hips, keeping from moving, yet the bulge in his jeans grew more prominent.

Honestly, the word *bulge* wasn't adequate. *Bulge* had the connotation of a small protrusion. Like a hot dog or a bratwurst. Brody had a whole hard salami in his jeans. A summer sausage at the very least.

Hand splayed along his jaw and cheek, I ran my teeth down the opposite side of his neck, sliding my tongue out to touch and taste his skin all salty with just a hint of sweet.

His fingers dug into my hips harder, and the sound he made... Mercy. That low, guttural whisper of "uunnhh" from deep in his sternum that was so male it made my nipples chafe against my bra. It seemed entirely unfair to women everywhere that this man was as sexy as he was.

One hand moved from my hip to my back, the other tangled in the hair at my nape. Biceps straining against his Henley, Brody fit his mouth against mine.

That kiss was the perfect amount of wetness and depth, tongue and tease. I was fairly sure I whimpered as I disappeared into it. Lost myself in wine and chocolate and the beautiful man in front of me.

With a gentle grip on my locks, he tugged my head back, sliding his kiss-swollen lips the length of my throat entirely too slowly. "Damn, woman. Your skin is so sweet." But as I tried to shift my hips to find the pressure I craved, he slid an arm around my waist, lifting me the slightest bit and pinning me to his torso.

Chapter Fifteen

*I have an "immense dong." No, no, that's not
my ego talking—that's what SHE said.*

Brody

I needed to stop this before it went too far. There wasn't
a chance in hell I was taking this woman to bed when
I had even the smallest doubt about her sobriety or
ability to consent.

Then she'd whispered, "Let me get lost in you."

As much as I wanted her, I knew she'd regret it later.
No, I wouldn't be her regret. I also couldn't help the
flash of disappointment I felt.

Sure, I got what she needed. Whatever was bother-
ing her—sometimes you just wanted to blow off steam
and Lily wanted to use me to that end.

But that's not us. We're already more.

We weren't one-night-standing this. Lily wasn't
some chick I could screw tonight and watch her go
out with someone else tomorrow. No, I'd rip some poor
fucknut's head off before I let that happen.

I liked this woman. I enjoyed spending time with her. We were friends and I wanted to get to know her better. To understand how experiences like being Billy Costello's kid had shaped her. When I took Lily to bed, it would be when I knew she wanted *me*. Not number 58, not the celebrity, not to blow off steam with a guy she could trust, and not her friend whose help she needed to find a puppy mill.

I'd know she was in it for me alone.

Until then, I had no intention of letting this get any more hands-on.

Picking up on the shift in me, she studied my face. "Something wrong?"

Stroking her cheek with a finger, that violet hue hit me right in the gut. "Lily…" Instead of answering, I settled my forehead against hers, breathing in her intoxicating scent. Warm sugar cookies, and some exotic bloom. Cupping the side of her neck, I brushed my thumb over her swollen bottom lip. I wanted to be inside her. To know if that scent intensified when her most sensitive skin was damp from my lips. Yet, when she started to move against me—all that warm and soft against my hard and straining—I knew I couldn't give her what she needed. Not tonight. "Shit."

If I continued to stay under her in that chair, I'd cave. I'd arch into her and put the pressure on, letting her slide against me until she found the oblivion she was searching for. Instead, I gripped her waist and stood, letting her legs fall away from my lap, but holding her off the floor to set her against the kitchen wall. When a helpless sound escaped her throat, the ache at the base of my spine took on a life of its own. I knew she'd make that sound when she came for me.

The things this woman did to me... Setting an arm above her head, I wiped my forehead with my shoulder, trying to get a grip. Lily had other ideas. When she met my look with all the shades of violet and plum swirling in her gaze... Heat. So much heat, I nearly broke. I wanted my mouth on hers so damn bad. That look was too raw, too full of the need I felt, too.

Lips parted, she angled her head, waiting for me to drop my mouth to hers, and nothing in my life had ever been prettier, or harder to deny. "Fuck." Even on her toes she couldn't reach my mouth if I didn't meet her partway. And I didn't. Not that I didn't want another of those drugging, drawn-out kisses of hers that tasted like sin come to life. But there was a chance she wouldn't remember this.

I'd be damned before I'd let her forget another kiss that singed my very soul.

"Lily..." Why was doing the right thing so damn hard?

"Brody..." Her voice was like silk.

As I pried my eyelids open, she shifted her focus to my neck and brushed her lips over the hollow at the base of my throat, her little pink tongue slipping out to dip inside.

In all my life, I hadn't realized that would be such a turn-on or how perfectly a woman's tongue filled that unassuming little spot. *Not* a *woman's tongue*. This *woman's tongue*.

The sound that came out of me was somewhere between a moan and a caveman grunt. *Just one more kiss*.

Sliding my hand into the hair at her nape, I tilted her head back and sank my mouth to hers.

And I took. Slipping into her soft warmth, I ran my tongue through every inch of her mouth. Over tongue and teeth and every dark, damp crevice. In and out, back and forth. Each time I'd withdraw she'd chase, every new sensation uncovered, and she'd gasp, letting me swallow her sighs. Damn, we were good together. Lily Costello gave as good as she got.

Step by step, I was moving backwards, this woman who was so tiny compared to me pushing me back where she wanted me.

It was when she wobbled to the side as my ass hit the kitchen counter and her stomach pushed against my throbbing cock that I pulled up.

I tugged at her nape to find her wet lips parted and plum-colored irises heavy with barely banked heat. I'd never seen anything so sexy in all my life. When she spoke, I realized how drunk she was.

"Jesus fucking Christ, Brody. You have an immense dong. Whoops." She clapped a hand over her mouth. "Didn't mean to say that out loud."

A guffaw worked up my throat. Damn, the woman was cute.

My cock jerked against my jeans and her eyes widened before she collapsed onto my chest with a snort.

"Christ, you're not making this easy," I said, rubbing a hand over my face. But I hadn't missed the way she leaned against me. "Lily, how much did you drink?"

"Dunno, wasn't countin'. Had kind of a shitty day."

Aww, hell. "Let's get you to bed, darlin'."

An innocent look crossed her face that I wasn't buying for a minute. "Comin' with?"

After a steadying breath, I slid an arm around her back and another behind her knees, scooping her up. "I'm putting you to bed. That's all. Now, where's your room."

"End of the hall on the right. Wish you'd come with me." Her head dropped against my chest.

I felt the wave of sadness wash over her. "What happened today?"

Her eyes turned watery and she spilled words I knew she'd wish she could take back. "Today's my daddy's birthday. I was supposed to have lunch with my mom, but…"

Halting my gait, I felt my heart crack wide open. "I'm sorry, Lil."

Running a hand over her face, she immediately looked embarrassed.

I shouldn't have asked. Not because I didn't want to know her—I did—but I hated that I'd made her say the words out loud.

I toed the door open. "But?"

"Huh? Put me down."

Doing as she said, I asked, "Why didn't you have lunch with your mom?"

"She, umm…she, she blindsided me with Dick." She snorted, laughed hard, forcing a grin out of me as I popped her feet under the covers. "I mean her husband. Not cock."

"I figured," I said, pulling the blanket over her shoulders.

"Oh, I gotta let the dogs out." She started to sit up.

"Shh. I got 'em."

"Mmm, thank you, sugar." With that, she snuggled in, drifting off at record speed.

After letting let the dogs out, I gathered up supplies for the night. I set the dishwasher to run, wiped down the table, washed the wineglasses. Nothing sucked more than cleaning a dirty kitchen with a hangover.

The entire time, all I could think about was the little peek into what it must have been like for her, being Billy Costello's daughter. How that would have shaped not only how she saw football, but what she thought of me, and I didn't blame Lily for wanting to stay away.

The sad thing was, now I wanted her more with every piece of herself she let me see. I didn't just like her. I was risking a hell of a lot more than just my job with Lily. I wanted her to see me for who I was, not just what I did for a living or who'd I'd been in the past. I needed her to understand I wasn't her dad. Because I cared about her.

You think Andra caused trust issues. Imagine what Lil would do.

I harrumphed.

I'd *thought* I could love Andra.

With Lily, I *knew* I could.

Yet, did I want to go down that road again? It wasn't until after Andra had left that I'd become that guy—the one Lily didn't want to have anything to do with. The guy who chased tail and slept his way through the Metroplex because it was easy to avoid attachment that way. The guy that didn't trust anyone because he didn't trust his own ability to judge character.

After hunting around the house, I found a trash can

in her bathroom that I sat next to the bed, then let the dogs in. Jet and Mack disappeared into Lily's bedroom.

Leaving her door cracked, I went out to the couch, where I tossed a decorative pillow to one end before I toed off my shoes and lay down, pulling a throw off the back.

CC took it upon herself to climb halfway on top of me. On Lil's small couch. Suffice it to say, sleep was fitful with monster dog half on top of me, blue balls, and thoughts of the woman in the next room.

But at least if she needed anything, I'd be here.

And I didn't even want to contemplate the implications of that thought.

Lily

When my alarm went off the following morning, the first thing I noticed was a glass of water and a bottle of aspirin. Next to me on the bed, Mack continued to saw logs while Jet jumped down to stretch. Before I reached for the lamp my head started to pound.

Fun.

Kicking my legs over the edge, I found my feet next to a trash can.

Damnit. Why did he have to be so thoughtful?

What happened between us crashed over my brain and oh, how I wished I didn't remember. At least I hadn't slept with him. I'd wanted to. Like, really, really wanted to. I wanted to grind up on his pole like a stripper. His enormous pole. I could still remember the feel of that thing against my stomach. "Jesus H, Lily." I slapped a hand over my eyes.

Downing the water and aspirin, I made use of the bathroom before stumbling into the kitchen for more water. It for damn sure wasn't in this state last night.

Brody didn't just put my drunk, loose-lipped ass to bed. He'd cleaned up my kitchen, too. Even my dog's food bowls were washed and sitting on the counter. The smell of coffee hit my nose. Brody had left a clean mug sitting in front of a freshly brewed pot with a note propped against it.

Morning, darlin',
   Figured you might want some of this first thing. I wanted to stay last night in case you needed anything, so I slept on your couch. I fed the dogs breakfast and took them out. Promised I'd meet Hayes for an early run before it gets hot, but I'll be home after that. Call me later, okay? Lord knows I've been where you are this morning, and I don't envy you one bit, but we've got things to talk about, Lil.

Thinking about you,
Brody

One of my throw blankets had been folded neatly and placed next to a throw pillow on the couch.
Seriously? Is this dude even for real?
Despite the hangover, I felt more hopeful than I had in a long time.
Perhaps I'd sold him short. Maybe Brody Shaw was the real deal...
Or is he too good to be true?

Chapter Sixteen

She'd charge hell with a bucket of ice water.

Brody

I sat parked half under a streetlight with the engine in my truck turned off, watching the rental from two houses away. The free-to-a-good-home ad had resulted in several inquiries. Most people were just good folks who wanted to give a dog a home. Between Lily, Melissa, and Kate, they'd been able to weed them out to focus on the more worrisome contacts. Of course, they'd always give them a gentle nudge in the direction of a local rescue before making their excuses.

Three inquiries had been particularly suspicious. The first two, one was possibly looking for a bait dog. He took one look at Everett's old Boxer, Maddie, and left. The second gave Melissa and Kate the creeps. They said he scrutinized poor Maddie like he was a serial killer in training. Everett, Hayes, and I decided that we wanted at least one of us on hand in the house after that. Not that the women weren't fully capable of handling themselves, and anyone else. Just as backup.

That split me and Hayes up for tonight. He was hanging back at the house while the next inquirer visited. I was waiting to follow them in my truck when they left. Hopefully they'd lead us to the mill. If not, we'd at least get a license plate or an address when they left.

Without Maddie, of course.

We never had any intention of giving Maddie to anyone.

Lily whipped open the passenger door, startling me. "I've got a feeling about this one, Shaw." She climbed into the cab and shut the door. "They were elusive on the phone and… I don't know, and asked a lot of questions about if Maddie had been bred. Which, yeah, Everett bred her twice after her grand championship title. They'll be able to tell if they check her undercarriage."

Seriously? Lily was all business, like we hadn't made out like teenagers then she ignored the note I left her. She hadn't even texted me since then. I was feeling a little used, and when I didn't give up the goods, she wrote me off. I didn't think that was it, of course. One, I didn't let anybody use me, and two, my gut told me she was embarrassed that she got that drunk and tried to ride me like she was breaking a young horse.

We'd save that for later. One issue at a time. "What do you think you're doing?"

"Coming with you."

I brushed a hand over my face. "Yeah, you sure that's a good idea?"

She sent me a *what the hell* look. "Why wouldn't it be?"

Truth was, I didn't want her with me if this person managed to figure out they were being followed. If they did lead me to the mill...well, by her own admittance she'd lost her cool and got her ass arrested. "I, uh...we can't approach these people, Lily. No matter how much you want to. We can't burst in guns blazing and start popping open cages."

She crossed her arms, glared straight ahead. "I'm going. They can't use me in there because there's a chance I might be recognized. Y'all aren't cutting me out of this. It's my plan, my mill to take down. I'm not going to sit in the back bedroom with my thumb up my butt."

"Your mill to take down? I thought this was a team effort. You need to depend on everyone else to do their part."

She huffed out a shitty laugh. "Yeah, sure. Because I've had so much luck with that."

"We're here, Lily. All these people. Helping. See, that's the thing about having a team. You don't have to do it all yourself."

Looking down at her lap, she nodded. "I'm not great...at that. Depending on people, I mean. I'm trying, though." Her voice was nearly a whisper as she flicked her eyes to mine and the streetlight reflected back at me. It damn near took my breath away. The soft scent of night-blooming jasmine and warm vanilla tickled my nose and was making my jeans too tight.

That fragrance of hers haunted my dreams. Would it be stronger in the crease of her thigh? Darker?

Blowing out a quick breath, I tipped her chin up. "I get it, darlin'. I have a hard time trusting people, too. I feel like everyone wants something from me. But, please let me help. Let me do my part. I'm here to back you up, Lil. You can count on me. I'm not trying to cut you out, I'd just feel better if you weren't with me if something goes wrong, is all."

Shit. The more I knew this woman, the more I wanted her to let me in—the more I wanted to let her behind *my* curtain, too. "I would never tell you that you can't, Lily. You're a grown woman who can do as she pleases, but I'd feel better if you stayed here." Not capable of stopping myself, I cupped her jaw, stroked my thumb over her cheekbone.

There was nothing I wanted more than to kiss her.

However, when headlights whipped around the corner making their way toward us, it all became moot.

She and I watched as a dark pickup truck parked on the curb in a shadow in front of a neighboring house. Our visitors were early.

"That's got to be them." We both scrunched down in my cab, watching two men get out.

Both were sizeable. One wore a baseball cap, the other had the hood on his sweatshirt flipped up. It was a bit warm for a sweatshirt this time of year. The truck was hard to see, too. Maybe black or navy blue…

I squinted. "Damn it. They don't have a plate on the front."

Both men walked up the drive, the one in the cap

ringing the doorbell while the other hung back several steps.

He looked in our direction, then at the back of his partner.

Followed by another turn in our direction as if he were staring right into the cab.

His attention shifted to Kate's SUV sitting across the street before refocusing on my truck.

"Something's wrong," Lily whispered.

"Yeah, the guy hanging back seems spooked." I didn't think he saw us sitting in the truck…besides, it was a neighborhood. There were other cars on the street, too.

A beat later, the guy tugged on the jacket of the man in front of him and they were cutting through the front yard back to their truck. By the time Melissa opened the door, the one who had watched my truck was sliding in the driver's seat.

High beams hit my windshield, and an equally bright passenger side spotlight turned toward the rental house. Lily and I both shielded our eyes. I would find out later, Melissa had too, but it was enough. With quick efficiency the driver whipped a U-turn and I caught a quick flash of orange on the truck's quarter panel before they took off the way he came. I also thought there was something written across the tailgate, but my field of vision was filled with white dots.

Lily grabbed my arm. "Can you see the plate?"

"Fuck. No, they blinded us on purpose."

"We should follow."

I was already ahead of her, turning over the engine

as they made their turn around the corner, but by the time I got to the corner, the truck was gone.

We drove all over the growing town for the next two hours looking for any signs of them, but it was the proverbial needle in a haystack. Pickup trucks were a dime a dozen around here. I was fairly sure it was an F-150 and I was ninety percent sure about the orange coloring and lettering on the tailgate. But the main road was lighted and was a hive of activity. Off the main road were lots of new neighborhoods, old ranches, and dark country roads.

We got nothing.

As we drove back to the rental house, Lil stared out of the side window. "What do you think spooked them?"

Glancing in my own rearview, I shook my head. "No idea. I couldn't see their faces, so I know they couldn't see us all scrunched down. Maybe it was a feeling."

She dropped her head against the window. "This didn't stand a chance. We don't know these roads like someone who lives here, or say, runs a puppy mill on one of these ranches."

I nodded. "Maybe, but I think we're on the right track, Lil. It was a solid plan. Otherwise, why would they run off like that?" A tear glistened against her creamy cheek. I reached across the seat to take her hand in mine.

She studied our joined hands but didn't let go. "I wasted time doing this. A lot of time—the dogs are the ones that will suffer for it."

"No, you didn't. This isn't your fault, darlin'. It was

a good idea. We couldn't have possibly accounted for every variable."

Pulling to a stop in front of the rental house, I lifted my arm across the back of the seat. "We'll have to rely on plan B is all. I promise we'll find them."

Without prompting, Lily slid across the seat under my outstretched arm, resting her head against my shoulder. I wrapped her tight. It felt so perfectly…right. Her hand on my chest. Her heartbeat against my side. I brushed a kiss across her hair meant to comfort that I had no right to give. When she turned her face up to mine, those sad eyes squeezed my heart.

I dropped my mouth in the direction of hers, just short of touching, letting her choose.

She chose to meet my lips in the softest, most tender kiss of my life. Our mouths slid against one another in feather light brushes with warmth and affection, feelings—on both sides—that were as clear as the ache that developed in my chest.

This woman.

Taking her chin between my thumb and index finger, I pulled back to see her face was a reflection of everything I was feeling. The same pull and recognition, the same desire and affection.

The same unease, too.

Lily

We were playing a dangerous game with both Brody's career and my heart. In truth, I was as much at fault as he was. More so. He didn't try to dry-hump me in his kitchen, after all.

I sat up and he ran a hand over his face. Throwing a wrist over the steering wheel, he stared out the windshield into the night.

I studied his profile. Inky hair curled around his ears from underneath his ball cap. The powerful line of his neck, the dark scruff on his sharp jaw. Longing erupted in my stomach as I remembered pushing the tip of my tongue against the hollow of his throat, my fingers threading into the hair at his nape. What it felt like to have his big arms around me. The single thick vein that ran up the length of his forearm and over the mound of his bicep before disappearing into a gray T-shirt pulled tight over his shoulders.

"We need to talk about what happened."

"I'm right here listening." His voice was deep, warm, that little bit of Texas Southern curling around my ears the same way his woodsy scent teased my nose.

I mentally hit the reset button, pinching the bridge of my nose and clearing my throat so my voice did come out husky. "I, uh, I drank too much, as if you didn't already know that. I shouldn't have done...what I did."

The dimple in his cheek made an appearance. "What? You mean make out with me?" His chuckle was easy. "Didn't mind that part at all. You're an adorable drunk, by the way."

Ugh. "I dumped my shit on you and you had to put me to bed and take care of my dogs—"

"Didn't mind that, either. Didn't even mind sleeping

on your couch." His tongue peeked out to roll over his lips. "But not calling me? That, I minded. And don't tell me the dogs ate my note."

Wait, did I hurt his feelings? Truthfully, I didn't think he'd even notice I hadn't called. "I found your note. Thank you for everything." I put a hand on his bicep. "You're a really good guy, Shaw. And a good friend."

A pink tinge climbed his cheeks. "'Friend,' she says."

That was the moment I felt the lid on the chest where I kept my heart blow wide open. I really had hurt his feelings. "I'm sorry. I should never have taken advantage of you. I tried to use you to forget my shitty family for a while and it was out of line. I'm sorry I didn't call. I'm…having someone take care of me—I'm not used to that. I've always taken care of myself. It embarrassed me. That I was so needy, I crawled into your lap like that and then you had to put me to bed. That's not usually me."

He slapped the wheel with his palm. "Dammit, Lil. I want to be mad at you, especially after the friends comment… I know you're not used to being taken care of, darlin'. I can tell you're not comfortable with it. Shit. Honestly, I'm not all that comfortable with the fact that I care enough to do it, but that's my shit." He turned his head to meet my eyes. "But I don't make out with my friends like that, so don't you dare try to friend-zone me. We are more and you know it, too."

Turning in the seat to see him fully, I noticed the clenched jaw and tension in his shoulders. "Brody." I steeled my resolve and my voice. "I should have never climbed Mount Shaw like that."

He barked out a laugh. "Mount Shaw? Christ, my emotions get whiplash when I'm around you."

Smoothing back the hair escaped from my ponytail, I let out an audible exhale. "I'm the one who said I didn't want that kind of strain on this relationship because I didn't want it to interfere with the dog search. Then I go and try to grind on you like a pillow-humper. I—"

He put a hand up to stop me. "What's a pillow-humper?"

"A dog that runs around humping everything. Couch pillows, toys, beds, legs, et cetera. I was all, 'Oh, big doggo haz nice hiney. I shud do a hump.'" *Ohmygod. I can't believe I said that out loud.* "Not important."

Seriously? Now I was babbling in doggy voices?

He barked out a laugh that didn't end, and the sound was my favorite music. "Aww shit, Lil." He wiped an eye with the back of his knuckle. "I'm so glad I asked."

I shook my noodle to clear my thoughts. As a general rule, I only geeked out like that in my head. This whole conversation had me shook and shit started pouring out of my mouth at record speed.

"Dude, I'd have to be blind to not want to bang you… I mean, for Christ's sake." I gestured to all of him at once. "It would be like not flicking the bean to that one picture of you in the Sports Illustrated Body Issue, the one with the football in front of your junk. Christ, between you, and Tyler Seguin—"

His head whipped around with sheer goddamned

glee on his face. No other way to describe it. "Me and Tyl—are you shitting m—"

I needed to stop talking, but I couldn't. So, in true Lily Costello fashion I overcorrected my course. "In the history of bad ideas, you and I wouldn't quite be as bad as Jelly shoes, but definitely worse than Crocs."

Turning away from me, his smile faded.

"You are enough trouble, and I…" *Might be falling for you.* "…am not willing to risk all this."

A muscle jumped in his jaw. "You think that little of me?"

Whoops. Freudian slip. "In. You're *in* enough trouble."

He nodded, but I could tell he didn't believe me.

I scrubbed my face with my hand. "I'm sorry for the mixed signals. That's on me. But if we let sex get into this…you *are* my friend, Brody, and I think *too much of you* to sour that."

Brody's jaw muscle twitched. "Aren't you tired of the excuses? I am. We've both been making them for so long it's like second nature and when one doesn't hold water anymore, we have another at the ready. When, in reality, you're scared of way more than damaging our friendship, and I'm scared of a hell of a lot more than losing my job. I'm just so tired of all of it. The Bulldogs organization. The excuses to keep people out. How much it stings when you believe the bullshit the media says. I won't lie to you and tell you I have never been that guy, but I am not that guy anymore. I don't screw around anymore. I haven't in a while."

But how was I supposed to know if that was the

truth or not? The owner's granddaughter wasn't that long ago, and the pictures from the fantasy suite spoke for themselves. "What about the owner's granddaughter, Shaw?"

His eyes went wide, before a line appeared between them.

"Yeah, I know about that. What about the pictures from the fantasy suite?"

I hated that I'd brought it up. That I'd bothered to point out the exceptions to his claim simply because it meant that I cared that he did screw around, that he was lying to me about a part of his life that was none of my goddamned business.

He ran a hand through his hair and his face smoothed. "The granddaughter was a mistake. The fantasy suite is utter bullshit, but the truth is, it doesn't matter what I tell you. You're going to believe the worst of me because that's what keeps you from getting hurt. I get it. I've been doing it, too. The thing is, that persona? It never really bothered me before. Not until right now. Not until you. Because all I want is for you to see me and all you see is football. This thing." He gestured between us. "This could be real, enduring. Beyond football and legacy. Beyond rumors and mistrust." He started to open his door. "But, hey, thanks for the reminder, Lil. I needed that kick in the nuts."

I grabbed his forearm. "What reminder?"

"That I'm still Brody Shaw, star middle linebacker for the Dallas Bulldogs."

As he spoke, something on Everett's SUV caught my eye. "Shit. I know what spooked them."

He whipped back to me and I pointed through the windshield.

"The sticker. On Everett's window." I nodded in the direction of the SUV where Everett had a sticker for the Unruly Dog Training Center.

He leaned forward. "Sonofabitch. I think we had the right guys."

"Can't be certain, but yeah, my gut tells me that was them." And they slipped through our fingers.

"We should go tell everyone else."

"Brody."

"Yeah." He kicked something nonexistent in the road.

"Look at me."

He did, I could see the shadow of pain lingering there. Brody wanted me to believe him and it hurt him that I didn't. The thing was, he hadn't really given me a reason to believe him because all evidence was to the contrary.

Yet, he was right about what we had between us. "I know you want me to take you at your word. That you think I've always got my guard up, but I'm not the only one, Brody. If you decide to want to tell me your side of the stories, I'll listen and try not to judge."

His expression turned thoughtful as he adjusted the bill of his ball cap and seemed to mull over my offer. With a soft nod, he climbed out of the truck and the two of us went inside to tell the others about the orange and black truck that escaped.

Chapter Seventeen

The Care and Maintenance of Damaged People:
A Dog's Guide to Rescued Humans

Brody

It was hot as balls outside. Texas in July was miserable, I didn't give a shit what anyone said. I'd lived here my whole life and I barely tolerated it. With training camp a week away, Hayes and I had only one pet shop left on our list in the immediate vicinity. We could always widen the circle later if we needed to. We both had our roles down pat, but each one of these shops made my stomach roll now that I knew where the puppies came from.

Hayes pulled the door open, a bell dinging overhead. We walked past the toys and birds in their cages, through damp air heavy with the smell of newspaper and urine. Guinea pigs darted away from their glass as we walked by while ferrets slept in an aquarium that needed to be cleaned. Hayes nodded toward the rows of kennels against at the back. A glass wall separated them from the rest of the shop.

All Puppies 20% Off was scrawled on the glass in brightly colored window paint. There must have been forty kennels total. Only a few were empty awaiting their next tenant. Some puppies slept curled in balls on top of wadded up blankets while others walked gingerly over their grated kennel floor, waste pans below them for easy cleaning. A few barked incessantly. A few had toys. Most didn't. Several kennels had sale signs clipped to the front: Rare Lilac Merle French Bulldog, $4800 For a Limited Time.

He was older than some of the other pups.

Another read American Staffordshire Terrier On Sale! $2000. He was older, too, and crammed in a kennel he could barely stand up in. Then there were the younger ones. The ones that were barely old enough to be weaned.

My teeth ground together as I took in the Bull Terriers and Pit Bulls. A Dogo Argentino and South African Boerboel. Bulldogs. Boxers. Boston Terriers. Doodles of all kinds. Each place we'd been to in the past couple of weeks had some version of this set up.

Each time, I had to fight the urge to slap a card on the counter and buy every dog here. Or beat the holy hell out of whoever owned the place.

But that defeated the purpose. Buying the dogs here would only line their pockets and perpetuate the cycle. Lily taught me the only way to put a stop to the mills was to stop making it profitable.

Stop buying.

Hayes nudged my shoulder, nodded at a Basset Hound pup who kept circling his kennel trying to find a place to lie somewhere other than on the exposed bars. When he turned to me, I knew he was having a moment. He wanted to take the pain away but knew why he shouldn't, too.

"Hiya, see a pup you're interested in?" The dude was short and a little round, he wore a blue shirt with the pet store's name embroidered on the pocket. "We've got visiting rooms back here, you can spend some time with one of them if you like." He sat the rabbit he was carrying into a glass habitat filled with bedding and three other rabbits.

I affixed my fake smile. "Possibly."

His face went slack, eyes like silver dollars. We'd seen this in several of the places we'd been to, but the awe factor hadn't gotten us the information we needed.

"Good God Almighty. You're number fifty-eight!"

"I am," I said affably. "This is my teammate, Hayes Walker." I nodded to the man next to me, who wasn't smiling. Instead, he crossed his arms over his chest and tipped his chin. I knew that look. If Hayes spoke, he was going to go batshit on the guy.

"We were checking out the pups. Got lots of bully breeds," I said, gesturing to the kennels.

The guy rushed forward, sticking out his hand. I only shook it because I didn't have a choice. "It's an honor to meet you two!" One look at Hayes, and the dude thought better of offering his hand to him.

"I'm a huge Dallas Bulldogs fan. I'm the Bulldogs'

biggest fan." Hands settling on his hips, his smile was wide and genuine.

We could use this. "Well then, it's an honor to meet you…" His nametag said *Randall* with *Sales Manager* printed underneath. "… Randall. So, lots of bully breeds, huh?"

"Yeah, is that what you're after? We've got some rare breeds, too. Lots of folks wanting bullies around here. That, and the doodles, and anything that says, 'Teacup'. Are you looking for something unusual? Did you see the Lilac Frenchy? They're going for eight large in L.A. Maybe a bulldog for the Bulldog?"

Hayes grunted again, turned back to watch the Basset Hound puppy circling.

"Oh, he's beautiful for sure. Why's he on sale?"

Randall's mouth screwed up. "Eh, he's almost four months old. But his parents were AKC champions."

My bullshit meter went on high alert. Sure, they were. "Actually, I was hoping to find Cane Corsos." I deliberately didn't use the correct plural.

Randall's mouth formed a little O. "You wanting to breed your dog?"

He'd seen the news. "No, not her. I put her down after that, but I have some property north of here and I'd like to have a breeding pair."

"What'd you want to breed for? Just for you or are you selling? Maybe you had something else in mind?"

I put on my biggest, friendliest *aww shucks* smile, thickening my accent. "Well, now. That there's my business."

He chuckled, probably thinking it was for fighting. "True enough."

"You wouldn't have any breeder names, would you? Maybe of somebody willing to sell off some of their breeding stock? Not that the pups aren't cute, but I'd like to get started sooner rather than later."

"Hmm." His mouth pulled tight as he studied me and Hayes. "Don't generally do that here. Could get me in trouble with the owner."

"Tell you what, Randall? Let's do this. I've got a couple of footballs in the truck Hayes and I could sign for you. The owner would never have to know."

He was tempted, but I could see the hesitance. "I don't know, man. That could get me fired. I'm supposed to be selling the dogs we got here, but we won't be getting any Canes in for a while. What about a Pit, instead?"

He glanced at Hayes, who was watching the Basset Hound. I could feel the menace rolling off the tight end.

I shook my head, leaned in. "A Pit won't do. They have to be Corsos." Rubbing a hand over my beard, I pretended to think. "What if I threw in a couple tickets to the home opener for you and the missus?"

He paused a beat. "Would those be fifty-yard line, ya think?"

"I can probably arrange that." I put on my Southern boy grin.

"I don't know…" He brushed the back of his head.

Hayes blew out a breath. "How much for the hound?"

I sent the tight end a quick warning glance.

Jaw tightening, he ignored me.

"She's $1600. I'd come down to $1400 for a Bulldogs player." Randall winked.

"If I take her, *and* we give you the signed balls?" Hayes got a little too close for the dude's comfort, crowding him with his size.

The manager took a step back. "A—and the tickets?"

"And the tickets," I returned, wearing a smile that made me want to throw up my lunch. This is exactly what Lily said not to do. She was going to have our nuts for this.

After scrolling through the phone, I found the team's PR department while Hayes whipped off cash for the dog. Two signed balls later, and a set of fifty-yard-line tickets at the will-call, and we had a name—Andrew Brower—and a phone number.

"Lily's gonna kick our asses for that. What were you thinking, man? And what the hell are you going to do with a dog?" The squirming pup was currently licking at Hayes's chin while we walked back to my truck.

"He wasn't going to give it up unless we bought a dog. And I couldn't watch this one circle that cage a minute longer, could I?" He nuzzled the puppy's head. "No, I couldn't, sweet pea. Not one damn minute. My sister and her boyfriend have been thinking about a dog. Now they have one."

I shook my head.

Hayes slapped his free hand on my shoulder. "I know. I know what I just did. But, the greater good, Shaw." He smiled. "We've got a lead."

We sure as hell did.

I could only hope Lily saw the greater good, too.

I pulled into a parking space at the Unruly Dog and left Hayes in the retail shop for everyone to fawn over the baby basset. He'd called to tell his sister and luckily, she'd been ecstatic. She was going to drive down this weekend to pick the dog up.

I pecked on the office door.

"Come in," came Lily's voice.

She glanced up from her desk and the butterflies in my stomach stirred. Actually, it felt more like a hornet's nest in there. As much as I wanted to tell her what we'd found, I dreaded telling her how we got it. Plus, we hadn't really been alone since the night at the rental house. We only made polite conversation at the center or if we needed to discuss the pet shops, but we never talked about what happened in my truck. It was driving me batshit. I wanted her so bad, and I knew she wanted me, too.

"Hey, good classes today?"

Her smile gave me a twinge in my chest. "Yeah, my favorite novice level agility class is today. They're a lot of fun."

"I'll have to stop and watch that one." Gently, I closed the door behind me.

"What's up? Did you start a new class today?"

I ran a hand over my scruff. "No, we're finishing up Intro to Agility on Tuesday, but with camp starting, the next class will have to wait until I get back. I think we can get through all the Agility Fundamentals classes before playoffs. Which means I should be able to keep up with the Tuesday night schedule and move CC into novice before the playoffs. I might have to make up a class here or there if the team is traveling."

Lil nodded. Put down the folder she was holding. "Rob said CC is doing well. That her confidence is really coming along, and the class is too slow paced for her. You know you can take private lessons to speed up her training. Plus, it would probably fit your schedule better."

It took sheer force of will not to roll into the flirty banter and suggestive grin that came so easily around Lily, but she was the one who pumped the brakes. I respected that, even if it was based on her misconceptions. She obviously wasn't comfortable with trusting me.

It didn't mean I didn't want her anyway.

We'd been doing a decent job not breaking the unspoken rule, but it took constant vigilance for me to pretend there was nothing between us.

I missed her. Her friendship, her sense of humor. Her lips. I blew out a heavy breath, trying to get a grip. This was what she wanted. For us to keep our distance. Wasn't it?

She leaned her ass against the lip of the desk. "What's up? Hey, did you find someone to watch CC for camp? I can keep her if you need me to."

I thought about it. Lily was the perfect option. "I'd owe you one. I really don't want to board her yet. My sister took one look at the slobber on my walls and started making excuses. I even thought about asking my neighbors—they'd do it—but she'd have someone to play with at your house."

"Sure, it's no problem. Her and Mack will have a blast. I'll be able to keep up her training, too. Was that what you needed?"

I need you. "No, Hayes and I caught a break today."

"No!" Mouth dropping open, she jumped up and swatted my chest. "Why didn't you lead with that! Tell me."

I couldn't help grinning at her enthusiasm. "The pet shop over by the mall had a lot of bullies for sale. The owner wasn't there, and the manager was a fan. It took a couple of signed balls and game tickets, but we got a name and phone number."

"Ohmygod, Brody!" Jumping up, she did a little booty shimmy that I wished I'd been behind her to see. "This is fantastic. I am so stoked! Finally, a break." Swinging her arms around my neck, she squeezed as she bounced on her toes. "You're amazing, Brody Shaw. Thank you."

Fuck. She was rubbing her body against me. A desperate groan slipped from my throat, and she realized what she was doing, because she stopped with the bouncing, but she didn't let go of me. Instead, she turned her face into my chest.

Pressing my palms to her back, I didn't let go either. The last thing I ever wanted to do was let her go.

"Brody…" Her voice was strained, her cheeks flushed. A question hung on the warm breath between us. It would have been so easy to close that distance and sink into her kiss. I could feel her heart racing against my sternum. The almost imperceptible tilt of her head as her eyes questioned.

"Son of a bitch. Friends, my ass." A person only had so much willpower in a given day. Today, I'd visited three pet stores and resisted buying approximately one hundred twenty cute little puppies. I had none left. I moved her backwards and Lily's butt hit the desk, scattering papers to the floor.

What was between us was beyond chemistry. It was the chemical reaction, a connection of particles realigned to create a new organism. For the first time, I understood down deep that being with Lily Costello was worth losing my job. But was she worth losing my heart?

I stepped back, letting my arms fall away.

Chemical reactions could have catastrophic results. They burned out buildings and razed cities to the ground. I didn't know if I could handle that.

"Lil, I gotta tell you something."

"Oh?"

Just do it, you pussy! My attention wandered to a piece of paper we'd pushed to the floor. It was time I came clean. "The manager at that pet shop…he wasn't going to give us the info unless we made it worth his while."

"Yeah, you said. Tickets. Balls."

"Not just tickets and footballs. Hayes bought a puppy. He's giving it to his sister," I added to soften the blow.

Her mouth fell open. "Brody—"

I held a hand up. "He wasn't going to give us the

info unless we bought a dog." I told her what had happened, expecting her to rain fire down on me. We'd supported the mills we were trying to stop. If Hayes hadn't bought a dog, I would have. We needed the info, and all those pups curled on themselves... CC would have had a sibling.

Only, Hayes broke first.

Lily's expression turned warm and inviting, as she settled a hand against my chest. "Brody, it's okay. I mean, it's not. But it is. I get it." She patted my chest, started to pull away. Gently, I circled her wrist, brought her hand back to my chest.

"I'm sorry." I poured my sincerity into those words.

A soft smile graced her lovely face. When she hugged me this time, it was in comfort. I dropped my chin on her shoulder. "If Hayes hadn't have done it, I would have."

She whispered next to my ear. "I know, big guy. It's okay. Hard on the outside, marshmallows in the center."

The door behind me swung open. "Hey, Lil—whoops."

Slowly, she pulled her arms from my shoulders and I stepped to the side.

I didn't turn around but stayed focused on that slip of paper on the floor.

"It's fine. What's up?" She focused on the other trainer.

"You've got a student that wants to schedule a private lesson. Do you want me to have them call you?"

"No. I'll take care of it now. This will only take a minute." She patted my arm.

I nodded, bent to pick up some of the papers thrown over the edge of the desk as she left the office.

I didn't mean to read the note.

It was one of those things. You pick something up and a word or two catches your eye, drawing it to the next. Then you go back to start at the beginning.

Bitch, I know you're looking for me.
BACK THE FUCK OFF!
You mess with my money you'll pay with blood—
yours, and your dog's.

"What in the holy fuck?" The bottom dropped out of my stomach as the blood rushed from my head. It was written in magazine clippings glued to printer paper like somebody watched too much CSI. It had to be from the mill—who else would've threatened one of my girls?

Whoa. What?

I wanted Lily. I cared about her…but, 'my girl'?

I'd have to revisit that shit later.

I had too much adrenaline swirling around in my system rapidly converting into a seething, dark anger. My teammates liked to say that I was two different guys. One dude most of the time in my everyday life. The other only came out when I put on pads, and I set the monster loose. The only time I was the monster was on the field. He was separate from me as far as I was concerned.

Now, I could feel him doing his damnedest to take over my meat suit.

Nobody fucks with Lily. Over my cold, dead body.
I knew I needed to get a grip. But FUCK—tell that to
the barely restrained monster currently beating at the
inside of my skull.

Focus, Shaw.

After a couple of deep breaths, I shoved him down
again. When had she gotten this? Today? Yesterday?
"Goddamn it, Lily, why didn't you tell me?" How did
they know it was her searching for them?

The guys at the rental house. They probably connected the sticker on Everett's car to the training center. Lily had said she was burned in certain circles. I
needed to pull my shit together so I could talk to her
calmly.

Maybe there was another explanation.

"Another explanation for what?"

I turned, the warmth of her smile usually welcome,
but at the moment, frustrating as hell.

"That puppy, though. Ohmygod, poor Hayes didn't
stand a chance against those basset eyes. Cutest puppies in the world."

Leaning my ass on the desk, I crossed my arms over
my chest. "Shut the door."

Puzzlement crawled across her face as she did as
I asked. "What's up? I'm not mad, Brody. Promise."

"No, but I am," I said in a low voice. "Wanna tell
me about this?" Holding the note up, I watched her
closely for a reaction.

And there it was.

A quick flick of the eyes to the left, a squeeze of her
fist, a swallow. "Not really."

"It's from the mill."

"Yeah, I figured. We must have had the right guys at the rental house."

We were both visibly trying to relax. I crossed my feet. She rested her butt on the folding table against the wall opposite, mirroring me.

I rolled my neck, trying to loosen the muscle. "They know we're looking for them."

She nodded.

"When did you get this?"

"A few days after we followed them."

Christ. That meant she'd had it for over a week. I felt my jaw tense as I stared holes into the floor between us. Anywhere but at her.

Lily was never in danger from me—unlike the people who'd threatened her. But I was pissed, and I knew, at my size, I was a scary motherfucker when I was pissed. When I thought I had it under control, I studied her face.

No, Lily Costello was not afraid of me. She was meeting my glare with her own, fire turning her normal violet to a rich plum as she refused to back down. Pack leader, through and through.

"Were you going to tell me?" My voice came out grated through clenched teeth.

"Nope," she snapped back. "Not your problem. It's mine."

What was truly foreboding about this whole standoff was the absolute moderation of our voices. Mine was low, calculated. Hers, steady and cold.

But that was about to change.

"What the hell are you thinking, Lily? Not telling me about something like this?" I knew I was getting loud, but I couldn't rein it in. "Jesus Christ. Did you think this through at all? Where did you get it?"

"I was thinking it's not your problem!" She moved off the table, throwing a finger out while glaring holes through me. "That I can damn well take care of myself, and I don't need you or anyone else to handle my business for me, Shaw. Back. Off."

"Bullheaded—" I ran my fingers through my hair, tugging at the curls. "Home? Did you find it at home? What if Hayes and I had just escalated this shit by asking in pet shops? Did you think of that? Fuck, do they know where you live?"

She rolled her eyes. "It came here. No return address, with a Dallas postmark." She smoothed her hair. "Man, are you a drama queen."

"Damn it, Lily, you can't just roll your eyes and act like this didn't happen! Did you think about the pet shops making matters worse?"

She clenched her jaw, glared at the wall over my shoulder.

Hell, yeah, she did. "Fuck me. You did think about it. But didn't tell me because you wanted to charge ahead without me pissing on your parade. *Your* plan."

When she scowled, I knew I was right.

"Does anyone else know? Tell me you at least told somebody. Anybody. The police or the rest of our team?"

"No. This is a scare tactic, is all. I won't run off that easy or back down from this, and I didn't need anyone trying to convince me that I should. I'm not afraid of these assholes."

"Not afraid, she says." I pushed off the desk to pace so I didn't punch a wall. "Sonofabitch. What happened to us being a team, Lil? I know you know how to work as a team. You do it with Jet. But beyond that you're being goddamned selfish withholding this from me and everyone else! It's about more than you and your fucking bent to never depend on another human being as long as you live."

Her lips parted, angry color cresting her cheeks, and as angry as I was with her, she was fucking spectacular to see in that moment. "That's not what I'm doing! Of course, we're a team." She motioned between us. "I didn't think it was a legit concern, is all. Those dogs have much more to lose than I do."

Hands on my hips, I stopped a couple feet in front of her. "Oh, really. What about Mack and Jet? They threatened your dogs, too. Ever think that if they know where you work, they know where you live?"

I didn't give her a chance to answer. "You seem to think you're the only one in this room that cares about finding those dogs, the only one responsible for seeing this through. Well, I fucking give a shit, too. Not only about them, but about you! I care about you, Liliana, and so help me God, if you get hurt because your stubborn, yet very nice, ass seems to think you have to do it all alone just to spite the world…"

Her eyes dropped away, her anger draining. "You… what? Brody—" she said with a softness that wasn't there before.

But I wasn't done. I knew I'd gotten too loud, too, and people could probably hear me.

I didn't care. If it meant getting her to see reason, I didn't care who heard. "We're also not a team of two anymore. Kate, Melissa, Carrie, Everett. They've all got a stake in this. Did you ever stop to think that if these guys know who you are, they might know who they are, too? Are you willing to risk their safety like you're willing to risk your own? Fuck!" I tangled my fingers in my hair.

That's when the door popped open and Hayes walked in. "Dude. Everything okay in here? They're starting to worry out front."

I blew out a deep breath. "Yeah, I'm almost done."

Hayes pushed the door the rest of the way open and leaned on the frame with a sleeping puppy cradled in his arm.

I let all the worry I felt for this woman blanket my stare. "It's not all about you, Lily, and whatever it is you think you need to prove to who the fuck knows, other people are sticking their necks out for you. For us. The way I feel about you…" I hesitated. "Swallow your damn pride or *you're* going to lose more than the dogs that need rescuing. Because I'll be damned before I sit and watch you get yourself hurt in the process."

Her eyes were glassy, but if that's what it took to make her understand she wasn't alone—that she mattered—so be it.

Without another word, I walked around her and shut the door behind me.

Damn her.

I *did* care about her. No, care was what you felt for a cousin. I had feelings for her. Maybe I was starting to fall for her.

Hayes nudged me on the way to the truck. "You okay?"

I wiped my bottom lip with my thumb. "Fuck, I don't know."

"You were pretty hard on her in there."

Unlocking the truck, we both crawled in the cab. I wasn't blind. I knew I wasn't the only one in the room that didn't trust easily. I was afraid, too. After we found the mill, she wouldn't need me anymore. I was a means to an—albeit, justified—end.

Yet here I was.

She was the first person I thought about in the morning and the last one before I fell asleep. Yet, she couldn't tell me about a threat to her damn safety because she was afraid I might step on her toes.

Is what I feel for Lily deep enough to get past my own shit and let her into my heart?

Deep down in my bones, I already knew the answer. It's why I'd told her how I felt about her.

Lily Costello was my perfect inevitability. I could only hope we wouldn't raze any cities or each other's hearts, when we came out on the other side. And if one of us hadn't let our guard down soon—invited the other inside our own personal shitshows—we might never find out.

I'd cracked the door for her. I just hoped she'd take the invite.

Chapter Eighteen

Clean up on aisle six.

Lily

Well, shit.

"Hey, you okay?" Rob, the center's senior trainer, stood in the doorway.

"I'm fine."

"You guys got pretty loud. You sure?"

"Yes, Brody would never hurt me." I chewed the inside of my cheek. "Hey, can I ask you something and you give me an honest answer?"

"Yikes. That sounds like a dangerous proposition."

I shook my head, hair brushing my shoulders. "I promise it's not. Am I...do I refuse to let people around here help me?" I knew I refused to depend on anyone, but did I push people away to the point that I didn't ask for, or accept help at all? "Like, say, if I had a dog I couldn't handle?"

He considered. "Hmm. You like to do things on your own. Most of the time you can, but on occasion, you get in over your head because you overestimate what you can do alone."

"Yesterday, I asked you to help me reposition the A-frame."

He nodded. "Yeah, but you tried to drag it across the ring by yourself first." He shifted to sit on the desk. "Do you remember Linus?"

I couldn't look at him, felt the sting of shame. It was the scariest incident of my career. The dog, a Leonberger, had aggression issues. During a private lesson, the giant dog broke away from his owner, attacking me with no warning. He pinned me to the floor in a matter of seconds, stood over me, holding me down.

"Linus was dangerous because of his size alone. He was also highly aggressive, agitated, and his owner had zero control over him. Yet, instead of asking for backup during the lesson, you decided to take it on by yourself. If I hadn't been keeping an eye on the situation, there's a distinct possibility you wouldn't have a throat right now."

"You wouldn't have asked for another trainer's help, either."

He huffed out a sigh. "Yes, Lily. I would have. I never would have stepped into the room with a dog that size if I didn't have a couple of extra pairs of hands. You, however, acted like you had something to prove. It was reckless."

I brought my head up. "I thought I could handle it."

"And you got yourself in way over your head. 'I thought I could handle it'? That's your pride talking. Not your brain. And definitely not your training."

Walking toward the doorway, he put a hand on my shoulder, but stared ahead. "Pride goeth, Lily. We all need help now and then. It doesn't make us weak. It makes us human."

I let that sink in. One after another my brain coughed up incidents where I'd shaken off help or didn't ask when I should have.

I owed Brody an apology.

After running home for a shower, I fed the dogs. Pairing my favorite black skirt with a plum-colored top, I swiped on a deep purple eyeliner, mascara, and a little lip gloss. I missed him. I missed us and the way we were together. While I was driving to his place, my phone vibrated.

I let it go to voice mail.

The fluttering in my stomach was too much to deal with.

I opened my window, letting the warm air and the lights of urban sprawl soothe me. This time of year, the sun didn't set until nine or so. The ginger-colored sunset was a beautiful backdrop for all the new construction. New. There was such newness to this part of Dallas. It made me want to follow suit.

Lily Costello is Under Construction. Caution: Hard Hat Area. The thought made me smile as I let my hand dance through the wind out of the driver's window and sang along with Alabama Shakes to "Sound & Color" letting the words wrap around my ears. It was amazing how much energy it took, how much weight I carried because I wouldn't let myself depend on anyone but me. I was tired of it. I was tired of shutting Brody down whenever he started to crack my shell.

After parking in a visitor's spot, I headed for Brody's apartment. It wasn't until I was in the elevator that I remembered the voicemail and listened as I walked down his hall.

"Hey, Lily. I'm sorry for the way I acted earlier. I just... I'm worried about you."

I knocked and Brody answered before the message was finished. Before he could say anything, I held my index finger to my lips.

"I care about you. A lot, Liliana. Okay, give me a call when you get this. Talk soon."

Hitting save on the message, I slipped it into my purse. "I was listening to your message."

He scratched his stubble. "Yeah. I'm sorry. I... The thought of someone hurting you. I didn't handle that well."

I cocked my head. "You care about me." It wasn't a question.

"I do." Brody's cheeks turned pink.

Warmth bloomed in my chest. When he held the door open wider in invitation, I walked in under his arm.

CC was lying on the couch. All four paws in the air, snoring like she had sleep apnea. It made me smile. Brody shut the door, and I could feel him behind me.

"Does she always sleep like that?"

"Like that. Or curled into a ball pushing against my ribcage."

I grinned up at him, the butterflies returning. "She

feels comfortable. Safe and protected. She's at ease. Curling into your side means you're hers. She's bonded to you. I'm so glad, Brody. She depends on you. You've really put your heart into helping her find her way."

"More like she stole my heart right out of my chest. You can depend on me, too, Liliana."

His eyes held mine.

When I didn't respond, he turned toward his kitchen, but not before I caught the disappointment. "Glass of wine?"

I followed him, my sandals tapping against the floor. That was the tricky part, wasn't it? I wanted to depend on him. To trust that he would be there when I needed him. And I knew Brody would be there for the dogs. But being there for me… "Yeah, that would be great."

He pulled an open bottle from the fridge, filling two glasses. "I'm glad you're here, Lil, but what's up? Something happen with the mill?"

As I slid on to a barstool at the kitchen island, he pushed a stemless glass in front of me. I felt myself wishing there was a stem to fiddle with. The man was all kinds of yummy.

Bare feet, loose shorts sitting low on his hips with *the* outline. The one that meant he was freeballing it. A threadbare UNT Football T-shirt stretched across his chest. Freshly trimmed scruff with the ends of his hair still damp.

And a heat radiating from him that I couldn't ignore. But why else had I cleaned up? I liked the heat. That tug in my abdomen, and the ache that came with it. The fact that this man wanted me as much as I wanted him.

I couldn't reconcile the Brody I knew with the one the media hounded. My Brody had a big heart in that big body. He'd been a man of his word and was smart and thoughtful. My Brody was a guy spending his Saturday night with a dog that had him wrapped around her little nubbin. That was my Brody—the one that mattered to me.

My Brody. Jesus.

"Actually, it's me that owes you an apology." Clearing my throat, I tracked his movement as he came around the counter to sit on the bar stool opposite me. "I know I'm not good at asking for help or letting people in. Anytime I've thought I could depend on someone, they've let me down. I've learned if I assume the worst of people, then I'm disappointed from the start, right?" I knew my smile wasn't hiding my pain. "I know I have my baggage—leaning on someone, trusting them to be there, it's like acknowledging I can't do it all. But self-preservation tells me that I *have* to do it all because everyone else will let me down." I pushed out a heavy breath.

"My dad took full advantage of the football lifestyle. Cheated on my mom, partied too hard, drank too much, and took too many pills. Hell, *I* am the product of my father knocking up a Bulldogs cheerleader." I chuckled, but even I could hear the sarcasm. "Sometimes I wonder how many half siblings I have that I don't know about. The fact that you play football makes it even harder for me to trust, but I'm trying. I promise I am."

"What about your mom?" His voice held such concern.

"After my dad died, inside of six months, Audrey

Costello dumped me at a boarding school with what little money we had left so she could find her next cash cow."

The muscle in his jaw ticked. "Then she married the Dick Head—who treats everyone like shit on his shoes."

"My mom included. Dick likes to hold money over her head. He thought he could do that to me, too. He even cut me off financially a while back because I wouldn't let him manipulate me with money like he does my mother." I sniffed. *Do I tell him about Trey, too? That Dick cut me off financially when I refused to marry Dr. Chase?* As much as I wanted to, I couldn't. If Brody knew that the team's head orthopedist had cheated on me then harassed me for years... I couldn't taint the working relationship between them. "Dick has never warmed to me, never tried to be a father to me. I am simply my mother's baggage, and I have no idea why. There was a time when I was younger that I wanted him to accept me, but he never did."

He rolled his lips in as he wet the bottom lip with his tongue. "I'm so sorry Lil. I can't imagine the pain you must have felt losing your dad, but not being able to count on your mom..."

"Anyhow." I shrugged. "That's why I don't let myself depend on other people, and I guess... I'm afraid you'll let me down, too. I don't want that."

I met his eyes for my next words. "Because I care about you, too."

Elbow on the counter, Brody rubbed his thumb over his bottom lip as he listened without interrupting.

"I'm sorry I didn't tell anyone about the note. I should have, I know that. But I was afraid you all might back out on me or try to talk me into slowing down. I didn't realize how selfish it was until you pointed out I'm not the only one who could get hurt. I never want to put my friends in danger. I realize this is more than a friends vibe between us, but even if we were *only* friends, with nothing else between us, it would still break my heart if you were to turn out like everyone else. Understand?"

With a soft touch, he turned my face back to his. "Better than you think I do. When you're in the lime-light, everybody has a handout or a fucking agenda. Every screwup you've ever had follows you forever and gets dredged back up at every chance. The grand-daughter thing… I didn't know you knew about that, but it set off a chain reaction with the team. Hell, I half think they want to get rid of me."

"Brody, you want me to trust you, but I can't do that blindly at this point. I'm not built that way. Tell me your side. What happened with the granddaughter?"

He sighed, pinched the bridge of his nose. "I had no idea she was Barnett's granddaughter. Ashlyn approached me in a bar after an away game we'd lost. I'd been drinking, I hadn't been with anyone in close to a year. I just needed to blow off some steam, is all. I slept with her once. But she misled me on purpose. I thought she was older than she was. I didn't know her last name, didn't give her my number, but she'd planned out this grand life with me she told her granddad all about. We were going to have babies together and she was moving in with me. Honestly, I think the old man knew she was making shit up, but he had to save face, ya know? It's stuff like that that makes me skeptical of everyone around me. The media…" He shook his head. "Boring Brody doesn't sell magazines the way man-whore Brody used to." The muscle in his jaw twitched. "I shouldn't have raised my voice, though. I'm sorry."

"You don't scare me, Brody Shaw."

He blew out a frustrated breath. "That's the problem, Liliana. You're concerned for your friends, for your dogs, but not for yourself. You're not invincible, damn it. Neither am I." Brody cupped my jaw, pleading with me. "I care about you too damn much to watch you get yourself hurt because of all this."

I pulled back, my own forehead furrowing. "I'm not walking away, Brody. Those dogs need us."

"I'm not suggesting that. I can't be complicit either. I want you to slow down, is all."

He slid off his stool. Those warm chocolaty eyes penetrated my every cell. "Ease off until after camp is over, Lil. That's all. We'll make them think you took the threat seriously. Do the research, work on our next step, but leave the rest until I get back. That's all I'm asking. Please."

"When you get back, you'll go straight into the season. You won't have time for any of this!" I shoved back, got to my feet to put distance between us. I couldn't think straight with him that close.

"I promise I'll make time. We may have to do things at odd hours, shuffle stuff around, but I promise I will be there every step of the way. We're a team, darlin'.

I don't leave my teammates' asses hanging out in the wind. Especially when the ass is as nice as yours." He grinned.

I'll never know unless I try. "I'm counting on you, Shaw. Don't let me down."

"I won't," he said in earnest.

My mouth kicked up. "Okay. Me and my ass will wait until you get back."

"Thank fuck," he whispered as he closed in on me with that big body. When his scent teased my nose, what had been kindling when I walked in lit on fire.

"Brody…" It wasn't a prelude to my dissent. It was a yearning I wouldn't deny.

He cares about me.

Brody Shaw had wormed his way into my heart despite my best efforts. This man would leave me devastated; I was sure. Pulse kicking up, my breath escaped in a rush.

Brody reached for my waist, stopping short as he balled his hands into fists.

"If you want me to stop, tell me now, Liliana. Because I give zero fucks about anyone or anything outside this room at the moment. I only want to bury myself in you."

The only time I'd enjoyed being called Liliana was when it rolled off Brody's lips. Lips I wanted against my own. Along my neck. Lower. "Don't stop."

"Be sure."

I rested a hand against his chest, slid it to his sternum. "I want you, Brody. Only you." I let my hand drift lower, over his abs and belly button until I felt the rim of his shorts. "If you're not going to fight it anymore, I'm not either." Leaning up, I feathered a kiss along his jaw, down to his Adam's apple.

"Shit," he whispered. Pushing his hand into the hair at my nape, he angled my head. Brody's mouth brushed mine, once, twice. A whisper of feathers against my skin.

I let out a breathy sigh when he captured my bottom lip and scraped his teeth over the sensitive flesh.

Our mouths were an endless slide of velvet tangling together, and the kiss got more desperate, more primal. Deeper. My hands gripped his hair. Fisting his shirt. Marking his biceps and dragging along his ribs. When I dipped the tip of my tongue into the indent at the base of his throat, that purely male sound of his vibrated against my lips.

Brody's palms circled my waist before dipping down over my cheeks. Gripping. Kneading. Pushing them together before pulling them apart in a feeling that I can only describe as naughty as hell. "Fuck, Lily. This ass…"

Grinning against his mouth, I slid my hands under his shirt. His abs tensed as I ran my fingers through the delineations.

Brody's hips jerked, his erection rubbing against my stomach.

Heat ran through my veins as my body ran slick. The need in my core was both pleasure and pain.

I ached for this man. Above me. Beneath me. Inside me. His scent, his salty-sweet skin against my tongue. The slope and curve of his muscles.

Tracing the vein in his biceps with my tongue, I let out a husky chuckle as he pulled my A-line skirt up with his fingertips only to grip my butt tight in his hands, lifting me off my feet.

I wrapped my legs around him. Locked my ankles over his butt. That crazy hot football ass I couldn't wait to see. A squeeze of my thighs and I was rubbing my center against him like a cat in heat.

Brody hissed, and I dropped my head back only to have him drag his mouth up my neck. "Jesus. I want you inside me."

His smile was naughty as hell. "When you see it, you might change your mind."

"Mmm, you poor man." I ran a finger over his scruff. "See, women like me—with all our soft spots—we were custom designed for…bigger things."

"I can't tell you how often I've thought about how your thighs will cradle my hips. The way your ass will shake when I take you from behind." When he lowered me to the floor, he made sure my body stayed pressed against his. "The color changes in your eyes as I look up at you from right…here." He ran a finger over my damp panties and my hips surged forward.

Christ, this man.

"As often as I've thought about straddling you. About the sounds you'd make when you came for me. Will you stretch me far enough that I'll feel it when you come, Brody?"

Eyelids rolled shut, he tipped his face to the ceiling. "Jesus, fuck. I wanna do this slow. I wanna explore, savor you, but—"

"Next time." I sat on the bed, tugging his shorts down. "This time is about need." Letting my eyes drift down, I checked out what Brody brought to the table.

"Christ on a cracker. That is an immense…"

"Dong?" He chuckled.

The man was thick, long and rock hard. The shaft was granite covered in silk, his veins high under the skin. The ruddy head, with its pronounced crown, had a bead of moisture pearled at the tip, and trimmed thatch of black hair surrounded the base. God, I couldn't help rubbing my legs together. Feeling the slide of my wet skin as I thought about him pushing into me.

I wondered what he tasted like. His cock was at the right level. I could swipe the liquid from the tip or cradle my tongue underneath, tickle the vein on the underside to see if he squirmed. Would Brody be salty or sweet? Both?

He must have seen my thoughts churning.

"Uh-uh." Stepping back, he tugged his T-shirt off and stepped out of the shorts. "Next time. Down and dirty, remember?" Wrapped a hand around his shaft, he ran his palm root to tip.

God, I'd never seen anything so sexy in my life as this man stroking himself while he watched me with fire in his eyes.

"You want to be *fucked*, Lily?" Grabbing a foil packet from the nightstand drawer, he threw it on the bed.

I whipped my shirt off. "Yes."

Brody moved forward until he was right in front

of me. Hands on my ribs, he guided me up the bed. "Please, let that be a front clasp."

"It's your lucky day, Shaw."

In a matter of seconds, he was pushing my skirt up around my waist. My sandals—well, I wasn't exactly sure when they came off. "Give me a second, I'll take the skirt off."

"No, leave it. It's like opening a present." His grin was all kinds of mischievous, but his calloused fingers were at my hips, tugging my underwear past my knees. His warm brown gaze fixed on my center, making me squirm.

He brushed a single finger over my slit. "Goddamn you're pretty, Liliana. You ready for me, darlin'?"

"See for yourself."

"I intend to." When a thick finger dipped inside me, a gasp escaped my throat. I arched off the bed, chased his hand as he pushed in and out of me.

"Fuck, Lily. So damn wet."

"I guess I'm ready," I gritted. I ripped open the condom, holding it up to him. Instead of taking it, Brody slid forward until his knees were under mine and his shaft bobbed over my center. "Put it on me."

Sitting up, I pinched the tip and rolled it up his length.

"Shit." Brody's hips arched forward. "I like your hands on me," he hissed through his teeth. Sliding his fingers into my hair, he took my mouth in a deep, penetrating kiss that left me with heavy lids and flushed skin. The ache in my lower belly turning painful. Guiding him to my entrance, I rubbed the crown through my soaked folds, over my engorged bud before positioning the tip where I wanted it most.

Popping the clasp on my bra, Brody palmed my breast, rolled my nipple with his thumb and forefinger as he put pressure on my opening.

This man would be the death of me. "Brody…"

"Yeah, I'm with you." Strong arms reached under my knees and cradled my legs in the bend of his arm.

With entirely too much caution, Brody sank the tip into me.

I'm fairly sure my eyes rolled back in my head. The sting of the stretch, the bliss of the pressure—a throaty moan tumbled from my throat. "More. All of it."

"Lily, shit. So tight." Irises turned the color of coffee, Brody's neck and shoulders corded with power.

I ran my hand over him, all that strength he held in check. "Brody, I want you to fill me up. Let me watch your body disappear inside mine."

"Not yet." Letting one of my legs go, the wicked man put a thumb against my swollen nub. He circled around it, inching into me, rocking his hips in short, quick strokes. "Jesus."

"You gonna come for me, Liliana? Already?" His lips quirked up on one side as he pushed in deeper, a little more sting and pleasure with each thrust.

"Yessss, just—"

Brody rolled my clit between his thumb and index finger.

I didn't tip over the edge. I detonated.

The muscle contractions were so sharp and deep they took my breath away. "Oh, God. Brody." A low moan broke free as my body rippled around Brody's thickness, drawing him in. Waves of pleasure, sharp and deep, crashed into me. My body shook. I couldn't control my own movements. All I could do was let the orgasm take me along for the ride.

Brody mumbled obscenities, his abs clenching in time with each pulse of my orgasm.

God, the man was gorgeous.

Only when I'd started to come down—my body lax and pliable—did he finally push inside me to the root. When his hips met mine, a new rush of arousal coated me. I never came more than once, but this man…

I'd wager we'd have to change the sheets by the time we were done.

Chapter Nineteen

Everything

Brody

"Ah, goddamn. Look at that." Seeing my cock seated in her was too much. Clenching my teeth, I rolled my face to the ceiling. "You feel so damn good, darlin'." Lily's body was warm and so very snug. Never in my life had a woman fit me this well. Perfectly.

It took all my self-control to keep from coming when she did. Drawing me in so completely. The woman had serious strength in her inner muscles. Combined with how responsive she was, it was a miracle I hadn't blown my load.

I wanted to taste her. To see her eyes up close when she came. Find out what made her gasp and what made her laugh. Did she have that little rough spot inside that could make her see stars? I also wanted to be privy to how her mind worked. There had been more when she told me about her mom and dad, but she held something back. I wanted everything.

What was scarier was I wanted her to know me, too. I wanted to tell her about Andra, but now wasn't the time. Now, she wanted to be fucked and that's what I'd do.

No matter how much she squirmed, how much I needed to move, I didn't. She needed to adjust to my size whether she knew it or not. But she didn't have to tell me that the softness of her thighs was made to bracket my sinewy hips. The sweet roundness to her belly would cushion my abs and ribcage. Those amazing pink nipples that were made to fit between my lips. "The way we fit…"

"I know." Her eyes were glazed, her brows drawn together as her cheeks and neck took on a soft blush. She watched me unhindered and with absolute confidence.

Maybe she'd been right when she'd told me this was a bad idea. Because I'd never get enough of this woman. I'd never walk away. Never be satisfied with what she gave me. I needed all of her—body, mind, and most definitely heart.

And I wanted to give her all of me in return.

I was falling for Lily Costello and there wasn't a damn thing I could do to stop it.

I rolled my hips, testing the give of her body. "Jesus, the way you grip me."

Her lips parted on a low moan. "The way you fill me. Nothing like it, baby. Nothing."

Leaning on my forearms, I started to curl my hips back and forth in long slow strokes. Her nipples scraped against my chest. Shifting my weight to my good arm, I took one hard bead between my fingers, circled, palmed the flawless mound.

She tightened around me. "Uhn. Jesus, fuck."

"I love that sound, baby."

My hips surged forward.

Lily gasped as she arched against me. "Like that, Shaw? When my body tugs on yours?" Christ, she was pure temptress.

I couldn't hold back anymore.

"So much. Seriously, do you work that thing out or what, because you got some grip there, Costello."

With a sadistic grin, she flexed her muscles around my cock and pleasure shot down my spine. "Shit, Lily…"

Nails scraping down my back, she dug them into the swell of my ass. "Mmm, football butt. Best get to work, big guy. I need at least one more."

The brazenness, the way she wasn't afraid to tell me what she wanted—she was real. Raw. Unencumbered. So fucking hot.

Sliding my hand up, I palmed the side of her neck, my thumb sure but gentle against her throat. "Careful what you wish for."

I thrusted in, backed out all the way to the tip and shoved forward again into her silky oblivion until I was balls deep.

And I. Did. Not. Stop. I set a quick pace, my sac drawing tight against my body, the throb in the base of my spine damn near uncomfortable while I watched her for signs that she was getting close.

"Ahh, Jesus, Shaw."

Her pulse under my palm, I leaned into my elbow and tugged her bottom lip between my teeth. Slid my free hand down to pull her thigh further up my hip. And then I went on the hunt for that sweet spot, curling my hips with every stroke.

I knew when I found it.

Lily's mouth fell open, her torso arched as the muscles of her sheath contracted around me. "Fuck. That's it." The words were a whisper. I shifted back on my heels, gripping her hips tight as I held them off the bed and pulled her against me as I pushed in. I hit that little sweet spot with each plunge.

The most satisfying moan broke from her throat.

I wasn't gonna last. "Lily, touch yourself. Show me how you like it." Sliding a hand down her belly, she found her hard nub and circled as I watched. "Christ."

Then, I felt it—that slow tightening around my shaft as her mouth fell open on a wordless cry. She shattered around me. Gripping me, squeezing me as her legs shook and her body fluttered.

Fuck. That feeling, watching her come apart. She was the prettiest thing I'd ever seen.

I buried myself deep and felt every pulse, every tug, and every millimeter I fell further for this woman.

As she came down, I was so ready to come, but with a wicked grin she sat up and pushed me backward to the bed. Her knees tight against my torso, Lily guided me inside her entrance, her skirt pooling over our joined bodies.

When she started to rock, I was lost. Lost to the warmth and sensations. Lost to the depths of her eyes and connection of us. I gripped her strong thighs, her hips as she found a rhythm that sent me right to the edge.

"Together," I told her, as she pulled my aching dick inside of her then slid back out to the tip.

Leaning forward, her lips hovered just out of reach. "Now."

I tugged her mouth to mine, lost myself while I arched into her. When her muscles contracted around me, I swallowed her gasp and groaned with every sharp throb of my cock inside of her. "Liliana. Jesus. It's everything."

"Everything," she repeated.

The hardest orgasm of my life.

Lips brushing mine in a final kiss, she rolled to her feet with absolute grace. I pulled off the condom and knotted it while she unzipped her skirt and let it slide down her hips to pool over me.

The sexy, satisfied expression was so damn perfect. Like she'd just climbed Mount Everest or slayed a dragon. With a swift move, I wrapped my arms around her knees, twisting to the side.

She landed on the bed next to me with a giggle and I had one thought.

I might love this woman.

Chapter Twenty

If it walks like a duck, and quacks like a duck...

Lily

I felt like I was sitting around with my thumb up my butt.

Brody and Hayes were leaving for camp this evening, and the fact that I'd promised to basically do nothing was making my skin crawl.

I got it. I really did.

No one else had received a threat. But, it made sense to pull back and let these assholes relax a little. But six weeks...it was another six weeks those dogs spent in hell.

We were so close. But I'd made a promise I intended on keeping. So, I'd teach my classes, and go to trials. Work on my house and try not to diddle myself raw.

That was the other thing. It had been nearly a week since I'd crawled out of his bed to go home to my dogs, and I couldn't stop thinking about Brody. He'd asked me twice to meet him this week, but one of the trainers was on vacation. I'd picked up two of her evening classes.

Dear God, having that man between my legs was nothing short of the divine. Yesterday, I'd been humming Doja Cat's "Candy"—without realizing it—during our playgroup. Melissa and Kate accused me of getting laid. With a tap to the side of his nose, Everett had sent me a playful wink.

That wily old cuss knew exactly who'd put the smile on my face. But I didn't tell him. Didn't tell anyone. Not even Olive, who hadn't been able to give much time to the mill search. Her newest high-profile client was the brat to beat all redheaded stepchildren. She's slowly been pulling her hair out.

"Uhh, I swear, this girl." She soft-whistled into the phone. "She's for damn sure lucky she ain't my child."

I chuckled. I could hear the Texan poking at the edges of her cultivated accent-less voice.

"Why don't you cut her loose? It's not like you need the business."

"It's not *her* business I want. It's access to her mother's charity committees. Are you going to the trial at Will Rogers Memorial Center this weekend?"

"No, I'm keeping CC. I don't want to leave her alone her first weekend. I'm headed to pick her up now." I checked my blind spot before moving into the left lane.

"Mmhmm."

There was way too much side-eye packed into that sound for my taste. Time to cut the call short. "Hey, I'm in the parking garage. Talk later, okay?" After hanging up, I shut the car off, opening the driver's side door, and July smacked me right in the face. Even in the shade of the open-air garage, it was too much. The kind of heat that sucks the will to live straight out of your pores along with every ounce of sweat you had to your name.

Add that to the generous amount of dog slobber I was sporting today, and the artfully greasy way my hair mashed to my skull because I'd been sweating all day, and I would have loved a shower before I came over. Perspiration was for thin women with flawless makeup, and deodorant commercials. I sweat like a sinner in church.

My life was so glamorous.

Maybe I'd check out Brody's shower.

I pushed his doorbell and tried smoothing my hair into some semblance of a ponytail, but when his door opened, my stomach turned into milk left on a hot sidewalk.

"Can I help you?" It was her. One of the women from the photo in the *Spotted* column. Tall, lean and strong—in Lululemon with no bra—her feet were bare, and her blond tresses made her look recently fucked.

"Uh." It was all I could say.

My heart plummeted into the pit of my stomach. To think Brody had told me the truth? Or that I was the *only* woman he was screwing? Yeah, right.

I ground my teeth together to keep from snapping.

"Are you here for the laundry? I know he sends his laundry out." She turned back over her shoulder before saying, "Staci, do you know where Brody left his laundry bag? She's here for the laundry."

Seriously? The laundry?

I heard the other female voice. "Umm, yeah. Hang on." A second later Unidentified Blonde Number Two—aka, Staci—stood next to Number One trying to hand me a bag full of dirty laundry. And she had on less clothing than the one who'd answered the door. Tiny workout shorts that I had no doubt, if she turned around, would reveal perfectly toned ass cheeks, and a crop top that slid off one shoulder to showcase her sculpted stomach.

I forced myself to stop clenching my jaw. "I'm not here for laundry, I'm here to get the dog," I snapped, trying not to lose my shit. After all, it wasn't their fault. It was Brody's.

Trust is a two way street, Lily. Trying my damnedest to throw off my initial reaction, I did something I hadn't done in a very long time. Prepared to give Brody the benefit of the doubt.

"Oh, CC! Yeah!" Blonde Number One said. "He left her bag and leash over here, hang on."

Staci grabbed the other woman's arm but stared at me to the point it was uncomfortable. "Oh my God, Erica, check out her eyes. They're purple. Like, Elizabeth Taylor purple."

Erica turned back to me. Leaned in. "Oh wow. They're gorgeous, darling. Are you wearing contacts?"

I cleared my throat. "Is Brody here? Where's CC?" I did not want these fucking supermodel lookalikes complimenting me in my current state of bedraggled.

"He's in the shower, CC is back there with him. Hang on. CeeeCeee?" Erica called.

In the shower? Seriously? You are not making this easy on me, Shaw. I really didn't want to overreact, to fall back on the assumption, but this whole situation was sketchy as fuck.

"Do you want to come in?" Staci studied me with an expression I couldn't interpret.

"Yeah, I think that's a good idea," I said, trying to rein in my temper. I needed to hear his explanation, and if it started with *it's not what it looks like*, so help me God… Only, as I stepped inside the door, CC barreled down the hall going full out. Before I knew it, I was on my butt and covered in dog kisses.

That's when I heard Brody. "CC!" The dog glanced back as he rounded the corner of the bedroom soaking wet with a towel he held around his waist.

Red fucking handed.

When he saw CC sitting on me, he ran a hand through his soaked hair. "Shit, Lily, are you okay? Let me help you."

I ignored his extended hand only to stare at his tiny towel. A scowl settled over my face. Deliberately, I swept my gaze up to his face and back to the towel, then over to the half-naked women before I pushed myself up off the marble. "Do you want to even try to explain this away, or should I just sit with the fucking assumption that's on the tip of my tongue?"

Jaw ticking, Brody's face hardened. "Lily…" He stood there looking all broody, as if he had a right to be pissed that my brain would jump there. No *let me explain,* or *they're not who you think they are.* No, there

I was, giving him the opportunity to tell me his side, but he wasn't talking. Again.

Maybe he didn't feel like he owed me an explanation. Which, I guessed, he didn't. He wasn't mine; we weren't a couple and he hadn't professed his undying love. I didn't have a ring on my finger. We were just two people who'd screwed and that was it.

I was only one more notch in Brody Shaw's bedpost.

"Do you have her leash?"

"Got iiiiitttt!" Erica handed it to me, and I clipped it on CC's collar.

"Lil—" he rasped.

"The bag?" I cut him off, directing the question to Staci.

"Here you go."

"Lily—"

I took the bag and stared at him, daring him to finish.

Go on and tell me it's not what I think. I gave him that heartbeat of space, which was more than I thought he deserved. *Going once. Going twice...* Instead, something like disappointment moved across his face. "Her bowl and toys are in there. Let me get her food."

You goddamned cliché. "It's fine. Text me what she eats and how much and I'll pick it up."

He nodded, scratched CC's head. "Be good for Lily. I love you, baby girl."

I slung the bag on my shoulder. "C'mon, sweet pea. Mack has missed you."

I didn't hear the door shut behind me when I turned to leave. But as the elevator door slid open, Brody stood in the middle of the hall with one hand holding his towel and the other sitting on his hip.

This was exactly why I didn't let myself get attached when I fostered a rescue.

Because you couldn't keep them. They always moved on.

This was on me. I knew who Brody was from the beginning, and I'd gotten attached anyway. I was the idiot falling for the starting linebacker for the Dallas Bulldogs while he was out banging the Doublemint twins.

It was a good thing he was going away to camp. Out of sight, out of mind. I needed time to repair the damage, to harden the shell that Brody had taken a sledgehammer to.

When he got back from camp, I would have all the info we needed, my feelings in check, and be ready to move on the mill.

By the time I got CC in my SUV, the tears I'd been holding through sheer will were all dried up.

Back to business as usual.

Chapter Twenty-One

*Does anybody answer their
fucking phone anymore?*

Brody

I barely made the team plane. Once I'd kicked the
rookie out of my seat, I put on my headphones and
crawled into my head, blocking everything out. The
Bulldogs always held camp in a small town outside of
Omaha. Peace, Quiet. Focus. Compared to the heat in
Dallas it was a nice reprieve.

And after today, I was ready to start hitting some
shit.

Anything to distract me from Lily.

I had linebackers' meetings, defensive meetings,
workouts, a playbook to help refine, films to watch,
and practices to get my guys and myself ready. Our
first scrimmage was a clusterfuck and I pulled a no-no.

I hit the red shirt. Full out.

I don't even know what I was thinking, which was
the problem. I wasn't using my head, and letting my

emotions rule me. Something I preached to my own guys about. It cost me $20K and a self-effacing apology in front of the entire team.

I didn't get to dress for the first pre-season game last week, either. Coach told me it was because they wanted to take it easy on my shoulder, but my fucking shoulder felt fine. Better than ever. I'd spent the game sidelined, going through scenarios and technique issues with my backups. I was the defensive captain. I knew the job was part teacher, but I felt like I was training my replacement.

Leaning in a hall outside the main auditorium, I thought about her again as another text went unanswered. It had been almost three weeks since she'd picked up CC, and if it wasn't about my dog, Lily wasn't responding. I'd decided to try calling her again, then saw a rookie corner back coming down the hall. He didn't realize my outside linebackers were a few steps behind.

Time for a little fun. "Hey, rook. I want the third seat in the eleventh row." Truthfully, I didn't even know where the seat was. I pointed at him. "You let anyone else sit there, I'll make you hand-wash my compression shorts after practice for a week."

He sent me a salute, shifting his backpack. Too bad the guys behind him heard me. They knew what was up. They were about to make his life miserable for the next hour, and my compression shorts would gleam like an ad for Clorox.

Not able to resist, I called Lily again. It went straight to voicemail. I didn't bother. Hanging up, I texted her instead.

Brody: We need to talk, Lil.

Brody: I miss you.

The three dots appeared only to disappear a few seconds later. They didn't pop back up again.

Staring at the ceiling, I banged my head against the wall behind me. Suddenly, I wasn't much in the mood for the rookie talent show. I went back to my room and grabbed my lifting stuff. Time to punish myself.

Why didn't you explain to her who the girls are, dumbass?

Because I was wrapped up in my own butt hurt. Lily didn't trust blindly, and she had good reason. Thing was, I knew how bad it looked to Lil, but a small part of me wanted her to give me the benefit of the doubt. Not fall back on her media-soaked idea of who I was. I wanted her to see me, who I was *now*, not who I'd been once upon a time.

I didn't know, maybe I was asking too much. It was one thing to see it in a magazine. It was something else to be slapped in the face with it in my apartment. If roles had been reversed, I'd have been just as closed off. In fact, I was. Lily was pissed but she'd tried to give me a chance to explain and I hadn't. I'd never had to explain myself to someone else like that. When I was with Andra, I didn't have the player reputation then. And before Lily, I honestly didn't give a single fuck what anyone thought of the reputation I'd earned post-Andra, either. Lily deserved an explanation at the very least—if she chose not to believe me, it was on her.

The weight room was empty except for a couple of trainers working out with Devon. He gave me a nod when I walked in, but I tapped the earbud in my ear, letting him know to leave me alone.

Wrapping my wrists, I stacked plates on the shoulder press and took my seat, anticipating the routine of it all. The space it gave me to think. The time to sort shit out. After pulling up my lifting playlist, I found my hand placement on the bar and hoisted over my head.

One. Two. Three...

I was falling for Lily Costello, and it scared the shit out of me. It fucked with my grand plan, didn't it. After all, it would be a shit-ton easier to let her make the decision to let me go than it would for me to decide between football and Lily. I wasn't naive enough to believe that if we continued down this path, our relationship would never get out. It would eventually, and it would be the end of my run with the Bulldogs. But was I even ready to give up football for a woman who seemed to think the worst of me? Would I always have to explain myself to her or would she ever give me the benefit of the doubt? That's why I'd hesitated to tell her who Erica and Staci were. If she didn't trust me, it would be a lot easier for both of us to walk away now. Before our relationship got out, my dream of retiring with the Bulldogs went in the shitter and I'd lost both my job and my heart in one fell swoop.

Half growling, I pushed off the bench to stack more weight on.

Was that six or seven plates? Eh.

Must have been an uneven number because when I lifted the bar the left side felt heavier. Whatever.

One. Two. Three...

I had this insistent part of me that believed when Lily got what she needed from me, she'd take off. Would she even need me anymore if I didn't play football?

That's when it happened.

It felt like somebody bumped the left side of the weight bar while I had it in the air. The bar listed to the left halfway above my head. My hand slipped, and I tightened my shoulders, reflexively.

POP!

Pain rocketed up my neck and down my arm. My ears started to ring, and my field of vision narrowed. I let the bar go, and it tumbled to the floor, but I barely registered the ruckus it made. Instead, today's early practice ran through my head.

We'd been running scenarios and were only supposed be going at seventy-five percent speed.

I called a new blitz. The play did what it was designed to do, creating a hole in the offensive line. The left guard read it and saw me coming.

We were both going harder than we should. Both twitchy for some real contact. He grabbed for the chest piece of my shoulder pads. I used a swim move to get around on him, throwing my left arm up and over his helmet.

But somehow his foot ended up on top of mine. The guard's weight shifted funny, but he'd managed to get ahold of a part of my pads. Brian rolled to my left on his way down, taking me with him. I landed on my left side, my left arm extended all the way out over my head, and all 320 pounds of writhing guard on top of it.

I lay there a minute and took stock. I heard two little pops and my shoulder hurt plenty, but it was fine.

I got up and walked away. Brian didn't. Broken ankle.

Now, I thought maybe I should have told someone about those two little pops earlier.

Slowly the ringing subsided and I heard Devon talking to me. "Brody, I'm sorry, man. My shirt…it got stuck on the bar. Shit, get Dr. Chase."

Ugh, not that *fucking guy.*

The pain wasn't the same as when I'd dislocated. That had felt wrong on so many levels. This felt more like soft tissue. It wasn't nearly as deep.

"Devon, stop. It was an accident. It's not your fault."

In the medical room, Dr. Douche gave me a shot of some painkiller and took films then sent me to the recovery room to ice it. I sat there like nothing. Just waiting to hear if my career was over. I didn't think so. I was moving okay. It just ached.

Half an hour later my ice had melted, and I hadn't heard anything. Sitting up from the table, I went to find out what was going on. Outside the PT room and down a hall, I finally heard the first voices.

I didn't think anything of it when I stood poised to knock and heard Dr. Chase say my name, or even when Dick's voice came from the other side of the door. But when I heard Lily's name, I pulled my fist back.

Why the hell would they be talking about Lily?

The voices were muffled, but it was definitely Doc,

Dick, and someone else, a voice that was familiar, but I couldn't place it.

"That girl's a pain," Dick said. "What…about Shaw?"

I was only getting bits and pieces of sentences.

"…some hyperextension…" Dr. Douche responded.

"… I need…sidelined," Dick said, but I missed so much of it I couldn't make heads or tails. Were they going to sideline me? My heartrate kicked into a gallop.

"…on the bench," Doc answered. "…it's a separation… X-ray or MRI. I'll put him in an immobilizer."

Okay, a separated shoulder. That wasn't too bad. It would take a little time to heal, but it wasn't a career killer. I might even make it back for the season opener.

"But… Lily…insurance." That from Doctor Douche. Again, with Lily. What the hell did she have to do with any of this?

"That was smart…real dedication, son," Dick intoned.

Then the third voice spoke up. It was also the hardest to hear. I pressed in close. "…lose my job…" He kept going but I could only make out the last few words, and I wasn't even sure of those. "…stepdaughter, you'd overlook this."

There was more after that, but the rest was so mashed up, I couldn't make anything out. I knew I should walk away. Go back to the treatment room before I got caught, but when I heard Chase's voice again, I stayed put. "How?"

"…said it…" That from the third voice.

Dick's next string of sentences were so tangled all I could make out was "proof" at the end of his sentence.

"I got it," Doc replied. "… Lily's fiancé…dust settles."

"Let me… Lily's fiancé soon," Dick responded.

Lily's fiancé. What the fuck? She never told me she was with someone. And how the hell could that possibly be tied to my shoulder?

Motherfucker. She's gotta be taking you for a ride.

But it wasn't anger that welled in me, it was hurt. A good old-fashioned ache in my chest that made my stomach drop to my feet.

"This is bullshit, right here." A new voice cut through—a woman, who must have been right next to the door. I didn't have any trouble understanding her. "You guys are screwing with people's lives for a damn game, and *he's* hiding something. That little prick is shady as hell."

Dick's voice got louder, clear as a bell. I could almost see his face, all scrunched up and red. "You'll do your goddamned job and keep your mouth shut, or I'll toss you out on your pretty little ass!"

When I heard a hand hit the doorknob, I folded around the corner into the recess. The door slammed, and at the last minute, she spotted me as she passed, her mouth drawn in a grim line.

I didn't blame her. Mariana Lopez was the team's Public Relations Manager, and this team had been one dumpster fire after another lately.

Slipping back into the PT room, I hopped up on the table. Was it possible Lily wasn't the person I thought she was? There were too many secrets. Too much she was keeping from me. Never mentioning she was engaged? I was falling in love with a woman that belonged to someone else.

I was trying not to go there in my head, but it sure as hell sounded like Lily could be playing me. Dick would give his left nut to get me out of here. It was a little farfetched, but I'd heard of crazier shit happening in this league.

Dr. Douche pulled open the medical room door carrying an immobilizer. I couldn't even look at Chase. How the hell did he know Lily's fiancé and why the hell would it come up in the same conversation as my shoulder?

His voice cut through, his face covered with disdain. This man truly hated me.

The feeling was mutual.

"Separated. Rest and ice. We'll reevaluate in four weeks. You can take the brace off to shower, but it stays on otherwise, with the exception of PT. No workouts. No practices. You're going to miss the season opener at least. Pack your bags. We're sending you home."

I cocked my head. "You sure? It doesn't feel that bad. A little achy, but usable."

"I have the medical degree here. What I say on player health is final. I'm going to tell your coach now. Check in with the office to get a flight home."

This was bullshit. Everybody knew what Dick said was final, not the doctor.

After a trainer helped me get the immobilizer on, I headed for my room to shove my stuff in a duffel. I pulled my playbook into my lap, flipping through pages. I'd designed several of these plays myself. Me and the defensive coordinator. I knew them like the back of my hand.

Dick would never release me outright because my contract was guaranteed—if they fired me, they'd have to pay me out for the last two years of it. I was valuable in a trade, too. But they couldn't do that unless I violated the conduct clause. Did they have enough to enforce it, or was Lily the missing piece?

Dallas had insisted on the clause with my first contract.

I'd screwed up bad my senior year of college. I got into a fight with a guy harassing a drunk girl at a party. I'd missed the last three games of the season, including the national championship, and scouts labeled me a troublemaker. It had cost me several places in the draft.

The clause was based on a strike system. If I behaved in a manner that violated our code of conduct, they could trade me. We'd never bothered pulling the clause out of subsequent contracts.

Right up until I banged the owner's granddaughter.

Technically, I wasn't in violation for that because it wasn't public knowledge. But it did put me at the top of the owner's shit list. Then the fantasy suite happened. Strike one. CC bit the sitter who decided to sue me, and I refused to put CC down. Strike two. If Dick knew about me screwing his apparently engaged stepdaughter, he'd get his strike three.

It was time to call my agent.

As I was about to hit her contact, Hayes smacked my foot and mimed pulling out my buds. "What?"

"You don't know?"

"Know what?" I wasn't in the mood to play guessing games.

"Wait, what happened to your shoulder?"

I balled a fist next to my leg and told him the story. "Chase said it's a separation, but it doesn't feel bad."

"How long?" He pulled the chair from the desk and turned it to face me.

"Four weeks. Then reevaluate. They're sending me home, dude."

"Shit." Knees on his elbows, he dropped his head. "I really don't want to tell you this now."

"Spit it out, Walker."

"Go to *Sportsworld*'s home page."

Navigating to their home page on my phone, I couldn't believe what I was seeing. "Fuck me running."

This was going to go down as one of the worst days of my life.

A woman from the fantasy suite was suing the team and the individual players. She was a Bulldogs employee and claiming sexual harassment. She'd named every player in attendance that night.

There was one problem. I wasn't there when things got dirty. I'd never even spoken to this woman before. I'd never seen her at the Bulldogs headquarters, even.

Yet, here I was.

Guess I'd be calling my lawyer before I called my agent.

Chapter Twenty-Two

Cupid is an asshole.

Lily

"Oh shit!" *Whoops.* Still at the training center, I slapped a hand over my mouth.

Brody was in it up to his eyeballs. In fact, the entire Bulldogs organization was in trouble from the looks of it. Olive had sent me the link as soon as the news broke. This woman who worked for the Bulldogs wasn't playing around. I didn't presume to know what actually took place in the fantasy suite, but this didn't sound like Brody.

I probably should have felt relieved that I'd dodged a bullet with him by getting out with minimal damage to my heart. Or so I'd thought. Apparently, when I'd dodged the bullet, I'd stepped into cupid's arrow.

Little asshole.

I couldn't get Brody out of my thoughts and had no idea how to harden my outer shell again. Deep down, I think I knew that the floodgates were open. Instead of the relief I thought I should feel, my heart hurt for him and what he was going through right now.

Brody may have been a manwhore, but he wasn't a predator.

"Lily, you have someone asking for you in the shop." Startling in my chair, I scowled at the break-room speaker and I shoved my cell into my pocket.

"Okay. Be right there." Probably a student with a question.

When I walked into the shop, my jaw hit my chest.

The last people I'd ever expected to see: the Doublemint twins.

They weren't half dressed this time, either. Erica had on a red power suit with black patent heels, and Staci wore yoga pants and a T-shirt that said The Boxing Academy—Head Trainer.

They both smiled, warmly.

"Umm, hey. Does one of you have a dog or something?"

Erica shook her head. "No, we were hoping to talk to you. Is there someplace we can go?"

"Okaaaay." I motioned for them to follow and led them past the agility rings to the door at the back of a storage area that led to a staff picnic table. "So…"

"So," Staci repeated. She seemed overeager, almost jumpy. "How have you been? Have you heard from Brody?"

I met her question with a glare. "We've texted about CC. That's it. If you're here to pump me for info—"

"Oh, God no. Sorry!"

Erica interjected. She was the calm one. All business. "I apologize for my wife, Lily. She tends to say whatever comes to mind."

Uh, WIFE?

"Oh. You two are together?"

Staci nodded. "Married four years next month." She took Erica's hand and held it in her own.

Ohmygod, did they bring Brody in for threesomes or something? I really didn't want to know that. Not that there's anything wrong with it, I just didn't particularly need to think about him having one with *other women*.

Erica set a manicured hand on top of mine. "We're not in an open relationship, darling. We're very much monogamous."

I was both mortified and felt instant relief wash over me in a way that told me I didn't *think* I was falling for Brody Shaw. I knew it in my soul.

"We're Brody's neighbors," Staci put in. "We watch things when he's gone. The picture you saw in the magazine—that was of a man who's like a big brother taking us out for Erica's birthday." She turned to her wife. "A good man treating two friends to a night on the town. That's it."

Erica nodded her agreement. "I know what it looked like when I answered the door. If it had been Staci with two half-naked women, I wouldn't have handled it well at all. It would have involved hair pulling. We'd just finished a workout, and dropped by to tell Brody goodbye before he left for camp. We let ourselves in," she said. "Should have called first. Lily, we wanted you to hear this from us. We don't see Brody that way. He's family."

"Besides, his equipment is all wrong." Staci made

an eww face. "All that man junk jumbled about on the outside. Just, no. Seriously, we'd be more inclined to invite you over for a threesome."

Mouth falling open, I guffawed. These two were something.

"Honestly, my first thought was 'who gives a shit what this chick thinks is going on,'" she continued. "Then, after you left, he told us who you are to him. Brody has eyes only for you, Lily. He told Erica he went by your house to explain before he left, but you weren't home. He barely made the team plane."

That was news. "I had a class. I brought CC back here with me." I should have asked him to explain. Instead, I'd judged, and I was so, so wrong. I met their gazes in turn. "Thank you. I appreciate you telling me what happened, but Brody and I…" I shook my head, examined my nails.

In a move that shocked me, Erica tipped my chin up. "For some of us, fear is a natural reaction to love. It was for me. It is for Brody. And I think it is for you, too."

"But Brody is a good man," Staci cut in. "All this shit on the news and tabloids, the lawsuits, it's bull. Most nights he spends with a beer and his dog."

"Unless he's camped on our sofa begging for chocolate and watching *Supernatural* reruns." Erica winked.

I laughed, nodded. That was my Brody. "I believe you, but there's a lot of baggage that comes with his job, too. My stepfather is the team's general manager. Seeing me could hurt his career. I also grew up with this lifestyle. It's not easy on anyone involved."

Erica nodded, searched my face. "I get your hesitance, Lily. He's afraid, too. Of more than your relationship getting outed. But you two either face your fears or you don't evolve."

I nibbled the inside of my cheek.

"Andra—" Staci blurted, but Erica squeezed her hand.

"They're not our stories to tell."

Staci nodded. "But they're worth hearing. He's worth it, Lily. Love is worth it, isn't it?" She turned to her wife, who returned her smile.

"Yes. Yes, it is."

"Anyway." Erica cleared her throat. "I'm representing Brody in the civil suit. The woman may have a suit against the Bulldogs and another player, but her case against Brody is baseless. Her lawyer filed blanket suits to see who'd pay. Once they know Brody will fight it, they'll drop the suit. I hope you'll let him tell you those stories, Lily. Brody is a good man."

"*If* he'll tell me his stories."

"He will. If you give him a chance."

With that, I peeked at Staci's watch. "Oh, shit. I'm late for class." Jumping up, I hugged them both. "Thank you. I admit I leapt to conclusions, and we've both got some secrets to tell, I think. But I'll listen."

Erica cupped my arm. "It's not easy, love. Nothing worth it ever is." With that, I led them back in and made a run for my class.

If he called again, I'd answer, and I would apologize for assuming the worst. He had enough on his plate right now when he should've been concentrating on football. If I didn't hear from him, when he got home from camp, I'd share my secrets and hope he did the same.

I'd also be able to tell him what Carrie had dug up about our possible puppy farmer.

Chapter Twenty-Three

Yo, can I get a luggage cart for all this baggage?

Lily

I'd just gotten home when I got the call from Brody.

Shit. I was nervous. Taking a deep breath, I stowed my nerves. "Hey."

"Hey. You actually answered." His velvety tenor soothed my nerves.

"Yeah. I was going to call you anyway when—"

"So, about CC," he said, cutting me off. Chilly. "Can you bring her home? I'm back in Frisco, but driving isn't easy right now."

"What? Why?"

"My shoulder. I'm out the rest of the preseason, maybe the first couple regular games, too." He was trying to mask it, but I could hear his frustration. Hell, I was disappointed for him. He had to be worried about his place on the team.

"Brody, I'm sorry. How'd it happen?"

"Long story."

When he didn't go into it, I got the hint. "Of course, I can bring her home. Consider yourself warned, she and Mack are connected at the hip. I'm afraid you might have to get another dog." It was meant to be a joke, but he didn't laugh. "When do you want me to bring her by? Tomorrow, or do you want a couple days to adjust?"

"Ah, I was hoping you'd drop her off tonight. It's kinda empty here without her."

He missed her. "No problem. Is there anything else you need since I'm coming?"

"No, I'm good. Just, miss my girls."

Of course, he missed his girl. Wait. Girl*s*. Had he said girl*s*? "Okay, let me get my guys fed, and I'll be over." I bit the inside of my lip. "Brody, I... I'd like to talk. If you're up for it. About us."

He sighed into the phone, sounded so tired. "Yeah, sure. Hey, can you bring me a couple of Hershey bars? I'm dying over here."

I chuckled into the phone. "You bet. Give me an hour."

After feeding the furries, I got a shower and changed into a band T-shirt and old cutoff shorts that fit like a glove. Forty-five minutes later, I was standing outside his door with CC in tow.

He answered the door without a shirt on, but an immobilizer brace in place. A wide band went around his waist that had a cuff attached at his bicep, and a strap went up his back flaring out into a soft pad. The pad covered the joint, then narrowed to a strap across his chest that held his lower arm in a sling.

CC darted inside, sliding all over the place as she ran from one end of the apartment to the other. "Hey, baby girl!" Brody yelled, and her legs went out from under her as she slid into a closed door while she scrambled to turn around. One-hundred-forty-pound dogs didn't exactly stop on a dime when the floors were slick.

"She's such a doofus." I smiled.

"I've been meaning to get rugs, so she'll stop doing that. She's already put one hole in the door with her head." He bent at the waist. "Who's a good girl, huh? Who's my best baby girl?"

"I'm the goodest girl, dad. Bestest. I like Lily, but *you're* my person." The dog dork in me leaked out of my mouth without thought.

"Yes, you are, baby girl. Who's the prettiest girl in the world. My big sweet doggo. I missed you, too, puddin'."

"Puddin'?" I laughed. It sooo did not fit CC's breed, but very much fit her personality with Brody.

"Says the woman who does dog voices." His lips curled into a smile. He had a dog dork in there, too. CC would get it all the way out someday.

"Don't even try to act like you haven't given her her very own voice in your head. You've become one of us, Brody. You're one of *those dog people*."

His dimples made an appearance.

When CC commenced with a happy dance, his smile could've powered the sun.

Until she poked him in the eye with her snout.

"Ah." He reared up.

It wasn't a hard poke. I lifted one side of my mouth,

shook my head. "Big dogs have big hearts, but also cause more collateral damage."

Kind of like her owner.

"True enough. Thanks for bringing her home. I can drive, but it's not easy."

I pulled her bowls out of her bag and handed her her favorite toy. Producing a six-pack of Hershey's with almonds, I slapped them against Brody's chest. "Here you go, big man. Sit down, eat your chocolate, and tell me about this shoulder while I get her settled so she doesn't knock you on your ass."

His expression was grateful. "Thank you."

I waved him off and walked to the kitchen to fill CC's water bowl.

"No, seriously. Look at me."

I shut the tap off, turned to him. Brody sauntered across the kitchen, stopping only when his chest brushed my arm. This wasn't the chilly Brody I heard on the phone.

"Thank you for taking care of my girl. When you have her, I know she's safe, loved, and well cared for. It means a lot to me, Lil. Even when you didn't return my calls, I knew you'd never mistreat my dog."

My voice came out a little hoarse, a lot nervous. "Anytime. She and Mack are buds. I'm happy to keep her when you travel. You said you won't dress for a while? What happened?"

Lines formed between his brows. "I think the team may put me on injured reserve." He shuffled over to the couch and sat, leaning his head on the back. "I don't get it. It doesn't feel bad. Achy. That's it. I don't need this thing." He gestured to the brace.

I slid down on the couch facing his side. He told me about practice and the accident in the gym followed by the diagnosis.

"Hmm. Acromioclavicular dislocation is the technical term. The clavicle is what dislocates, not the shoulder joint. Most of the time, it pops back in before you even knew it was out. It generally happens with an impact, so it's not inconceivable, but it doesn't sound like you had the right kind of impact in practice." I noodled on the options. "It's possible you could have had a small or partial separation during practice, then the weight bar pulled it the rest of the way out. But even after a partial, you shouldn't have been able to do shoulder presses the same day. The pain receded quickly?"

"Yeah, it was a sharp pain when it happened. It's still achy, but it doesn't feel like I need this thing."

I bit the inside of my lip, running through what I knew about shoulder injuries. "When you dislocate a shoulder, that happens at the big ball joint, here." I put my hand on the front of his right shoulder and pushed against the joint. "Separation happens where your clavicle meets your scapula. You feel it here." I moved my fingers to the top of his shoulder near the edge of his collarbone. "Can we take the brace off so I can poke around?"

He smirked as he slid forward to undo the Velcro. "Old habits, Lil?"

"Mmm, I enjoy this stuff. It's all the people I don't

like. Dogs are more loyal," I added as I moved to the table to sit in front of him.

"Loyalty is important, isn't it." It wasn't a question, but I nodded as I worked my fingers along his left shoulder.

No bruising. Mild swelling. "If it were a serious separation, you'd have a bump here." I circled the area with my finger. "Unless it snapped right back in, in which case it's not a severe separation and wouldn't need four to six weeks to heal." Walking my fingers to the ligaments around the clavicle, I pushed down hard. "That hurt?"

"No. The ache is all but gone, but it was up front. Not on the top of my shoulder."

I angled his elbow at ninety degrees tight to his body. "Make a fist." When he did, I rotated his forearm out and away from his torso while making sure the elbow stayed tight to his side. "Any changes in pain level?"

"No."

"Lift your arm straight in front of you, palm down." Putting my palm on top of his hand, I told him to push against me. "Now?"

He shook his head.

"Normally, I'd err on the side of caution. I'm not a doctor, Brody, but you don't have the classic symptoms of a separation."

Forehead wrinkled, he clenched one fist in his other palm.

"You want me to help you put that back on?"

"Nah. I'm going to leave it off. See how it feels."

No more stalling. It was time to do the hard stuff.

"Erica and Staci came by the training center today." I tried for nonchalant and failed.

Surprise on his features, he slid back against the sofa.

Getting up from the table, I pulled a leg under me before sitting on the couch to face him. "You've got good friends in those two. I know I jumped to conclusions about them being here, Brody. I let my own crap affect how I perceived you, and the situation. I'm sorry for that, and for not taking your calls to talk."

He turned toward me, put his elbow along the back of the couch. "I need to ask you something and I want you to be straight with me."

"Okay?"

The way he watched me, I felt like I was under a microscope. "Are you engaged?"

"Huh? No! Why would you think that?"

"I overheard Dick talking about you and your fiancé."

It was time to unpack some baggage for this beautiful man and hope he didn't run screaming from the room.

He says connected the police I was on a date. At one

...

Chapter Twenty-Four

Baggage

Brody

"I'm not engaged." She glanced at her lap. "I was once. A long time ago. I broke it off."

"What happened?"

"I walked in on my fiancé fucking one of my would-be bridesmaids. We hadn't announced anything, so there wasn't a lot of fallout, not publicly anyway. Privately, was another thing."

Ohhh. "Is this the ugly breakup you mentioned at the park?"

She nodded. "His father is a Texas bigwig, and my ex didn't take the rejection well. The more adamant I got about him leaving me alone, the more assertive he got about me being 'the one.'" She made the air quotes. "He harassed me for a long time. Kept saying we were meant to be together. That was never going to happen, but he just wouldn't hear the word no. He texted and called constantly, sent me outlandish gifts.

He even confronted me while I was on a date. At one point, I considered leaving Dallas, but I couldn't let him win, ya know?"

"Wait. So, he cheated on you, then harassed you." I could feel the vein in my forehead start to rise. "Is this the one who convinced you not to go to law school?"

"Yeah."

"Who is he? I feel the need to pay him a visit."

She shook her head. "No, no. He's… I have an order of protection now. He doesn't bother me anymore, but in the beginning, my mom pushed me to forgive him. She doesn't now, but Dick still tries to get me to patch things up. Lord knows he'd love to have a senator in his back pocket." Her eyes met mine. "I'd never do that. Even when he tried to use money to force me. He cut me off financially after that. The only reason he left me in his will was because he has no heirs."

Damn. That couldn't have been fun. Her reaction to Erica and Staci made more sense now. "And you get here, and it looks a lot like I'm screwing two women not long after I slept with you." Her fiancé, her dad. Men in Lil's world weren't faithful.

But I couldn't go around paying for their mistakes. "I get it, Lily. I really do. Between your dad and your ex…but I'm not him, and I'm sure as hell not your dad. I'm not a cheater, but you treated me like one. I kinda feel like no matter what I do here, I can't win with you. I know I have a reputation for sleeping around, but you are the only person I've been with or want to be with. Yet, I can't do that if you're always going to believe the worst of me. I am not that guy anymore, not your dad and not your ex, and it hurt me when you treated me like I was. I won't pay for their failings, Lil."

A little irritation bled into her voice. "I'm not an idiot, I know you're not them. But you can't ask me to trust blindly yet either, Shaw. My responses are conditioned a certain way and it takes time to break a pattern. I won't lie, when they opened that door, I absolutely thought the worst, but I broke that pattern and gave you a chance to explain, and you didn't take it. You didn't even try."

It was more than valid. "I should have. Some part of me knew I was screwing up, but I couldn't see past my own hurt feelings. I didn't want to give you any more of my heart if you weren't going to be able to trust me. I'm sorry, darlin'."

She sighed. "Oh my god, we're both so screwed up. You don't owe me an apology."

I couldn't help the little laugh. "True enough. Staci and Erica didn't know I was seeing someone. When I talked to Erica this morning, she asked if I'd cleaned up my mess yet. I told her you'd been sending me straight to voicemail."

Her focus shifted to the sofa back.

"I didn't ask them to come see you, Lily. But I know I shouldn't have let you leave without an explanation. Part of me wanted you to give me the benefit of the doubt and when you didn't, I pouted. I knew it was a mistake before the elevator closed behind you."

I wanted to reach for her, pull her to me, and without prompting, she slid under my outstretched arm.

She belongs here.

"I know I push people away, Shaw. I know it's stupid, even dangerous sometimes, but I promise I'm trying… I'm willing to try with you, if you are, too."

When she blinked up at me, tears rolled down her cheeks. "There's only you."

Sliding my hand over hers, I marveled at how tiny it felt. This brave, smart, strong woman.

She had me right then and there. Lily Costello owned my heart.

"I'm scared of all of this, Brody. I'm falling for you, and I'm afraid you'll let me down, too, and I know I'm going to screw up at some point." She rolled her lip between her teeth and searched my face as I wiped her tears with my thumb.

"I promise I won't."

Her eyes softened, but I could see the hesitance. "There's your career to think about, too. I don't want to put your job in jeopardy."

Leaning in, I cupped her jaw. "Then we'll do our best to keep it quiet until either the game, or the team, is done with me, whichever comes first." *It might be sooner than I'd like to admit.* "I want to retire here." If they didn't push me out first. "Now more than anything because I don't want to move away from you. So, we'll keep this our secret. And if we're found out, I'll deal with it."

When she nibbled the inside of her cheek, I brushed her forehead with a kiss. "Liliana, I'm so fucking gone for you. I knew it the moment you walked down that hall and got in the elevator. I don't give my heart away easily—if you want it, though, it's all yours if you'll be careful with it."

She met my gaze and let me see her sincerity. "Always."

With that, I let my lips slide over hers in the softest, sweetest brush, so wrought with emotion I felt it in my soul. I had niggling questions. But I locked those away for later in favor of the warmth I felt in my chest.

Now wasn't the time to think about Dick.

Well, actually, it was, but I had an entirely different dick in mind. One I couldn't wait to sink into my girl.

My. Girl.

Wiggling out from under my arm, Lily's smile turned naughty. She scooped up my brace and started putting it back on. "Just in case. I wouldn't want to put you in the hospital or anything."

A small groan rumbled in my chest. "Confident little thing, aren't you?"

Pulling me up off the couch by my good arm, she led me down the hall. "No more so than you, Shaw."

I raised an eyebrow, making her giggle. "True."

Turning me until my knees hit the bed, she gave my sweats a tug and I kicked them off.

Lily gave me a little shove in the chest that sent my ass to the mattress.

I grinned. "Somebody likes control."

"Have you met me?" she asked, giving me a flirty wink. Standing just out of my reach, she started working her clothes off. In a painfully slow move, Lily bent at the waist to push her shorts and panties down her legs. It was a perfect fucking view. That ass I'd fantasized about, but hadn't seen shake as it slapped my thighs. The plump lips that peeked out from between her legs, and the curve of her inner thigh into her cheek.

Goddamn. "That is the most spectacular thing I've ever seen." Little vixen.

"You can touch it, you know. I'd rather enjoy it."

"Just waiting for permission, darlin'."

"Oh, your mama taught you well." Normally Lily didn't have much accent—that was fairly common now—but she slid right into it like a pair of old boots.

"Please don't bring up mamas." I gripped her hip before I sank my teeth into the meaty globe. I'd wanted to do that for so long. Her high-pitched squeak was so worth the wait.

Soothing the bite with my tongue, I brought my hand around to her other cheek and swatted it with a thwack. Lily's moan made me do it again before I dipped a finger into the lips between to circle her clit before I rimmed her entrance.

Goddamn it, I didn't have enough hands. I wanted to lean her forward and taste her while I stroked my cock *and* circled her hard bud. But I only had the one hand to work with.

"Dear God, that's nice." Standing, she lifted her shirt over her head and popped the hooks on her bra, letting it drop. "Condoms?"

"Nightstand."

She bit the inside of her cheek. "It's time to have the talk, Shaw. I've always been safe, and I have an IUD. Do we need these?" She held up the foil packet.

She was trusting me at my word. Like the fucking

Grinch, my heart swelled in my chest. "No, I don't believe we do. Clean as a whistle here. I can count the number of times I haven't suited up on one hand, and those were a long time ago. I've been tested since."

Her dimples made an appearance. "Wanna go bare, big guy?"

"Fuck, yes. Come here."

She stalked around the bed with the kind of confidence that suggested I was only along for the ride.

Palming my shaft, Lily's hand made a long slow slide up and over the head while she slithered her tongue between my parted lips.

"I want you so bad, Liliana. You can't…" My breath hitched as she cupped my balls, rolled them in her palm.

"Can't what?" She chuckled against my mouth.

"…keep doing that."

She was a goddess. A lovely blush crawled along her neck and cheeks. Her generous hips flared out, begging to be squeezed, her sweet tummy calling to my mouth. Lily was strength and seduction wrapped in an air of the ethereal.

Letting go of my hard-on, she slid over my outstretched legs. Mouthed my neck, my jaw, my collarbone as her soft heat slid against my hard length.

"I love the way you fit here," she told me. "The way you nestle in against me?"

Jesus. So did I. Mouthing the base of her throat, I felt her pulse surge against my tongue. "Pieces of the same puzzle."

Rising up, she dragged her nails through the trail of hair under my navel, making my stomach clench.

"Lily, I'm struggling here." The look I gave her could have melted metal.

The look she returned was pure sin.

She crawled over the bed in front of me, pulling her knees under her torso and twisting her head to the side.

"Oh, damn. look at that." I tore at the brace's Velcro, wanting both of my hands. Her pussy was spread, and she was so fucking wet. Breathtakingly beautiful. She was fantasy come to life.

"Please be caref—" She didn't get to finish the sentence. Instead, she gasped as I sank my tongue between her folds. The scents of jasmine and vanilla permeated the air mixed with a heady dose of her arousal. I circled my tongue lazily, exploring before I slipped a finger inside and made her moan.

I wanted to give her an orgasm before I slid my girth into her, but that's not what she wanted. "Ohmygod, that feels good. I'm close, baby. I need you inside me when I come."

"Say the magic word," I teased.

"Please."

With a final circle of my tongue, I sat up and lined myself up with her entrance. The head of my shaft sinking through all her wetness to work the tip inside as I kneaded her ass was pure bliss.

Spreading her cheeks wide, I watched as my body disappeared inside hers so damn slow.

"Christ, Lil. So pretty." It had been a long time since I'd gone raw. Every sensation was multiplied. The heat and squeeze of her, the feel of her channel and the dampness easing my way.

Warm. Slick. So. Damn. Snug.

I pushed forward until she writhed against me, trying to get me to thrust, and a low moan erupted from her throat. When I didn't accommodate, she took matters into her own hands and rocked back, taking me in until my thighs touched hers.

She'd moved in a steady rhythm, chasing her orgasm as the head of me dragged across that sensitive spot inside her, but the angle wasn't right. And I needed time to play. To enjoy my view. A warning tingled at the base of my spine, reminding me I was close.

"Brody, God. I love the way you stretch me, sugar."

"Your body grips mine. I can see your body tugging against my skin. So good."

Her sheath flexed around me. She liked the dirty talk. So did I.

My hips began to swing in time with hers, my fingers digging into the flesh of her cheeks in a way I knew would leave bruises, but I couldn't stop.

I started with slow thrusts in time with hers but the faster I went the less her hips moved and the louder her moans got. "Broooodeeee."

I couldn't help but chuckle when she drew out my name. "Like that, Liliana? Want me to make you come?"

Twisting herself, she held me suspended with her plum-colored eyes. "Jesus. That's the sexiest thing I've ever seen."

This was nothing like what I'd felt for Andra. Andra was a poor substitution, a muted shade of blue when real love was a vibrant violet hue.

I was irrevocably, undeniably in love with Lily Costello.

I swung my hips faster, the slap of my thighs against hers rocking her forward. Her ass shook with every thrust, a jiggle of skin and muscle as she stared through my soul.

"Lily, I'm close."

"Me, too. I need…"

I knew what she needed. Angling my hips up, I hit that spot. Dragged the head of my dick across it over and over again.

"Oh, God, Shaw. Like that." Her moans got wild and deep.

Guiding a hand around her leg, I circled my finger around her clit and her muscles went tight all over. Lily's legs began to shake, her muscles clamping down on me with ever-increasing force.

"Fuck, Lily. Give it to me." Pressing down on her clit, I nudged that spot inside her in unison.

She came unglued. Shattered. Her canal pulsed and shoved me over the edge in the hardest fucking orgasm of my life. Lightning rode down my spine. My cock visibly jerked alongside my heartbeat with each throb inside my girl. *My. Girl.*

Her mouth popped open in a little O when she felt it, too, as the last of her spasms waned. "Holy shit."

Yeah, holy shit.

I was hers so completely, I'd never again be the same.

Chapter Twenty-Five

Collateral Damage

Lily

I traced the scar across his chin. Admired the thick onyx lashes. A mouth fashioned for sin.

I placed an openmouthed kiss on his injured shoulder before I snuggled into the crook of his neck on his good side.

Brody wasn't quiet when he came. The completely male sounds he made were half grunt, half moan and all Brody. I was addicted to that sound.

But something was off. He was so quiet I could hear the gears turning in his head.

"You okay, big guy?"

"Andra was her name, and she played me. Big time."

The words were said so soft, like he was afraid I wouldn't want this part of him, or maybe he was embarrassed to give it.

"Tell me about her?"

"We were together almost a year. She even moved

in. She was too perfect, that should have been the first clue. I didn't realize she was playing a part, telling me what she thought I wanted to hear. If I liked the movie, so did she. If I didn't like the dress, she didn't wear it. If I wanted to have sex, she never told me no. We never argued. Not once."

He ran a hand over his face. "Then the suggestions started. I should rent a loft downtown. I should get the new Lambo. Her ex had an account for her at Dior. If I'd just do the same, it would make life so much easier. She didn't want me. Andra wanted a lifestyle. I think I chose to not see it for a long time. When I didn't take the suggestions the fights started. I've never needed to flash the money around. I don't even like the fucking celebrity of it all. I got home from a road trip, and she was just gone."

I knew a little. They were photographed together a lot. I think she was the only relationship he'd had, and it was fairly early on in his career. She was engaged to a baseball player now.

I ran my nose over his collarbone. "If she only wanted you for your money, she never deserved you, sugar. You are so much more than that."

"It kinda set me up for the years to come, ya know? It's hard to know who your real friends are and who only wants something from you. Who's real and who's fake. Some of the other guys handle it like they were born to it—all the celebrity and other stuff. I just wanted to play football. I don't know… I'm just fed up with all the shit that comes with it."

I gave him a small nod. "My dad dealt with it poorly.

He needed the validation; I think that had more to do with the depression than anything. If you're the life of the party, nobody realizes you're riding the razor's edge. He hid it. Kept sinking deeper until I think he couldn't see a way out anymore."

Rumors about my dad's death had always persisted, but this was the first time I told anyone I thought my dad took his own life. He'd never sought help and didn't have any of the tools or knowledge about how to live with depression. Depression, likely exasperated by repetitive head injuries. But this wasn't about my dad.

"Did you love her?"

"No. I know that now. I hoped she was someone I could love, eventually. Maybe I hoped I could change her, too." His grin was a little sad. "Ironic, I guess.

"Then came Barnett's granddaughter, and tight on the heels of that dumpster fire, the fantasy suite hit the news."

Drawing circles on his torso, I stayed patient and quiet.

"I was in that hotel room maybe twenty minutes, Lil. Had one beer." Leaning up, he locked eyes with me. "I wasn't there when they trashed that suite, and I sure as hell didn't touch any of those women."

"Brody, I believe you."

He pinched his nose with his free hand. "Nobody else does. The woman who snuck the phone in was good with Photoshop, I'll give her that." I could feel the way his muscles tensed, the angry edge to his voice. "She superimposed my face on O'Sullivan's body— O'Sullivan, who happened to be sharing a woman with another player—simply because I was one of the highest paid players in there."

As a backup linebacker, O'Sullivan had a similar build to Brody, but he was deep on the team's roster and didn't make as much. It made me angry for him. "And now a harassment suit."

"Yep. She's saying Sherman invited her and insinuated the organization wouldn't want her to let the team down. *I* didn't see her and there were only a dozen people there while I was, but that doesn't mean anything. I think maybe she got there after I left. Erica says the suit against me won't stick—that they're probably just covering their bases. I get it, I wouldn't put it past Sherman. The dude is a dick and a half, and I hate that one of my teammates could've done this to her. She's not the first woman to complain about Sherman, and the team is way too good at burying shit like this. Last time, it was a female sports reporter in the locker room. The asshole waited until she was on air, walked up behind her, and rubbed his naked dick on her ass. Some of these guys, hand to God, they think they can get away with anything. Like they're invincible. Remember last season when Sherman was sporting two black eyes after the New York game?"

I nodded.

"Yeah, I broke his nose for that incident. I also told the reporter I'd give a statement if she wanted to file charges and she told me if she brought charges, she'd never get another job in sports. This fantasy suite thing... I'm tired of ending up collateral damage because of events that happened at a party after I left."

Sitting up, I rested my chin on his chest. "I'm sorry, Brody. I hate that you're going through this." I paused a beat. "I'd take it all away if I could. Just you and me, the dogs, and this big-ass bed of yours."

He chuckled, cupped my jaw as he arched up to place a kiss below my ear. "I get so tired of never knowing who I can trust. Of always being somebody's target."

And here I was in his bed. The person who could ruin his dream of retiring in his hometown. Yet, I don't think I'd ever felt so right as I did in Brody's arms.

It was an impossible situation.

One that would probably blow up in our faces.

That was his choice to make, not mine to take away. If he was willing to take the risk, I would, too.

"You gotta go home to the dogs, don't you?" He pulled me from my thoughts.

"I left them with my neighbor."

"Will you stay?" He rolled toward me, brushed the hair off my forehead.

I nodded, tried to push the worries away.

Right now, there was warmth to absorb and bare skin to explore. Chest hair to sift my fingers through, and those rich velvety kisses. Lush brown eyes to fall into. Fantasies of having it all.

Even if only for a short while.

"Thank you for sharing with me."

He traced my lip with his finger, and I felt the bed shift as CC jumped up to join us, curling up next to Brody.

He whispered, "With all three dogs, we might need a bigger bed."

I giggled. Contentment I'd never felt before settled into my bones as I drifted off to sleep.

Yet, later that night, I found myself on the balcony staring into the inky sky while I contemplated the uncertainties. I wouldn't forgive myself if Brody's dream got crushed because of me. Would he resent me for it? Or if push came to shove, would he choose the game? I could only pray I never had to find out.

When his arm slid around my waist, and his mouth skated over the nape of my neck, all the worries fled.

He was good at that.

Chasing away the worries for another time.

Chapter Twenty-Six

Why do I want Mexican food all of a sudden?

Lily

I checked Brody's shoulder before I left the following morning, but I didn't think it had been separated. His range of motion was too good. He'd decided to get a second opinion away from the team.

Honestly, I was completely exhausted. Muscles I'd forgotten I had were sore. After I pulled into my drive, I went next door to get the monsters.

"Hey, were they good dogs?" My neighbors were retirees who loved dogs but didn't keep pets because they liked to travel. I watched their house when they were gone.

When I'd explained to Mrs. Edmonds that my pinch was a man built like a brick shithouse, she'd said it was about time.

"Always. Your babies are no trouble at all," Mrs. Edmonds said. "There was one thing."

"Oh?"

"Jet started whining in her kennel, which isn't like her. Dan thought maybe she needed to go out. When he let her and Mack out back, she got really upset."

"Whining? Like in the house?"

"No. Barking and growling. Snarling as she ran the length of the fence between our yards. Mack whined, wouldn't go off the porch, but even he woofed a couple times."

"Hmm. Did Dan call her back?"

"Several times, but she wouldn't come. He had to go out and leash her to get her back inside. Animal, maybe? We heard the coyotes howling last night before we went to bed. Last week we had a bobcat out on the patio."

I chewed on the inside of my lip. "Could be. A big animal like that in my yard might set her off. I'm sorry about y'all losing sleep. Is there anything I can do to make it up to you?"

Mrs. Edmonds waved me off. "Hush, girl. Dogs will be dogs on occasion. Even dogs like Jet. It wasn't a bother, just thought it was odd enough that you should know."

That was true. I'd never seen Jet behave like that. Not even as a pup. After I got the dogs leashed, we went home. When I opened the front door, they darted inside, whining and sniffing.

Something was very off with my pups. I walked into the kitchen, saw the note on the counter written in sloppy scrawl on my own damn notepad.

You keep asking questions and I'll make you watch while I gut your dogs.

Then I'll bleed you, too. You got lucky this time. BTW, 12DA was a piss poor stud and too small to sell as bait.

So, I shot him.
Can't believe the little bastard lived.

Ohmygod that was the brand on Mack's belly.
12DA.
CC's brand read 63DA.
And these motherfuckers came into my house and threatened my dogs! Threatened me! Well, this shit just backfired on them. Because I had their number. Literally. Something I'd waited to tell Brody because of all the other feels last night.

I *wasn't* scared of them. I was fucking pissed. Rage coursed through me. When I opened the back door for the dogs, I saw the busted window in my laundry room. *Damn them.*

Whipping out my phone, I dialed Brody as I walked around the house to see if anything else had been touched.

"Hey, darlin', I'm getting ready to go to the doctor. Miss me already?"

"Those motherfuckers broke into my house and threatened to gut my dogs!" I turned back to the living room, scanning over everything.

"Say what now?"

"I found another note. They broke into my house last night. Threatened me, and the dogs, and said I was lucky I wasn't here."

I felt a rage like I'd never experienced before building under my skin. This must've been what a mother felt like protecting her young. It worked up my spine, over my shoulders and up my neck, down into my arms that were tense as a bow string and into my hands that I'd balled into fists.

I'd never been in a fist fight and had wondered from time to time about my fight or flight. Would I flee like Mack or would I go batshit like Jet?

I had my answer.

"Lily, calm down. You need to call the police. I'm on my way now."

That snapped me out of it. "No. You can't come, Brody. Not with cops. Not if we're going to keep us a secret."

"Shit. Goddamn motherfucking shit!" He pushed out a heavy breath, trying to get a grip on his own temper. "Okay. How'd they get in?"

"Hopped the fence and broke a window. And before you ask, I have a video doorbell and cameras for the front and back of the house that I haven't installed yet." Walking into my bedroom, I noticed my jewelry box open. "Shit. Please, please, please no."

"Lily, what's wrong?"

I picked through my jewelry, searching for the only thing that meant anything to me. "No. Please, no. Brody...they took my daddy's championship ring."

It wasn't until I hung up and called the cops that I noticed the other thing that was missing.

The slip of paper on the edge of my desk with the name and phone number Brody and Hayes had managed to get out of the pet shop owner.

* * *

"We'll check with neighbors to see if any of them have cameras that could have caught the thief. I'll check into the name you gave me, but it's only speculation at this point. Whoever came in got out clean. I'll have forensics examine the letter for evidence." Officer Johnson held up the plastic bag.

I told him about the mill and gave him the name and number Brody had gotten at the pet store. Come to find out Officer Johnson was a dog lover. He had a retired K-9 at home. "I'll do some research into the mill, Ms. Costello, but you should let the professionals handle it. File a complaint, hand over your evidence, and let the appropriate authorities investigate."

Yeah, because that won't get buried and never happen. Besides, how did I file a complaint about animal abuse when I had no animals and no way of knowing when the next would show up?

I played along to get rid of him. "I'd just really like to get my dad's ring back. What are the odds you guys will find it?"

His sympathetic smile made me want to smack him no matter how nice he and his partner were. "We'll do our best." His mouth said one thing, but his face said don't bet on it. "You got someplace you can go for a few nights? Or maybe someone who can stay here with you?"

Nodding, I fidgeted with the inside of my lip.

Please leave so I can call Brody. I still needed to tell him what I'd told the cop.

Finally, he left, and I sank down on the step in my backyard, phone in hand.

Twenty minutes later, he showed up sans shoulder brace. "What did the cop say?"

"They'll look into Andrew Brower, but unless they can connect him, they can't do anything. They got out clean, but they're going to check the letter. I feel like I got a very polite blow off. Takeaway: No blood or bodily harm pushed me way down the priority list."

"Yeah, but your dad's ring…"

I fiddled with a hangnail. "It's insured, but that's not the point."

Brody pulled me into his arms. Lines were etched into his face that I'd never seen before. "I'm so sorry, darlin'."

"I didn't get to tell you last night because we were…" I cleared my throat.

"Playing hide the salami?" he added.

It had the desired effect.

A laugh burst from me and I leaned back to see his face. "While you were gone, I came up empty on Andrew Brower. What I did find, I didn't think was our guy."

"What makes you say that?" Brody picked up Mack's ball, hurled it into the yard, and the dog darted after it.

"The first guy was an engineer relocated here from Seattle. The second was a journalist. Not exactly the guys you'd expect to be running a puppy farm. I gave the officer the name and number you got at the pet shop, and copies of my research. But what I couldn't tell him was I gave the name and number to Carrie, too."

"Why Carrie?" he asked.

"Um, because she's a white hat hacker. She consults. Companies hire her to test their internet security systems for weak spots."

Brody's mouth dropped open. "Sweet little Carrie? I'll be damned." Brody guffawed. "I wouldn't have guessed."

"Yeah, you don't want to piss her off, trust me. She can clean out your accounts and have you declared legally dead inside of five minutes. I'm sure what she did must have been all kinds of illegal, but she managed to find out that Andrew Brower is most likely an alias, the phone was a burner phone someone paid cash for. BUT, she was able to pinpoint recent calls from that number to acreage about five miles northeast of the practice facility." Brody's grin began to stretch. "The land belongs to an elderly woman in an assisted living facility, land is still used for livestock, but it's run by a farm manager who did a stint in Huntsville."

"Anything else?"

"Yeah. She did a satellite view search and there's an outbuilding set in the middle of a small wooded area on the property that happened to be where Carrie pinpointed a cluster of phone calls. The dirt road leading in turns into pavement, and it's wide enough for cargo trucks."

"We got 'em?" The delight on Brody's face was near comical.

I couldn't help but return it. "Yeah, I think we've found the mill."

He plucked me off the step and spun me around while Mack and Jet danced around our feet. "Hot damn, darlin'!" Brody's lips landed on mine, teasing the seam of my mouth open for a quick but intense kiss before he sat me back on my feet.

"But," I said, grabbing his arm and dampening the moment. "With the break-in, taking that slip of paper? They may know we know, Brody."

"Which means they might close up shop. That's not a bad thing."

"It's not, but we need the people running the mill to be prosecuted and hopefully sent to jail. Puppy farming is lucrative, and this one is most certainly a cash business under the table. If they close up shop in one place, they'll just pop up somewhere else."

I chewed the inside of my lip. "Think the pet store manager ratted you out?"

"Possibly. If he did, these people know you have backup with pull *and* muscle, and they don't give a damn." Brody's hands dropped to his hips. "Shit." He spit the word, turned away to pick up Mack's ball and nearly hurled it out of the yard.

I pinched my nose. "We need to move fast. We don't want to give them the chance to disappear." I stooped to scratch Jet's chest. "But with me calling the police because of the break-in, it complicates how fast we can go. I'd hoped we'd get proof of where they were and the condition the dogs are in, then call in the police. But I can't give up *how* we got that information."

"Yeah, we can't put Carrie at risk." That line between his brows returned. The one that was always a dead giveaway that the gears were turning. "You said Officer Johnson was a dog lover, right?" Brody turned his eyes on me, and it struck me how absolutely breathtaking this man was.

"He has a retired K-9 at home, and a rescued Pit mix. He even showed me pictures."

Brody brushed his hair back, rested his hands on his head. A move that should have been painful for someone who'd separated a shoulder. "What if we give him a day or two? If he comes back with nothing, we'll go poke around."

"That was my thought, too. I just…" This was so incredibly frustrating. "I hate waiting at all when they could be hurting those dogs. Moving them, or…disposing of them." I tried to keep the panic out of my eyes.

Pulling me against his chest, he tipped my chin up. "I know you're worried, but I think it's the only play we've got. I'd say let's sneak out and get the evidence we need tonight, but this whole break-in thing is too damn fresh for me. These people are probably on high alert. Besides, it will give me time to call the cop and tell him I'm your partner in the mill hunt. *That's* no secret at least, and maybe it will help move things along."

I nodded absently. "I'm supposed to go stay with a friend or have them stay here with me. I can ask Olive."

"No. I want you with me. At my place." A hardness crept into his tone, one I didn't particularly like.

"That's not bright," I snapped back. "Me coming and going from your apartment every day."

Brody arched his neck and took a deep breath. We were both having visceral responses to the strain.

"Sorry, I didn't mean to snap at you, but if I stay at your place, we're more likely to be photographed. I feel safest with you, Shaw. But if it's going to be you with me, you should stay here. Your pickup truck is a dime a dozen, but you can put it in my garage if you want. I'll park in the drive."

I gestured to the end of the house, but he didn't seem convinced. "Besides, I have a yard for the dogs and my neighbors know I kept CC for a friend. They won't think anything of it."

"Yeah." His voice sounded weary. "That makes more sense. I know you're strong and capable of taking care of yourself. And all that. But the caveman in me needs you with me."

I nodded, remembering he had a doctor's appointment. "What did the doctor say about your shoulder?"

"Range of motion, strength, all that, looks good, but he wouldn't tell me if he thought it was separated or not. Said to follow the team doctor's orders." His lips thinned. "The feeling I got was that he wasn't going to step on anyone's toes for me. I've got to see a PT guy today. How 'bout I bring some stuff over after that."

"I have classes this afternoon, anyway. I'm going to take care of those so nobody else has to cover for me."

I backed up on the step, using the front of his shirt to pull him to me. The way his lips curled, one dimple winking at me—he was all arrogance and swagger— but in the eyes is where I found *my* Brody. The tough guy with a soft heart and a gaze the color of molé that melted me faster than butter on a hot tortilla.

Chapter Twenty-Seven

Where was Hayes when you needed him?
At training camp.

Brody

It had been a fucking day. The break-in at Lily's house had me unsettled. These scabby-dick-tip motherfuckers threating my girl and her dogs? I'd never felt that kind of anger before. Not even on the field.

Shit was not sitting well, and I was walking a fine line with my temper as I headed into the Bulldogs practice facility for Devon to treat my shoulder. With a couple of players besides me injured, Dr. Douche had decided Devon would accompany us back to Dallas for treatment. Seemed odd to me. We had therapists who didn't travel to Nebraska with us this year—one of which had been with the team a lot longer than Devon.

While I stood in the hall outside the medical room waiting for my appointment, I checked the clock on my phone. Team should be taking lunch about now. It gave me a chance to hit up Hayes.

"Hey man, how's the shoulder?"

"S'okay. I'm waiting on PT, but I'm fine. No residual pain past the forty-eight hours. How are you doing, old man? Getting the start against Miami?" The Sharks were our third preseason game.

The sigh Hayes let out made him sound drained. "Hell, I don't know. Same shit, different day around here."

"How's Jensen doing in my spot?" Jensen Bishop was the rookie linebacker out of Miami who held it down when I got hurt last year. He'd played fifty percent of last week's game while I'd continued to ride the bench for a fucked-up shoulder I didn't have. Sonofabitch. I was proud of the kid. He was doing his job like the a pro he and he was a quick learner. None of this was Jensen's fault. It was just the nature of the game.

"Yeah, well, they're not publicizing this, but he took a nasty hit during practice yesterday. It was just a bad tackle. Helmet to helmet. Kid's definitely got a concussion. I heard him throwing up in the locker room. But Chase gave him the okay to start this week."

"That motherfucker. Dick's just pulling Chase's strings. Dick wills it, so shall it be. Swear to God he's the dirtiest general manager in the league. And Chase needs an ass whooping, I'd be glad to give him."

"Get in line. Hey, how's your girl?"

I ran a hand over my face. "Yeah, someone broke into her house and left another threat, but thank fuck she wasn't home."

"I meant the dog, but no shit? When was this?"

"Last night."

"Where was she?" I could tell Hayes was choosing his words carefully and I appreciated it.

"Guess."

"Ahh. You okay, man? You sound like you're walking the edge. I mean, I would be too with everything."

He didn't know the half of it. "Yep. Pretty much. Keep me posted on shit there, okay? If the quilting bee mentions my shoulder, or anything about the girl?"

"The one suing you?"

"The dog trainer. Something weird happened before I got sent home. I overheard some talk about her, and I can't put the pieces together."

"Umm, okaaay." I didn't blame Hayes. I was confused, too.

"We'll talk when you get back."

As I let Hayes go, Darius—a senior team trainer—rounded the corner. "Shaw, you're with me today." He unlocked the room and I followed him in.

"Where's Devon?"

Irritation darted across his face that was gone as fast as it came. "He had a family thing come up. So how is it?" Feet spread, arms crossed, he nodded at my shoulder. "You're supposed to be in an immobilizer. Where's it at?" Darius's tone was all business.

"There's nothing wrong with it. That's not my ego talking, Darius. Something is shady here."

His focus shifted back to my shoulder. "Lift your arm straight out."

Fifteen minutes later he'd run me through much of the same routine Lily had. "You may be right. But

I'm not a doctor." Shaking his head, he looked like he wanted to say more but stopped himself.

"Fuck."

"Yep. You certainly are. Look, man." He readjusted his arms. "I didn't say this, but they need you sidelined for Bishop to gain experience."

Dropping my head to stare at the floor, I just couldn't figure it out. The pieces didn't fit. "Why go through all this, Darius? Why not just bench me?"

"I don't know, my man. Your rehab with the dislocation was ahead of schedule, too. Were you benching the same weight you did before the dislocation?"

I grunted. "More."

Darius harrumphed. "There's nothing I can tell you that you don't already know, except that if you think Dick Head and Adam Chase are scheming to keep you out...well, you've always had good instincts, bro." He slapped me on the shoulder.

After I left the Bulldogs facility, I picked up CC, packed a duffel, and told Staci I would be gone a few days. Figuring Lily would be wiped out, I also did my damnedest to adjust my mood.

She didn't need one more thing to worry about.

"Lucy, I'm home!" I called as I carried a bag from the Blue Goose through the back door.

My girl wanted Mexican food.

Standing in the kitchen with her cell to her ear, she waved me in.

"H-hang on. Officer Johnson, my partner just

showed up. If I put you on speaker, can you start again?"

I hadn't expected to hear from him so soon. Lily pulled the phone away from her ear, putting it on speaker as I set the food on the counter. "Ya got me, Ms. Costello?"

"Sure do."

"Hi, Officer Johnson. I'm Lily's friend Brody. Thanks for getting back to us so quickly."

"No problem. I have a soft spot for dogs as Ms. Costello knows. My Malinois was the best partner I've ever had. Okay. Bad news first. I dug into Andrew Brower and I'm fairly sure it's an alias, but I was able to pull some footage from a CCTV camera and a neighbor's doorbell camera. The perpetrator was dressed in a black hoodie and gloves. We never got a clear face shot from the camera. Fingerprints from the house also didn't turn up anyone in the system. It doesn't mean they're *not* in the system, just that they were careful. I've got nothing on the letter yet, but chances are they won't find anything there either. This guy was careful."

With every sentence, Lily's shoulders sagged a little more.

"However. We did get a make and model on the truck. 2019 Ford F-150 Raptor."

Lily bit the inside of her cheek. "That makes sense. It would fit with the body style of the truck we saw at the rental place."

"Unfortunately, that's all we've got so far," the officer continued. "I called a few local contacts and put feelers out about your daddy's ring, Ms. Costello. You might also check pawn shops over the next few months and keep tabs online."

She nodded. "Okay, I can do that."

"I hate to see Billy's championship ring go missing like this. He's a legend. I even saw him play a few times. But I digress…

"Now, about the mill. The phone number you gave me for Andrew Brower is a prepaid that's gone quiet. They've likely dumped it. We were able to pinpoint a location near the Bulldogs practice facility where the phone was getting a lot of use, but it's out of Frisco PD's jurisdiction. I put in a call to a county deputy I know, and she said what I already suspected—not enough probable cause to get a search warrant. But the *Davis Ranch* outside *Prosper* is already on her radar for other complaints. Whoops, I guess I shouldn't have told you where that was." Johnson went quiet, letting the info sink in.

After a heartbeat, Lil asked what I was about to. "Let's say, hypothetically, the sheriff's department received photos, anonymously, of dogs coming and going or the conditions inside the mill. Would that give the sheriff probable cause?"

"Indeed, I believe it would," the cop said. "In which case, the sheriff's department could get a warrant and confiscate the dogs if the conditions are inhumane. As well as pursue prosecution if they can locate the responsible party. I don't think it's Mrs. Davis, given her advanced Alzheimer's."

Lily's smile was sunshine through the clouds as she

read between the lines and grabbed my biceps. "Okay, then."

"Ms. Costello, I'd be remiss if I didn't advise you, Mr. Shaw, and whoever else might've been helping you to let the authorities handle this. My cousin—*Deputy Angela Lee*—is certainly qualified."

And there was who to contact. "Of course, officer. We understand completely and thank you for the update."

"My pleasure. Be careful, you two."

It took only one glance at Lily to realize we weren't going to get much sleep tonight. As much as I wanted to wait until it was Hayes sneaking around on private property with me—particularly in a state where people would shoot you for trespassing without blinking an eye—I wasn't going to convince Lily to wait.

The way she'd set her shoulders, she was already gearing up for an argument. "Shaw, don't you even—"

"Okay."

She lit from within. Plopped down on one of her kitchen chairs and pulled food out of the bag. "Fucking finally."

Chapter Twenty-Eight

The Fighters

Lily

Finding the dirt road off the main road was the hardest part. It was well hidden. But a good way in, the overgrowth gave way to fenced pasture down each side and the dirt turned into pavement.

We were lucky to have a nearly full moon. Brody killed his headlights.

Trees cropped up sporadically, then got thicker the further we went. The structure, if you could call it that, was an older metal building hemmed in on three sides by brush and trees, with a pasture on the fourth. It resembled something you'd see in a bad horror movie and yell at the dumbasses on the screen not to go inside. And guess what we were about to do.

Twenty-five yards from the front, a padlocked gate blocked the road and Brody pulled to a stop.

We moved quickly and quietly, climbing the gate.

But something was wrong. My heart dropped before we ever made it inside.

"There's no barking, Brody. No noise."

He took my hand. "Yeah, I noticed."

The two garage-style doors on the front had rusted handles. He gave one a try, then the other, but neither would budge.

"There may be another door," I said, and we traipsed through the pasture hoping to find another way in. The uniform windows we found, one of which was partially broken, were covered in dirt. They bracketed a back door. "There. Look."

His eyes followed my finger to the jagged shards.

"In for a penny," he said, and walked to the edge of the trees, came back with a branch, and broke a good part of the window out.

We were in the middle of the property and at two a.m. there was nobody around to hear, but I shushed him anyway. Pulling off his shirt, he threw it over the broken glass and made the precarious climb through the window.

I stood there trying to watch every which way for any indication we'd drawn attention, but all I heard was a couple of cattle mooing in the distance.

A light inside came on and I wanted to scream at the man. I settled for a whisper-yell. "Brody, turn the light off!" Then the door popped open and there he stood, pulling his T-shirt on, which now had a few holes. His face was a mask of anger. "The dogs are gone, but they were here."

The smell hit me. A mixture of piss and shit, vomit

and illness. It took everything I had not to retch when I stepped inside. "No. No, no, no. Please, no. God-damn it."

They'd been busy.

Empty shelves big enough to hold medium-sized and smaller kennels lined the perimeter of the build-ing. The space underneath the shelving was big enough for large and extra-large. Walking to one shelf, I found where a puddle had soaked into the wood, recently. Dabbing my finger in it, I held it to my nose and the tears fell. "It's urine."

"Yeah." I turned to find Brody squatted on the ground underneath the shelving. "There's poop on the wall over here. Look around to see if you can find fur or food or anything."

I studied the shelves. At the back, in the crack, black muck stuck to the wall. I pulled over a milk crate and flipped it over, stepping on top. The muck was a mix-ture of fur and poop and God knew what else.

That's when I lost it. I stepped off the crate as a quiet sob racked my chest. They'd been here until very re-cently, probably earlier today.

And we'd missed them. We'd waited too long and missed them. I could have done this. Came out here while Brody was at camp and gotten everything I needed. Last night, while I was safe in his bed, they were here. Waiting. My legs started to wobble, and tears streamed down my face.

"All this…" I turned in a circle, letting my eyes fol-low the shelving. "So many dogs, Brody. So many… and they're gone. What if they've been dumped like

Mack?" I tried to swallow the knot in my throat. "Or worse?" I couldn't even allow myself to give voice to the meaning that implied.

If I'd just gotten here sooner. If I hadn't promised to wait.

I'd never felt so beaten, so absolutely desolate in my life. Despair was a monster in my abdomen clawing up my chest cavity, creating wound after wound.

I'd failed them. Again.

I ran to the door and vomited my despair. My rage for the monsters who did this to these poor dogs. My self-loathing for my failure.

There was no air-conditioning or heating in the building. I could just imagine dogs crammed into a metal building in the Texas heat, one on top of the other, and lucky if they were only one to a kennel. Most kennels would have several.

Females bred every time they came into heat for the entirety of their lives, only to have their babies ripped from them way too young.

Dogs that had never touched grass, never smelled freedom, had never known a kind touch. I wasn't so sure death was the worst fate. At least it would've brought them peace.

But the cycle would start again with new dogs, in a new location.

Brody pulled me into his arms. "Shhh. We're gonna find them, Lily, I promise. They won't destroy their investment that easily. They likely moved them elsewhere."

That was probably true, but… "Is that really the better fate, Brody? Look at this place."

"It is. Because we're going to find them." With both hands, he framed my jaw. "And they will know love and safety and care in their lives because we won't quit on them. We can't. They need us. They'll just have to wait a little longer, is all."

I let myself drift back to watching CC interact with Brody the first time. The first time Mack had asked me to play. The expression on a dog's face when it found its very own person.

I hated this feeling. It was heartbreaking, and for every ten times I felt this heartbreak, the one time we won, and a dog went to a good home or made a break-through or learned to trust again… That feeling would always outweigh this heartbreak.

Always. No, I'd never give up on them.

There was another problem. A big one. This wasn't some small operation that only supplied local pet shops. The bay doors. The heavy truck tires that rutted the sides of the road. "This is… It's big. More than a hundred dogs, maybe. They're not only supplying to local shops and selling online. This mill could have a pipeline with brokers selling all over the place."

Even if we managed to find the dogs again, there were way more involved than I was prepared to handle with my connections. Even if local shelters and rescues could take on that many dogs—which wasn't likely—these were bully breeds. They were going to be very under-socialized dogs that didn't trust humans. Rescues wouldn't adopt out a dog that might bite. How many of them would have to be destroyed because they weren't trustworthy around humans through no fault of their own? Even at a no-kill shelter, they'd be cared for, healthy, but just trading one cage for another.

I wiped at my tears.

I had no idea how to handle a mill this size.

"We need to get out of here. Let me get some pictures."

I was in over my head.

"Lil."

"Huh?"

Brody kicked dust and grass over my puke pile. "We have to go, darlin'."

That's when I heard the saddest whine. So small and hoarse. Both of our eyes widened. "Did you hear it?"

"Yep." Within a fraction of a second, Brody moved inside to a pile of milk crates and wooden pallets. Bending down, he slipped his arm behind the pile.

"Brody, it could be rats."

"Nope." The most desperate little squeal prickled the air as he pulled his arm back and cradled something to his chest.

A tiny brown bulldog puppy, maybe four or five weeks old. "Ohmygod."

It wasn't much bigger than the hand holding it. "Shhh, buddy. It's okay. Shhh," Brody whispered, trying to soothe a baby calling for its mama.

Fresh tears tracked down my cheeks as I stroked the puppy's head. Its own little eyes were crusted over with god knew what. With extra care, I pulled the skin on its back away—it didn't snap back. The pup was badly dehydrated. As gently as possible, I lifted its lip to check the color of its gums and found them pink with tiny milk teeth, but not as hearty as they should have been. "We need to get it to a vet."

Brody passed me the pup. "You head back to the truck. I'll close this up."

After carefully crawling over the gate, I wrapped the pup in a shirt from Brody's back seat and settled him on my lap. No, they wouldn't kill their cash cow.

Watching the little pup wiggle, I knew I couldn't give up. If I had to start all over again, that's what I'd do. These dogs deserved justice.

Not every aggressive dog could be rehabilitated, but I was damn good at what I did, and confident that I could train quite a few dogs that other agencies might put down for being aggressive.

What I needed was my own place. A rescue to house the dogs that would be deemed unadoptable elsewhere. Dogs like CC and Mack that took more than a regular rescue could handle. If I had to work with them one at a time, that's what I'd do. I knew if I told Rob, he'd volunteer to help me. So would the other animal behaviorists I knew.

The problem would be feeding, housing, supplies and medical costs. Money.

Little dude wiggled in my lap. "Shh. It's okay, baby. We're going to get you patched up."

The door opened, and Brody slid in, but I kept comforting the pup. "And when you're old enough, we'll find you the bestest home ever. Then we're going to find your mama and get her patched up, too."

"How is he?"

"Weak, but *she's* a fighter."

"Let's get her to the vet, then." Exhausted, the little pup settled into the blanket and fell asleep as Brody turned and left the way we came.

We got the baby into Dr. Avalos's care and made it back to my house physically and emotionally exhausted.

As overcrowded as my queen-sized bed was with dogs and a hulking man, when Brody slipped in and slid his arms around me, there was no place I would have rather been.

Tomorrow, I needed to start making calls, do some research into other organizations, but for tonight I'd sleep in this amazing man's arms. The one who wanted to make sure I knew I could depend on him. Who'd told Dr. Avalos he was paying for all of the bulldog's vet bills.

I was completely in love with him. Unequivocally.

Tonight, there was just Brody, and sleep.

I'd save the tough stuff for tomorrow.

Chapter Twenty-Nine

I thought the full moon was last night.

Brody

"Okay, thanks for the update, Dr. Avalos. Anything she needs, just send me the bill," I said as I stepped out of my truck. Lily came through the backyard gate as I hung up the call. Relief washed over me. The bulldog pup was getting stronger. I'd even given her a name—Laila, after Laila Ali. Because she was a fighter through and through.

Lily launched into my arms, kissing the shit out of me. Eventually, the whine of a passing car's power steering in the alley at the back of Lily's yard brought my head up. She lived in an old part of Frisco with a big yard, but cars were forever traveling up and down the streets and back alleys. Especially with the park across the street from her house.

"Why don't we take this inside," I said.

She nodded, hit the keypad to close the garage door before she led me through the backyard and into the kitchen. We barely cleared the door before I slipped an arm around her waist and slid my lips over the back of her bare neck. "Damn, I can't imagine ever seeing you and *not* wanting to do that." She arched her back, pushing her ass against me.

"Mmmm, ditto." We were at it like rabbits. Every night except the first. We should have been exhausted, but whenever she was near, my cock sprang to life.

"In fact…" I kept walking her forward, whirled her around and sat her butt on the counter with me between her thighs.

"You're lucky I have a strong sex drive, Shaw. Otherwise, I'd have to kick your ass out just to get some rest."

I sucked at the skin below her ear, making her hum. There wasn't a single inch of her I didn't know. "Why, Ms. Costello. I'm surprised at you." I feigned offense, but her hands were under my T-shirt exploring my skin and my hands were pulling at her shorts trying to work them off her legs without taking her off the counter. "What's it gonna be? Make love to me or fuck me till neither of us can walk?"

She winked an eye shut. "Hmm, how bout 'grr, hrr, thank you, sir.'"

A laugh bubbled out of my throat. "A quickie it is. Lift your butt so I can get your shorts down." I wanted to tell her I loved her so many times, but every time I got close, I swallowed the words.

She did the same.

Yet, the only reason I cared about keeping our secret was so I could play in Dallas to be near her, and with the civil suit against me looking more and more like it would fold, things were promising again. I'd have to go back to my apartment soon. The last preseason game was this weekend, then camp would break.

She was still breathing heavy from her orgasm when I lifted her off the counter to find her shorts and swatted her butt.

"Was that Regina? How's Laila?"

She was already gone for the puppy, too. "It's going to take time for her to heal but she's doing better. Gina said she had a female that lost her entire litter yesterday. She won't eat or sleep, but if Laila does well the next couple of days, the Golden Retriever might take her on as her own. I didn't know dogs would do that."

Lily buttoned her shorts, poured iced tea from a pitcher. "Sometimes. It's good news. There are things a mother can teach her that people can't. She needs that socialization, but we shouldn't have any problem finding her a forever home."

Finding her a forever home? I thought she already had one. Right here with us. Then, again, this wasn't my home.

If Lil wasn't thinking about Laila in terms of forever, maybe she wasn't thinking about me that way either.

I shook the thought off. We'd talk about it later. Between classes, the animal welfare agencies she'd contacted the last few days, and me keeping her up at night, she was probably exhausted.

I wasn't going to read into it.

"I heard back from the sheriff today." She handed me a glass of tea.

"What did she have to say?"

Lil's disappointment was written on her face. "They got anonymous photos but can't get a warrant because the barn was empty. She said it's probably been scrubbed at this point anyway."

"What about the pictures of Laila?"

"Who's to say whoever sent her the photos didn't bring the puppy with them? The judge isn't going to grant a warrant on that alone. No dogs, no case. And they can't direct resources to search for dogs that are no longer there. Especially with the Davis family having ties in that community."

"Fuck a duck." I spat the words.

"Pretty much. The deputy told me they'd add it to their case file on the Davis ranch."

The irritation in my system made my skin feel tight. Walking to the back door, I watched my girl lying in the shade with her buddies. "Did you hear back from the ASPCA?"

Lily's arms slid around my waist, her head against my back. "Similar to what the deputy said. They understand our predicament, but they can't direct resources into finding dogs that may or may not be there. And they're more large scale in their responses."

"This isn't large scale?" I was a tad incredulous.

"Not in the grand scheme. ASPCA steps in for big things. Huge mills. Natural disasters. Although, if we do locate the dogs again, we can contact them, and they can put someone in to gather evidence on site. They'll even coordinate with law enforcement and local shelters. But until we have a bead on the dogs…"

I rested my forehead against the glass, pushed out a breath. "Damnit, I'm sorry, Lil."

"Shh. This isn't your fault."

"If we hadn't have waited…but with camp."

"Brody, look at me."

I turned.

"This isn't on you." I could see rather than hear the unspoken *it's my fault* on her face. "What we need now is to regroup. Even if we do find them, and the ASPCA gets involved, there are special considerations for the bullies that have never been socialized. But we'll dig back in, keep our eyes and ears open. When some morsel of evidence turns up, we'll be there. In the meantime, you need to focus on your shoulder and your job." She picked at something on my T-shirt that wasn't there. "We need to get back to routine. Which means…"

I brushed my knuckles along her jaw. "You trying to tell me something, babe?"

"It's time for you to go back to your place. Not that I want you to, but—"

"But if I care about playing football for the Bulldogs this year this arrangement is risky?"

She nodded.

That's when CC chose to slap the back door with a paw asking to come in. Lily shifted her weight, and I turned to open the door. The whole gaggle busted in and did their happy doggie dances complete with slobber.

"I'm surprised they didn't come say hello as soon as you got here," Lily said.

"They were comfortable out there in the shade."

Retrieving the water bowls—there were two now—she filled them both before replacing them on the floor.

I pulled a chair out from under the table and sat rolling my shoulder around to loosen it up.

"Brody, the longer you stay here, the higher the likelihood we'll get caught."

"Not sure that's a bad thing at this point."

"Oh, no." She poked me in the chest. "No, you don't. That can't have anything to do with me. You want to walk away from twenty-four *million*? That will be on you alone, buddy. I don't even want to be a whisper of a consideration in that decision."

Hooking a finger in her shorts, I pulled her toward me, rested my forehead against her stomach. "If the Bulldogs put me on IR, that gets cut in half."

Pushing a hand into my hair, she gripped it firmly and cranked my head back until I was forced to look at her. "And if you walk away, it's zero. If that is what's in your heart, I want you to follow it, but I know that you love this team and this town. I can't be the reason you walk away from that."

When I was drafted by Dallas, we were a team I was proud to be a part of. The head coach loved the game and his players—he wasn't anyone's marionette. The former general manager cared about us, too. She built a strong bond with both the players and coaches—one where we wanted to win for her. We would sweat, and bleed, and break our bones for her.

But she retired; her replacement let the coach go, then our quarterback.

Shit rolled downhill.

Old man Barnett turned a blind eye to how Dick operated in favor of a higher ROI and more playoff berths.

This wasn't the team I loved anymore.

Still, Lily was right. I only had two more seasons. That was a lot of scratch to the poor kid with a single mother from Denton. I didn't want to leave that on the table if I didn't have to.

"How 'bout I go in the morning. One more night?"

She held up her index finger. "One more night."

The following morning, I packed up my duffel and my dog. The sun was creeping over the horizon in shades of yellow and orange as I pulled out of the garage when there came Lily. Out the front door wearing nothing but a T-shirt that said Property of Dallas Bulldogs #58 and toting a dog bowl. Goddamn, she was something, all messy hair and creamy flushed skin.

After rolling down the window, I adjusted my ball-cap and draped my wrist across the steering wheel. When I dragged my tongue across my lips, I could still taste her there. "Miss me already?"

Stepping up on the running board, she handed the bowl through the window and I'm sure flashed half her ass at the old man next door. "You forgot this," she said, then nibbled on that plump bottom lip.

"Well, you forgot something, too." Before she stepped off the running board, I checked both ways and stuck my head through the window, snatching a scorching hot kiss.

"I love you, Liliana." It slipped right out without hesitation.

Her fingers came up to cover a soft smile as she stepped backward off the running board and giggled. Lily's gaze turned the most radiant shade of mauve in the morning light as she laughed like a little girl. "I lo—"

"Uh-uh. No, you don't. You save that till you can tell me properly. Naked. In bed." I rolled up the window and put the car in drive, watching my rearview as I pulled away.

With a quick scan of the block, she turned her back to the truck and flipped her T-shirt over her butt, then tossed her head back and laughed.

I slammed on the brakes. My tires screeched to a halt. I probably woke half the neighborhood and CC slid off the bench behind mine onto the floor with a thud.

She just mooned me. And disappeared into the house before I'd even gotten the truck into reverse.

That was my girl.

Chapter Thirty

The Unlovables

Lily

I'd gone back and forth in my head a million times over the last week. I weighed the positives and negatives over and over again, considering all possible options. The problem with having Brody here was that we were so new we couldn't keep our hands off each other. It wasn't his fault, mind you, but I needed time to think and strategize, figure out the best path to take.

When we located the mill again, the ASPCA and SPCA of Texas said they'd step in and help. But I couldn't fathom all those unsocialized, so-called dangerous breeds, being put down by their respective shelters. Or mentally deteriorating in a no-kill shelter until they succumbed, never knowing a life with love in it.

I knew I was the person who could keep that from happening. I needed my own facility. A place for dogs nobody else could handle or train. The ones nobody would adopt because of breed bias and under-socialization.

Those were the dogs I wanted in my care, and not just for *this* mill. It would be a haven for the dogs other shelters couldn't handle. Dogs Like Mack and CC. Mill dogs, dogs from fighting rings, strays, dogs that had been abused and didn't trust humans—those were the dogs I wanted in my shelter to get the medical treatment, love, and care they needed.

Those that I couldn't rehabilitate, I would filter into working programs that curbed the worst of their issues or redirected them into more acceptable behavior. Every abused and mistreated dog deserved a chance to heal from the physical, emotional, and psychological traumas of their lives.

Every. Dog.

There was one problem. I needed money I could never go to Brody for. The last thing I wanted was for Brody to think I was using him for his money. Besides, even if he gave me every penny he had to his name, it might not be enough.

Running a shelter wasn't cheap. It would take millions in capital just to open the doors—I'd need paid employees, medical and operational costs, I'd have equipment and facility expenses. I estimated at least twenty million just to get the doors open for fifty dogs.

There was only one person I could ask for the money, and I knew what I'd have to do to get it.

Which was how I ended up at the Dallas Bulldogs corporate headquarters instead of teaching my eight a.m. class. "He's ready for you, Ms. Costello."

Stiffening my spine, I grabbed my folder, prepared to

make a deal with the devil himself. I only hoped I came out with my soul intact. I also knew how far I would go where I was concerned, but Brody Shaw was off the table. His career was his, not mine to gamble with.

Dick's office looked down on all of Oz—it was very J.R. Ewing. Expansive windows. Brown leather couches and chairs where I'm sure he banged his secretary. Enormous oak desk and wet bar with crystal decanters.

The ick factor was high.

"To what do I owe today's visit, Liliana?" He met me with a repulsively haunting grin that prickled the hair on my neck.

When I was young, I loved to read Little Red Riding Hood with my dad. I always read the little girl's part aloud. "Grandmother, what big eyes you have!"

Dad read the wolf's part in a grumbly voice. "All the better to see you with, my dear."

Seeing Dick smile like that, all I could think was, "Grandmother, what big teeth you have!"

Shaking off the willies, I walked directly to his desk and dropped the file on it. "I need your help." The words came through gritted teeth with my jaw locked and a little bit of bile sitting on the back of my tongue.

"Oh, you do, do you?" He chuckled, flipped the folder open. "A rescue." He took a seat in his monstrosity of a chair.

I preferred to stand. Avoiding all details about Brody, I gave Dick my pitch. I told him about my mill search, and the resulting discoveries. How the mill would be too big for one shelter, or one trainer to handle, but that I could arrange to take only the least adoptable dogs. "As you've said before, the Bulldogs are always looking for charitable causes to fund. Why not a dog shelter? Think of the tax write-offs, branding tie-ins, et cetera. The Dallas Bulldogs would fully fund their own dog shelter where players and staff would volunteer. It would be unprecedented. The commissioner would be all in."

He flipped through the papers I'd prepared, scanning over the numbers. "I'm aware that you and Mr. Shaw have been searching for this mill. Let me be blunt." He stared straight through me, but I didn't flinch. "Are you sleeping with Brody Shaw?"

I'd expected this question. He'd already asked me to rat on Brody. I lied with psychopathic precision and cold calculation in my voice; it did not waver. Nor did my eyes stray from Dick's.

"No, and frankly I'm offended you asked. You know damn well I'm not my mother." *Sorry, Mom.*

Dropping the fingers propped on his chin, he raised an eyebrow. "This is a handsome investment, Lily. You can't possibly think I'd do this without quid pro quo."

I had expected that, too. I was fully expecting to leave this room with my tail tucked between my legs. I would posture, negotiate, beg, borrow, and lie my ass off at world-class level in the hope of keeping a sliver of my integrity intact. But the truth was, he had the upper hand and we both knew it.

In my head, I'd already agreed to the Head Trainer's position.

But, a girl's gotta try. "Of course. You'd never do it simply because it's the right thing to do. Tell me what you want, and I'll tell you what I'll give." I sank into the chair across the desk and crossed my legs, tapped my fingers against the tufted leather that was an exact match to the color of a football.

Dick put his elbows on the desk. "You will leave your dog training position and come to work for me as my head trainer. You'll be given a fitting salary, and you can remain the figurehead of the Bulldogs animal shelter because it's good publicity for *my* stepdaughter to have a pet project of that magnitude."

So far, it was what I'd expected and I'd get to work with the dogs at the shelter.

"However, you will find someone else qualified to attend to day-to-day operations and oversee construction." That gave me pause. "You'll also have to choose another trainer to work with the dogs. Any time you spend at the shelter will be outside of your hours here, and unpaid.

"In addition, in your function as head trainer, you'll work closely with me, *Trey*, and select medical staff to provide the players with outcomes that will best benefit the Bulldogs organization."

Whoa. There it was. He'd try to manipulate me into gaslighting players and coaches like he and Trey had done to Brody to benefit the organization's bottom line and championship hopes. And why was I not surprised my ex-fiancé was under Dick's thumb? Adam Chase III was nothing if not slippery as fuck.

"Last but not least, the Bulldogs will not break ground on this shelter until you've reached your third anniversary in your position and I'm satisfied with your performance."

Nope. "Let me tell you what I'm willing to give." Leaning forward, I planted my elbows on the corner of his desk, mocking him. "I will leave my position at the training center and come to work for the Bulldogs, but I will oversee all phases of the shelter's development. When it's ready to accept dogs, I'll hand day-to-day operations over to someone of *my* choosing who reports directly to me. I want two days a week, paid—three during the off-season—to work with the dogs at the shelter myself. I will not report to Trey. Figure something else out there. Oh, the Bulldogs will break ground on the shelter as soon as I identify a suitable space to build or renovate, and I want it close enough to this campus that the players and staff can give freely of their time. And I want it all in writing, Dick."

He laughed. Literally fucking laughed. In my face. "It's good that you have that backbone, Lily. You're going to need it. It helps that you're not a half-bad liar as well."

"What's that supposed to mean?"

He ignored the question. "And player outcomes?"

I shrugged, but kept my eyes locked on his. "It is what it is. The dogs are what matter." The answer was short, noncommittal, and easy to twist. There wasn't a chance in hell I was going to gaslight the players for Dick. I suspected he thought he could force the issue later.

Eh, let him try. Poor Dick. He'd brought a bulldog to a Cane Corso fight.

His lips split into a slimy grin. "Your father always knew when to roll over, too."

Asshole!

"Here's my best offer, Liliana. You can oversee the shelter planning and construction You can even pick your replacement and they can report to you. You get one day a week at the shelter—two in the off-season—

unpaid. I will break ground on the shelter in one year and I will put most everything in writing. You will work with Trey, and whether you think you can hold out or not, you *will* 'rat' for me, Liliana."

He made the damn air quotes with his fingers. What a douche. "Six months and you break ground. The shelter should be up and running nine months from then. And if I have to work with Trey, you have to tap some of your resources to help me locate the mill."

"It's a deal. I'll get it drawn up and take it to the board." He stuck out his hand and I clasped his palm, but for the first time in my life, I wondered: if this was a win, why did I feel so utterly hopeless? Lost, empty, completely beaten down, and badly in need of a scalding hot shower with a side of Clorox bleach.

For the dogs, Lily. For CC and Mack and Laila, and all those dogs in the woods that didn't make it out like Mack did. For all of the underdogs, the unwanted, the throwaways who are out of sight, out of mind. For the mamas that never run on the grass with their babies, and the males that are met with the end of a cattle prod instead of a loving hand.

You did it for the unlovables, Lily.

I did it for the unlovables. Because it was what was best for the dogs.

I made it into the elevator and watched the door shut before I let my tears fall.

Chapter Thirty-One

The Ashes of Brody Shaw

Brody

"You're cleared to play. Your shoulder is fine." Dr. Chase snapped off his gloves and turned to throw them away.

Should have been exactly what I wanted to hear. The first game of the season was tomorrow. Not only did it mean I'd get to play, but they couldn't put me on injured reserve. "Was there ever really anything wrong with it?"

Darius tried to hide his grin. I hadn't seen hide nor hair of Devon in the last several days. Honestly, as the most senior trainer on staff and Devon's boss, if Darius thought the other man was a problem, it was probably for the best.

Chase spun on me, though instead of the distaste I'd expected to see, he wore a shitty smirk that made me want to cram my fist down his throat. Pulling off his glasses, he wiped them with soft cloth. "Oh. I nearly forgot. Mr. Head wants to see you in his office as soon as we finish your exam. Take your playbook."

My stomach plummeted, my head going a little light. I'd just been cleared for trade.

"Why, you weaselly little motherfucker." I hopped off the table, made a grab for his button-down. "I ought to beat your crooked little raggedy ass for the hell of it with all the shit you've done to the guys on this team."

His eyes widened ridiculously as he realized he had nowhere to go.

"Whoa, Brody." Darius stuck an arm between me and Chase, pushed against my torso. "You know that's not a smart move, my man."

With a growl, I punched the drywall next to Chase. Letting go of his shirt, I whipped the door open. The glass rattled when I slammed it behind me.

I hit the locker room and started stripping clothes off. Ten minutes later I was pushing my wrist wraps into my gym bag as my hair dried. As soon as I got out of the locker room, I tried to call Lily.

It went to voicemail.

Knowing what I sounded like at the moment, I figured a text would be better than a voice message.

Brody: Call me as soon as you can.

After a stop at the truck to stuff my playbook in my bag, I texted again.

Brody: Lily, I need to talk to you. I'm about to go into a meeting with Dick.

No response.

I tried to call one last time before I went into the building that housed Dick's office. I had a glimmer of hope that this meeting wasn't what I thought it was. When the call rolled over to voicemail, I did my best not to scare her for no reason. "Give me a call as soon as you can, darlin'. I need to hear your voice."

With that, I pulled open the door and took the elevator up to Dick's office. His assistant was waiting for me. "Mr. Shaw, you can go right in."

I pushed through the doors. Sitting in a leather executive chair so big I was sure he was compensating for something, Dick turned from his bank of windows. "Brody."

"J.R. How is everything in the land of Ewing Oil today?"

"Funny." He didn't smile.

I didn't give a shit. "Thanks, I thought so." The last thing I ever wanted was to give Dick the satisfaction that he'd gotten to me, so I tacked on a smile for good measure.

"Mr. Shaw. I'm aware you're sleeping with my stepdaughter."

Sonofabitch. "Oh? Not that I wouldn't *like* to sleep with your stepdaughter, or just about anybody for that matter, but what makes you think that?"

He had zero proof.

"I have proof."

Fuck me running.

Dick slid a folder across his desk at me. "I'm particularly fond of the one with half her ass hanging out."

I flipped open the file and my brows creased. It was full of photos of Lily and me.

Locked in a kiss next to her garage.

Her on the running board of my truck when I told her I loved her.

Wrapped in my arms against the railing on my balcony the morning after I'd told her about Andra.

Nearly the exact same pose the night before, when she'd gotten out of bed in my T-shirt and I'd found her on the balcony.

In her backyard after her house was broken into.

I ground on my molars, sat the folder down.

"Not funny now, is it, Shaw? Those will be released tomorrow to several media outlets, both local and national. Shortly thereafter, we'll be releasing the news of your trade. You're going to Miami, son. Not all that bad, considering. It's a good deal. They pay out the remainder of your contract. I get a tailback, and first *and* second round draft picks next year."

There was a faint buzzing in my ears from the rage building inside me. "Why not bench me? Why all the shoulder bullshit?"

He leaned forward. "Truthfully, we didn't think you'd make it back from the dislocation at all. We needed Bishop to take the reps if he was going to start this season. But, not only did you recover, you did it in half the time. That meant paying out your contract in full, even if you rode the bench. We needed to slow you down, Mr. Shaw. When Dr. Chase told your trainer to keep you limited, you didn't listen."

"My contract isn't fully guaranteed. You thought

you'd be able to put me on IR this year and cut my pay in half. Me coming back fucked that up."

He steepled his fingers. "Exactly. And Chase says you're as dumb as you look. Fortunately for us, the last year you've had a run of bad luck. That got me thinking about your trade clause, Mr. Shaw. You were two strikes in. Arranging a trade would be even more lucrative for the organization than having your contract reduced. The accident at camp was purely a stroke of luck, but it was the opening I needed to both send you home so I could get these for your third strike—" he tapped the folder with the pictures "—and set you up to go on the injured reserve list, if I couldn't get the photos. We knew the civil suit wouldn't stick before you even knew there was a lawsuit." He leaned forward like he was imparting a secret. "In fact, the criminal case won't either. The girl has character issues."

Jesus. The way this man's mind worked. If he weren't so fucking evil, it might be admirable. Might. "Mmhmm, and you didn't have anything to do with that either, right? For all you know that woman could have been forced into sex at that party, and you'd find a way to make that go away, too, wouldn't you?"

He spread his hands wide. "It's a football town, son."

It was taking everything I had not to jump across the desk and punch in his eye teeth. "I'm not your son. I want my release. Free and clear. The Bulldogs don't have to pay out the last two years on my contract and I'll announce my retirement early. I'll even say it's medical if you want."

"Now, why would I do that? I need you healthy now, Mr. Shaw. This deal with Miami hinges on it. As much as I'd like to be free and clear of your contract, you're worth a lot in this league. First and second round draft picks *and* a tailback. Three players for the price of one when Bishop can do your job just as well as you can. Miami is desperate for you. I'd much rather have talent I'm going to use than let you go free and clear. Now, if you'd have asked me before the trade was possible, this conversation might have gone differently."

Dick rocked back, rested an ankle over his knee as he sipped brown liquid from a crystal tumbler. "Don't take it personal, son. This is a business. Bishop is younger, faster, and he took a smaller contract just to come here and learn with you. I'm in high cotton."

The sonofabitch threw his head back and laughed. "Of course, I also have it on good authority that, should you stay healthy for the duration of the two years, Miami is prepared to offer you an extension to keep you from retiring."

Miami was desperate after their starter retired without much warning, and their backup had more brains than ability. With them tossing two picks at Dallas, they'd be praying they could convince me to stay a couple more years.

Not that I gave a shit.

"See, everybody wins, Brody. More money for you, more money for me, and Lily gets her dog shelter." Shifting in his chair, Dick clasped his hands behind his head. "Besides. You might not want to ask for that release. Take this trade for the blessing it is." Glancing at the photos, he tipped his chin. "How do you think I came by those, anyhow?"

Was he implying that... Oh, no. No, Lily wouldn't.

"She wouldn't do that, you sadistic fuck!" I jumped from the chair needing to move only to find my legs shaky as I paced. "Lily wouldn't sell me out."

"She wouldn't, would she?" He kept a hand poised under the edge of the desk, I'm sure with a finger on his panic button. "Not even for the dogs she loves so much?"

Shaking my head, I clasped the back of my neck as my stomach bottomed out and I fought back the bile.

Lily used me. She set me up.

"Now, she can finally get back to planning the wedding."

She lied?

She'd fucking told me she loved me, and she was planning on marrying some other guy? One she said had cheated on her, but fuck, was that even real or did she lie about it, too? Was any of it real with her?

No, you couldn't fake the kind of chemistry we had.

Maybe she has it with him, too.

Dick's smarmy grin was salt in an open wound. Rage flooded me. Gut-searing, all-consuming, black-out hate for the bastard. I'd never wanted to crush another man's windpipe so much in my life. To feel it give underneath my palms until his eyes bulged and he gasped for his last breath.

"You better hit that button now, Dick." In something out of a movie, I turned, reached across the desk and lifted him out of his chair by his shirt front. His face blanched. He clawed at my hands, tried to reason with me, but I blocked it all out. "You arrogant, narcissistic piece of shit. You *whored out* your s*tepdaughter* for a game. You really do think everyone else is shit on your gaudy-ass Lucchese alligator boots, don't you?" I felt people pulling at my arms, I was fairly sure I smelled urine, but it was all the buzzing of flies.

I knew I couldn't kill him.

But I would get one hell of a punch in on this diseased microdick who was a scourge on the game I loved. The woman I loved. "Well guess what, you sack of donkey shit. You bleed. Just like the rest of us."

I loaded up and punched.

But I didn't hit Dick.

Hayes stepped into it and I nailed him in a pectoral muscle.

That's when I realized I'd had a security guard on one arm, Hayes had been on the other, and a second teammate around the side of my desk was trying to pry my hand off Dick's shirt. I could hear his assistant screaming into a phone and the last guy had me around the waist with his feet braced against the desk. I put both my hands down.

Dick tried to straighten his shirt. "Get this asshole out of my sight. Your new team will hear about this, Shaw. So will the commissioner." Everyone turned to me like they weren't sure they should move. "Now!" Dick yelled like a recalcitrant toddler.

Leaning down, I picked up the folder that had fallen to the floor, and I walked out of his office like my life hadn't gone up in flames and the ashes weren't floating all around me.

Chapter Thirty-Two

Wear your brown pants, Dick Head.
I'm coming for you.

Lily

Brody wasn't answering his phone.

I left him voicemail after voicemail, texted him, tried calling again. Nothing.

I spent a solid hour in the shower crying. Thank God for tankless hot water heaters. My classes—all those dogs and people. I wouldn't get to see them two or three times a week, watch my puppy class grow up, and my agility students at their first trial.

I wasn't sure I'd even have time to trial anymore. There was no national team in Jet's future if I didn't have a career that allowed me to run my own dogs between classes. Now, they'd have to stay home.

After drying my hair, I put on clean clothes and got in my car to head over to Brody's place. If he wasn't there, then I'd wait until he got home.

I'd have to tell Brody about Trey, too. I'd been trying

to avoid that. I knew Brody had regular appointments with him and I didn't want to taint things if I could help it. But part of me was embarrassed, too. He'd cheated on me before he worked for the team, and my stepfather hired him after the fact. Dick chose my cheating ex-fiancé over me because Trey's father was a senator. I guessed politician trumps stepdaughter.

I rolled down the window and cranked up Post Malone, letting my hand dance through the wind.

The dude wasn't right. At first, it had been pleas to come back and pledges of undying love, but it had eventually progressed to repetitive phone calls and texts where he was verbally abusive. He even tried threatening my livelihood with false accusations. Trey threatened to tell my clients that I abused my own dogs unless I came back to him. When I refused, he went as far as to report me to animal control who showed up at my home to search for signs of abuse. It came to a head when he confronted me while I was on a date. He screamed in the middle of a crowded restaurant that I was a cheating whore, then punched my date. Trey's daddy covered the arrest up for him, but not before I managed to file an order of protection. Dick had asked me not to, spouting some bullshit about uniting two great families in a bid for world domination or whatever.

I had zero doubts this job with Dick would reescalate things.

My one bright spot in all of this was being able to tell Brody I'd leveraged the Bulldogs into funding the rescue *and* helping us locate the mill. I'd tried him back several times, but the calls were going to voicemail.

Pulling in the garage, I noticed Brody's truck was in

his spot. I checked my eyes in the mirror. The change of attitude and fresh air had taken out most of the redness. When I knocked on the door, Staci answered.

"Hey, hi. Is he here?" I put on a smile.

She didn't return it. Instead she called over her shoulder, "Babe, I think we should give them some space." Stepping back from the door, she motioned me in, and Erica sent me a sad smile on the way out. Brody was in his bedroom packing a bag.

He didn't acknowledge me when his eyes darted up. Something was very wrong, here.

"Shaw, what's going on? I tried to call you back about a million times."

He didn't look up.

I walked his direction and he didn't answer. Instead he slipped past me, going out to the living room. Following him, I stood behind the couch as he tucked several suits into a garment bag. "Brody?"

His head came up slow. "Just don't."

"Don't what?"

"Don't play dumb. It doesn't suit you." He zipped up the bag. "You should go."

CC didn't get up to greet me. She was lying on a bed by the balcony, head between her paws.

"Nope." I didn't know what was wrong, but I wasn't in the mood to make nice with some surly asshole who was being as petulant as a thirteen-year-old girl. "To say I've had a shitty day is putting it mildly. I'm not playing games with you, big man. I don't know what you're mad about, but unless you tell me why you're pissed, I can't apologize, either."

He didn't respond and all the wind went out of my

sails. Turning away to lean my butt on the back of the couch, I was too tired to hold the tears off anymore. "They traded you, didn't they?"

He picked a folder up off the coffee table, threw it on the couch. "Miami."

Peeling myself up, I walked around the couch, putting a hand on his bicep. He stopped moving but didn't look at me. My heart was breaking for him. For us. "Brody, I'm so so—"

He nodded at the folder. "Open it."

I did and my heart split in two. My legs failed me, and I slid to sit on the couch next to his garment bag. "Dick knew about us? How?" It came out in a whisper. My hands shook as I leafed through the photos. Shock settled into every muscle of my body. There was picture after picture of Brody, holding me. Kissing me. Pictures of him taking my trash out. Playing with my dogs in the backyard as I watched. Me hugging him from behind in nothing but a T-shirt. The night I'd gone out to his balcony. God, that must have been two a.m. Me leaving his building the morning after I'd taken CC home.

The one that truly broke my heart, though, was of him sticking his head through the window of his truck to kiss me.

He looked so young. So open. Like a college kid sneaking out of his girlfriend's dorm. I remembered exactly what I felt then. Everything would be okay. All hope was not lost because I had the most amazing man in the world, and he was in love with me. This sweet, big-hearted football player who would be there for me because I was loved.

Brody's voice came out soft, pained, shattering the moment in my head. "You used me. I took a leap of faith. Told you I loved you, and you were using me to get shelter funding out of your stepdad."

"What?" Mouth wide open, I turned to him. The shock was a ball of dread sitting in my stomach.

"I know about the rescue, Lily. What I don't know is was it the plan from the beginning, or only since we found the empty building?" His hands were on his hips as he stared into the duffel on the table.

"What are you even talking about?" I was so utterly horrified he'd been traded. Because of me.

He met my eyes and I didn't care that he saw the fat tears or dark circles. "When I heard them talking about your fiancé at camp, I should have run in the other direction. But I'll give it to you, you're a decent actress, sweetheart, and hey, we lucked out with all that chemistry in the sack, right? I know you didn't fake the orgasms, so at least there's that much."

"Brody, stop. This isn't—"

"For the life of me, I couldn't figure out why *you* would come up in the same conversation as my shoulder at training camp of all places."

"You think I *knew* about this?"

"Stop, Lily." He threw a hand up. "Nobody but Hayes and my neighbors knew, and they had nothing to gain by telling Dick about us. But you did." His face was a mask of disappointment, and I could see the ache hiding beneath.

He had so much wrong, I didn't know where to start.

I wasn't even sure it mattered. He wasn't interested in listening, anyway.

Running a hand through his hair, he sat down on the couch, elbows on his knees. "Why didn't you come to me about the money, Lily? If you didn't know anything about this, why wouldn't you just come to me first about starting a rescue?"

I spun to face him, not only hurt, but angry. The longer this went on, with each word that left his mouth, I knew how wrong I'd been about Brody. He didn't trust me, and I couldn't count on him. "Really? Come to you for money—right. The dude that is sure everyone in the world wants in his pockets. Brilliant idea."

"Bullshit. *You* could have asked me for the moon and stars, and I would have found a way to give them to you. I would have emptied my bank accounts, given you the shirt off my goddamned back. I would have left football for you, just to stay here. With you." His head sagged forward on his big shoulders. "I tried." The words came out soft. So soft, I wasn't sure I'd heard them right.

"You what?" Circling around, I tried to see his face. Everything in my body wanted to reach out and touch him. But I couldn't. Not when he thought I did this to him.

He steepled his hand over his nose. "I asked for my release. When Dick told me he arranged a trade, I told him I wanted my release."

Pushing the folder over, I sat on the table facing him. "*This* is exactly why I couldn't come to you. You're accusing me of using you, yet you think if you could give me everything I've ever wanted, we'd live happily ever after. Don't you think I know you would always wonder if I loved you for what you could give me instead of for the man you are?"

When he didn't respond, I knew it didn't matter what I said. His mind was made up before I ever walked through the door.

Shit got hard for Brody, and it was time for him to flake. Imagine that. "I always thought it would be my baggage that got in our way." I just wanted to be done with this. I couldn't trust a man that didn't put his faith in me, no matter how much I loved him or how much my heart hurt. A man that would leave without hearing my side of the story? He'd written me off so easily. Taken the word of someone like my stepdad. At the first sign of trouble, he was running. Like everyone else I'd loved.

Really, Lily? Couldn't he say all those same things about you?

I supposed I never really let go of my own baggage either. I guess I'd expected this moment all along.

"Why you didn't mention a shelter, Lily? Seems like something you'd tell someone you love. Unless he wasn't part of your plan." His raw voice sounded incredulous, and he had every right to be. Not because I'd used him like he thought, but because deep down, I wasn't any more capable of checking my own shit than he was.

With a slow shake of my head and a continuous flow of tears, I met his eyes. My voice came out choked, full of what might have been if we both weren't so screwed up. "You're right."

He searched my face, a tear tracking down his own cheek that broke my heart anew.

"It's only the why of it you've got wrong, baby."

I spotted the picture of us kissing through his truck window on the edge of the table, and picked it out of the pile. Held it to my chest.

The absolute anguish in them…so conflicted, so wounded. Like CC's eyes months before. When I'd seen her eyes while she was huddled in her kennel, I knew I could help her to trust her human. But people were a different story. They were much too complicated.

Dogs were easier. Loyal. They never let me down the way people did. As long as I remembered the golden rule of rescue.

Don't let yourself get too attached, because they'd be moving on soon.

I should have never gotten attached.

"Brody, if you truly believe I could use you as a means to an end…" Pausing, I tried to clear the lump from my throat. "…then you don't know me at all."

Steadying myself, I put my palm over his heart. Pressed my mouth to his. The salt from our tears mingled on our lips, and I allowed myself a few seconds before pulling away.

"Lily…" He pressed his forehead to mine.

I reached down to pat CC, who had been worried enough about her people to join the fray. After placing a kiss on her head, I whispered, "Take care of him for me, puddin'. I love you, and I love him, too."

Wiping my face, I stood and left, the picture in my hand.

The following morning, I turned in my notice at the training center. Funny that the hardest part hadn't been leaving the dogs I taught, but the people on the other end of the leash.

With some vacation time stored, I took a week off that Rob was happy to give me. Honestly, I needed it.

I wasn't doing great.

I slept. And I slept. Then moved out to the couch to stare at the idiot box and slept some more. I also took to living off generic cereal and Blue Bell ice cream.

My wake-up call came by way of the last person I wanted to see. My mother. When she knocked and I didn't answer, she used her key.

"Liliana, when was the last time you showered?"

I rolled my eyes. "Oh, Mom. Go fuck yourself."

Quicker than I could blink, she reached out and slapped my cheek. It wasn't hard; it wouldn't leave a print. It was meant to shock me, and it did its job. "Now listen here, girl. I know I'm not going to win any prizes for mother of the year, but I brought you into this world and you will treat me with respect. You think you're the only one who's ever had a rough go of it, Lily?"

Stunned, I reached up to hold my cheek. In all my years, my mother had never laid a hand on me.

"My own mama was a stripper and a drug addict who cared more about her next fix and her next boyfriend than her children. I will never tell you the horrors I endured in the house where I grew up. When I started up with your daddy, I wasn't in college like he told people. I was on the pole at night and in a cheerleader's outfit during the day because I had no other way to feed myself."

It was like being slapped again. My mom never

talked about her life. My dad told me what little I knew, and apparently, I got the fairy princess version.

Audrey sat on the arm of the chair. "I know you think the worst of me for marrying Richard so soon after your father died, but I loved your father, Liliana. Very deeply. Not because he provided for us, but because he was larger than life, he had an amazing heart and spirit and for whatever reason, he wanted to be with *me*. In the beginning, I constantly thought to myself, 'Dear God, please don't let him change his mind. Being in his orbit was like standing in sunshine that never set on the world.'"

Her smile slipped away. "But the longer he played, the worse the depression got… His death broke me in a way I never expect you to understand. Every day it hurts, every day I miss him. And every day, I pray you'll find the courage to let go of all the harm the three adults in your life did to you, so you find a love like that. I'd hoped that might be Trey, but clearly he wasn't it, and I'm glad you saw what I didn't and took care of yourself."

A sad smile touched her lips as she ran a hand over my cheek. "I'm sorry for what I did to you. For leaving you. I never wanted you to have the kind of life I did when I was your age. Can you understand that?"

I nodded, slipped my hand into hers. "I'm sorry."

"So am I, my love, more than you will ever know. Now, I find it perfectly acceptable to wallow for three days. I gave you a fourth, because I've met that young man a time or two, and Brody Shaw is… Mercy." She fanned herself. "But it's time to remember whose daughter you are, Liliana Costello. You've never hidden, never felt sorry for yourself, never wallowed in your entire life. You stand up, shake off the grass, and go back to the huddle. If there's anybody in the whole of this city that can walk into Bulldogs headquarters and tell *Dick* to shove it right up his ass, day in, day out, it's you. I'm quite sure that backbone you inherited from your father is why Richard never warmed to you."

A little grin flitted across her mouth. "Do you know, when your daddy was at the top of his game, and Richard was a glorified water boy, that he came on to me? This was before I got pregnant with you."

"No! Really?"

She nodded. "When your father found out he'd groped me and several of the girls on the squad, Billy pinned him to a plateglass window. By his neck."

"Oh shit."

"That's what he did, alright." She guffawed, laughed in a way I hadn't heard since before my father died. "That's the backbone you inherited, Liliana." She squeezed my hand.

"Mom, did you really just tell me to rub some dirt on it?"

"Indeed, I did."

After she left, I got in the shower. I took my dogs for a walk, and something occurred to me between making notes about the rescue and pulling my old anatomy books out of the attic to brush up.

For a long time, I'd pitied Audrey because I thought she was weak.

But there was more strength and depth to my mother than I had ever known.

Chapter Thirty-Three

Fuckstick, party of one?

Brody

I let the water beat on my aching neck trying to wash away the remnants of another shitty game. In fact, that's all I'd had in Miami—one shitty game after another.

Running my hand through my hair, I bumped the bridge of my nose and hissed. During the fourth quarter, somebody in a pile-up had taken a cheap shot and split the skin on the bridge of my nose.

Cranking around, I tried to see the bruise on my ribcage. I understood how guys like Billy got hooked on pills. Tomorrow, I'd have to swallow enough ibuprofen to give an elephant an ulcer just to get out of bed. More bruises would come out, too. I'd feel the strains and pulls I hadn't earlier today.

Football held no appeal for me anymore. I was tired of all of it—the pain, the politics, feeling like I couldn't trust anyone on or off the team.

Turning off the water, I stepped out of the shower and slipped trunks and a shirt on to take my girl down to the water's edge. I would side arm a stick into the surf—she would dash in after it and let the waves carry her back to shore for me to throw it again.

It was peaceful. Gave me time to mull over my mistakes. The defense was out of sync, and it wasn't their fault. It was mine. My teammates were understanding and patient, but they wanted leadership on the field, and I wasn't giving it to them.

Because Lily was all I thought about. I had a constant inner monologue with questions I had no answers for. What class would she be teaching right now? How were the shelter plans coming? Had any more dogs shown up, or did she have any more leads on the mill? How was Laila?

Did she miss me? Did she still love me? And the biggest blank of all. Why? Why didn't she tell me about the shelter? Why did it feel so real, if it wasn't? Surly bastard that I was, I refused to contemplate the possibility of Lily getting married. It simply didn't exist in my orbit. Complete denial.

She'd told me I was right to be angry, but my reasons were all wrong.

When CC came out of the water walking instead of running, I knew it was time to quit. I rinsed the saltwater off her in the footbath and filled her bowl with fresh water. Pulling another beer from the fridge, I grabbed my phone and the pictures I tortured myself with off the counter before I settled into the lounger next to CC.

Part of me understood why Lily had gone to Dick.

The dogs. What she wouldn't do for those dogs. Hell, what *I* wouldn't do for the dogs. I could see why she wouldn't come to me for the money, too. She was afraid it would make me question her loyalty. *So, what do I do? Oh, I question it anyway.* But, why not tell me about the shelter if she wasn't setting me up with Dick?

It sure as hell wouldn't have been out of character for Dick to lie to me about it—to manipulate me *and* Lily to his own purpose. If she would have just trusted me—

Like you trusted her? I fingered the picture of us on the balcony. It was the one I came back to over and over. I hadn't trusted her. I'd believed the worst and didn't even ask her to explain. I just assumed she'd kicked me where it hurt the most…because that's what people do.

Golly, Karen, I wonder why she didn't let you in? Maybe she held on to a little of her fear, the same as you did.

I was right to be angry that she didn't tell me about the shelter, but the reason she didn't wasn't because she cut a deal with Dick to sell me out, it was because deep down she still worried I wouldn't be there for her.

And that's exactly what had happened.

Self-fulfilling prophecy much?

"Ah, fuck. We both held on to the bullshit." CC lifted her head to stare at me like I was nuts. I was fairly sure my dog understood everything I said, thought I was an idiot half the time, and as such, it was her job to protect me.

Mah humanz a doooofus.

"It's okay, girl. Go back to sleep. Daddy's inner voice is an asshole, is all."

Still, there were so many holes. What about the fiancé? And if Lily didn't sell me to Dick, why did he agree to the shelter?

Picking up my phone, I thumbed up Hayes's number.

"Well, well. You son of a bitch. Finally decided to answer the phone, huh? Good to know you're alive, asshole." His voice was teasing, and I could hear his crooked smile, but there was an undertone that was clearly *hey fuckstick, I've been worried about you*!

"Yeah, I've been trying to get up to speed here and it's taking a lot of my time." The truth, but also man speak subtext for *I'm sorry I've been a twat because I'm nursing a broken heart*. "I saw the hit you took against San Diego. How's the knee?" *I care about you and you are my bestie.*

"Bruised. Sore. But okay. You've had a rough go lately, too." *You're my bestie, too. I really don't want to talk about it.*

I sighed into the phone. "Yeah, my head's not in it." *I am a fuckstick. I see you noticed my fuckery. Thanks for that.*

"The girl?" *Get your head out of your ass, dude.*

"Probably." *I'm lying. It's totally the girl.*

"What do you mean, probably? You're so in love with that woman you don't know your ass from your elbow." *This was completely self-explanatory.*

I grunted. Took a deep swig from my bottle.

"Lil's not real cray-cray about her new job either. I

mean, she's good at it. She doesn't take shit from Chase or Dick. But you can tell it's wearing on her."

I choked, sprayed beer all over my lap and the pictures lying there. Coughing, I tried to shake off the worst of the damage. "Lily isn't at the Unruly Dog anymore?"

"Dick made her the head trainer. I thought you knew."

"Why would she do that? She loved working with those dogs. Lily doesn't always people well."

Fuck me on a cactus. Lily didn't sell me out to get her shelter. She sold herself and went to work for the team. I didn't understand why Dick would want her working for the team in exchange, but I knew down to my very marrow that Lily Costello didn't set me up.

See? Fuckstick.

"Sorry, I assumed you knew. But no shit about the peopling. Half the team is afraid to piss her off for fear of an ass chewing. They're all scared of your girlfriend, Shaw. She does not put up with shit or excuses. Wallace hurt his thumb horsing around during walk-throughs and Lily lit into him. It was funny as hell. I think he's half in love with her now. He's definitely a bottom."

I broke into a belly laugh that I hadn't felt since I left. "That was my girl. Pack leader all the way." I scanned over the picture of her that took the most of my beer-fountain damage and a flash of color caught my eye. "Oh shit. Is that? Hayes, let me call you later, okay?"

"Yeah. Hey, don't drop off the Earth this time, okay?" *I love you, man.*

"Later." *I love you, too, bro.*

After I hung up, CC followed me inside and I flipped on the island light, putting the picture down on the counter. *Please tell me it wasn't my imagination.*

Using the empty bottle, I angled it back and forth over one photo trying to get a better look. It had taken the majority of my beer fountain. The photo was grainy and a little far off, so I hadn't really lingered on it before.

It was of Lily leaving my building. A side profile of her walking to her car with a to-go coffee in her hand. Behind her, parked bed-first inside the garage, sat a black pickup truck.

The splatter on the photo made the colors richer, and I could see the custom paint down the side panel, paint that only just wrapped around the brake light to the edge of the tailgate.

It was either burnt orange or a deep red.

The word Ford stretched all the way across the tailgate in flat black letters.

"Son. Of. A. Bitch."

I rolled the bottle around and saw something that nearly had me in tears.

My building's garage had a teal-colored metal barrier—an architectural thing meant to function as a safety barrier to keep cars from running over the sidewalk. The barrier ran in front of the truck, between Lily on the sidewalk and where the truck was parked.

The barrier was made of long steel railings set on the horizontal that ran between larger vertical posts maybe ten feet apart.

Through two of the railings, I could see a license plate number.

I couldn't read it. It was too small, and a couple of the digits were obscured by one of the posts.

But it was there.

It was right fucking there.

Whoever owned that truck owned the mill.

And we had a partial license plate.

Setting the picture aside, I smiled to myself. *Finally.* I decided to kill two birds with one stone and pulled up my contacts list.

"Dallas Bulldogs Public Relations Office."

"Hi, can I speak to Mariana Lopez, please?"

"Who may I say is calling?"

"Brody Shaw."

There was a pregnant pause on the other end. "One moment. I'll see if she's still here."

"Brody?" Mariana sounded out of breath. "What can I do for you?"

It was time I got some answers about what my shoulder had to do with Lily.

Hopefully, Mariana would take pity on me, and just maybe…do me a solid?

Chapter Thirty-Four

Can't Fight This Feeling

Brody

The windshield wipers flicked back and forth, the dog snored in the back seat, and REO Speedwagon played soft in the background. Most of my belongings were getting drenched in the bed of the truck as I jotted a note next to another name on my legal pad and ignored most traffic laws.

It had taken me only two hours to draw up my play-book, and I was executing as I drove. My brain buzzed with all the things I needed to do, all the pieces that needed to come together for everything to work.

I had only one goal.

To give my girl the world and hope she didn't throw it in my face.

But some of the biggest risks in life, like love…they had to be taken with a leap of faith.

My lawyer told me that.

I pushed the phone button on the steering wheel. It

was going to be a long night, I had more calls to make, and only one person on my mind.

"Hey, man. It's Brody Shaw. Sorry to wake you, but…"

Chapter Thirty-Five

Well, that was entertaining, but now what?

Lily

"You've got a small tear in the lateral ankle ligaments." Hitting a button on the portable ultrasound keyboard, I re-angled the transducer I held to Shaun Jackson's ankle. "Right here. See?" I pointed to the screen.

He leaned forward. "So, a grade one sprain?" The running back had a medical background. He'd been in a PT program at Michigan State before he was drafted.

I shook my head. "Given the swelling, I'm calling it grade two. I'd rather be safe than sorry." Pulling the transducer away, I wiped it off with a paper towel before also using it to clean the jelly off his skin. "I'll tape it instead of giving you a brace as long as you take it easy. I catch you overusing it, I'll slap a brace on it. Walk-throughs only for three days. Ice, ten to fifteen minutes as often as you can. No heat. I want to see you again in two days." I met his eyes to let him know I meant business.

He nodded. "Thanks, Lil. It's nice to have staff that actually cares about our bodies. Billy Costello was your dad, right? Is that why you got into this?"

I started pulling out supplies. Tape, scissors. No pre-wrap. "Something like that. Sit tight. I'll be right back."

Damn, this job was demanding. Balls to the wall from 5:30 a.m. till every last player with a concern or a sore muscle had been seen for the day. On game day, sometimes, I didn't get home until one or two in the morning.

I missed Jet and Mack. Away games were even harder on them.

I'd managed to skate on Dick for the first two away games, but he was pissed. We'd screamed at each other in the trainer's office and half the team heard it. At least it earned me some street cred with the players and staff.

They knew I wasn't afraid of Dick.

Of course, I never passed up a chance to scream at Dick. He thought he was going to make *my* life tough until I folded? Fuck him. I made his equally miserable. He'd either back off or fire me, and if he fired me, I still got the shelter. I had it in writing, and nobody out-stubborned me.

Hayes flagged me down coming out of the supply room. "Hey, Lil. I need you to come with me. It's kind of an emergency."

"Can't Darius handle it? I need to tape Shaun up." Everyone knew as the most senior trainer, Darius was the boss. I followed his lead. I also promised him I wouldn't—under any circumstances—put the players at risk because of my stepfather. He was a decent guy, and understandably wary since he'd recently fired a guy who had done exactly that.

"Sweetheart, it has to be you." Hayes's look pleaded with me.

"Hayes, we're friends, and I actually don't mind when you call me sweetheart away from here, but try not to do it here, okay? It kind of undermines this whole badass thing I've got going on that has everyone afraid to piss me off."

He gave me a little salute. "Got it."

"Hey, Vanessa," I yelled down the hall. She stuck her head out of the office. "Can you tape up Jackson's ankle for me? Apparently, sugar britches here needs help elsewhere."

She smiled. "I gotchu." She was a good trainer. Efficient. No nonsense. They were a little scared of her, too. And Shaun had a major crush on her.

Handing off the pre-wrap, I gave her my thanks.

I followed Hayes up the hall, through the weight room, out into the corridor by the locker room. "Where are you going? This better not be some kind of STD you picked up on the road. I'm not checking out your junk. Ever. No matter how much it burns when you pee."

He laughed. "We're going next door. And for somebody who doesn't like it here, you sure as hell fit in."

"Eh, I grew up around football players. I can talk shit as well as any of you."

When we got into the other building, he pushed the button to call the executive elevator.

I stopped dead. "No. I don't know what's going on,

but I'm not going up there unless someone's dying. And if it's Dick, he can just fucking die."

"Sweetheart, you're gonna have to trust me on this."

He held out a hand I grudgingly took, and I let him pull me in to the elevator. When we stopped climbing, the doors opened into the waiting room for Dick's office. His secretary gave me a thumbs-up as I walked by.

Huh? What was that about? "Hayes?"

He ignored me, pecked on the door, and a deep male voice answered, "Come in." It wasn't Dick's vomit-inducing tone I heard, either. Walker opened the door and made an after-you gesture, following me in.

Dick was behind his desk trying to look like the king of the castle, but I could see the way he tapped his fingers on the desk. He was uncomfortable.

But the other man wasn't.

He leaned a hip on the credenza. I hadn't seen him since I was a little girl. I was seven, and my father's team had just won the championship.

Mike Brennan had been on the field with the players and families while confetti rained down on our heads. He was nearly as big as my father. I didn't know his name at the time, but he bent down on one knee and booped my nose. I giggled. "I've got a secret," he said. "Would you like to know what it is?"

I nodded, and he leaned forward to whisper in my ear. "You can't tell. Not even if Dad tickles your ribs, or says he'll buy you a pony. Promise?"

I nodded. "I promise."

"Very soon, I'm going to tell the world that your daddy is the Most Valuable Player. And in a few weeks' time, Mom and Dad are going to take you to Disney World to celebrate."

I nearly screamed with excitement, but the man put a finger over his lips and winked. Then, he stood and shook my father's hand before turning to the stage in the middle of the field.

"Look at you all grown up!" Mr. Brennan's voice rumbled through the office. "We shared a secret once. Do you remember?"

My smile was wide and soft. "I do. Hi, Commissioner Brennan. It's good to see you again. I hope you've been well. How are the knees?"

"Ah, you know how it is. I'd have them replaced, but I don't like the knife. I've been told your home was robbed recently, and your father's ring was stolen?"

Dick's eyes widened. Apparently, he didn't know. "Yes. I reported it to the police, and I'm sure they're doing their best."

"I'm sure they are." He turned to Hayes. "I assume you're joining us as the team's collective bargaining representative, Mr. Walker? Is the Collective Bargaining Association aware of the meeting?"

Hayes nodded. "We're aware this isn't a formal injury complaint, but a jumping off point for the CBA to decide if an investigation is warranted."

"Good. Good. Have a seat." He nodded to the couch on the opposite wall.

What the hell am I doing here?

Hayes nudged me and I followed him to the couch.

"Commissioner, if you don't mind me asking, and not that we don't appreciate the visit, but what's this all about?" Dick was trying hard to play it cool, but as my dad would say, he looked like a cat shittin' peach seeds.

There was another knock, and the door opened. "Ahh, you're about to find out."

In waltzed Darius, carrying a folder. He was followed by Mariana Lopez, the team's public relations manager. I'd met her a couple of times trying to get things with the shelter moving. I wanted the announcements made, but Dick was stalling.

Brody walked in, and my skin prickled with awareness, the shadows under his eyes making me worry. Yet, when that whiskey color landed on me, all the lines and angles of his face softened, and he was that college boy in a pickup truck again.

When his stare skated to Dick, my stepfather's face leeched of all color.

The league commissioner lifted his chin at Brody. "Ready?"

Brody nodded.

"Your floor, Mr. Shaw."

Brody casually crossed his arms. "Mr. Head, I contacted the commissioner because of concerns I have about player health and how particular members of the Bulldogs organization are dealing with player injuries."

Oh, shit! I'm fairly sure I gasped, and my mouth was nothing but a flycatcher.

Brody continued. "Commissioner, this year during training camp, I was examined for the possibility of a separated shoulder. As is my right, I got a second opinion and that doctor wouldn't refute or confirm the diagnosis; however, Ms. Costello and Mr. Paul also examined me and didn't believe the shoulder had been separated. I realize they're not orthopedic specialists, but I wasn't the only person suspicious of my diagnosis.

"After the injury occurred, I waited for some time in the treatment suite for our head orthopedist, Dr. Adam Chase the Third…" His gaze flitted to mine and I bit down on the inside of my cheek. He knew. "…to hand down a diagnosis. I wandered around to see if I could find out what was taking so long and overhead voices in Dr. Chase's office discussing my injury. One was Dr. Chase. The other was Richard Head. The third voice, I couldn't identify. I could only make out small groupings of words, but my shoulder was mentioned. As was Ms. Costello and her supposed fiancé.

"I believed those three were the only people in the room until the end of the conversation, when I overheard a woman's voice. It was the Bulldogs public relations director, Mrs. Mariana Lopez."

The commissioner nodded at him. "Brody, I appreciate a good yarn much as the next person, but speed it up. I'm not here to listen to how good of a snoop you are."

"Yes, sir. Mrs. Lopez?"

"Commissioner, yesterday, Brody called me with a favor to ask, but he was also curious about the content of the meeting he overheard since he knew his shoulder *and* Ms. Costello had been a topic of the conversation. You should know that I've resigned my position as PR director because of the following events."

Dick flew out of his chair. "This is absurd. What

two ex-employees have to say is irrelevant and likely fabrication."

The commissioner stood from the credenza to his full height. "Richard. Sit. Down. I will hear this out."

Dick slid back into the chair, face falling as he fidgeted with his shirt collar.

The commissioner lifted a hip and sat on the edge of Dick's desk. "Mrs. Lopez, please continue."

"During that meeting, the third person was an assistant trainer named Devon Taylor. Devon was concerned he might lose his job because of an accident he caused in the weight room that re-injured Brody's shoulder."

"Is this the supposed separation?" Mr. Brennan looked to Brody.

"Yes, sir."

He turned back to Mariana, and she continued. "Devon was aware of Brody's romantic relationship with Ms. Costello. He claimed Brody told him, though Brody says he never told Devon such a thing, but that's neither here nor there. He took the information about the relationship to Dr. Chase and Richard, afraid he'd lose his job for causing Brody's accident.

"After the fantasy suite scandal broke, Brody was tasked to stay out of the media and away from women completely. It wasn't a secret to anyone in the organization. Then his dog bit the pet sitter, who filed a lawsuit." She shifted in her chair, recrossing her legs.

"After being warned about the dog and the scandal, Brody's decision to have a sexual relationship with Ms. Costello would become his third strike, as a violation of the conduct clause, when it became public knowledge."

She glanced back at me then turned back to the commissioner. "*I* was brought into the meeting in Dr. Chase's office for two reasons.

"Years ago, the Chase family tasked me to hide Dr. Chase's indiscretions and questionable behavior when Ms. Costello broke off her engagement with Dr. Chase. In fact, I did it so well, I was offered this job as a result. Dr. Chase's father is not only a sitting senator, but one of Richard's golfing buddies.

"The second reason I was called to the meeting was to control the flow of information when evidence of Brody and Lily's relationship was leaked. I was also tasked with finding an investigator to collect evidence of the relationship. You should know that Brody wasn't aware of Ms. Costello's connection with Dr. Chase until I told him yesterday.

"Dick...uh, Richard," Mariana continued, "wanted to force Brody into a trade, and the conduct clause was how he planned to do it."

The commissioner's brow furrowed. "It's shady, but not a policy issue, Mr. Shaw. You broke the rules you were tasked with and agreed to. You had the relationship anyway, and you got caught. You told me this was about player health, not your love life."

Dick had been relatively quiet up until that point. "See? This is superfluous and I'm so sorry these people have wasted your time, Commissioner. I—"

Brody tensed. "I regret having to thrust my relationship with Lily into the light, but it does have bearing on player health, sir."

Mariana spoke up. "Mr. Brennan, if I may, I can connect the pieces."

He tipped his head. "Please, Mrs. Lopez."

"During the meeting, Richard and Dr. Chase struck a deal. Dr. Chase admitted in front of everyone present that Brody's injury was most likely a scar tissue problem. A rather simple, but painful, non-injury of sorts. However, Trey Chase agreed to tell Brody his injury was worse than it was in order to create the possibility of putting him on injured reserve if a trade couldn't be made. In the meantime, Brody would be benched, and his backup would get field time."

"And IR would reduce his contracted salary." The commissioner eyed Dick over his shoulder. "That's a problem, Mr. Head."

Hayes stood up, walked over to where the commissioner had been. "Yeah, it is."

"In exchange for lying to Brody about the severity of the injury," Mariana continued, "Richard would pressure Ms. Costello to move forward with a wedding she didn't know about."

My mouth fell open. This motherfucker told my ex that I'd marry him if he lied about Brody's shoulder, so they didn't have to pay him? "Are you fucking kidding me right now? Of all the jacked-up sh—"

Everyone turned to me. "Um, sorry?"

Mr. Brennan grinned. "Actually, Ms. Costello, I think that's a rather accurate reflection."

Brody smiled, and Hayes turned to Mariana. "So, if I've got this straight, Dr. Douche—uh, Chase, and Dick colluded to provide Brody false information about his health and used Lily as a bargaining chip?"

"You have no proof. It's her word against mine." Dick's face was as red as a tomato as he pointed at Mariana.

Brody slid down on the couch, elbows on his knees. "Unfortunately, he's right. I requested my medical notes from Darius, and my case file only says possible separation *or* scar tissue was the culprit. But last night, I called a few of my former teammates that are current Bulldogs players."

Brody turned to Darius. "You're up."

Darius opened his file and pulled out several printed emails. "This is where I come in, and I believe Lily might, too. Dr. Chase has approached me about lying to players and coaches in regard to possible injuries on more than one occasion." He turned to me. "Lily, has anyone approached you about doing the same?"

Slowly, I nodded. "Dick came to me and asked me to gloss over injuries or not to note the full extent of an injury so a specific player could continue to play. I refused, and I can give you the player names and dates. I believe my stepfather wanted me in this position as head trainer because he thought he could force me to help Dr. Chase manipulate player health issues to the team's advantage."

Brody had figured it out. I hadn't sold him out for the shelter. I'd sold myself and was miserable because of it. Still, this was career suicide for him, and very possibly the end of my shelter hopes. Dick wasn't going to push any shelter funding for me after what I'd just said. Although, I had the distinct feeling that a lack of funding would be the case until I played ball.

Darius stood, handing a thick folder to the commissioner. "I received these last night. Emails from four current team members who shared their interactions with Dr. Chase and believe health procedures weren't properly followed. Everything from concussion protocols to repeated cortisone injections. In fact, in the previous season, Mr. Shaw was given a cortisone injection in his left shoulder before eleven of the thirteen regular season games he played, all done by Dr. Chase or Devon Taylor. He's said that Dr. Chase assured him there were no side effects with the steroid injections.

"Recommended cortisone dosing for a non-athlete is no more than once every four weeks. It's quite possible that excess injections of corticosteroids weakened the soft tissue around Mr. Shaw's shoulder joint and contributed to his atypical dislocation. Without the injections, the dislocation was unlikely."

Ohmygod. For, like, the eighteenth time, my mouth fell open and I slapped a hand over it. Trey nearly ruined Brody's career? Jesus.

"Well, Mr. Shaw," the commissioner cut in. "This is a lot to take in. I can assure you a thorough investigation will be made into the collusion and health procedural concerns. Walker, how do you feel about scaring up Dr. Chase?"

As everybody but Dick and Mike filtered out, the commissioner handed Brody a piece of paper I assumed was a card, but I felt like I was walking through a haze.

"Lily, wait up!" Brody called as I made my way to

the elevator. Hayes leaned over next to my ear. "Here comes the big finish. You're not going to want to miss it."

"*That* wasn't the big finish?"

Hayes only smiled in answer as Mariana handed Brody a folder and he turned to me.

"Can we talk, Lily?" The eloquent, confident linebacker from Dick's office was gone. The man in front of me was a ball of nervous energy shuffling his feet and scratching at his scruff.

As entertaining as this whole thing had been, the problem remained.

Brody was afraid I'd use him, and I was afraid he'd flake on me.

Plus, Brody might have put Dick over his knee, but I had no mill, no shelter, and after all this, more than likely, no job.

He could have at least given me a heads-up.

Chapter Thirty-Six

Rule Number One.
Start at the beginning.

Brody

My palms were sweating. My goddamn palms. What was it about this woman that made me revert to a thirteen-year-old boy scared to death to ask a pretty girl to the dance?

Because it's not a *pretty girl. It's* the *pretty girl, asshat. The one you want to spend the rest of your life with. And you don't deserve her.*

Man, did she have to be so stunning? Her hair had grown out a little and was gathered in a ponytail at the base of her neck. She had on a training staff performance T-shirt and yoga pants that stopped at her calves and were snug enough to show off all her curves. We walked along the concrete path around a retention pond behind the main building. The city was finally getting a reprieve from the triple digits of summer, but I was sweating bullets, and Lily was letting me. She hadn't said a single word. I wiped my forehead on the hem of my T-shirt trying to figure out what to say first.

Where do I even start?

Lily stopped, crossed her arms below her breasts. "How about at the beginning."

Her violet eyes scanned over the pond, and my heart skipped in my chest.

My hand drifted to her cheek all on its own. "I'm so sorry, darlin'." I wanted her to see how much I meant the words, how much I regretted every single moment of my life since she'd walked into my apartment for the last time. I knew my eyes pleaded with hers to see my sincerity. What a dumbass I'd been.

How much I loved her with every single breath and heartbeat.

When the tear slipped down my cheek, I didn't wipe at it. I didn't try to hide it. I cleared my throat of the lump and my voice came out grated. "I think I know, but will you tell me what happened in the meeting with your stepdad. I already know I was wrong, I just want to know what you went through that day. I fucked up, Lily. I've been protecting myself so long that I didn't even give you a chance to talk about what you went through. I'd like it if you'd tell me, though?"

Fat tears rolled down her cheeks as she exhaled a heavy breath. "That's a good start, Shaw. My deal with Dick was that I'd come to work for the Bulldogs—leave the Unruly Dog—and he'd fund a rescue for dogs too aggressive for most other shelters. You need to know that I knew what he wanted from me. I knew he expected me to lie to players. That's why he wanted me to work for him so badly, but I wouldn't do it. After my dad, I could never—" A tear caught on her lashes. "Honestly, I don't think he had any intention of building the shelter, either."

I couldn't help it. I had to brush the tear from her cheek.

"The first time he came to me about a player, he wanted Douglas's hyperextended elbow downplayed so he could have him on the field against Las Vegas. I wouldn't do it and he told me, 'If you don't scratch my back, I don't scratch yours.'"

Sniffing, she shook her head. "I may have made a deal with the devil, Brody, but you were never on the table. Your career wasn't mine to bargain with. Ever. I gave up everything I loved that day trying to do the right thing for the dogs: the center, training, spending time with my own dogs, agility…and you accused me of using you anyway. The very thing I was trying to avoid by going to you in the first place."

Lily shuffled her feet. "So, I lost you, too. Pretty much the worst day of my life so far."

She pulled in a shaky breath. "The more I think about it…it wasn't all on you. I was still worried you might flake on me. Whether it was money, or celebrity, cheating, or getting traded, or hurt, or…worse. So much of the hurt in my life leads back to this game. It has taken so much from me, and I've never played a single down. That's why I couldn't let go of the fear. I think I always knew it would take you, too."

Turning to a bench in the shade, Lily sat, pulling one foot onto the edge.

I stared out over the water. The thing was, Lily was right. The game gave me a lot, but it took a lot, too. For her, it had taken even more. When I thought about all my own bullshit—the shoulder, the pain, the trust issues and lawsuits, the paranoia about being used— my common denominator was always football, too.

"I have something for you, Lily."

Chapter Thirty-Seven

Hey, Dick Head! Take a flying fuck.

Lily

"I have something to share with you." Brody slid down on the bench next to me, pulled a photo out of the envelope Mariana had given him and handed it to me. "I, uh, I found something in one of the photos Dick had taken."

I rolled the paper over. It was a photo of me leaving Brody's building with a cup of coffee in hand.

"I accidently spit beer on it, so it's not like I'm some super sleuth or anything, but if you look close, you can see that the truck behind you looks exactly like the one from the rental house, the one that we tried to chase down."

"Oh my God. Ohmygodohmygodohmygod. Brody… is that what I think it is?"

"Yeah." He slid another picture into my hands. One with an enhanced view of the truck's license plate. "I figured maybe you could give that to Officer Johnson and see if he can run the partial plate matching that make and model of truck."

I turned to him, but I was absolutely speechless. My mouth hung open, tears tracking down my cheeks. There would be a ton of footwork, I'd need to call the ASPCA and the county sheriff and, and…my brain was on complete overload. "This is them. This is a name and an address and not just a suspected location. Authorities can chase down an actual lead on a person or people. Find where the dogs have been moved. SPCA might be able to get someone in undercover. These motherfuckers are going to get prosecuted." Finally, I noticed Shaw watching me with an amused smile on his face as I babbled incoherently. "Brody, did you just save these dogs?"

"No, darlin'. We're going to save them together. As a team. We're a team."

I squealed and latched on to his neck. "Fuck yeah, we are!"

His laugh was a balm for my soul.

"I need to give you something else, Lil. And I need to give it to you before I try to plead my case, because I need you to know it doesn't come with strings."

Fishing several folded papers from his back pocket, he plucked out a piece of yellow legal paper and handed it to me. "This is given freely, Liliana. It's yours. Whether you and I are together or not."

I stared at the lined sheet, the scribbled names and numbers, flipped it over and the back was covered, too. "What is this?"

His shoulders rounded, his brows drew together

as Brody focused on the sidewalk. "The real reason I came."

"What about all that?" I waved a hand in the direction of the building.

"That was a byproduct. When I talked to Mariana yesterday, I started putting things together, and as I made calls to people on that list, I found myself in the right place at the right time, is all. I called Darius to ask about my medical file. He's the one that noticed the cortisone shots."

"I should have told you Trey worked for the Bulldogs. I didn't because—"

"Because you didn't want it to affect how I treated the good doctor."

I nodded.

"It was smart. Much smarter than I would have been had I known. I already didn't like him, and he knew it. I'm worried about the harassment, though. Has he bugged you since you've been here?"

I breathed out a sigh. "Nothing I couldn't handle. Honestly, I think Dick took advantage of him, too. My stepdad knew I'd never consider marrying Trey. He told him what he wanted to hear."

"Imagine that. Dick. Lying." He huffed out a laugh, nudging my knee with his elbow. After a beat he nodded at the paper. "I didn't want you to have to give up everything you love to do what's right. Last night on my way here, I called every athlete, agent, team owner, celebrity, and philanthropist I know who happen to be dog lovers."

I recognized several of the names on the list. "Brody..."

"I told them about the shelter, that it needed funding."

When I figured out what the numbers meant, I about fell off the bench. Gripping his shoulder, I dug my nails into the muscle. "Brody!"

"You've got your funding, Lil. Enough to get the doors open, I think. You can tell Dick to take a flying fuck. Go back to the Unruly Dog if you want. You don't need this team's money, and you sure as hell don't need to put up with Dick." Brody's smile was sunshine through the clouds. "You're gonna get your shelter, darlin'. And you better get to work, because you're gonna have a whole bunch of mill dogs that need a place to crash for a bit while they get their feet under them." He opened a much smaller piece of paper. The one the commissioner had given him, and when he flipped it over, I nearly fainted.

"Here's your start-up capital."

So many tears. I could barely see to count the zeroes. Six. All lined up behind the number five. The check was from the league, not the commissioner.

"I don't even know what to say. I can never..." I was a shaking, breathless, babbling mess. The sheer joy that poured through my very soul was alive and warm.

I jumped on Brody. I mean, like, jumped, jumped. A flying tackle leap that he wasn't expecting and that knocked us both off the bench into the grass.

"Oww." He rubbed the back of his head with me

sprawled across his chest. "You throw down a pretty good hit, Costello."

"Got it from my dad." I'd never felt so light.

No, not true. I had, once. When Brody told me he loved me.

He laughed, sucked in his breath as I buried my nose in his neck, breathed in deep.

"Thank you," I whispered, letting my lips brush his neck. This big, beautiful, tenderhearted man. "Why, Shaw?" I expected him to say because he loved me, or because he wanted to make me happy, or to apologize for the way he treated me. But what he said was the most perfect response I could have hoped for.

"For the dogs. Because it's the right thing to do for the dogs." He'd flipped my world upside down with a piece of legal paper and I was quite sure Brody Shaw had one of the most genuinely kind souls I'd ever know. Human or dog.

"If this is the reaction I get with that check, I can't wait to see what you do when you open this one." He kissed my temple and held a second check in front of my face.

I bit the inside of my lip. Sat up on my butt.

"Lily, what's wrong."

What was wrong was that money wasn't going to solve the issue between Brody and me. As I stared at the second cashier's check for five million that was from Brody's personal account, I knew we hadn't fixed the problem. Not really. We were only covering it up.

"I can't take that from you. I can't do this again."

Sitting up, he dusted off his hands. "I thought you might say that. Which is why I've prepared a rebuttal."

"Huh?"

"I've had a while to think. Really think. About my own issue. It's not about money."

Cocking my head at him, I lifted a brow. *Are you losing it, buddy?*

"I mean, don't get me wrong. Money comes into play a lot, but it's more than that. People want to use me. For my money, for my name, for my influence. When they're up front with me, like you were the first time we talked about the mill, it's not an issue. I don't mind buying things for the people I love, giving money and lending my name and time to a cause. It's the underhandedness I can't get my head around. The people who try to worm their way into my life, or Photoshop my head onto somebody else's body because I have the deep pockets."

Ahh. I got that. "Or sue you for six figures because they weren't smart enough to read CC's body language and got nipped."

Chapter Thirty-Eight

Thank God for small miracles.

Brody

"Exactly. They don't know and don't care who I really am, but only what I can do for them. When I accused you of being one of those people...there's no excuse for that. I was wrong. I was out of line, Lily, and I might as well have been telling you that you couldn't count on me because I pushed you to let me in, then I shit all over it."

It was something I'd regret forever. Because I hadn't only made her doubt me, I'd made her doubt herself, too. Dammit, I was screwing this up.

I ran a hand over my face. It was time to blitz. "I closed myself off for so long that I couldn't tell genuine from fake anymore, and it cost me the genuine article. It cost me you.

"Your trust. Your love. Your laugh and smile. I will never forget the taste of your tears on my lips, or the sorrow in your extraordinary eyes. *I* put that there. I took the shine away."

Dropping her head, she pinched the checks between her fingers. The tears she was trying to hide dropped down her cheeks.

What I wouldn't give to take the pain away. I cupped her jaw.

She sniffed, lifted her head. "After Trey, I quit peopling all together. Unless they were dog people. And I don't really let them in, either. Part of the reason I wanted you to go back to your place was because it was all getting too comfortable. Too real. I should have told you my plan to go to Dick, but a small part of me wondered when you'd let me down. Would it be after we found the mill? Or a month before the wedding? Or when our daughter was twelve and you drove off a bridge?" She wiped at her tears. "I was also beating myself up for losing the dogs again. It threw me right back into *I* have to do this, *I* have to do that. *I* can't let other people interfere because then my heart gets broken."

My stomach churned at the thought. "And I let you down. The one thing I swore I'd never do." We'd taken each other's deepest fears and breathed them to life. "I wasn't there when you needed me most, darlin', and I can't promise that I'll never let you down again. I know that now. I'm human. I'm going to screw up."

I tipped her chin up and her watery eyes hit me in the gut, but I needed her to see my truth. "If you choose this." I gestured between us. "There will be screwups and apologies, arguments and nights where I'm relegated to the couch, but I will not leave." I shifted, held both of her cheeks in my palms as I let my gaze move back and forth between hers.

"Because I am totally in love with you, Lily. I'd rather hold you in an empty barn than sack a thousand quarterbacks. Or have you in my arms than money in my bank account. I don't need a stadium full of fans screaming my name if I have your laugh to listen to. I'd rather sit on your porch and watch the dogs play than play two more years of football, because the way the game makes me feel doesn't hold a candle to the way I feel with you."

"What are you saying?" Her face was so open, so bright.

"All the bullshit, the ancillary crap, that comes with playing this game—fame, loss, pain and tears, the worry." I shook my head. "It's not worth it for me anymore. The game itself has brought me a lot of joy over the years, but football is also the main factor in all the scars our souls bear. It's time for me to move on from this game while I'm healthy enough to enjoy my life. I know you loved your father, Lil, but I never want to walk his path. The drinking and the pills to cope with the pain and what this game does to you mentally."

I brushed my mouth against hers. "I'm saying, if you can forgive me for being a dumbass, I'm currently unemployed—I asked Miami for my release and they gave it to me. I was hoping there might be a job for me at your new shelter. I'll clean poop and walk dogs. Wash kennel walls and scrub floors. I'm great at tug games and I do excellent doggie commentary."

My heart skipped several beats when she started

chewing on that lip. "Football isn't the only problem, Shaw. We weren't communicating with each other. Neither of us was used to being open with another person. We've both been guarded, and we can't do that anymore. We need to go into this with open hearts and minds and have patience with each other."

I nodded my agreement. "Absolutely. Let's make a deal. At the first sign one of us is slipping into old habits, we have a come to Jesus and lay it all out so that we can fix it together."

Lily smiled through her tears, a smile that made my heart light and my head dizzy.

She slipped the checks in the pocket of her leggings and shifted on to her hands and knees. Her nails dug into my bicep. "What about baths, Shaw. Can you do baths at *our* rescue? Getting those Mastiffs in and out of a dog tub is not easy."

She slipped her tongue into the dip below the base of my neck and my jeans got way too tight. When she swung a leg across my thigh and settled on my lap, my breath hitched. "I can do baths."

"I don't know, have you tried to get a 150-pound dog into a dog wash when they've never had a bath? It can be tricky."

My girl punctuated the sentence with the slow drag of her hips over the seam of my jeans.

"I…uh, shit, that feels good. I, um, bench…weight. A-a lot. I meant to say a lot of weight. I'm strong."

"Well, then, Mr. Shaw, you have yourself a job." Scooting back, she unzipped my fly and pushed her hand in.

"Lily. Out here? Are you sure?"

She shrugged a shoulder. "Eh. Zero fucks. I quit."

"Christ, that feels good."

With that I dug a hand into her hair and gripped it firm, bringing her mouth to mine.

Standing, she kicked off her sneakers before she shimmied her pants off.

"Lily! We're gonna get caught."

"I don't care."

Oh my God, this woman. I shifted my jeans down my ass and Lily settled astride my hips, her core slick and so hot against me. "It should be illegal how good you feel."

A smirk spread over her face and with a tilt of her hips, I was buried inside her.

I could already feel the throb in the base of my spine. "Not gonna last long, darlin'."

I guess I'd have to wait till later to tell her about the ring in my glove box. Bonus. I'd likely get rewarded by sinking into her again.

Lord knew she was all about the positive reinforcement.

When she shifted back so we could both see down the front of our bodies, I knew I wasn't going to last more than a couple minutes. Pushing a hand between us, I brushed her nub with the tip of my finger. "Liliana. Look at me." She gave me those deep purple eyes, and I fell in love all over again. "I love you, darlin'."

Her channel fluttered around me, her little muscles squeezing as her body shook and her lips brushed against mine and just as she started to come down, I followed her over the edge.

She bracketed my jaw with her hands as my legs shook, and I emptied inside her. "Brody. I love you so much."

We exchanged heavy breaths and mischievous smirks, a tender kiss before she stood and started to dress while I tucked myself in my jeans. It was a miracle we didn't get caught out here in broad daylight. "CC will be happy to see Mack."

"Mmm. Laila will be happy to see you. She comes home next week."

"You adopted Laila?" Sheer joy filled me.

"I adopted Laila."

Swinging my arm around Lil's waist, we headed for my truck as I thought about my little family. All my girls and Mack under one roof. That was my happily ever after.

Then it dawned on me. Mack and I were outnumbered.

"Lil, I think we need another male."

She pushed out a sigh. "No more dogs, Brody."

Eh, she'd come around.

There were always dogs out there that needed good homes and a second chance.

Chapter Thirty-Nine

Happily Ever After

Lily

I dried the Boxer pup with a towel to stimulate its breathing and settled it back in the whelping box where its mother and siblings waited. The smallest of the litter, he had been sluggish to breathe and I was checking on him often. Soft cries and grunts danced over the air in the small room dedicated to mothers whelping their pups.

Iris nosed her baby as it wrestled with the other four to find a nipple. She'd be a good mama.

She'd been a handful when she came in.

Skinny, hungry, with wounds on her shoulders and sides I was sure were cigarette burns. She'd been dumped, likely because she was pregnant, and she'd attacked her male rescuer but had gone to a female rescuer with relative ease.

It wasn't hard to figure out her abuser was a man.

The whelping room had a temporary sign on it that

said Women Only. We'd start Iris's socialization once her pups were older. For now, she'd hang with the girls.

Shutting off the light, I closed the door behind me, and regarded the shelter I'd named the Unlovabulls Canine Rescue Center. It was smaller than I'd originally hoped. We were set up for thirty-five dogs at a time, but we never turned one away. Somehow, we always found room for the dogs that needed us most. There wasn't a fancy ribbon cutting or a glitzy celebration, either.

No, the money went where it was needed most—the dogs.

I walked over to the fold-up cot that would be my bed and prepared myself for a long night. I needed to stay close to Iris tonight to make sure she didn't have any complications. She wasn't a spring chicken. Dr. Avalos—Regina or Gina, as most of us called her—thought she was at least eight, and this definitely hadn't been her first litter.

Our shelter didn't adopt many dogs out directly. They came here to get the care and skills they needed to be companion animals, and when I was sure they posed no more risk, they went back to the rescue organization that brought them to us to be adopted out. We'd adopted out only forty-three dogs directly. Dogs from the mill that weren't suitable for other rescues.

I scanned over the Original Unlovabulls wall. Each survivor we'd rescued from the mill had a framed picture up there. The ones that hadn't made it out with their lives had a plaque in my office with their breed type and a name we'd given them. The top of the plaque read You Were Loved. It was the truth.

Brody's picture had yielded results.

Officer Johnson was able to identify who the pickup truck was registered to.

The red and black Ford F-150 Raptor belonged to Devon Taylor.

I scrunched my pillow under my head, trying to get comfortable, when the soft padding of doggie feet and tennis shoes down the hall made me smile. I glanced up to see Brody toting an air mattress.

"What are you doing here? You don't have to sleep down here with me. Go upstairs with the dogs, Shaw." I started to sit up. "You've got an agility trial tomorrow."

Discovering Devon was one of the guys behind the mill had come as a shock, but after a little digging, it all made sense. Brody had never told him we slept together. Devon knew because they'd been keeping tabs on me since they got spooked at the rental house. It wasn't only the sticker on Everett's car that had spooked him that night, either.

He'd recognized Brody's truck.

Devon had flipped on his cousin in exchange for a reduced sentence. They'd moved the dogs to a rural warehouse a couple of towns over. Mrs. Davis turned out to be their grandmother, and the farm manager. He took a cut in exchange for letting Devon and his cousin, Colton Andrews, use the barn.

The letters in the brand finally made sense. DA. Devon Taylor and Colton Andrews. The ASPCA, SPCA of Dallas and Collin County Sheriff's department had joined forces once we had a location. We rescued 104 breeding dogs, most of the females pregnant or nursing. That number didn't include the pups.

"We're not sleeping upstairs when *their* mom"—he

pointed to the dogs—"and my fiancée is down here on a cot. Now, come on down on this mattress. It's a lot more comfortable than that cot. I'll be back, I've got to get a dog bed."

Fiancée. It wasn't a title I'd ever thought I'd wear again. I admired my modest engagement ring for the millionth time. This time, I had the right man. The only man. The wedding would be small. Out on our ranch outside the city, nothing fancy. Picnic tables and straw bales. A band in the barn and an open bar. Dogs welcome, people tolerated.

It'd be fun to watch Hayes and Olive dance around each other all night, given their history and their statuses as best man and maid of honor.

That man was relentless when it came to her.

Laila's happy little face made me smile as she tried and failed to jump up on my cot. She was full grown, but she was still a bulldog, with short little bulldog legs and a chubby bulldog butt. Smiling, I slipped down to the air mattress, where she buried her big wrinkly head under my arm.

Hearing Brody's steps and more doggie feet coming down the hall, I kissed her snout. "Your daddy spoils you rotten, little girl."

"Damn straight. My princess deserves it. All my girls do." He put the dog bed down at the head of our makeshift bed. Jet crawled in, and CC snuggled in half on top of her, half in our bed, with her butt in my face.

Such is life with dogs. I reached up and patted my girls.

Brody kicked his shoes off and got situated on the other side of the mattress, and Mack jumped on top of him, rolling on to his back and pushing my fiancé to the edge.

Chuckling, I nodded at my good boy. "What's your excuse for how spoiled that one is?" Mack snorted and wiggled his head under Brody's hand.

"That's all you, darlin'."

"Oh, you're full of shit, Shaw." He and Mack were buds, best buds.

"Hey, he's the only other guy in the house. We need each other. We bond."

"You feed him off a fork."

Brody closed his eyes and true to form, he and Mack were snoring in a matter of minutes.

Nineteen.

That was the number of breeding dogs we couldn't save, and the number of names on the plaque in my office.

Six.

Six dogs I deemed unfit for adoption. Two Corsi. One Pit Bull. One Bull Mastiff. A German Shepherd. And a Bull Terrier.

We sold my house and bought the ranch for them. They'd never be trustworthy around most humans because most humans didn't know how to read them, how to handle them. But I did, and Brody had learned. And Officer Johnson—David—he knew how to channel their work ethic into something productive that gave them peace. They had good lives with us on the ranch. Full lives, with fresh air and sunshine. A pond and plenty of food and water and trees to sleep under and climate-controlled housing. Warm beds, and goats and ducks and chickens to guard——for those who'd mastered their prey drive.

They would live that way until they went over the bridge.

There was no doubt the life of a rescuer was hard. The lows were very low. But the highs…the dogs that went to good homes or into working dog programs. Seeing them explore grass for the first time and feel the sun on their faces. Pick up a toy and bring it to me. The pictures that covered the other three walls of my office—successful adoption stories and updates from families.

I'd take a hundred of the bad days in exchange for the feeling I got when one of our dogs found a home.

Because they were our dogs. All of them.

I reached over, tapped my snoring husband-to-be.

"Huh."

"I love you."

"Mm, love you, too," he mumbled.

"Shaw, thank you."

He opened his eyes, and he reached over to squeeze my hand. "For what, darlin'?"

"For loving these Unlovabulls every bit as much as I do."

* * * * *

Reviews are an invaluable tool when it comes to spreading the word about great reads. Please consider leaving an honest review on your favorite retailer or review site.

To find out about other books by Tricia Lynne or to be alerted to new releases, sign up for her monthly newsletter at https://tricialynnewrites.com/about-me/

Acknowledgments

Authors say it's always harder to pen your second book than the first. For me, it absolutely was. Beyond the crippling imposter syndrome and the constant anxiety that I couldn't do it again, the actual words-on-paper part never seems to get easier.

But I had an exceptionally hard time with *Protective Instinct.*

In 2019, while I was writing this book, my husband and I said goodbye to my five-year-old Clumber Spaniel quite unexpectedly. In fact, he was the second dog we lost last year. I also held the sweetest Basset Hound ever born while he went to the rainbow bridge, too. After losing my boys, it was nearly impossible for me to write about dogs. My dogs are my children, you see. And I couldn't dig into this book without finding myself awash in a new wave of sadness and loss… In fact, I'm still grieving. But I know I never could have finished *Protective Instinct* without a rock-solid support system to see me through.

I am forever grateful to Carina Press and my editor, Stephanie Doig. You were beyond understanding of how losing my dogs, combined with the current state of the world, affected how quickly I wrote. Thank you so, so much for nursing me through. I'm lucky to call myself a Carina author. I'm also beyond thankful to my agent, Saritza Hernandez, who stayed true to her principles in this difficult time, and for sticking with me when I struggled to get through the sophomore slump.

My All The Kissing family—Shannon, Lindsay, Maxym, and Alexa—who helped with early brainstorming, I don't know what I'd do without you all. An extra special shout out to Gwynne Jackson, who not only read the early stuff for this book, but was there when I needed both feedback and a really good friend. Thank you, my sister. I'm in your debt.

A huge thank you to my beta-readers, Haley, Paris, Janet, and Cassie. I'm lucky to have had your eyes on my words and your invaluable notes to guide me. I'm even luckier to call y'all my friends and peers.

A huge thanks to my own agility instructor, Ryan— you are so much stronger than you know. I'm so blessed to have access to a wonderful training center in Frisco, TX. The staff and facilities at What a Great Dog are unparalleled. Your knowledge of dog training and canine behavior is only second to how you treat us like part of the family.

To Shutt'er Down Ranch, thank you for choosing us to adopt Brennan from the extensive pile of applications for her. We can't imagine our lives without her. Simply put, she's my best friend.

To Mom and Dad. Thank you for being proud of me, and for letting me adopt my first pound puppy. Dad, I'm sorry Orion ate your Gortex boots and stole your socks.

To my dear friends and OG agility crew—Kim and Antoine, Michele, and our very own Yoda, Connie—I'm so grateful to have met you all and made life-long friends who are crazy dog people like us. I wouldn't have gotten through the last year and a half without you …and the wine. Let's not forget the wine, or Cards Against Humanity.

To my husband. Thank you for putting up with my moody ass, eating too much fast food when I'm on deadline, caving when Brennan chose us to be her for-ever home, and for not getting too pissed when I ran-domly bring home another dog. I'm also grateful for your linebacker shoulders and your football turned cy-cling butt. Love you.

Orion. Guinness. Sadie. Jake. Murphy. Gus. Jock. Sugar. Holmes. Each night I look up into a starry sky and feel grateful you were a part of my life. Thank you for being our stand-in children and bringing us such un-complicated love and joy. Each of you has taken a piece of my heart with you when you went to the bridge, and I'm better for having had you in my life. You will al-ways be in my heart.

Last but not least, to my Velcro Corso, my precious, goodest girl who has come so far in the last two years. Brennan, my inspiration for The Unlovabulls. Thank you, sweet pea, for being so patient with your new little brother, Smitty, for all the Corso snuggles, and each and every night you sleep curled into my legs.

Mama loves you forever, Brennie Lynne.

About the Author

Tricia Lynne is fluent in both sarcasm and cuss words and has little filter between her brain and mouth—a combination that tends to embarrass her husband at corporate functions. A former competitive cyclist, she's a tomboy at heart who loves hard rock, Irish whiskey, her Midwestern roots, and will always prefer her Vans to her heels. She's drawn to strong, flawed heroines, and believes writing isn't a decision one makes, but a calling one can't resist.

Tricia lives in Dallas with her husband, a rescued Cane and a Clumber Spaniel. She is a co-founder of the All The Kissing blog for romance writers, #FridayKiss—a Twitter writing prompt, and #KissPitch—the Twitter pitch event for romance and women's fiction. In addition, she contributes to The Curvy Fashionista blog, was a 2016 Pitch Wars mentee, and is constantly trying to talk her husband into more dogs.

To stay up-to-date on what Tricia's working on next

and get awesome doggie content in your feed, you can follow her at:

http://tricialynnewrites.com
https://www.facebook.com/TriciaLynneAuthor
https://twitter.com/tlynne67
https://www.instagram.com/tricialynnewrites

HARLEQUIN

Heartfelt or thrilling, passionate or uplifting—Harlequin is more than just happily-ever-after.

With twelve different series to choose from and new books available every month, you are sure to find stories that will move you, uplift you, inspire and delight you.

HNEWS2021

Love Harlequin romance?

DISCOVER.

Be the first to find out about promotions, news and exclusive content!

Facebook.com/HarlequinBooks

Twitter.com/HarlequinBooks

Instagram.com/HarlequinBooks

Pinterest.com/HarlequinBooks

YouTube.com/HarlequinBooks

ReaderService.com

EXPLORE.

Sign up for the Harlequin e-newsletter and download a free book from any series at **TryHarlequin.com**

CONNECT.

Join our Harlequin community to share your thoughts and connect with other romance readers! **Facebook.com/groups/HarlequinConnection**

HSOCIAL2021